The Awakening

"One must have chaos within to enable one to give birth to a dancing star."

- Friedrich Nietzsche

To those who stood by me as I dared to dream and
put my thoughts on paper. This one is for you.

Prologue

At the beginning of time, three gods were born. Astraliam, the Sky Father and usher of day and night; Malignos, the ruler of the hellish domain known as Infernus and king of the damned; and Terralynia, the creator of life. Although minor deities would spawn as the years passed by, The Supreme Three have existed since the planet Sacarnia was formed.

Seeing that Sacarnia was void of life, Mother Terralynia began to create several sentient races in her image during the year 3000 BC. By 1000 BC, Terralynia's first two races, the vilek and the álfrolk, were thriving. Living on an island off the mainland called Florella, these two races coexisted harmoniously. However, the longstanding peace these peoples experienced deteriorated when a dragon attacked the ancient álfrolkian capital of Snøvern in 20 AC. This, along with the subsequent events occurring soon after, has since been labeled "The Great Dissolution."

Because Terralynia promised to not interfere with her creations after 0 AC, she was helpless to watch as half of the álfrolk population was wiped out during the dragon's onslaught. The leader of the álfrolk during this challenging time was King Hakon, who was forced to divide the surviving álves into groups and put them in the care of his three children; Laufeia, Snaerr, and Fenrolf. With his kin entrusted to his children, King Hakon stayed in Snøvern while his offspring led the groups of survivors to various areas of the land.

Laufeia, the eldest child and only daughter of King Hakon, led her group of survivors to Florella's southern reaches,

1

predicting that the unexplored landscape would prove bountiful in shelter and supplies. Along the way, the survivors encountered a group of stranded outcast mages, also known as Terralynia's chosen, who could change into the shape of a single animal. Finding allies amongst these pariahs, the groups merged and formed settlements across the southern expanse of the island.

Snaerr, the second child and King Hakon's first son, led his group towards the Snøthorn Mountains, deciding that the expansive mountain range would provide ample shelter and resources to create weapons and armor should Snaerr and his kin choose to hunt the dragon in the future.

Fenrolf, the third child and King Hakon's second son, led his group to an area of the island no álfrolk had ever dared go before: the Whispering Grove, a small section of the Glimmering Wilds that was said to be the home of the vilek. Various álfrolk scouts had surmised that the fairy women wielded immeasurable power that could help Fenrolf and his kin fight back against the dragon destroying their homeland. Because of this intel, Fenrolf summoned his courage and led his people to the vilek capital. Their arrival tore the vilek apart politically, as some sympathized with the álves' story while others were disgusted by the outsiders' presence in their serene sanctuary. Although their presence was a divisive matter, Fenrolf and his kin were allowed to stay—a decision that led to a brutal uprising and separation of the vilek people into two councils: the Light, or "Welcoming," Fairies, and the Dark, or "Unwelcoming," Fairies. The women of the dark council fled to a small, uninhabited island adjacent to the Florella, isolating themselves from the rest of the world but vowing to return one day and reclaim their homeland.

As the generations went by, the descendants of the three groups of survivors began to evolve, resulting in drastic changes to the original álfrolk genome and culture. Today, the descendants of the ancient álfrolk now belong to one of three vastly different subraces: the Dokkalrolk (descendants of Snaerr's group), the Magijarolk (descendants of Fenrolf's group), and the Sylvanrolk (descendants of Laufeia's group). With such massive differences separating the three subraces, no one thought it would ever be possible to gather the álves under one united álfrolk banner for a shared cause...

Until now.

The Stranger
16th of Red Moon, 1300 AC

A twig snapped in half, the noise piercing the serene atmosphere of the forest with a sharp crack. Frightened squirrels scattered to and fro across the dirt path, retreating into the bushes with a chorus of chitters and squeaks. Standing in the center of the sun-bathed trail was a lightly tanned, lean álf named Idal. His body twisted at the sound of the broken stick, his ebony hair swaying to the side.

"What was that?" the male inquired uneasily, his gray eyes darting every which way. "Who's there?"

The source of the noise, a she-álf named Cymbelina, sat hunched over in a pair of bushes off to the left. She eyed her friend cautiously, trying to assess his level of discomfort and whether or not her prank could still be salvaged.

Dammit, that was louder than I thought it was going to be. I hope Idal doesn't put too much thought into what he heard.

All hopes of her friend ignoring the noise vanished once Cymbelina noticed the male reach for the bow on his back, his thin, dirt-caked fingers sliding an arrow out of the quiver.

Well, there goes that idea.

"It's just me, Idal!" The brunette called out from her hiding spot. "There's no need to get jumpy."

The disheveled female emerged from the foliage, the sunlight filtering through the fiery leaves illuminating her frame. Her light brown skin shone under the brilliant autumn sun, her long, hickory waves swaying as she shook the leaves off her head. Brushing some of the remaining orange-speckled

4

leaves off her leather armor, her pine-green eyes met Idal's gray ones, her hands raised in a defensive position.

The male sighed in relief, shaking his head as he put away his weapon. "One of these days, I'm going to end up lodging an arrow into your chest. You know better than to sneak up on me like that when I'm in a foul mood."

"You? Foul mood? Never," the female álf teased, doing a quick once-over of her armor to ensure she hadn't missed any stray leaves. "So, what areas are we patrolling today?"

Idal chuckled, motioning ahead as the duo walked down the dirt path. "We, is it? Last time I checked, you were supposed to be with Master Arvel in his tent, learning about your patron animal so you can eventually get your OWN patrol duties. Not sneaking up on me and stealing mine."

Idal was right. Cymbelina was supposed to be with her patron teacher, Master Arvel, in his tent today. In fact, the she-álf had every intention of visiting him this morning and even headed in that direction. However, the looming threat of boredom awaiting her in her teacher's abode caused the Wood Álf to unceremoniously retreat into the Sunshade Forest. She couldn't stomach the notion of dull lessons on such a beautiful day.

"Stealing your duties? Oh, Idal, I wouldn't dream of it. I just want to be helpful."

"Ha…sure you do."

As childhood friends, the duo was accustomed to being told they were doing something wrong nearly every time they hung out, whether they meant to cause trouble or not. However, both Cymbelina and Idal knew that what they were currently doing was against the rules of not only their clan, the Glenrolk, but every Sylvanrolk tribe that dotted the surface of Florella. Only álves were allowed to go on patrols, and according to the Sylvan Tenets, Cymbelina was still an adolescent álf—an álfling—because she had not mastered her patron animal yet. Not only had she not become one with her patron, but she also had no idea what it was—a foreign and vexing concept to Cymbelina and the rest of the Sylvanrolk community. No matter how annoying the female thought the situation was, she did not allow it to hold her back from doing what she thought was right, even if that meant ignoring the Sylvan Tenets.

The songbirds sang a melodic tune as the álves waltzed down the path, the brisk wind caressing their sunkissed faces. They followed the road onward under a canopy of trees, the leaves glittering like the dying embers of a fall campfire. Falling to the ground, the leaves crinkled under the duo's boots, which padded against the dirt in sync. Animals ran amok in different directions as the friends continued down the road, Cymbelina's thoughts lost in the moment.

Listening to the sparrows sing while patrolling the edge of Sunshade with my best friend? Yeah, this is MUCH better than one of Arvel's lectures.

Cymbelina remained in her thoughts as she and Idal approached the end of the path as it bled into the shoreline. Turning to say something to her ally, she was startled when he shoved her behind a bush to their right. Landing in the dirt with a loud thud, the brunette shot her friend a bewildered glare.

"What was that for?" Cymbelina hissed, rubbing her injured wrists as she attempted to stand up.

The male quickly stopped her. "There's someone on the shore up ahead. I didn't want to risk it seeing us, so I acted without hesitancy. Sorry."

The female laughed. Idal had always been a bit tense, but he had never done something like this before.

"'It'? Why didn't your mother ever tell you not to reference people in that manner? It's awfully rude."

"I'm serious, 'Lina. I've never seen anything like it before."

"Oh, come on, surely whatever you're referring to can't be that shocking."

"No? Take a look for yourself. Quickly, though, I don't want it to notice us."

Cymbelina slowly peeked around the side of the bush beside her and Idal. Her green eyes scanned the sandy shore until they rested upon a figure huddled beside a modest rowboat. The creature had cotton-white hair that cascaded in a braid down its bony, leather-clad back. The morning sun shimmered on the creature's grayish-yellow skin, which contrasted against the shore's white sand. Although far away, Cymbelina could see the being's lips moving as it muttered to itself while digging through the contents of the vessel.

"What do you think it could be?"

The female ducked behind the orange-leafed shrub, staring at her perturbed friend in bewilderment. "I...I have no idea. We should return to camp and tell Kinlord Emyr about this."

Idal emphatically shook his head in disagreement. "We don't have that kind of time. What if it leaves while we return to camp and share the news? And even if one of us goes, the other might be in danger if the creature finds out we've been spying on it. We don't have any choice but to make the first move."

The male álf grabbed his bow with one hand and an arrow with the other, preparing to stand up. Before he could position his shot, Cymbelina grabbed the hand that held the projectile.

"Please, Idal, listen to me. I don't think confronting this person alone is a good idea. How do we know they're hostile? I mean, they might just need help."

Batting the brunette's hand away, the male repositioned his arrow and stood up. "It's better to be safe than sorry."

Idal let the arrow loose as he and Cymbelina watched it whiz through the crisp air of the forest and toward the beach. Perfectly avoiding all the branches in its way, the projectile was just about to land home when the yellow being froze. Cocking its head to the side, the stranger waved their hand, creating a strong gust of wind. The stream of air made the arrow miss its mark, causing it to bounce off a nearby stone. Unfazed by the arrow, the creature continued to rummage through its things as if it had merely swatted a bug away. Disturbed by the nonchalance of such a feat, the two álves stared at one another.

"I...uh...I think now would be a good time to leave," the male mumbled, his eyes glued to the mysterious stranger.

"It's about time!"

The duo slowly backed away from their former hiding place, starting to retreat into the depths of the Sunshade Forest. The friends repeatedly gazed backward and forward as they tip-toed away from the edge of the beach, ensuring their presence had gone unnoticed by the stranger and that a clear path was in front of them. However, Idal focused too much on the way behind them as he eventually tripped over a log and let out a startled yelp before tumbling to the ground. A murder of crows, nestled in the trees adjacent to the fallen one, cawed and flew toward the shore. Cymbelina quickly looked toward the sea to determine if the being had heard her friend's cry.

The yellow-skinned outlander was no longer there.

"Idal, you need to get up this minute. I think that...thing...knows we're here."

The clumsy male grumbled from his prone stance on the ground, spitting out the dirt caking his tongue. Although he attempted to get up, Idal had gotten the wind knocked out of him, making every one of his movements staggeringly slow. Desperate to get moving, Cymbelina grabbed the ebony-haired álf underneath his armpits, hauling him to his feet. As she helped her friend regain his footing, a rush of wind knocked them down as a cackle floated on the breeze. With a renewed sense of urgency, Cymbelina swiftly stood up and unsheathed her short sword. Idal dazedly followed behind her and opted for his sword instead of his bow. The friends pushed their backs together, their eyes glancing hurriedly from side to side to see if the violent wind would strike again.

"Look what you've gotten us into," Cymbelina grunted, the sweat on her skin causing her dark brown hair to stick to her forehead.

The sounds of Idal's retort died on his dry lips as another whirring wind sped toward the friends. Unlike the last time, this gale was accompanied by the metallic sound of blade meeting blade as Idal blocked the creature's attack. His hands trembled as Cymbelina pirouetted and swung her steel sword downward, cutting through the air as the creature quickly dodged her attack. It appeared seconds later on Idal's left side, attempting to carve into his midsection. Escaping in the nick of time, the male created the opening the she-álf needed to try another attack on the strange being. The sharp tip of the brunette's weapon bit into the skin on the creature's arm, a sparkling cobalt liquid blossoming forth from the flesh wound. The yellowish-gray being let out a shrill cry as it moved to the side. Swinging its clawed empty hand at Cymbelina, it missed the she-álf's forearm by a hair.

Dodge; missed attack. Dodge; a slight jab. The fight carried on this way for minutes on end, with all three participants obtaining a myriad of gashes and bruises. With each subsequent attack, both parties' movements became progressively sloppy, their energy quickly draining as the encounter continued.

As the creature went in for a fatal stab to Cymbelina's heart, an arrow flew past the female's body and lodged in the mysterious creature's right shoulder. The being dropped its weapon and backed away, stunned by the fluid-coated arrow. Black ooze formed around the wound as the being was brought to its knees, screeching in pain. Kicking the stranger's weapon away, the friends turned around to see the source of the arrow. Instead of seeing an álven archer, the friends saw a horse surrounded by a green aura as it charged through the fiery forest foliage. The pale horse snorted as it slowed down and stood next to Cymbelina and Idal, looking between the two álves with an overwhelming sense of disappointment emanating from its deep, amber eyes. The horse then trotted towards the wailing creature, gracefully kicking it on the side of its head and knocking it unconscious.

If this were any other continent besides Florella and if the two friends were not of Sylvanrolk origin, they might have been surprised that a horse came to their rescue in the midst of battle. But the two álves knew by looking at the stallion that it wasn't your average steed. The horse's coat was the color of cream, which contrasted with the all too familiar black horse tattoo that was revealed when the wind whipped up the horse's umber-hued mane.

"Master Arvel!" Idal exclaimed, recognizing the patron form of the teacher at once. "I was wondering when you would stop by to retrieve your wayward pupil."

The horse shook its head before it slowly morphed into the form that the younger álves were more accustomed to. A towering male álf stood where the stallion had stood before, his periwinkle patron robes rippling in the wind as his amber eyes bore into the two individuals standing before him. The man Cymbelina had tried her best to avoid earlier this morning was now in her presence, irritation masking his soft, alabaster features.

"What in Mother Terralynia's name are you doing here? You two should know that if you spot anything suspicious, you are to return to camp immediately and fetch help."

"I tried telling him that, Master Arvel, but—"

"You're not even supposed to be out here with Idal, Cymbelina! You are an álfling! It is forbidden to assist others during their patrol routes, no matter how you may feel about the subject."

"I told her to go back, Master Arvel, but—"

"Hush," Arvel interrupted. "You two can settle this with Kinlord Emyr when we return. For now, I want you two to carry the stranger back to camp so we can show Healer Vevina and the others what was lurking on the outskirts of our settlement. Hurry now, before it wakes up."

With disgruntled grumbles, the two álves unwillingly carried the body back to the Glenrolk camp. Luckily for them, the creature was lighter than it appeared, but that didn't raise the she-álf's spirit much, considering the conversation that awaited Idal and her when they arrived home.

A part of me is glad I accompanied Idal during his patrol today, and a part of me isn't, the female thought. *I'm relieved that I was able to help him avoid a potentially deadly situation, but I'm dreading the lecture we're about to get.*

A gloomy sky slowly rolled over the region of Florella known as Terralynia's Folly as the trio of álves made various stops around the Glenrolk camp. Dropping the body off at

Vevina's tent, Master Arvel ushered the younger álves to Kinlord Emyr's abode, the wind slowly picking up. Guiding Idal and Cymbelina into the kinlord's hearing room and briefing the clan leader on the situation, Master Arvel left the duo to their fate.

The wind pounded against the fabric of Kinlord Emyr's tent, the walls billowing as raindrops hit the roof, sounding like tiny bells. On one side of the noisy room sat Kinlord Emyr on his twig throne, laced with the most vibrant wildflowers from across Terralynia's Folly. On the other side of the room knelt Cymbelina and Idal, positioned on Emyr's prized cave bear rug.

The leader sat tall on his throne, his kempt silver hair framing his pale, chiseled face. His mint-green eyes bore into the álves before him, his weathered hands clasped together on his lap.

"What exactly gave you two the right to disobey the Sylvan Tenets and try to decide an unknown creature's fate without consulting me?"

The young álves looked at the floor, neither one eager to be the first to talk. Annoyed by their lack of initiative to articulate a sentence or even glance at their leader, Kinlord Emyr called on Idal.

"Well, Idal? You were the one who proposed to attack the creature, were you not?"

The ebony-haired álf nodded and looked up to speak, his gray eyes meeting Emyr's green ones. "I was, sir."

"And what was your reason for doing so?"

"I was afraid that if Cymbelina and I left the stranger alone, it would disappear, and if only one of us came back to the camp, the person left behind might get hurt."

Emyr rested his right arm on his armrest, his chin nestled in his palm. "Is that not the duty of a Wood Álf? To report to the Kinlord or Kinlady and get their input instead of acting like an uncouth assassin?"

Ignoring the lessons she'd received about hearing room etiquette, Cymbelina interjected: "Grandpa, Idal did what he thought was right. Isn't that another lesson the Sylvan Tenets seeks to teach us?"

Both of the male álves in the room turned their focus to the brown-haired female, Idal giving her a thankful look while Emyr gave her a look born of agitation.

"You know better than to speak out of line and address me by that title in a hearing, Cymbelina. Do so again, and the consequences you two shall receive will be increased twofold."

Cymbelina shifted her eyes to the floor once, staying silent for the sake of her friend.

The flap of fabric covering the entryway into the hearing room was pulled to the side as Emyr's advisor, Phalena, entered the room with a scroll clutched in her hands. Genuflecting, she whispered, "I'm sorry to interrupt, Kinlord Emyr, but I have news regarding the specimen found on the shore this morning."

"Thank you," Emyr muttered with a slight smile, taking the scroll and placing it on the wooden table beside his throne. "Anything else?"

"Yes, sir. Deirdre asked me to tell you she wishes to speak to you and Cymbelina once you have finished speaking. Master Arvel spoke to her after leaving your tent, and she wishes to talk to the two of you about what happened in the Sunshade Forest earlier this afternoon."

Cymbelina's heart dropped into her stomach upon hearing her mother's name.

Excellent...three lectures in one day.

"Thank you, Phalena, that will be all."

The bubbly advisor smiled and bowed, leaving the room as swiftly as she entered. The slow pattering of the ever-dwindling rain accentuated the silence in the room after Phalena's departure. Once Emyr was sure his assistant was far from the hearing chambers, he continued his questioning.

"Now, Cymbelina, what do you propose we do with the insubordination you two have disgraced the Glenrolk clan with today? In other words, what would the Sylvan Tenets have me do? According to Master Arvel, you have been skipping your lessons lately, so you must be confident enough in your current knowledge."

Suppressing a mouthful of sarcasm that threatened to spill from her lips, Cymbelina put on a fake air of confidence and addressed her grandfather. "Since we broke one of the minor laws by not informing you of the stranger on the shore, we should be fined, given extra guard duty, or have one of our other privileges stripped away: whichever punishment you see fit to administer."

"That is correct. Wow, maybe you are learning something from the few patron sessions you've decided to attend."

The female álf closed her eyes to avoid rolling them.

"Now, for your punishments. First, let's start with Idal."

The tall álven male stood up from his throne, approaching the kneeling forms of his granddaughter and her friend. His pale, bony left hand hovered in the air above Idal's head.

"Idal, you shall remain at the Glenrolk camp and act as a guard during the Eldenfield Festival."

A sense of sadness filled the female álf's core as she glanced to her right and saw the disappointed look on her friend's face. *The event starts in two days, and Emyr is changing Idal's schedule? But it's his favorite time of year!*

"Yes, Kinlord Emyr," Idal responded despondently, accepting his punishment without quarrel.

The elder álf then raised his right hand above his granddaughter's head. "Cymbelina, you shall attend double the required patron lessons after the Eldenfield Festival since you are not eligible to act as a guard."

"I understand, Kinlord Emyr."

"Good. You two may rise."

Once Cymbelina and Idal were on their feet, Kinlord Emyr placed his hands on their shoulders as a seemingly deceptive smile spread across his stubble-covered face. "Remember, these consequences are not an act of retribution but of love. You two are dismissed."

With dismissal granted, Cymbelina and Idal headed out of the tent. The drizzling rain had ceased altogether, leaving

13

behind a damp, brisk wind and a gloomy gray sky. Leaves tinted with autumnal hues were scattered across the dampened steppe on which the Glenrolk camp sat. The usual bustle of activity that accompanied the late afternoon hours was absent, most likely due to the spreading news of the odd, yellow stranger. Usually, Cymbelina would be happy to take a break from the large crowd, but its absence allowed her to see the person she dreaded seeing the most at the moment; her mother, Deirdre. Sitting on a bench underneath the blacksmith's canopy across the road, Deirdre's cerulean eyes shone angrily as she glanced at her daughter.

Recognizing the negative emotions culminating inside his best friend's mother, Idal began to plan his retreat from the situation.

"I'm sorry about earlier today, Cymbelina. We should've returned to camp when you suggested it instead of confronting the stranger."

"You were right to be cautious, Idal. I just feel bad that you have to miss the Eldenfield Festival now."

The tanned male álf turned and shrugged his shoulders, working his way down the path toward his family's tent. "What can you do about it, ya know? Just make sure to see me before you leave for Eldenfield tomorrow. Anyways, good luck with your mom!"

Cymbelina winced, turning her anxious stare toward her mother, who was approaching her with a sense of vigor. Deirdre's chocolate curls bounced against her sand-colored shoulders with each stride, the space between the mother and the daughter steadily decreasing. When only two feet of ground separated the pair, Deirdre called out to her child.

"What kind of lunacy has ensnared your mind, 'Lina? You could've been killed!"

"No lunacy, Mother, just my rebellious sense of justice," Cymbelina joked. "By the way, Grandpa will be out in a few minutes."

"You're not taking this situation seriously, Cymbelina."

"I am. I just process things a bit differently than you do."

"By making jokes after the fact? Ugh, you're just like your father in that respect."

Cymbelina's eyes drifted to the ground, all sense of humor evaporating from her countenance. Before she could find the words to respond, the rustling of cloth caught her attention. Turning her gaze toward her grandfather's tent, the younger brunette saw Kinlord Emyr emerge from his dwelling with a smile spread across his weathered features. It was as if the past few hours never happened.

"Oh, Daughter," the elder sighed, hugging his daughter. "It's so good to see you."

"It's great to see you too, Dad. If only it were under better circumstances."

Staring at the two older álves, the younger she-álf remained silent. *It's as if I'm not even here.*

Ending their embrace, the two álves split apart, Deirdre's cerulean eyes glancing at her daughter.

"Maybe you can talk some sense into your granddaughter. I don't think she fully comprehends the gravity of the situation."

"I do, Mother. In fact, I'm the only one here who went head-to-head against that creature, so I fully experienced the gravity of the situation. Speaking of which, did you read the scroll about the stranger before you came out here, Grandpa? If so, what did it say?"

Kinlord Emyr folded his hands, giving his granddaughter an expectant expression. "You fought against the creature, didn't you? You should know all you need to know about it."

Cymbelina snorted. "Alright, keep your secrets then," she joked, backing away from the two álves, sensing a possible opening to exit the conversation. "I have some packing that I need to attend to anyway."

There was a moment of silence as the female álf made her nonchalant getaway until her mother's resounding voice cut through the peaceful air. "This conversation isn't over, 'Lina, not by a long shot!"

Of course, it isn't. I wouldn't be so lucky.

The dirt path Cymbelina took to head back to her family's

15

tent zig-zagged between businesses and other familial abodes. The makeshift buildings came in shades of green, brown, and white, the signature colors of the Glenrolk clan. On the right side of the path lay the tents where families resided, and on the left sat tents used for various business-related activities. The most common trades among members of the Glenrolk were bakers, blacksmiths, and tailors. With such a vast world to explore, Cymbelina wasn't sure how anyone would be content wasting their days working inside a tent, but their services benefited the community, so she was thankful for them.

After all, I don't know what I would do without Tadhgmaris' poppy seed loaves.

Reaching the first fork in the road, Cymbelina took the right-branching path, her boots sinking into the fresh mud with each step. As she approached her family's ivory tent, the squelching of her leather shoes drew the attention of Cymbelina's younger sister, Una, who was waiting inside the home.

One of the tent's side flaps opened, exposing Una's head. Her fawn skin and frizzy, inky waves shone in the sunlight coming from a part in the gray clouds, her right arm flailing wildly out of the opening.

"It's about time you got home, 'Lina! Come in; I have something to show you."

"Aren't you gonna ask what I've been up to today?"

"I don't have to! The entire clan knows about it! Now get your butt in here already!"

Entering her family's abode, Cymbelina kicked off her boots. Before her eyes could adjust to the dim entryway, the brunette was overwhelmed by her shorter half-sister, who gave her a bear hug from behind. The eighteen-year-old laughed in elation behind her older sibling's back as she spun her around before releasing her from her tight grip.

"Wow," the older sister coughed, recollecting her breath as she stared at Una in stunned amazement. "I can't remember the last time I received one of your back-breaking hugs. Why are you in such high spirits?"

16

"Well," the black-haired she-álf said, folding her hands behind her back and swaying back and forth, "I might've done something today."

"Oh? And what 'might' you have done?"

Pulling up the fabric of her left sleeve, Una shoved her forearm into Cymbelina's face. The shape of a red squirrel was etched in black ink into her younger sister's fair skin.

"I got my patron animal tattooed today!"

A pang of jealousy gnawed away at Cymbelina's heart as she stared at the jet-black squirrel tattoo on the navy-eyed woman's arm. Unlike Cymbelina, who has never known her patron animal, Una has always known that her patron was a red squirrel and recently mastered it; thus, the tattoo. It is a sacred custom for Sylvanrolk álves to get a tattoo of their patron once they have learned their powers and communicated with them. Although Cymbelina was happy for her sister for reaching such a milestone, a small part of the brunette found it increasingly difficult to look at the tattoo and be ecstatic for her sibling.

"What do you think, 'Lina?"

Cymbelina pushed Una's forearm down so she could look into her younger sibling's eyes. "It's beautiful. What is your patron's name? Also, I thought you were going to get the tattoo done next week?"

"His name is Tully. He's a chipper little fellow. And I was going to get the tattoo done next week, but I wanted to show it off at this year's Eldenfield Festival."

Giving her younger sister a pleased smile, Cymbelina turned to leave the room. "I see. Well, speaking of Eldenfield, I need to pack."

Una frowned. "But you just got home. Don't you want to talk about what happened earlier?"

"Not really, if I'm being honest."

"Are you sure? It must've been frightening to see—"

"I'm ok, Una, really. I think I just need some time alone to process what occurred in Sunshade earlier. Maybe I'll talk to you about it later, ok?"

The black-haired woman nodded, leaving her sister alone so

she could leave the living room.

Once Cymbelina was in the bedroom she shared with her sibling, she dove for her travel bag. Dashing about the room, the brunette grabbed the supplies she would need for tomorrow's journey to Eldenfield, hoping the negative thoughts would ebb from her mind.

Hopefully tomorrow will be a better day.

To Eldenfield
17ᵗʰ of Red Moon, 1300 AC

The autumn trees dotted the expansive Sunshade Forest, which housed the sprawling path the Glenrolk clan trotted upon. Row after row of álves huddled together as they walked down the leaf-ridden path, their traveling supplies in tow. The carts' wheels rumbled across the bumpy woodland ground, the grumbling noise fading under the cacophonous voices of the talkative voyagers. The clan had been traveling down the uneven road for three hours already, with another three grueling hours remaining ahead of them.

Cymbelina and her family, aside from Kinlord Emyr, who was shepherding the Glenrolk, were located toward the back of the group, along with a few other álves.

"Oh boy, do my feet hurt. Why couldn't I be born with a patron animal with the ability to fly, like a pigeon or something?"

"A pigeon? Ha! You're too unique for that, Una."

"I heard that, Séacael! Some of us here have pigeon patrons, you know."

"I know that, Talfryn. How could I forget? You never stop talking about it!"

Cymbelina sighed, witnessing the pre-festival row her stepfather, Séacael, was already getting into. Unable to refrain from commenting, she leaned over to whisper in Una's ear.

"It took three hours for Dad to get into his first argument. I think we just witnessed the breaking of a record."

The black-haired she-álf snorted. "Hey, I'll take an

adolescent argument over more talk of the creature you and Idal found yesterday."

Since the moment Cymbelina got out of bed this morning, news of the grayish-yellow-skinned stranger had been the topic on everyone's lips. According to Idal, who told her about the situation before she departed the camp this morning, the being had roused in the night, thrashing about in its restraints and screeching unintelligible words. The guards monitoring the being scoured through old Sylvanrolk texts to see if they could attempt to decipher what the creature was saying, but to no avail. Frankly, Cymbelina thought the situation was severe enough to warrant the postponement of the Eldenfield Festival, but no one else seemed to share the brunette's opinion on the matter.

"Aren't you the least bit concerned, Una? I mean, I'm doing everything I can just to keep my mind off of what might be happening back home as we speak."

Una shrugged her shoulders. "Sure, the entire situation is a bit unnerving, but if there was anything to truly be worried about, Grandpa wouldn't hesitate to contact the other clans and reschedule the festival. I trust his verdict, and I think you should, too."

"I guess," Cymbelina lied, trying her best to avoid starting an argument with her sister. In reality, the independent álf had never understood people who put their trust in one individual. Because of this mindset, the verdict of one person—even if that person was the leader of her clan and her grandfather—meant little to the brunette.

"Hey, Cymbelina!"

The brown-haired álf shuddered as the all too familiar discordant voice landed upon her pointed ears, her feet coming to a halt along with Una's. Cymbelina turned to the side, her green eyes landing on the source of the annoying voice. A flaxen-haired she-álf with a pair of deceptively inviting hazel eyes stood in the center of the road, one of her hands resting on her hips. The one person in Cymbelina's clan who did everything in her power to remind Cymbelina of her shortcomings stood before her, a condescending smile plastered on her face.

"Yes, Malaveen?"

The pale woman sauntered closer toward the sisters, her gaggle of followers following close behind.

"Are you and Idal the ones who fought that weird creature that everyone's been obsessing about this morning? Or should I say found? After all, I'm sure Master Arvel was the one who did all the fighting."

"Why are you asking a question you already know the answer to?" Una answered defensively.

"Because she likes to hear herself talk," Cymbelina responded, a teasing smirk gracing her lips.

The snobby álf narrowed her eyes. "Although I have an affinity for talking, at least I contribute to the clan by possessing a patron animal. You don't even have one."

"YET," Cymbelina corrected. "All Sylvanrolk have one, even Half-Sylvanrolk such as myself. My patron just hasn't revealed itself to me yet."

"Kind of like your father, right?"

The competitive edge dropped from Cymbelina's demeanor upon registering Malaveen's cruel remark—which even the blonde's friends tried to distance themselves from. It was common knowledge among the Glenrolk that Deirdre's first lover was a man from outside the clan, who disappeared after Deirdre became pregnant with Cymbelina. Or at least, that's what everyone had always told Cymbelina when she asked questions about him. Hell, Cymbelina didn't even know her father's name or race. But in Sylvanrolk culture, if a child had one parent who was a Wood Álf, that was enough for the child to be considered one, too. Even though most people in the Sylvanrolk clans adhered to this ancient belief, Malaveen and her parents did not, and they were not afraid to be vocal about the subject.

The air around the cluster of she-álves seemed to still as Cymbelina's gaze centered on her aggressor. "What did you just say?"

21

"Why ask a question you already know the answer to?" The blonde spat, a malicious smile plastered on her face.

Before the situation could escalate, Deirdre, who had returned down the path to see why her daughters were no longer with their father, stepped in between the two she-álves. "Girls, that's enough. Cymbelina, you and Una should be helping Séacael with his things. And Malaveen, aren't you and your friends supposed to be helping Findella with her cart?"

Malveen's unwavering gaze bore into Cymbelina as if taunting her to respond. When the brunette didn't give in, Malaveen exhaled, gazing at Deirdre.

"Why, Deirdre, you're absolutely right. It must have slipped my mind with all this talk of the strange creature and whatnot. Well, come on, ladies, we have work to do."

"Yes, Yes," Deirdre replied, watching the girls walk up the path and catch up with Findella. "After all, I would hate to see your...contributive... patron animals go to waste."

"You ok, 'Lina?" the black-haired woman asked, sending a look of concern in her older sister's direction.

"Yeah, I'm alright, Una. Just an unpleasant conversation, nothing I can't handle."

"Some people never grow up," Deirdre added, placing her hands on the girls' shoulders. "Speaking of which, why don't we catch up to your father? I would hate to see him get wrapped up in another one of his petty disagreements."

Agreeing with their mother, Cymbelina and Una marched forward, following the forest path for another three hours until they arrived at the Glenrolk clan's usual campsite in Eldenfield.

The autumnal moon shone brilliantly upon the clan's corner of the glade, which housed lush, wispy grass that fluttered under the crisp breeze. The hooting of the owls roosting in the nearby trees entertained the álves as they toiled away, setting up the necessary communal arrangements. Throughout the toiling, the spirits of Cymbelina and her kin were kept in check by the scent of the sizzling dinner the clan's chef, Tadhgmaris, was preparing.

Cymbelina finished setting out her bedroll and lantern early, fleeing to a distant section of the glade to seek solace underneath the starry sky. The babbling of the nearby brook and the distant murmuring of her Glenrolk kin filled her mind as she sat atop a section of soft grass and set her eyes on the Tree of Remembrance.

Located in the center of Eldenfield, the Tree of Remembrance—a large oak tree—serves as the symbol of togetherness for the three Sylvanrolk clans, who meet under its boughs every fall for three days. The three clans are called the Glenrolk, or Valley Folk; the Forrolk, or Forest Folk; and the Durolk, or the Jungle Folk. Their three-day-long gathering is known as the Eldenfield Festival. During this time, the kinlords and kinladies of the three clans gather underneath the tree to review the Sylvan Tenets and discuss pressing matters. The other members of their septs celebrate the survival of the Sylvanrolk through songs, stories, and crafts. The Eldenfield Festival is also the time of year when the newly recognized adult álves are honored, along with their mastered patron animals. In Cymbelina's opinion, this was the most exciting part of the fall event—a ritual that she couldn't wait to be included in someday.

If that day ever comes, the she-álf thought, her deep green eyes gazing across the sprawling field.

The twinkling glow from the other clans' campsites illuminated the outer rim of Eldenfield, creating a tenebrous pool of darkness underneath the central oak. Cymbelina's gaze was locked onto the dark abyss until she heard the pattering of approaching footsteps.

"How're you doing, 'Lina?" Una greeted, taking a seat beside her sister. The aroma of freshly roasted veggies filled the older álf's nostrils as her sister presented a basket of assorted vegetables to her. "Tadhgmaris just finished cooking his first round of vegetables, and I figured you would want some. It's been a long day, and I'm sure you're hungry."

"I appreciate it."

The sisters ate in silence, basking in the serenity of the scattered orchestra of crickets in the expansive field around them. Ever since the confrontation with Malaveen earlier in the day, the girls had been a bit distant and quiet, with Cymbelina unaware of what to say and Una unaware of how she could console her older sister. Having had enough of the silence, Una masticated the food remnants lingering in her mouth before speaking up.

"What are you looking forward to the most this year?"

Cymbelina smiled warmly at her sister as she chewed on a stalk of broccoli. *Una's clearly trying to put my mind at ease, and although that's easier said than done, I might as well play along.*

"Well," Cymbelina started, scooting around in the grass to face her sister. "I would have to say that I'm most excited to see you have your moment to shine."

"What do you mean?"

"What do I mean?" The older sister said, playfully scoffing. "I'm talking about how you recently mastered your patron animal, silly. I know how hard you've worked over the past few years to connect with Tully, and now that you have, it's time you got some recognition for it."

There was a moment of stillness as Una looked at her older sister, happiness gleaming in her dark blue eyes. Tossing her empty veggie basket on the ground, she brought Cymbelina in for one of her signature back-breaking hugs. "Thank you, 'Lina. I, well…just thank you."

The duo's moment of sincerity was cut abruptly short by an ear-piercing shriek originating from the other side of the Glenrolk campsite. The sisters' embrace broke apart instantly, giving Cymbelina the space she needed to take to her feet and run, Una following close behind. The black-haired she-álf dashed toward the noise in a fit of excitement and wonder. Cymbelina headed toward the noise in a dash fueled by fear and desperation.

That noise sounded an awful lot like the one the yellow creature let out when it was in pain yesterday. The brunette thought to herself, leaping over a series of bedrolls. *Dear Goddess, are there more like her on Florella?*

The women sprinted around the lanterns strewn throughout

the campground, occasionally leaping over more sleeping bags as they got in their way. Their feet thudded against the soil, akin to the thumping of a drum. With each step forward, the sisters drew closer to a gathering of álves near the camp's northern edge. Realizing the group's purpose, Una dug her heels into the soil to come to a stop, but Cymbelina charged her way through the gathering, too focused on the racing thoughts in her mind.

Please let my brethren be safe, Mother Terralynia; please ensure none of them are harmed.

"Wait, 'Lina, stop!"

Una's plea fell on deaf ears as Cymbelina pushed her way through the murmuring crowd, her racing heart lodged in her throat. A myriad of glares and grunts were shot the concerned female's way as she carelessly threw the complaints of her kin to the wind. Once Cymbelina reached the front of the crowd, she realized why she had received so many dirty looks. Kneeling in front of the string of onlookers was a young male álf, who was bestowing a gleaming river stone to a woman standing before him. Cymbelina had not infiltrated a mass of worried álves but a pack of witnesses to the betrothal of two lovers.

I was so caught up in the possibility that one of those creatures had returned that I forgot that the Eldenfield Festival is a popular time of year for couples to become engaged.

A wave of shame rose up the embarrassed álf's spine, crimson spreading across her light brown cheeks. A bony elbow dug into the right side of Cymbelina's ribcage, causing her to jump and look to her side. Positioned beside Cymbelina was none other than Malaveen, who had nothing but malice plastered on her hardened features.

A sardonic huff emanated between the blonde's lipstick-coated lips as she whispered into Cymbelina's ear, "How do you manage to ruin everything?"

Cymbelina kept her lips sealed, refusing to sully the beautiful moment unfolding before her any further.

Once the proposal concluded and the lingering álves

dispersed, Cymbelina apologized to the engaged couple before retreating from the scene in embarrassment. Una waited for her older sister in the same patch of grass she was left in, her dark blue eyes giving her older sister a look of sympathy.

"I tried to warn you, 'Lina, but it looks like you were so wrapped up in your thoughts that you didn't hear me. I'm sorry."

Cymbelina tucked a stray strand of hair behind one of her pointed ears, trying to regain her composure. "You have nothing to be sorry for, Una."

The sisters walked back toward their bedrolls, the gaze of their neighbors weighing heavily on them.

A brisk breeze swept through Eldenfield, causing the long, lush grass to sway to and fro. Lanterns were dimmed around the camp as members of the Glenrolk camp went to sleep, desperate to start the next day's festivities.

"We should probably go to sleep," Una said, yawning as the sisters approached the beds. The black-haired she-álf plopped down on hers. "I wouldn't want either of us to be exhausted before the fun of the Eldenfield Festival even begins."

"You're right," the brunette replied, sliding into the sleeping bag and pulling the plush covers over her.

Maybe some extra sleep might even help to clear my mind.

"Goodnight," Una said, tucking herself in and extinguishing the flame in her lantern. "Sleep well."

"You too," the brunette followed, closing her eyes.

Hopefully, tomorrow will help me forget today.

* * *

"Has the issue been remedied, Kazimiera?"

"Not yet, Monarch Vukasino. However, the two warriors you requested have been sent to the western shore of Florella, where you sent the scout, Petiča. In fact, they just confirmed their arrival via an affirmative call moments ago."

"Excellent," the ruler spoke, stroking the head of his rook, Tajni, who was perched upon his armrest. "It's about time I know what Petiča has been up to, considering she hasn't been giving me any updates on the progress of her mission."

The sconces adorning the walls of the gloomy throne room flickered as a burst of wind whooshed in. The gigantic wooden doors leading into the royal chambers banged as they hit the stone walls and closed, a stomping female emerging through the opening the doors allotted. Her yellowish-gray skin glimmered in the faint glow of the muted flames, her white hair swishing from side to side. The woman continued her anger-fueled approach toward the stone throne on which the monarch sat, only halting when one of the leader's bodyguards stepped in front of her. Unaffected by the guard's daunting frame, the woman addressed the leader of her people.

"Monarch Vukasino, I have something to say to you."

The guard in front of the forthright woman snarled, raising her javelin and pointing it toward the yellow-skinned woman. "You won't be saying anything if you address our lord in such a manner."

"Morana, please. Let the woman speak. She clearly has a pressing matter to discuss." The man leaned forward in his seat, resting his slate-gray hands underneath his pointy chin, a humored glint emanating from his coal-colored eyes. "What's your name, woman, and what did you come here to say? I have little time to spare, so speak quickly."

"My name is Urskana, and I'm here to ask about my sister, Petiča. Rumor around Elderfell is that her scouting mission on Florella went awry. I demand to know what you're going to do about it."

Another bodyguard visibly tensed at Urskana's aggressive words as the floor of the room began to tremble. Before the warrior could do anything to Urskana, Vukasino spoke up.

"Kazimiera, I can handle her. What kind of ruler would I be if I couldn't deal with the concerns of the rabble."

"The 'rabble'?!" Urskana yelled, fuming from how the leader of Elderfell spoke to her. "I'll have you know—"

"SILENCE!"

The monarch's raucous exclamation bounced off the walls,

causing all his attendants to stand a bit straighter. His eyes closed in exasperation as he released a cough, two of his skinny fingers massaging the shaved side of his head. Tajni squawked.

"Although I don't owe you an explanation, Urskana, I'm feeling mildly generous this evening, so I'll indulge you. Shortly before you so inappropriately interrupted my meeting with the knights, I was informed that the two warriors I had sent to fetch your sister had safely arrived on Florella. In fact, they're searching for Petiča as we speak.

"Will the group return to Elderfell after the rescue mission has concluded?"

"After they've completed another mission I've assigned them, yes."

"And what mission might that be?"

Monarch Vukasino momentarily sealed his lips in a tight line, his patience becoming increasingly scarce with each syllable that left the his subject's mouth. Narrowing his eyes, he rose from his throne. His splendorous wings, which resembled those of a peacock moth, untucked themselves from his regalia, briefly fluttering.

"The details of the mission I have sent the warriors on should be none of your concern," Vukasino said, his gaze still glued to Urskana. "If I decide to share any information with the common folk, I'm sure you'll be one of the first ones to know."

The answer the monarch supplied Urskana with was clearly to her disliking, as she soon began to rattle off a barrage of insults directed at him. Vukasino brushed the meaningless drivel off as he adjusted his garments, turning away from the raving woman and towards one of the throne room's exits. Looking over his shoulder, he addressed his bodyguards.

"I grow tired of this menial conversation. Bojana, Kazimiera, and Morana, please escort Urskana to the courtyard. I think it's about time she left."

"You're nothing like Matriarch Zlatana! She never would have abused her power in this fashion! She was the ruler of Elderfell, but she was not above her subjects!"

Vukasino felt his eyes twitch as he turned his head to peer at Urskana. In a flash, the monarch appeared before the woman who had offended him, one hand twisted in the female's white tresses and another clenched around the hilt of his curved blade. His solid black eyes bore into her purple ones, Urskana's hands coming up to clutch the ruler's broad shoulders.

Vukasino lowered his chapped lips to the pointed shell of the woman's left ear before hissing into it. "You're right; I'm not like my mother." He paused, his hot breath tickling the hairs inside Urskana's ear. "I'm not afraid to reclaim what rightfully belongs to our people."

With his parting words out of the way, Vukasino buried his blade into the astounded woman's abdomen. Blood-filled gurgles bubbled in Urskana's mouth as she let out one final surprised squeak, her balled fists unclenching around the monarch's robe-clad shoulders. Pushing the dying woman to the ground as if she were a sack of flour, the leader of Elderfell backed away from the felled corpse, cobalt pooling around its twitching frame. He groaned in disgust, flicking the blood off of his treasured sword.

"Change of plan, ladies," Vukasino started, popping his collar. "Kazimiera and Morana, I want you two to take this wretch," he motioned to the dead Urskana, "to the laboratory. Bojana, I want you to fetch Tihana from the war room. Tell her our meeting will be conducted later: she has a new test subject to assess first."

The Festival
18th of Red Moon, 1300 AC

Tapestries dyed in innumerable shades rippled in the brisk winds flowing throughout the festival square. Merchants from all three Sylvanrolk clans strategically established their stalls alongside the trails that wove throughout the clearing. The haggling of eager consumers and the euphonious tunes from the excited flutists permeated the air as Cymbelina approached the entrance to the event.

The waterskin hooked to Cymbelina's belt bounced against one of her moving legs as she and Una walked underneath the entryway banner. A merry festival organizer greeted the older álves walking in front of the sisters, stretching an arm out to the girls as they attempted to walk by. The morning sun shone down on the array of flower crowns attached to his waistband.

"Welcome to the Eldenfield Festival, ladies! Would either of you be interested in one of this year's flower crowns?"

Una shook her head emphatically, taking one of the daisy crowns and placing it on her head. Cymbelina politely declined.

"If you want to know more about today's events, feel free to take a gander at the board to your right. Now, be on your way and have a merry day!"

"Thanks. You too!" Una yelled, grabbing her sister's hand and attempting to drag her toward a row of stalls. "Now come on, 'Sis, we have a lot of ground to cover. We don't want all the goodies to be bought before we even have a chance to look at them!"

Cymbelina dug her feet into the ground, tugging her distracted sister backward. "Aren't you forgetting something, Una?"

The younger sister cocked her head to the side, her deep blue eyes assessing the look on her older sibling's face. The confusion written on the younger álf's soft features spoke volumes—she had clearly forgotten that they were supposed to help Séacael with his stall today. Because he couldn't set up his archery shop last year due to his assigned guard duty, he missed out on many potential clients, a situation he hoped to rectify this year since his schedule was free. To make up for last year's absence in festival profits, he asked the girls to help him this year, his reasoning being that the more people he had crafting supplies, the more money he'd be able to generate.

As Cymbelina opened her mouth to rectify her sister's forgetfulness, a disappointed look perverted Una's once cheerful appearance. "Oh yeah, we have to help Dad with his stall."

"That's right. And the sooner we do that, the sooner we can do what we want. So come on, let's get going."

Una groaned, dreading the work cut out for them. Although Cymbelina would never admit it, she was secretly grateful for the task. Worries about the creature back at the Glenrolk base camp plagued her mind, and helping Séacael appeared to be an opportunity that could temporarily alleviate her fears.

If work can't take my mind off of the situation, I don't know what can.

The girls traversed down the stall-filled path, the younger álf's wonder-filled eyes frequently straying from the path ahead of them. Chipper autumn sparrows sang their melodies as they soared in the sky above, Una's eyes flicking from stall to stall as quickly as the birds changed their song. Admiring the wares the various shops had to offer, Una babbled about what she saw.

"Is that a glow lily from the Jungle of Solitude? Those look like the wings of a Florellan swallowtail. Oh wow, look how cool that armor looks. Please, 'Lina, can we look at that vendor's jewels?"

31

Cymbelina chuckled, glancing at her sister's mirthful appearance. Although Una turned eighteen recently, her childlike curiosity seemed to return every time she stepped onto Eldenfield soil.

"I promise I'll come back with you later today, ok? As I said, we need to get to the archery stall. Dad set it up a few hours ago, so I'm sure he has a fair share of orders he needs help completing."

"Alright, you win—but don't try to weasel out of your promise like you did last year. This time, I won't forget."

The brunette chuckled. "We'll see about that. Come on."

The women marched onward without uttering another syllable, reaching Séacael's stand minutes later. Decorated in the Glenrolk clan's signature colors, the male álf's shop was intricately embellished, just like the craftsmanship of his weapons. Each wooden post that held up the carefully sown, juniper-hued awning was decorated with various symbols associated with archery, such as bows and arrows. Underneath this elaborate construct stood the owner and a customer. The client had a grateful smile plastered on her face. Jumping up and down, she thanked Séacael before skipping away, her red bob bouncing as she delightedly showed her latest purchase to a group of álves awaiting her return. Since the customer had left, the graying male álf glanced at his daughters.

"Good morning, girls. Glad to see you've finally decided to help your old man out. I've received more orders than I initially anticipated, so I will need all the help I can get." Séacael walked away from the counter and sat at his workbench, wiping away the beads of sweat on his furrowed brow. Glancing over his list of orders, he sighed before pointing to a box on the counter in front of Una. "Una, my dear, would you do your old man a favor and bring me my box of engraving tools. I'll definitely need them for this next order."

As Una did what she was asked to do, Cymbelina glanced about, noticing the absence of a familiar figure. "Where's Mom?"

"Deirdre is serving as the record keeper for the meeting of

the clan leaders today. I bet she's REAL thrilled with that assignment," Séacael tittered, beginning to whittle a shape into the bow in his hands.

"I see. Well, is there anything I can do to help out?"

"Actually, yes." The man paused, stopping his project to look at the brunette. "While your sister and I work on these orders, would you do me a wee favor and head to Tadhgmaris' stall and get me some food? I heard from one of the customers that he's selling roasted chestnuts today, and since I neglected to eat breakfast before setting up shop, I'm absolutely famished."

"Wait," Una butted in playfully. "Why don't I get the fun job, eh? I want to run an errand."

"Because Cymbelina doesn't get distracted like you do."

"Hey!"

"I'm sorry, but it's the truth of the matter. Now, Cymbelina, go fetch those chestnuts before my stomach starts eating itself."

Avoiding the conversation at her stepfather's stand, Cymbelina began her trip down the trodden path, seeking the chef's stall. Tadhgmaris was one of only three cooks who inhabited the Sylvanrolk clans, so he was never assigned guard duty during the Eldenfield Festival. Because of this, the stands the chefs set up were one of the festival's highlights each year. Supposedly, each of the three chefs and their apprentices had one specialty, but all of Tadhgmaris' food was so good that the Half-Sylvanrolk could never determine which of his dishes was the best.

Following the wafting scent of delicious roasted nuts, Cymbelina found Tadhgmaris' shop, which had a winding line of álves waiting to be served. Promptly joining the queue, Cymbelina peered ahead to see who was working the counter. She became startled when she gazed into a pair of all too familiar marigold eyes.

Is that…Kayven?

Under the thick, cream-colored canopy covering the chef's workstation stood Kayven, Tadhgmaris's only child and

Cymbelina's childhood friend. The she-álf hadn't seen much of Kayven since eight years ago when they were both fourteen. Their separation was a disastrous result of his transfer to the Forrolk clan so he could live with his mother, Adair. It was heartbreaking for her back then, but as the years went by, it seemed like he had only been a hallucination in the brunette's adolescent brain. However, he stood before her now, an adult álf, his warm bronze skin sheltered from the sun's blinding rays. The lack of sun did nothing to detract from the brightness of Kayven's deep-set, yellowish-orange eyes, which gazed at the álf in the front of the line.

I can't believe it's really him. I can't recall the last time I thought about him, let alone heard anything about him from Tadhgmaris.

The line leading up to the counter moved forward inch by inch, the half-álf still lost in her thoughts. After twenty minutes of waiting, it was finally Cymbelina's turn to order food. Turning around to tell his father something, Kayven overlooked Cymbelina until he faced forward.

"Hey, what can I get for you today? Wait," the male álf paused, leaning over the counter. The sunlight hit his chiseled face, highlighting the obsidian locks draping over his shoulders. A falcon feather was dangling from one of them. "Is that you, Cymbelina?"

"In the flesh," the brunette laughed.

"Wow..." the male exhaled, looking the brunette over in astonishment. "How long has it been, eight years? It feels like I haven't seen you in an eternity."

"It has been quite some time; I haven't seen you since you joined your mom's clan. Speaking of which, what're you doing over here? Shouldn't you be helping the Forrolk clan's chef as their apprentice?"

The male smiled. "I could...but that wouldn't do much good for someone who has rejoined the Glenrolk clan, would it?"

Cymbelina blinked in astonishment.

"Can you order something and move on already?!" An álf toward the back of the line yelled, distracting the she-álf from what she was planning to say. "Some of us have things to do today!"

"I'll be with you in a moment!" Kayven replied, his eyes never wavering from Cymbelina's. "I guess we'll have to continue this conversation later, Cymbelina. What can I get for you today?"

"I'll take one order of roasted chestnuts, please."

"Coming right up," the male grinned, retreating into the depths of the stall to retrieve the brunette's order.

So Kayven has rejoined the Glenrolk clan. Maybe this is my chance to rekindle the friendship we once had.

"Here you go!" the male announced, returning with an overflowing basket of chestnuts in his hands. "Enjoy!"

Giving Kayven her thanks, Cymbelina departed the stall and headed back to Séacael's stand. Arriving at her stepfather's booth, she was greeted by the sight of two salivating álves, who dropped what they were doing at the first sign of food.

"Oh wow, would you look at that? Seems like Tadhgmaris outdid himself with this batch of chestnuts."

Cymbelina cocked an eyebrow in amusement. "That's what you say every time you eat chestnuts, Dad."

"But it's true! Tadhgmaris seems to outdo himself every time he steps foot into the kitchen."

"If they're so good," Una began slyly, sliding up next to her father, "you won't mind sharing them with me."

"Of course, I don't mind sharing with ya," Séacael answered, a humored grin slowly spreading across his face. However, as the black-haired álf reached over to pluck a delicious nut from the basket, Séacael swatted her hand away.

"Hey! You said you would share with me."

"Oh, and I meant it. You can have some...just as soon as you finish that bow you've been working on."

Una grunted. "Not fair."

"Life isn't fair!" The aging álf bellowed, laughing at his little prank. "You might as well get used to it before it's too late."

Cymbelina chuckled, tying her hair into a neat braid as she set up her workspace at the counter, preparing to jot down orders for the incoming customers.

The trio worked throughout the day, with Una and Cymbelina switching tasks occasionally to prevent the younger female from bickering. Orders came and left at an alarming speed, leaving an abundance of álves from all three clans content with their newly acquired weapons. The stall continued to make a handsome sum of profits well into the afternoon as the scintillating autumnal sun passed across the sky. Cymbelina worked fastidiously, jotting down the newest customer's order until a shriek echoed across the festival grounds. She dropped the quill she had been writing with, her eyes flicking from side to side before turning to face her stepfather and sister.

"Did either of you hear that noise?"

"I can't hear anything back here, 'Lina." Séacael motioned to one of his pointy ears. "Sometimes, I think you forget that your dad's sixty years old."

"I'm not joking. I think someone's in trouble."

"Come on, Sis…trouble? Do you mean the type of trouble you ran into last night during the couple's proposal? It's probably nothing."

The brunette sighed, leaning over the counter and gazing out into the festival center, where a horde of álves, both young and old, fervently danced in a circle, flower crowns bouncing atop their heads.

Una's probably right. I'm probably just overthinking again.

However, as the worrisome woman stared into the crowd, she ascertained a sudden shift in the revelers' mood. The tightly packed group of álves suddenly dispersed as the fearful people fled the scene. The lively music accompanying the dancers came to a discordant halt as the musicians joined their fellow álves in a getaway. Bloodcurdling screams echoed throughout the valley, the hairs all over Cymbelina's body standing on end.

Cymbelina backed away from the counter, moving toward her sister and stepfather. Terror flooded the brunette's veins, her eyes flicking to and fro across the crowd. "No trouble?" The older sibling gulped, her eyes never straying from the ever-dwindling crowd of partygoers. "Then what do you suppose is causing that?"

"Please, 'Lina, we have work to do."

"She's not kidding, Dad, look!"

Séacael grumbled, pushing his greasy, graying hair out of his eyes, his deep brown orbs expanding in shock as he witnessed the turmoil being sowed in the center of Eldenfield. The square's partygoers were replaced by the fighting forms of two Wood Álves and a pink-skinned being, similar to the one Cymbelina and Idal had found outside the camp.

"Oh, heavens above," the older male mumbled, clearly in shock. Dropping the project he was working on, he shakily stood up, his eyes full of fear. "What in the world is that thing?"

"Why does that matter?!" The younger sister screeched. "We should be focused on what we're gonna do!"

"We're going to fight," Cymbelina responded to her sister, fear flowing through her veins. With a trembling hand, the Half-Sylvanrolk reached underneath the counter to grab a bow and a handful of arrows Séacael had just made for a customer. She wasn't exactly thrilled to face off against one of those creatures again, but she refused to sit and watch her kin battle the being without her.

"Are you daft!" Séacael roared, watching helplessly as the brunette armed herself with various supplies. "You're going to get yourself killed. We don't need to fight; we need to flee. Now!"

"You two can flee if you want to. I'm going to get Mom," Cymbelina declared, grabbing one of her stepfather's extra quivers and sliding arrows into it.

"I want to come with you!"

"No!" Séacael and Cymbelina responded to Una simultaneously before the older male continued, "Deirdre's with the clan leaders. They're the strongest Sylvanrolk around! Your mother is in good hands—and that's ignoring the fact that she's capable of defending herself!"

"I'm not willing to take that chance, Dad."

Realizing that he couldn't convince his stepdaughter to come with him and Una, Séacael sighed, giving the brunette one last look. "Fine, but you better be damn careful out there. Come along, Una, leave everything behind."

Cymbelina dashed toward the festival center ahead of her, leaving her family members behind. Diving behind an abandoned counter adjacent to the chaotic quarrel, the she-álf crouched. Plucking a sharpened arrow from the quiver, she leaned to the side, assessing the skirmish occurring a few feet away from her.

The two lightly-armored Sylvanrolk were still battling the pink-skinned creature, but now they had transformed into their patron animals: one a furious bull and another a determined hawk. The altered álves charged toward the being, who smoothly dodged and blocked each of the fighters' attacks. Despite their failed attempts to land a blow on the strange creature, they kept trying, leaving Cymbelina little room to fire an arrow.

If only I had an opening.

As if on cue, Kinlord Emyr bounded around the broad trunk of the Tree of Remembrance in the form of his white stag patron animal. Galloping around the monumental oak, a brilliant purple aura encased the buck's sleek body as Emyr charged toward the pink creature. The thunderous sprint of the mighty kinlord caught the other two warriors' attention, and both fighters ceased their onslaught. Emyr took advantage of the space the bull and hawk created, speeding between them and toward the enemy. His spindly antlers pierced the being's flesh, unfortunately causing little harm as the stranger jumped backward just as Emyr began his attack. Extending an arm in the clan leader's direction, the creature let loose a stream of fire from her pink, spindly fingertips. The flames sputtered, licking underneath the stag's right eye. Emyr recoiled in agony, his right eye closing as he emitted a wail.

"Grandpa!" Cymbelina instinctively yelled, not thinking about the possible consequences of her outburst.

The other two fighters transformed into their álven forms,

rushing to the aid of the injured kinlord, leaving Cymbelina alone with the startled enemy.

The brunette's braid swayed to the side as she jumped to her feet, nocking an arrow on the bow and taking aim at the mysterious creature. Without a shred of hesitancy, the woman released the projectile, her green eyes glued on it until it sunk into the pink-skinned creature's toned left forearm, which it was about to use for another attack. Lowering the arm, the creature shrieked, its hate-filled grimace flicking to the Half-Sylvanrolk.

As the determined archer prepared to fire another arrow, the being's mouth unhinged like a snake, a raging inferno pouring out of it as it yanked the shaft out of its arm. The stream of fire spread out far and wide, causing Cymbelina to drop her weapon and duck. The heat of the fire warmed the nape of the álf's neck as she reached for her discarded bow, failing to grab it before the entity attacked again. Screaming like a dying banshee, the pink creature ran toward the prone Cymbelina, who tucked her arm down to her side before rolling to dodge the enemy's sharp fingernails. Dirt caked Cymbelina's sweaty skin as she rolled twice more, rising into a crouch before throwing a handful of soil in the stranger's face. The creature yelled again, furiously rubbing her eyes.

"Cymbelina!"

Looking to the source of her name, the brunette eyed the leader of the Forrolk clan, Kinlady Nairna, her white robes billowing in the breeze. Beside her sat Kinlord Quindlen, leader of the Durolk clan, coiled up in his anaconda patron form, ready to strike at the blinded being.

"Get away from that creature!" Nairna yelled, motioning for the brunette to move. "We have it covered."

As soon as Cymbelina followed the clan leader's orders, Kinlord Quindlen struck out at the dazed being, his ten-foot-long snake form tightly wrapping around the mysterious woman. As the leader's shiny, scale-covered body slowly squeezed the life out of the enemy's frame, Cymbelina tore across the field to kneel next to her grandfather.

Her grandfather had unintentionally returned to his álven form, the energy drained from his unconscious frame. The skin underneath Kinlord Emyr's right eye was a worrisome red, with blotches of an even darker scarlet dotting the surrounding area. Thinking on her feet, Cymbelina grabbed the waterskin from her waist, pouring a liberal amount of the cooled water over the fresh burn.

I hope this will suffice until he can receive more thorough care.

As Cymbelina continued to administer the best first-aid she could muster, the weak sounds of the whimpering pink-skinned being filled the air. The brunette ignored the pitiful sounds of the creature until, in its dying breath, it let out a final ominous threat:

"We...won't stop...until death has taken...all of the álfrolk."

With a final squeeze from Kinlord Quindlen, the creature died. Releasing her from his tangled coil, the leader of the Durolk returned to his álven form before approaching Kinlady Nairna, who stood behind Cymbelina's crouched frame.

"Come, my dear," Kinlady Nairna spoke softly, motioning for the two nearby warriors to pick up the unconscious kinlord. "These men will bring Kinlord Emyr back to his tent, where they'll help Healer Vevina treat his wound. For now, you must return to your family."

"Do you know where my mother is?" The brunette asked, tears glazing her pine-green eyes.

"She went looking for you and the rest of your family after she helped me bring down another one of these strange creatures."

"Perhaps investigating the Glenrolk campsite would be the best place for you to start your search," Kinlord Quindlen added.

Cymbelina nodded, not needing to hear another word. Glancing at her grandfather one last time, she headed off in the direction of her clan's camp.

"And you said you've seen one of those creatures before,

Cymbelina?"

"Yes, Kinlord Quindlen. In fact, my friend and I found one sneaking around the western shore not far from the Glenrolk base camp two days ago. We were able to apprehend the creature and detain it."

The kinlord hummed, his pewter-gray eyes moving toward his fellow clan leader. "What do you think, Kinlady Nairna?"

The woman was silent for a time, her tattooed fingers playing with one of her braids, her eyes closed in reflection. The barn owl on her shoulder hooted, its head cocking to the side as it gazed at Cymbelina. Opening her mahogany eyes, Kinlady Nairna glanced at the brunette. "I certainly feel like these creatures are worth investigating. I'm also wondering why this situation wasn't brought to our attention sooner."

"If I may speak freely, Your Lordships, " Cymbelina began, eyes darting between the two kin leaders. Neither objected. "I'm sure Kinlord Emyr believed that the creature was alone. If not, I think he would've sent you both a message."

Although I thought hosting the festival after discovering the strange creature was a bad idea in the first place.

"I'm sure that was his reasoning as well," Kinlord Quindlen said. "However, I still question his logic."

Kinlady Nairna sighed, petting the owl as it nuzzled against her neck. "Regardless of our joint opinions, the past is in the past. We must look forward to the future and plan our next course of action."

The sun had descended from its celestial pedestal, causing a thick shroud of darkness to envelop Eldenfield. Hours had passed since the two unknown beings wrought havoc on the Sylvanrolk clans, leaving several álves injured. Luckily for Kinlord Emyr, the flame that had wounded him only managed to burn the skin under his eye, an injury that Healer Vevina could treat within a few weeks. After the healer began the kinlord's treatment, Emyr was placed in isolation, allowing him to rest for the night. Due to his incapacitated state and Cymbelina's previous experience with the mysterious creatures, Cymbelina was forced to take Emyr's place in the clan leaders' tent, a position she had no desire to occupy.

Cymbelina looked between the two clan leaders, agitation slowly rising in her gut as their silence continued. *Mulling over what happened earlier will do us no good. We should be out there trying to find where these brutes are coming from and prevent them from harming any more of our kin.*

A flickering lantern doused the meeting area in an orange glow, the humming of the nocturnal bugs outside invading the space of the claustrophobic enclosure. Kinlady Nairna clasped one of her sepia hands around her waterskin, her dark eyes closing in reflection. After a brief sip of water, she spoke again, pushing one of her twin onyx braids over her shoulder. The owl hooted.

"The pink creature that attacked the festival square had fire abilities, and the one that attacked the festival outskirts was green and had earth manipulation abilities. Tell me, child, what color was the creature's skin that you and your friend fought on the beach, and what powers did it possess?"

"Well," Cymbelina began, "the being was yellow, and it moved very fast. It could also move objects with the swipe of its hand."

"Wind abilities, perhaps?" Kinlord Quindlen suggested, his long, pointy ears peeking out from between his layered crimson waves. He had a silver hoop in his right earlobe, which dazzled in the lantern's light.

"I was thinking the same thing. Did the stranger on the beach appear to be a woman?"

Before the brown-haired álf could respond, Quindlen's facial expression changed. "Oh, Kinlady Nairna, you're not suggesting—"

"I haven't suggested anything, Kinlord Quindlen. I'm just letting the cogs in my mind work their magic."

"Please don't try to deny your speculations from me. The questions you're posing are clearly skewed—"

"For the love of the Supreme Mother," Nairna uncharacteristically interrupted, placing her free hand on Quindlen's shoulder. "Let the girl answer my question."

Sensing that there wouldn't be any further comments, Cymbelina responded to Kinlady Nairna's inquiry. "Yes, the yellow creature appeared to be a woman. May I ask why the sex of the stranger is important?"

"The fact that the being appeared to be a woman alone does not particularly pique my interest." Nairna took a quick sip from her waterskin again before placing it down. "However, when you combine that observation with others—such as the beings' magical capabilities and range of skin tones—well, I can't help but say that I'm thoroughly intrigued. After all, the fact that these creatures possess these three qualities simultaneously makes them very similar to the vilek of the Glimmering Wilds."

"But why would the fairy women want to target the descendants of the ancient álfrolk? They allowed some of our predecessors to live in their sanctuary."

"I didn't say they were vilek, Kinlord Quindlen. The creatures that attacked our clans today didn't have wings, and I'm assuming the one on the beach didn't either?" Nairna glanced at Cymbelina for clarification.

"It did not," Cymbelina drawled, looking confusedly between the two clan leaders. Kinlady Nairna and Kinlord Quindlen's incessant babbling about the vilek made the she-álf's head spin. Unable to hold back, Cymbelina inquired, "Who are the vilek?"

Quindlen's almond-shaped eyes widened. "Do the Glenrolk storytellers not share tales of the vilek and their acceptance of our ancient kin?"

"No…"

"Well, it seems like Kinlord Emyr needs to set his storytellers straight. They've done a grave disservice to their peers by not sharing the stories of—"

"Calm down, Kinlord Quindlen. Let us not make expectations for those who are not present," Nairna interrupted. "Now, to answer your inquiry as concisely as possible: the vilek are a group of fairy women who dwell in the Glimmering Wilds. Unfortunately, we know little more than that in terms of the history of these women, besides the fact that they predate the álfrolk. However, our scholars know that the vilek took in some of our álfrolk brethren during The Great Dissolution—which is why I'm not certain these creatures are vilek."

"And because of the fact that these creatures don't seem to have wings."

"Yes, Kinlord Quindlen, and because of that tidbit, which I already established."

"Then what do you propose we do, Your Lordships?" Cymbelina queried, looking curiously between Quindlen and Nairna. "Should the rest of the Eldenfield Festival be postponed while you two seek a conference with the vilek? If they're as amicable as the tales suggest, don't you think they'd be willing to discuss the situation and discover what's going on?"

"Well, I certainly agree with you on postponing the event, young one, but seeking a conference with the vilek?" Quindlen shook his head, an amused smirk spreading across his fair face. "That's out of the question."

"Why, Kinlord Quindlen? Don't you think this is a serious enough situation to consult with old allies?"

Kinlord Quindlen took a steady breath as he gave the brunette a slightly peeved look. "I admire your enthusiasm, Cymbelina, but the vilek are practically unreachable. In fact, I've sent many scouting parties to the Glimmering Wilds in past seasons, and not once did my scouts come back with news of their whereabouts. I believe Kinlord Emyr tried to reach out to them at one point as well, but he was also unsuccessful in his endeavors."

A sinking feeling settled in Cymbelina's stomach, causing the female álf's vocal pitch to increase. "Well, there's got to be something you clan leaders can do. What if they attack again, and things go sideways? You can't allow your citizens to be needlessly slaughtered!"

Kinlady Nairna gave the brunette a warning glance, sensing where the conversation was headed. "We won't sit back and do nothing, but the first thing we should do before we plan any further course of action is to have the clans travel back to their respective camps, converse, and then communicate via mail if necessary."

"You can't be serious," Cymbelina replied, looking incredulously between the two clan leaders. "Splitting up is the worst thing we can do at this point in time."

"I'm sorry, Cymbelina, but this is how joint leadership works. Snap decisions are not an option."

Nairna stood from her cross-legged position on the ground, her owl flapping its wings. Quindlen followed his fellow clan leader seconds later. Walking behind Cymbelina, Nairna opened the tent's entry flap, exposing all three of the álves inside to the cool night breeze.

"Now, I think it's time you returned to the Glenrolk campsite, Cymbelina. I'm sure your parents are anxiously awaiting your arrival."

Cymbelina wordlessly ducked through the opening and into the dark night, desperate to flee the gathering. She still couldn't wrap her mind around the decision-making process that occurred during the meeting. Did the lives of her Wood Álf kin mean so little to the leaders that they were willing to sit on the threat looming in the shadows? What if more enemies were waiting for each clan when they returned home? It was impossible to know what the future had in store for them, so why not investigate the situation now?

What a bunch of cowards. I'm frightened, too, but I'm not opposed to doing what's right instead of heading home with my tail between my legs.

The soft grass crinkled underneath Cymbelina's stomping feet as she crossed the glade and entered her clan's camp. The sound of the crackling campfire was her only greeting, as all the other Glenrolk álves were fast asleep, besides the occasional guard patrolling the grounds. Tucking herself in her bedroll, the she-álf turned on her side, facing Kinlord Emyr's tent. Images of his injured form flashed before her eyes, her stomach churning in disgust.

Don't worry, Grandpa. I'll help to stop those creatures, no matter what it takes.

Vengeance
19th of Red Moon, 1300 AC

Although Cymbelina never had the opportunity to disclose the clan leaders' decision to her grandfather, he came to the same conclusion that they did without any debriefing from the she-álf. Ignoring his injury, Kinlord Emyr woke up the rest of the Glenrolk and signaled to the other clans that they would depart Eldenfield shortly. Much to Cymbelina's chagrin, her kin barely seemed phased by the attack, talking more about their disappointment in the festival's cancellation than the creatures' ambush. A deep feeling of disgust welled in the brunette's core as she heard the words of her brethren, who seemed to disregard the wounds of their fellow álves.

With each passing day, I realize just how little I know about the people around me. Why is everyone focusing on the fact that the festival was canceled while we should be worrying about where our aggressors are coming from? How come I'm one of the only people taking the threat our enemies pose seriously?

The dreary mood of the travelers seeped into nature's heart. The sun was tucked behind a thick wall of gray clouds, the sky opening up as the Glenrolk began their withdrawal from the glade. The downpour of chilled raindrops continued an hour into the clan's journey through the Sunshade Forest, the sheets of descending water muddying the dirt trail. Twigs crunched underneath the shuffling álves, who cloaked themselves from the torrents of rain. Most of the travelers had their eyes cast to the ground as if looking at the road ahead was too difficult to bear. One exception to this phenomenon was Cymbelina, her eyes drifting from side to side, scanning the area for possible attackers as she walked behind her grandfather.

Before yesterday's attack, the young álf was scared of the stranger she and Idal found on the beach. Its existence in Cymbelina's life was new and mysterious, full of possibilities. However, after the attack and her discussion with the other clan leaders, a new feeling sprouted in her soul: fury. Fury toward the clan leaders and their inability to grasp the urgency of the situation. Fury toward the creatures lurking in the shadows and seeking to spill more blood. Fury toward the fact that regardless of how willing Cymbelina was to fight for her clan, she still felt weak and powerless. Irrespective of the poignant mixture of anxiety and frustration in her chest, the she-álf promised herself that she would maintain a brave face.

"Cymbelina," Kinlord Emyr whispered, stirring the brunette from her thoughts. Her dark green eyes bore into her grandfather's light green ones, which peeked out from the shadows of his royal purple cloak. "I would prefer you to dwell beside me rather than behind me."

She hurried to her grandfather's side, pulling back the left side of her golden hood to get a better look at the older man. The burn around Emyr's right eye was startlingly noticeable, the pale pink skin and the red spots around it moist from the gel he had administered hours before. Emyr looked at Cymbelina from the corner of his eyes before turning his head to fully face her.

"I saw you guarding me back there, protecting me as if I were a mere álfling. Although your effort is appreciated, I'm sure my guards can help me with any situation that should arise."

"You mean the two álves who were nowhere to be seen yesterday when you received the brand on your face? That's doubtful."

Emyr chuckled, his stubbly laugh lines creasing. "I see your point, but yesterday was an extraordinary circumstance. The guards are more alert today. So please, stay up here with me."

Cymbelina wordlessly complied with his request, allowing her presence beside Emyr to be her display of agreement.

The vibrant leaves of the surrounding foliage rustled underneath the weight of the droplets, which came in larger scores by the minute. The increased rainfall decreased the visibility of the álves leading the traveling clan, ultimately slowing the group's pace. The forest birds, which would typically be singing their afternoon melodies, were silent, opting to use their bodies to shield their hatchlings from the rain. The lack of birdsong created a tranquil void in Sunshade, which Kinlord Emyr sought to fill through conversation—a tactic few travelers were currently employing.

Emyr asked Cymbelina to recap the clan leaders' conversation, the duo's voices increasing in volume under the pounding rain. This was the first time in a while that the female álf had been able to talk with her grandfather one-on-one, and although she wasn't a fan of the topic they were discussing, she was glad to be spending some time with him.

"Now that you've given me the gist of the conversation, I have one question left to ask you: how did it feel to be in the clan leaders' tent for an official meeting?"

The brunette snorted. "Let me put it this way: I don't know how you can stomach the abhorrent protocols of being a kinlord. I can't tell what's worse: the stuffy formality or the boring lectures."

"Welcome to politics, Cymbelina," Emyr started, guffawing. "Some Wood Álves spend their entire lives craving power while ignorant of the fact that it's not all fun and games. So they seek leadership like a pack of starving dogs, ravenously devouring every scrap of authority they can sink their teeth into. But you...you discovered the truth of leadership at the young age of twenty-two. Consider me impressed."

"I never expected leadership to be all fun and games: in fact, I'm a little shocked at just how relaxed Kinlord Quindlen and Kinlady Nairna were about yesterday's incursion. They're not even planning to seek out any allies the assailants might have. Do you not object to this inaction? After all, álven blood was spilled yesterday." Cymbelina's train of thought disintegrated, a plan emerging through the smithereens of her previous notions. "We could interrogate the stranger we have back at camp and see what she says."

Kinlord Emyr sighed, ignoring the plan the young álf had proposed. "My feelings about the event that occurred yesterday are unimportant in the grand scheme of things. And even if I did outwardly object, I would be in the minority: one against two. I am effectively powerless in this situation, even if I did decide to share my notions with the other leaders."

"So you do object to their reasoning. Well then, why don't you establish your own group of álves to seek out the creatures and try negotiating with them."

"My hands are bound. The Sylvan Tenets clearly state—"

"Grandpa," Cymbelina began, turning angrily towards the kinlord. "Has it ever occurred to you that some situations might necessitate bypassing the Old Laws? Like, I don't know, a situation where a group aims to destroy all álfkind?!"

Emyr was silent, his pale green eyes displaying a sense of helplessness unfit for words. He quickly turned his face away from his granddaughter in shame.

Why won't he do something? Why won't anyone do something about the threat looming over our heads?

Roused by the tense exchange between the grandfather and granddaughter, one of Emyr's personal guards sped ahead, falling in step with Emyr and Cymbelina. "Is there an issue up here, Kinlord Emyr?"

"No," the she-álf answered for him, her voice dripping with disillusionment as she walked away from the male álves. "I was just leaving."

The brunette left the stream of Glenrolk and stepped to the side, waiting to rejoin the rest of her family as they passed by. When she spotted Una's cloaked frame, she entered the crowd again. Like the rest of the clan, her family was quiet, their eyes glued to the ground underneath them.

Wiping away a stray raindrop that had found its way onto the tip of her nose, Una looked up. Giving the brunette's tense frame a once-over, the younger álf whispered, "What's wrong, 'Lina?"

"Is 'everything' a valid answer to your question? After all, there's not much that's gone right these past few days, is there?"

"I suppose you're right," Una sighed, looking away from her sister and back at the ground. "I'm just glad the two of us left Eldenfield unscathed."

I'd be even more glad if Grandpa would come to his senses and decide to investigate the culprits behind the recent attacks by the time we arrive at camp, but that's doubtful.

"As am I," the brunette responded, keeping her thoughts to herself. "Hopefully, the rest of our journey home will be as uneventful as it has been thus far."

"We can certainly hope."

The sisters kept their mouths closed for the remainder of the trip, the silence between them becoming painfully obvious as the rain slowly decreased its descent. The rain shower had ceased entirely by the time the Glenrolk reached the border of their base camp, the group's dejected pace pushing their arrival time to the hour of twilight.

Shades of pink and purple filtered through the trees lining the edge of the Sunshade Forest, the hilly valleys of Terralynia's Folly vaguely visible in the distance. The weak braziers surrounding the forest perimeter of the clan's camp crackled, casting jagged shadows across the muddy woodland trail the álves trod upon. Besides the squelching of leather boots sinking into sludge, the forest air was chilly and devoid of noise. The stillness left Cymbelina feeling unsettled, anxiety gnawing away at her core.

Usually, there are guards who patrol this region, especially at dusk. Where could they be? The half-álf thought, inhaling deeply to try and steady her troubled heart. *And why are the flames of the braziers so weak? It's as if they've been flickering for hours, and nobody has tended to them.*

Clinging to the hope that the absence of sentries was due to changing shifts, the brunette remained silent, keeping in step

51

with the rest of her clan members as they approached the camp. With each step Cymbelina took and each flick of her wandering gaze, the dread lingering in her stomach continued to fester. There were no guards in sight; not only that, the area surrounding the Glenrolk home seemed devoid of all life, an unnerving placidity hanging in the autumnal air.

What is going on here? Where is everyone?

About ten feet away from the campsite, the cluster of álves came to an abrupt halt. A wave of murmurs floated over the tightly packed crowd before Kinlord Emyr silenced everyone with a hair-raising outcry.

"I need five álves to investigate the camp! Yestin, Aurnia, Gallven, Wynne, and Séacael, come up here to see me."

The brunette's eyes worriedly looked at her stepfather as he pushed through the crowd, trying to navigate his way to the clan's leader. Moments of silence followed until Kinlord Emyr spoke to the five summoned Sylvanrolk loud enough for everyone in the Glenrolk to hear.

"Yestin and Wynne, I want you two to investigate the camp's surrounding areas. Make sure we did not miss anything as we approached the camp. Séacael, Aurnia, and Gallven: I want you three to search the campgrounds; we need to find out why no álves are patrolling the area."

The selected Wood Álves spread out, doing as the Glenrolk leader instructed. Cymbelina and the rest of her kin were left to wonder what was happening, praying to Mother Terralynia that nothing terrible had occurred at the campsite in their absence.

"What do you think is going on?" Una whispered, huddling close to her mother and sister.

"I'm not sure," Deirdre mumbled, hugging her two daughters close, "but keep your eyes open."

Cymbelina's eyes followed Yestin as he searched a shadowy thicket only a few feet away from her and her family. She could tell the male was just as nervous as she was because he hurled a dagger into the bush when it started to rustle. A faint squeak was heard seconds later.

"Way to go, Yestin!" A male álf to the right of Cymbelina

exclaimed. "You saved us from a squirrel."

A wave of hushed giggles arose from the crowd, easing some of the tension amongst the gathering.

"Quiet!" Emyr responded, concern dripping from his gruff voice.

The álves quieted upon hearing their leader's tone of voice, tension filling the air once more. The search continued for what felt like forever, many álves becoming fidgety as they awaited some news on the state of their camp. If the circumstances were different, tons of álves would join the search parties to patrol the land, seeking answers to the questions plaguing their minds. However, the possibility that one of those creatures was lying in wait for a foolish álf to discover its hiding spot made the members of the Glenrolk practice a bit of restraint.

Such notions of self-restraint were thrown to the wind minutes later when Aurnia called for Kinlord Emyr.

"Kinlord Emyr!" Aurnia yelled, her high-pitched scream piercing through the still night air, disgruntling some nearby birds as they fled from their nests in the dark trees. Disgust laced her voice. "I think you're going to want to see this!"

The crowd of Glenrolk surged forward as soon as Kinlord Emyr headed toward Aurnia's voice. Scurrying after their clan leader, Cymbelina and the rest of her kin ended up in the center of the dim campsite.

Whatever possible scenario the female could've conjured in her mind about what awaited the Glenrolk in the center of their settlement paled in comparison to the carnage before her. Lying in the center of the town was a towering stack of burnt álven bodies atop a dead fire. A putrid smell emanated from the fly-ridden charred corpses, whose faces were so burnt that their identities were hard to discern, especially under the darkness of night. The scent of vomit soon joined that of the singed cadavers as the álves responded to the scene of brutality before them. Gasps and cries rang on the night wind, which whirled through the site of the unholy massacre.

Cymbelina's mouth fell open in a silent gasp of terror, her

bloodshot eyes glistening with the threat of tears. Her lips quivered, and her breath came in shallow, ragged bursts, each exhalation a shaky breath of horror. The sight before her was unlike anything she had ever witnessed—an unspeakable carnage that left her paralyzed with shock.

How did this happen?! Cymbelina swallowed, trying to keep her breakfast from coming back up. *Are the same creatures we encountered yesterday responsible for this? How were they able to overcome so many álves?*

Among a chorus of weeping and retching, the first person to utter a semi-coherent message was the kinlord, his voice laden with restraint as Master Arvel helped him to remain standing. "I...I want every able-bodied álf to investigate the tents and the perimeter of the camp. Find any clues as to what might've happened here. All álflings stay here with Master Arvel and me."

Cymbelina remained by her grandfather's side, not because she was trying to obey his command, but because she was too stunned to move. She was deaf to the world around her, her green eyes glued to the pile of charred corpses, both young and old. The contents of her stomach gurgled with each breath, the female slowly inhaling air to keep her composure. Her limbs shook, her heart pounding in her chest.

This can't be happening. This is some sick nightmare that I need to be woken up from. Oh, Supreme Mother, please let me wake up from this horrendous dream.

A mournful scream tore the brunette out of her daze, her gaze darting to the direction from which it came. Her eyes rested on Healer Vevina's tent, the same tent that housed the creature Cymbelina and Idal found the other day.

Cymbelina's eyes grew wide. Throughout this entire ordeal, she hadn't thought of Idal a single time. She needed to find him but, with the state of the camp, she wasn't so sure she would like what she saw.

Tearing away from the crowd of álflings, the brunette raced toward Healer Vevina's shelter, leaving Kinlord Emyr and Master Arvel to scream after her in vain.

Although Cymbelina wished for her companion to be alright with all of her heart, she knew that wouldn't be the case. As soon as the brown-haired álf flung open the tent's entry flap, she felt her heart plummet into her churning stomach, every vain notion of her friend's safety shattering in her fragile mind. On the table which the yellow-skinned stranger was formally strapped lay Idal. With his head turned to the right, Cymbelina's green, life-filled eyes met with her friend's glassy, lifeless ones. The brunette's gaze followed the dried stream of blood that trailed from the corner of his mouth and down his chin, her eyes eventually landing on the male's torso. His chest was covered in deep gashes and bruises, some of which Idal's mother, Rhoslyn, concealed as she bent over his deceased frame, sobbing in despair.

"No," the younger woman whimpered, her knees buckling as her limp body crumbled to the floor. Her cracked lips shakily emitted a litany of "no" from her dry throat, an overwhelming sense of nausea brewing in the pit of her stomach. She pounded against the dirt underneath her with bruised knuckles, letting out one final wail of woe.

The sorrowful disbelief the young álf voiced roused Rhoslyn from her own grief. With tears streaming down her flushed, golden-beige cheeks, the mother weakly raised her left arm, one of her trembling fingers aimed in Cymbelina's direction.

"You," the older woman moaned, her lips curling in disgust, "you're the reason my boy is dead."

Sniveling, Cymbelina lifted her head up, looking at Rhoslyn. "W-what did you say?"

"You heard what I said, you...you patronless wretch!" Rhoslyn spat, standing up to slowly approach the crouching brunette. "It's your fault my son is dead!"

"I...I..." The she-álf sputtered, taken aback by the older woman's outburst.

"Don't even say a word!" The mother yelled, inadvertently spitting in the brunette's face. "You're scum!"

Master Arvel, who initially followed Cymbelina to bring her back to the gathering of álflings, entered the tent, blanching at

Idal's body. Before fully digesting the sight before him, his eyes drifted toward Rhoslyn, who he quickly grabbed as she lunged at his student.

"I always knew you were trouble!" Rhoslyn screamed loud enough so that the whole Glenrolk population could hear. Struggling in Master Arvel's grip, she continued, "Since the moment it came out that Kinlord Emyr couldn't detect your patron animal at birth, most parents of the Glenrolk clan kept their children away from you. But not me! I was kind and let you play with my boy. Many parents thought I was crazy to allow such a thing; they said your birth was a bad omen." Rhoslyn tried to free herself from the patron teacher's arms, barely swiping at the air before Arvel restrained her again. "Turns out they were right! If not for you leading him astray in the woods, Idal wouldn't have had to stay behind for guard duty. If not for you," Rhoslyn breathed shallowly, freeing one of her arms and pointing at one of the walls of the tent. "The creature wouldn't be seeking vengeance!"

Cymbelina looked where the deranged woman was pointing, noticing that the word 'vengeance' was scrawled on the cream-colored fabric wall in dried blood. Rhoslyn continued to hurtle insults and threats at the overwhelmed Half-Sylvanrolk as Arvel led her away, leaving the weeping Cymbelina alone in the tent that reeked of death and despair.

* * *

"Did Urskana prove to be a viable test subject, Mistress Tihana?"

"Well, 'viable' is not exactly the word I would use, Your Lordship, but she did help me reach a valuable conclusion. Before I go any further, however, I have one question: do you want the good or bad news first?"

The kohl drapes adorning either side of the balcony doors billowed, ruffled by the cool breeze flowing through the entryway. Vukasino's gray fingers tapped on the ornate stone railing lining the porch, his coal-black eyes locked onto the murky sea below. The swaying waves lapped at the rocky cliffs surrounding the monarch's castle, leaving a repetitious roar in the gloomy night air.

"I don't care about the order of the news, just the haste at which you dispense it," Monarch Vukasino began, his head turning from the sea to the interior of the upstairs lab, his cavernous eyes meeting Tihana's orange ones. The alchemist was sitting at her desk, patiently waiting for the ruler's response. "Share."

A candle flickered on the desk, causing Tihana's grayish-blue skin to faintly twinkle in the dim light, along with the jeweled pendant hanging around her neck. Tucking a strand of her bobbed white hair behind her pointed ears, she stared at the leader of the Dark Vilek.

"Very well. You brought me a corpse to experiment on, which limited the observable results of the potion. When I injected the experimental elixir into Urskana's right bicep, it began to swell—which I was surprised by, to say the least. So I would say the good news is that, although the test subject was dead, the injection still managed to increase the size of the muscle it was administered to."

"And the bad news?"

Tihana paused before answering, "My lord...if you plan on giving the troops this potion for future battles, I'll need to test it on a living subject. After all, we'll need to see how the user's overall muscle mass and elemental abilities are impacted once the substance is transported via bloodstream."

The leader hummed, his eyes closing. "That seems reasonable."

The tall male sauntered off the balcony and into the laboratory, keeping the doors open behind him to let the chilly breeze follow him in. His studded boots clomped against the stone flooring as he crossed the threshold and passed a series of bookshelves, all of which housed a myriad of worn texts. Sliding his finger across the spines of the dust-covered tomes, his eyes remained fixed on the gurgling cauldron in the fireplace, where Tihana's elixir was brewing. Approaching it,

Vukasino peered into the black pot. The orchid-colored liquid frothed and burbled, the occasional air bubble bursting. The ruler's moth wings fluttered in approval as he looked at the glowing liquid, which sent a pink glow across his gray features. A foul smile etched itself into the man's twisted face.

Mother, being the fool that she was, said our forces would never stand a chance against the sheer number of álves that pollute Florella. With luck, the Elixir of Annihilmon will end up proving her wrong.

Trailing his fingers through the flowing white locks that cascaded down his lithe frame from the unshaven side of his head, the monarch continued to grin. His coal eyes flicked from the solution to Tihana, who had left her desk to stand beside Vukasino at the cauldron.

"How soon would you be able to perform another trial if I brought you a living subject?"

"I would begin immediately, Monarch Vukasino."

"Excellent," the male said, clapping his hands together. "I'll announce that the royal house needs a test subject and that any participant will be handsomely rewarded for their involvement. The first person that comes forth will be sent directly to you."

"But Your Lordship, the test subject you bring to me might not survive the test trial."

The male chuckled darkly, shaking his head at the alchemist's remark. "Of course, that's a possibility, but I wouldn't get any volunteers if I told them that part, would I?"

The sound of hurried footfalls echoed through the empty hallway and into the lab, disturbing the conversation between Vukasino and Tihana. A delicate voice emerged over the clamorous footsteps, repeatedly calling out the monarch's name.

Fantastic, Vukasino thought, gritting his teeth. *Dealing with the underlings is just what I need to be doing right about now.*

"I'll see you soon then, my lord?"

"Very soon."

Making his way out into the hallway, the ruler encountered a young servant. The pinkish-gray woman was bent over, her chest expanding and collapsing as she desperately tried to reclaim her breath. Her white curls fell around her sweaty face, her breaths broken up into a series of short pants. Vukasino crossed his arms as he looked at his servant, a grimace painting his sharp features.

"What is your name?"

"S-Sanja, Your Lordship," the servant answered, still struggling to catch her breath.

"Well, Sanja, you need more exercise. Now, I presume you're running amok and squealing my name for a valid reason?"

"Y-Yes, I am, Monarch Vukasino." The woman said, standing straight before sloppily giving the ruler a rushed bow. "You asked to be alerted right away if Petiča returned, and Knight Morana said—"

"Take me to Petiča."

The female nodded, her body now fully recovered from the arduous jog. Turning her tired frame around, she led the monarch down the hallway. The plum carpet covering the stone floor scrunched underneath the duos' feet as they traversed the corridor. Vukasino's eyes traced the portraits that hung on either side of him, the gazes of his female ancestors following his path.

If only those women could see me, a visi-vilek, a scientifically made fae, on the throne of Elderfell. If only they could see that I'm doing what none of them could ever fathom doing; taking back our rightful place on the shores of our ancestral isle.

Following Sanja down the long passageway, the ruler's gaze faltered from the stone walls and landed on the servant's back. Through the opening in the back of her dark jade dress, the ruler could see two large, film-covered wounds, which used to be the site of a pair of wings resembling those of a butterfly. The glimmering gloss over the wounds signified that the appendages were growing back, leaving Vukasino's upper lip to curl in jealousy.

"My dear," the monarch spoke cooly as the two stood under the doorway leading into the entry hall. Sanja turned around, her pink skin appearing paler due to her blanched cheeks. Vukasino placed both hands on her shoulders, his grip becoming excruciatingly intense in the blink of an eye.

"Yes, Your...Your Lordship?" Sanja asked, her lip trembling as she winced.

The man gave a deceptively welcoming smile as if to thank the servant for guiding him. His snow-white hair fell over his shoulder as he lowered his body to get on the young woman's level. His black eyes narrowed, his gaze as sharp as the curved blade at his hip. "If you see a future for yourself that doesn't involve the gallows, I suggest you get your wings clipped after your shift. Do I make myself abundantly clear?"

The girl nodded vigorously, her shoulders shaking underneath the male's tight grip.

"Splendid! Now, hurry along and get back to work. I saw some dust on the portraits, so that should give you something to do." He winked, watching the servant scamper away. After she was midway down the hallway, the ruler turned around to face the audience that awaited him. Instead of seeing four women in the entry hall, there were only two: Knight Morana and Petiča.

"When the servant said that Petiča was here," the monarch began, folding his hands behind his back as he sauntered into the grand entryway, "I didn't think she meant that it was JUST Petiča who had returned from the island. Explain yourself; where are the others?"

The shivering yellow-skinned woman looked up at Monarch Vukasino as he towered above her, her glassy lavender eyes shining with fright. "There was a mishap during the second assignment, Your Lordship."

"Tch. What kind of 'mis-hap'?"

"The...uh...the fatal kind."

"That much is obvious since the two women I sent to fetch you are not standing beside you. E-LAB-OR-ATE. I have little time for vague explanations, and my patience is wearing thin."

The vilek gulped. "After Vatrina and Travana saved me from the álven camp, we followed the clan's trail throughout the forest, their footsteps eventually leading us to a clearing.

They seemed to be celebrating an event with two other groups of álves."

The two groups must be the other Wood Álf clans Kazimiera's scouts have reported about, the monarch thought, his cold gaze still locked on the cowering woman.

"Go on, tell me what happened at the clearing."

"Travana wanted to take a closer look at the Sylvanrolk and told Vatrina to accompany her. I…I was tasked to stay hidden in the forest in case anything went awry. Soon after they went to investigate, they split up and w-were killed."

Vukasino balled his hands into fists, anger boiling in his gut. The fact that he had such incompetent women under his command was astounding. *I told them to stick together, and they chose to split up. Unbelievable. However, I suppose they paid for their idiocy in the end.*

Instead of allowing himself to lose control and execute the remaining member of the inept party, the monarch nurtured the bud of a blossoming plan in his mind. Unclenching his fists, Vukasino cleared his throat, trying to mask the anger in his voice.

"Have you told anyone else about your experience on Florella?"

"No, Monarch Vukasino, I didn't have time. As soon as Knight Morana saw that I arrived at the docks, she brought me in for questioning. I'm sure my sister, Urskana, is worried sick about me, though. May I return home to see her?"

"How marvelously fortunate for you," the ruler remarked, his stony gaze meeting Morana's. The knight nodded, not needing any clarification into what her boss was thinking. "Your sister is already here waiting for you."

"Really?!" Petiča's eyes lit up, her stature becoming more relaxed. "Where is she? Where is Urskana?"

The ruler of the Dark Vilek smiled diabolically. "In the incinerator in Mistress Tihana's lab: take Petiča to the basement lab, Knight Morana."

Morana grabbed the yellowish-gray woman's arms, hauling her off her feet. The Dark Vilek clawed at the air, struggling to free herself from the knight's grasp as she carried the frantic woman away. Strings of incoherent babble floated through the damp air, leaving the monarch to stare in amusement at the scene before him.

"Fear not about your sister!" Vukasino called down the hall, laughing blithely. "You'll see her again after Mistress Tihana is through with you."

Petiča's pleading continued for several more minutes until she was finally out of earshot. The monarch shook his head and chuckled, turning to the right to gaze out of the castle's front doors. Approaching them, the ruler stood on the landing to a large flight of stairs, his eyes following them down into the bustling town below.

I guess I don't need to make that announcement after all.

* * *

The weight of drying tears lingered on Cymbelina's face, her bloodshot eyes tracing over the watery trails of each drop as she analyzed her devastated reflection in her grandfather's mirror. Emyr's dimly lit tent was inhabited by three people beside Cymbelina: the kinlord himself, Phalena, and Master Arvel. The three latter individuals discussed the attack on the Glenrolk campsite in hushed whispers, not paying much attention to the mourning álf, who was kneeling next to her teacher. Ordinarily, the brunette would not be allowed into the clan leader's tent during such an important discussion. However, her grandfather gave her some leeway due to her connection to the recent events.

"If you don't mind my saying so, sir, this is a matter of utmost importance. Not only have some of our kin been slaughtered while we were away," Phalena began.

"But we also have shadowy assailants who know our location and most certainly intend to kill again," Arvel finished.

The older álf remained quiet, his eyes closed as his chest rose and fell rhythmically. He remained that way for a time, his still frame glowing under the moonlight pouring through the transparent roof of his tent. When he finally opened his eyes, he scanned the three álves before him, his eyes lingering on his granddaughter.

"I was initially hesitant about seeking out these creatures, but it seems they've forced my hand."

"So what is your plan, Kinlord Emyr? How shall we seek out our unknown transgressors?"

"They're not completely unknown," Cymbelina murmured, responding to Phalena's comment. "The other clan leaders believe that the strangers are somehow tied to the vilek of the Glimmering Wilds."

"The fairy women? Why would they play a hand in this?"

"My thoughts exactly, Master Arvel," Emyr said, adjusting his posture as he looked back and forth between Cymbelina and Phalena. "Your generation doesn't know much about the vilek because I didn't think implementing a learning plan about races that aren't actively communicating with the Sylvanrolk was important. So I don't fault you for not understanding what I'm trying to say, but you need to listen to me. The actions of these creatures are nothing like those of the vilek our ancestors met and took shelter with."

"People change, Kinlord Emyr, and right now, the fairies are our only lead."

"Cymbelina has a point, Kinlord Emyr," Phalena added, looking sheepishly between the clan leader and his granddaughter. "This is an emergency, and every lead is worth investigating."

"Not you, too, Phalena."

"I'm sorry, sir, but you always ask for my honest opinion— so now I'm providing it."

Kinlord Emyr's eyes drifted to the floor, his mind lost in thought.

He just has to do something now, Cymbelina thought, her gaze glued on her grandfather. *He won't listen to me, but he might listen to Phalena.*

Master Arvel coughed, sitting up a little bit straighter. "May I provide a suggestion, sir?"

"Please do."

"Perhaps you could send a team of scouts to the Glimmering Wilds to see if the Sylvanrolk clans can make contact with the vilek. Even if they're not responsible for the assaults, they might have recent experience with these creatures. I doubt we're their only targets."

"It's a nice idea, Master Arvel, and I thank you for bringing it to my attention. However, there is one problem with it: the location of the fairy women." The leader paused, taking a deep breath. "I, as well as the other clan leaders, have sent several scouting parties over the years to investigate the Glimmering Wilds, and the scouts have always come back empty-handed. Neither hide nor hair of the fairy women's settlement or their existence, for that matter."

"I still think it's worth investigating, sir. It's very possible that these attacks are indeed connected to the vilek, especially if the fairy women were in hiding and are now coming out of it. If our hypothesis turns out to be wrong, there is minimal loss. However, if our hypothesis is correct, many álven lives will be spared."

"I suppose you three are right," Emyr admitted. "But who amongst the Glenrolk would be brave enough to leave their kin and go out into the Wilds? I cannot spare any of my best guards in case the creatures attack again, so I'll have to send someone else."

"I would," Cymbelina volunteered, standing up. "Those beings killed my best friend, and I demand to know why and stop them from killing more álves."

Emyr gripped his armrests tightly, his green eyes casting a displeased look upon his granddaughter. "How many times must we go over this, Cymbelina? You are an álfling. You do not leave this settlement unless it is to go to Eldenfield until you discover and master your patron animal. You will—"

"Find my own way to the Glimmering Wilds if I must," Cymbelina interjected, tears brimming in her eyes. "I am twenty-two years old and I am not a fledgling álf, regardless of what the Sylvan Tenets say. I WILL seek retribution for Idal's death and avenge you for what those creatures did to your eye."

"I do not need avenging; I need an álfling who will follow the Old Laws. And I also need—"

"You to trust me," the brunette interrupted again, balling her fists. "I won't change my mind on this, Kinlord Emyr. You know I won't."

The she-álf and her grandfather were locked in a heated exchange of glares, their eyes unwaveringly still. Moments passed as both individuals waited for the other one to add more fuel to the fire.

"What if I were to accompany Cymbelina and the other scouts to the Glimmering Wilds?" Master Arvel proposed penetrating the tense atmosphere of the hearing room. "That way, I could simultaneously support the team on their journey and continue to conduct Cymbelina's patron lessons. That's if she decides to go, of course; I'd be happy to help the scouts either way."

Although the she-álf despised the idea of undergoing tedious lessons while on the road, she was willing to accept Master Arvel's proposed terms if that meant she had her grandfather's blessing to head to the Wilds.

Emyr didn't respond to Arvel's inquiry immediately, opting to wait until the fired-up she-álf standing before him softened her facial expression. When Cymbelina's face didn't change, the kinlord gave a defeated chuckle.

"I know Cymbelina won't follow my instructions or the Sylvan Tenets unless I offer a punishment, so here it is: you are indeed a twenty-two-year-old álf. I cannot physically force you to do anything. However, if you decide to leave with the scouting party tomorrow, you will be banished from the Glenrolk clan. Do I make myself clear?"

Although Cymbelina's face didn't show it, a pang of sorrow rocked her shattered soul. Her ears rang from the sound of her grandfather's words as she cringed, her eyes drifting to the moon shining down on her through the transparent ceiling.

I don't know when, if ever, I'll discover and master my patron animal, and I may never have another chance to right Idal's death and save my fellow Sylvanrolk. Even though it hurts to leave my family behind, I'll accept banishment if that means I saved álven lives.

Cymbelina swallowed, her eyes returning to her grandfather's as she shifted her weight from her right to her left foot. "You do, Kinlord Emyr."

Nodding his head and lifting his arms, Kinlord Emyr gave Phalena and Master Arvel a chance to stand before he stood up from his throne.

"I plan to have a group leave at sunrise tomorrow, Master Arvel, so you should go home, pack, and get a good night's rest. Phalena, you stay with me so we can ask for candidates willing to venture into the Glimmering Wilds. And Cymbelina," Emyr paused, his weary eyes resting on his granddaughter. "I look forward to seeing what you decide to do tomorrow, now that you know the consequences if you should choose to leave. Cymbelina and Master Arvel, you may be dismissed."

Cymbelina opened her mouth to address her grandfather on a more personal level but quickly changed her mind. Masking her sadness, the brunette swaggered out of the tent, trudging along the settlement's swirling paths to head back to her family's abode.

I guess I have some packing to do.

The Journey Begins
20th of Red Moon, 1300 AC

A cock crowed along the edge of the Glenrolk campsite as the brilliant fall sun peeked above the eastern horizon. Its rays doused Terralynia's Folly in an orange glow, which filtered through the thin fabric of Cymbelina's family tent. The brunette was busy counting all the belongings she had gathered on her bedroll, ensuring she had everything she needed for the journey ahead.

A spare set of clothes, check. An extra waterskin, check.

Una's navy eyes wearily blinked as she sat upright in her sleeping bag and glanced at her sister, who was hunched over a row of items in the corner of their bedroom.

Yawning, Una inquired, "What are you doing, 'Lina?"

"I'm packing," the brunette whispered, stuffing some items into her favorite leather backpack, which had previously belonged to her biological father.

"For what?"

Cymbelina shoved her journal in her copper-toned sack before clicking it shut using the shiny silver buckle sown on the front.

"A trip."

The younger sister grumbled, turning her gaze to the outside world. Looking through an opening in the tent, Una saw the deep azure of the early morning sky, shades of orange outlining the horizon. The sleepy songs of the newly awakened birds floated on the chilly morning air, a slight breeze rippling the fabric walls of the bedroom. Una shook her head in astonishment, her black frizzy waves swaying from side to side. Draping the fur-lined covers over her shoulders, she drew her knees inward, preserving the bit of warmth that the blanket provided.

"What possible reason could compel you to leave the house at a time like this? It's cold and early, and those weird creatures could be roaming about on the outskirts of our camp."

Cymbelina stared at her shivering sibling, debating whether to disclose the truth of the matter. On the one hand, she felt that Una had the right to know what the kinlord was planning. On the other hand, Cymbelina knew her sister would attempt to go to the Wilds with the scouts if she knew the truth, and there was no telling what sort of dangers awaited the travelers once they entered the magical forest.

As much as it pains me to keep the truth from her, I know she'll have a better chance of staying safe here than she would in the Wilds.

"Well, are you going to keep me guessing?"

The older sister shook her head, approaching her agitated sibling to give her a kiss on the forehead.

"Just go back to sleep, Una. I'll tell you about it later."

The last part was a lie, and Cymbelina knew it. She knew that she was giving up her place in the Glenrolk clan by venturing into the Glimmering Wilds, so there was no way she would be able to tell Una about the trip later on. But she had to keep her younger sister safe, so she lied through her teeth.

The younger she-álf rolled her eyes, falling back into the warm comfort of her mat. She wrapped the blankets around her cold frame and turned on her side to face the wall.

"Whatever you say, Sis."

Taking one last look at her sister and their childhood bedroom, Cymbelina grabbed her supplies and left, making one last stop in her family's tent. Lifting the sheet of fabric that separated her parents' room from the main living area, she entered the bed-chamber, her eyes landing on the slumbering forms of her parents.

The older álves' bodies rose and fell sporadically, their faces expressing the bliss slumber always seemed to bring. Deirdre's silent frame was snugly tucked underneath the massive mat's quilt, while Séacael snored loudly with an arm thrown above his head. The amusing sight brought a small smile to the she-álf's face, the type of smile she did not expect to display again any time soon.

The brunette gave her parents two gentle kisses on their cheeks before fleeing the tent, afraid she might begin to second guess herself if she stayed any longer, which she couldn't afford to do.

Standing outside of the tent, the she-álf checked her stash of equipment. Bow and arrows: hanging on the sling that adorned her torso. Traveling bag: swung over her left shoulder. Daggers and other supplies: attached to her belt. Cymbelina had all the materials she would need for this journey except her steel short sword, which she opted to leave behind to avoid becoming encumbered. With all the necessary items on her person, she walked away from the tent she had occupied her entire life. The abandonment of her childhood home gave rise to conflicting emotions in her soul: a sense of freedom from the harsh Sylvan Tenets and sadness at the prospect of never seeing her family again.

I wonder if this is how Dad felt when he left Mom and me behind.

Cymbelina shook her head, erasing such musings from her mind. She couldn't afford to have her thoughts wander.

Because the she-álf had gotten an earlier head start than expected, she decided to tour a bit of the settlement before heading to the kinlord's tent. The nostalgic journey led her down one of the camp's many rows of darkened tents, which she had become accustomed to seeing every day. Her gaze lingered on each structure as she passed them by, engraving their appearances into her memory.

One of the abodes she passed belonged to Tadhgmaris. The rhythmic clanging of pots and the tantalizing aroma of roasted pumpkins drifted through the air from the fabric house, hinting at the promise of a sumptuous morning feast.

Maybe Tadhgmaris is crafting a grand meal that will distract everyone from what happened yesterday, as well as celebrate Kayven's return to the

Glenrolk clan. If only I could stay and enjoy the festivities.

From a nearby tent emerged the sound of unceasing bickering, along with the sound of objects being thrown. If the tent's immaculate outer appearance wasn't enough to indicate that Malaveen and her family lived within, the noises they made gave their presence away.

The woman chuckled, shaking her head. *Although leaving the clan fills my heart with sadness, the idea of never having to listen to Malaveen or the rest of her family's bickering again fills me with joy. I guess there is a silver lining to every cloud.*

The swerving path took Cymbelina up a grassy hill, one of many that adorned the surface of Terralynia's Folly. Her position at the top of the small peak allowed the she-álf to stare out into the depths of the verdant region, which was filled with scattered streams. The babbling of the nearby brooks echoed in the morning breeze, the grass quivering underneath its gentle caress. A few field mice scurried between the towering blades of turf, running away from the brunette. Scanning the scenery before her, the woman's eyes eventually landed on a vast meadow below the hill she occupied, a field she became well acquainted with in her childhood. The clearing she gazed upon was where Master Arvel used to take Cymbelina and her former peers daily for their patron lessons. Simply staring at the familiar field evoked vivid memories in the twenty-two-year-old álf's mind, most of which left a bitter taste in her mouth. One such memory pushed its way to the forefront of the brunette's thoughts, leaving her to visualize a scene she could never entirely forget.

"The Supreme Mother made you a Sylvanrolk and didn't even bestow you with a patron animal. Don't you think that shows what she thinks of you, Cymbelina?"

The female álfling sat cross-legged beside Idal in the meadow, her hickory pigtails swaying as she cocked her head to the side. Her dark green eyes analyzed the orange snapdragon she twirled between her fingers, ignoring the harassment from Malaveen and her friends. Cymbelina carried the dried-out flower everywhere because, according to her mother, it was one of the last things her biological father had in his possession before he went missing. Plus, it made the álfling feel special, as snapdragons were not native to Florella.

"My mom doesn't want me to hang out with you, Cymbelina. She's afraid I'll catch whatever disease you have."

"It's not a disease, Gaildwynn," Idal responded, sitting up a bit straighter to show that he was ready to defend his friend. "She's the only one in her family who doesn't have a patron animal. So clearly, you can't catch what she has."

"How do you know that? You've never met her dad! None of us have. Even Cymbelina doesn't know what her dad is like."

"Stop it, Olenell, or else I'll get Master Arvel."

"And say what, Idal? That I'm repeating the truth? He won't do anything about that."

Cymbelina remained silent as her best friend stood up for her against Malaveen and her malcontents. The young she-álfling was too transfixed by the flower's magnificence to pay any mind to the venomous comments aimed her way.

Idal continued to argue back and forth with Gaildwynn and Olenell, not paying attention to Malaveen. The flaxen-haired álfling gazed upon the fiddling Cymbelina, a smirk spreading across her face. Telling her friends to hush, the blonde directed them to look at what the brunette was doing. The trio exchanged glances before Malaveen addressed Cymbelina.

"You haven't said much since we've come over here, 'Lina. Care to make any comments?"

"No," Cymbelina murmured, her gaze unwavering from the flower head. "Not really."

The ringleader of the bullies scowled, quickly bending down to snatch the bloom from the quiet álfling's grasp. Once the delicate bud left the young girl's fingertips, she turned her eyes toward the thief.

"Hey! Give it back, Malaveen."

The blonde girl took her time making her own observations of the flower, her hazel eyes glancing over its dried-out, fragile petals.

"You do know that this thing is withered away, right? Why would you keep it?"

"I don't care about the state it's in," Cymbelina said, uncrossing her legs and jumping to her feet. "It's one of the only things my dad left behind, so give it back!"

"Ew, your dad?" Gaildwynn's nose crinkled. "Drop it, Malaveen! It might have poison on it."

Idal scoffed. "Poison? That makes no sense."

"Yes, it does! Cymbelina's dad abandoned her and her mom, after all. I bet he didn't want Cymbelina in the first place! He could've left the flower as a way to kill her!"

"Destroy it, Malaveen," Olenell chimed in, "before the poison rubs off on you!"

"No, please—just give it back!"

Cymbelina's request meant nothing to the cruel álfling, who unceremoniously dropped the flower on the ground. Snickering, Malaveen stomped her right foot down upon the dried plant, crushing the wilted petals instantly. With each grind of the blonde's shoe into the torn flower, another piece of the brunette's heart broke.

"Why?!" Cymbelina wailed, her dark green eyes brimming with tears.

Malaveen removed her foot from the flower, revealing that the snapdragon had been torn to pieces. The orange petals were crushed and ground, their remnants scattering as a brisk wind swept over the meadow. Idal took off to chase after a couple of petals the wind had blown up a nearby hill while Cymbelina scuttled to grab the bits of the flower lingering nearby, her hands shaking in the process.

"Why?" The she-álfling repeated, whimpering this time.

The gaggle of bullies formed a circle around the crying girl, some bearing blank expressions while others didn't even attempt to hide their laughter.

"You should be thanking us, Cymbelina. We just rescued you from your dad's trap."

Cymbelina's hunched-over body shook with anger and sadness, her tear-filled eyes glaring up at Malaveen. Snot dribbled over her lip and down her chin. "H-He wasn't trying to kill me, you...you idiot!"

A wave of fake gasps rippled through the group of álflings, making fun of the brunette's choice of words and helpless demeanor.

As the group of kids reveled in the anguish they caused, the sound of running footsteps caught their attention as Malaveen told her friends to quiet down. The source of the sound was the sprinting Idal, who cupped his *hands close to his chest.*

"I told on you guys! Master Arvel says he's coming over here after he's done with Kayven's lesson."

The mean álflings ran off in glee without another taunt, their sadistic giggles ringing in the patronless álf's ears as the bullies traveled across the field. Their departure left Idal and Cymbelina alone, the former approaching the latter with a saddened expression.

Idal poured the few petals he could catch into his friend's hands. The she-álfling whined when she saw he hadn't been able to catch them all.

"I'm sorry, Cymbelina, I tried to catch more, but the wind was too strong."

Although the brown-haired child was thankful for her friend's effort, she didn't have the emotional strength to utter her gratitude. All she could do was bury her head in her hands, praying that her tears would magically stitch the snapdragon back together.

When Cymbelina's flashback ceased, she noticed that the top of the sun had risen above the edge of the horizon. Startled by the passage of time, she fled the hill's peak, kicking up bits of the dirt trail as she went on her way.

The she-álf arrived in the town square just in time to see three cloaked figures conversing with Kinlord Emyr. Traces of solemnity penetrated Emyr's neutral expression as he watched his granddaughter approach the three people from behind.

"Ah, I see you've decided to join the expedition. How unfortunate."

Cymbelina stood beside the shortest member of the group, who looked in her direction after the kinlord spoke. A pair of hazel eyes gleamed through the shadows the mauve hood cast upon the wearer's face, leading the brunette to laugh internally.

Of course, Grandpa chose Malaveen as one of the álves to search for the vilek. He's using her as a deterrent. Unluckily for him, I won't allow her presence to repel me from the task at hand.

The disgust on Malaveen's face was plain as day as she turned to the clan's leader to question his motives. "Why is she coming with us, Kinlord Emyr? Doesn't her participation in this quest violate the Sylvan Tenets?"

"How very astute of you, Malaveen—it certainly does. However, she and I have reached an understanding. Care to elaborate, Cymbelina?"

At the mention of the brunette's name, the second figure to Cymbelina's right turned. Lowering their cobalt-hued hood, the individual was revealed to be Kayven. A look of shock was plastered across his chiseled features.

Before Kayven could say anything, the brunette answered, "The kinlord has agreed not to fight me on joining the expedition to find the vilek as long as I give up my place among the Glenrolk once our task is complete."

Malaveen's look of disgust rapidly changed to one of delight as she let out a hearty laugh. "Well, isn't that a surprise! If those are the terms, I certainly don't mind tolerating Cymbelina's presence during our journey. After all, the further she is away from the camp, the more likely our clan will be safe!"

"Hush," the third figure in the juniper cloak said in a voice that was recognizably Master Arvel's. "Whether you approve of her accompanying us or not matters little. She's still our Sylvanrolk kin by blood and will be coming with us, so please show a modicum of respect."

Malaveen immediately shut her mouth, an embarrassed flush spreading across her pale cheeks.

"As I was saying before Cymbelina arrived, I've prepared four maps of Florella for you all to keep," Kinlord Emyr spoke. "Master Arvel has toured the Glimmering Wilds before, so the maps should mainly be used for emergencies or lapses in his memory. Remember, your group's primary objective is to find where the vilek live. Return home immediately if you cannot find any traces of their whereabouts." Emyr's gaze, which had avoided Cymbelina's throughout most of the exchange, finally rested on her. "Although it saddens me to see you go, Cymbelina, I believe this mission will serve as a great opportunity for you to find a home outside the camp."

The brunette balled her hands into fists, the desire to sink into her golden cloak rising. Malaveen chuckled.

Turning away from his granddaughter, Kinlord Emyr addressed the three other scouts. "Do any of you have questions for me?"

Cymbelina and her fellow party members remained silent.

"Well, then, I bid you all farewell! And good luck. Walk with a firm step and an open heart, and remember: each action you take should align with the Sylvan Tenets."

Cymbelina remained silent as the other three álves said their goodbyes to the kinlord. Finding his granddaughter's lack of parting words unacceptable, Emyr called out to the brunette as the group left the campsite.

"I'm saddened that you've chosen this path, Cymbelina. May the ancestors guide you and enlighten you along the way!"

The Half-Sylvanrolk cringed, looking behind her to gaze into her grandfather's eyes. *I refuse to allow Emyr the satisfaction of making himself feel better about shunning me from the clan. He would never admit it, but he's scared that I don't view the Old Laws the same way he does. The difference between him and me is that I know what I'm doing is right; I don't need some ancient rules to tell me that.*

"I'm saddened more of my kin aren't taking the path I've chosen today. May the ancestors guide you, Kinlord Emyr!"

The four travelers left without further ado as the Glenrolk leader gazed upon the departing group with a disheartened but hopeful glance.

The rising sun shone upon the winding dirt path the álves trotted upon as they walked past the tents on the outskirts of the camp, the inhabitants within just beginning to stir. The first clangs of the blacksmith's anvil on the other side of the settlement echoed in the fall wind, and Tadhgmaris' holler that breakfast was almost ready drew a crowd toward the town square. Cymbelina saw Kayven cast a longing glance backward, clearly stirred by his father's voice. However, the male remained silent, just as all the other group members did.

The main trail eventually bled into a downhill slope, a dense field of grass bordering either side of the dirt road. Cymbelina continued onward with the group, her eyes resting on the fall wildflowers that sprinkled the surface of the pasture, their stems dancing under the autumnal breeze.

"Let us be thankful for a moment," Master Arvel said, stirring the first snippet of conversation between the travelers. "As you all know, Terralynia's Folly doesn't have much foliage, meaning we'll have little protection from the rising sun. This would spell out a hot journey ahead if we had been traveling earlier in the year. However, since the four of us are going to the Glimmering Wilds during autumn, the rays that douse this region in light will be less harsh and, therefore, more bearable."

"You make a valuable point, Master Arvel," Kayven responded, his gaze turning toward the vast blue sky above. "It's always good to look at the bright side of any situation."

"Why don't we dispense with the pleasantries, yeah?" Malaveen said, her eyes landing on the two male álves in the group as she adjusted her purple cloak. "It's still a bit chilly outside, and I've just woken up. I'm not in the mood to be talked to."

"Be glad that nobody was speaking directly to you then."

"You know what I meant, Kayven."

With each step the álves took, the sun rose higher in the heavens, its beams beginning to warm the travelers' chilled limbs as they pressed forward on the winding road. The path meandered through a rolling landscape of hills, each varying in size and shape. The group's footfalls stirred the elusive creatures hidden in the tall grass, releasing a symphony of squeaks and rustling sounds from the verdant undergrowth. Despite the region's breathtaking lushness, Terralynia's Folly harbored only a sparse array of wildlife. At the top of the local food chain were the Glenrolk álves, with non-venomous snakes occupying the second tier. Apart from these small snakes, the land was dotted with rabbits, field mice, and various insects, while the meandering brooks harbored small fish.

This lack of wildlife left little to be discussed amongst the scouts, who felt familiar enough with their task to leave the topic alone for the time being. However, this lack of conversation soon changed when the adventurers encountered the realm's most noteworthy feature: Terralynia's Gorge.

Running horizontally through the center of Terralynia's Folly, the rocky canyon sat between two steep inclines: the one on which the álves currently stood and the one to the north. Either side of the ravine was connected by a rickety bridge, which slightly swayed back and forth in the wind. The afternoon sun shone down upon the structure and the crystalline river underneath it. The burbling of the rapid water echoed off the rocky walls below, the thunderous sound stopping the scouts in their tracks. Cymbelina's heart leaped into her throat, her eyes unwavering from the derelict crossing ahead.

I have heard tales of Terralynia's Gorge, but I never expected it to be quite like this. The idea of crossing over such a drop, especially if it involves a decaying bridge, is not in the slightest bit pleasant.

Looking over the cliff's edge and back at his fellow travelers, Master Arvel was the first to speak. "Since I've crossed the bridge before, I'll go first. It's imperative that you three pay attention to my actions as I cross to the other side, as the decaying thing is known to be temperamental."

The blonde shook her head. "Pfft. With all due respect, Master Arvel, if you think I'm crossing that bridge, you have another thing coming."

"What do you intend to do then, Malaveen? Are you giving up on the journey into the Wilds already? Do you intend to head back to camp?"

The blonde closed her eyes, her lips widening into a cocky smirk. "Watch and learn, everyone: watch and learn."

In the blink of an eye, the conceited álf changed into her patron animal, a swan named Flora. Gracefully flapping her white wings, the pen ascended into the chilly air. A glittering gray aura cloaked the transformed woman as she soared over the dilapidated bridge. Doing a single twirl in the air, Malavenn landed on the other side, reverting to her álven form with a flourish.

"I forgot that her patron animal is a swan," Kayven remarked, crossing his muscular arms over his chest. "Well, that certainly explains the honking she's been doing."

Cymbelina laughed at her companion's remark, which was funny enough to distract her from the anxiety gnawing at her stomach. Master Arvel suppressed his own amusement by coughing into his hand.

"Be civil now, Kayven. Now, you two watch as I cross the bridge. Make a note of my form and what I do if there is a strong passing breeze."

The older álf turned sideways, his right foot stepping on the first worn wooden plank and his left foot preparing to replace the right one when he stepped forward. Lightly clasping the ropes on either side of the structure, Master Arvel began his journey across the bridge. His long, umber hair flicked in the wind as he stopped on the fifth plank, his head turning to the side to call back at Cymbelina and Kayven.

"Notice how I stop when the wind blows through? You two must do the same when the time comes in order to preserve your balance."

Sunlight shone upon the teacher's alabaster skin as he continued his passage, shimmying across the few planks in front of him. His amber eyes meticulously switched between the boards underfoot and the path ahead, which was relatively smooth until he reached the halfway point of the overpass. Another wind blew through the gorge, this one a bit more fierce than the last. A lump began to form in the brunette's throat, her eyes looking away from her teacher to look at Kayven. The tall male was calm, an attentive look plastered on his sunlit face.

Well, at least one of us will be able to get across the bridge without having an anxiety attack.

Once the breeze ceased, Arvel continued his walk until he arrived on the other slope. Now that the bridge was empty, it was up to Kayven and Cymbelina to decide who would traverse the unsteady walkway next.

The tall álf looked at the woman beside him, motioning the brunette forward with a polite smile. "Ladies first."

"Ladies? I-I don't see any ladies here, haha." Cymbelina

joked, trying to mask her nervous energy with humor.

Kayven cocked an eyebrow, vaguely amused by the Half-Sylvanrolk's nervousness. When Cymbelina didn't make another comment, he shrugged his shoulders before wordlessly walking toward the mouth of the bridge. Pushing one of his tight locks behind his right ear, the male álf journeyed across the bridge, perfectly mimicking the posture Master Arvel demonstrated. Luckily, he didn't experience any sudden gusts of wind, making his journey relatively easy and quick. Unluckily for Cymbelina, it was now her turn to cross the ravine.

Dang, a part of me wishes I had gone first now.

Stepping forward, Cybelina gazed over the edge of the cliff and into the rapids below. Some loose pebbles underneath her boot fell into the gorge, bouncing off the rocky walls of the ravine and dropping into the raging stream hundreds of feet below.

Malaveen, who had been silent during the passage of the male álves, released an annoyed grunt before calling out, "Are you coming or not?!"

"Yes, I'm just—"

"Well, hurry up! The sooner we reach the Wilds, the better."

"And The sooner you stop squawking, Bird-Brain, the sooner I'll be able to cross!"

Placing one unsure foot on the first plank, Cymbeina's peered through the slit between the first creaky board and the second. The jagged stones of the gorge glistened with water in the autumn sun, taunting the she-álf with their sharp edges.

I hate everything about this, the brunette thought, her heart racing in her chest.

Taking a deep breath, Cymbelina copied the actions of her teacher and Kayven, her left foot following her right as she walked atop the weathered pieces of wood. An unsettling song of creaks and groans erupted from the bridge, causing a pool of anxiety to gurgle in the woman's stomach. Although the worry threatened to consume her, she continued moving forward, attempting to reach the other side as quickly as possible.

Cymbelina's eagerness to reach the other cliff proved to be her undoing as she accidentally sped forward as a breeze swept over the ravine instead of standing still. Her actions caused her to place too much weight on her right foot, making the rotten board give out from underneath her. Her right leg fell through the gap that the broken board created, the structure swinging from side to side violently as she stumbled forward.

"Cymbelina!"

The she-álf gripped the support ropes for dear life, her knuckles turning white. The bridge continued to sway from side to side as she remained as still as possible, her breaths coming out in frightened pants. Her right leg dangled above the rocky abyss as her left knee fought for her to remain upright. A series of creaking groans from the bridge echoed off either cliff, the roaring waves below seemingly calling out the Half-Sylvanrolk's name as she squeezed her eyes shut, refusing to look at the tumultuous stream at the bottom of the pass.

Don't look down, don't look down, don't look down.

"Do you need help?!" The male álves screamed unevenly.

"N-no, I'll be fine!"

Shaking her head and rolling her shoulders, Cymbelina leaned to the left, carefully pulling her right leg from between the planks while avoiding a glance at the dizzying drop below. With a shaky breath, she stood unsteadily and placed her right foot on the next plank, her heart racing as she navigated the precarious path. Each step sent a rush of adrenaline through her, her pulse pounding in her ears and her chest heaving rapidly. Once safely on the opposite cliff, she doubled over, her skin glistening with sweat under the afternoon sun.

Arvel and Kayven rushed to be at the brunette's side, praising the Supreme Mother for allowing Cymbelina to complete the rest of her journey without getting hurt or losing any items. Malaveen stayed where she had been standing the entire time, gazing at the trio in displeasure.

"Hmph. Only Cymbelina would nearly fail a task as simple as crossing a bridge."

"You flew over the bridge and avoided the trek entirely,

Malaveen. So, in a way, you failed the task too."

The blonde rolled her eyes at Kayven's remark. "Whatever. We're all safe and sound now, and that's what counts. What's our next move, Master Arvel?"

"We move onward, of course. We'll call it a day once we reach the edge of Terralynia's Folly that separates it from the Glimmering Wilds. Camping in this region will be safer than in the Wilds."

"And then what?" Kayven questioned.

Master Arvel released a wearied chuckle. "Why don't we just get where we need to go first? Then we'll discuss our next move. After all, rushing won't do us any favors."

"As we saw on the bridge," Malaveen added, looking over at Cymbelina. The brunette simply shook her head in response.

"No need for drama, Malaveen. So what say the rest of you, eh? Shall we be off?"

The trio of younger álves nodded in affirmation, following the patron guide down the trail.

The following hours crept by at a snail's pace, the sun slowly creeping toward the horizon. The travelers passed hill after sprawling hill until they chose a spot to settle in for the night. The selected area was near a large lake that had innumerable streams branching out of it. However, this wasn't any average body of water. This particular lake was considered sacred to the Sylvanrolk people. In fact, the Wood Álves had named it Laufeia's Sorrow long ago. The body of water's name came from the founding pioneer of the Sylvanrolk, Laufeia the Kind, the daughter of the last united álfrolk leader, King Hakon the Last. Sylvanrolk legends claim that Laufeia and the álfrolk survivors that accompanied her as they fled from the ancient city of Snøvern camped next to this lake as they headed south. During the night, Laufeia's companions were kept awake by her mournful prayers to the Supreme Mother to protect her homeland and family. From then on, the lake and its rivers became an embodiment of the Sylvanrolk founder's endless stream of tears. By camping next to such a historical landmark, Cymbelina and her fellow scouts hoped they would have good luck on their journey, as well as a tasty dinner in the form of one of the river fish.

After the álves set up their camp for the night, the group split up. Malaveen and Master Arvel headed to the lake to reel in fish, while Kayven and Cymbelina stayed behind to prepare the supplies needed to cook dinner.

The fire crackled and hissed as Cymbelina added more kindling to the budding inferno. Kayven whittled away at one end of a stick, which he planned to impale the fish on. Once finished, he dropped the stake on the ground, his marigold eyes turning toward the brunette as he grabbed another piece of wood.

"Nice night, isn't it?"

The she-álf cringed. Now that the stress of leaving home and crossing the bridge had subsided, Idal's death came to the forefront of her mind. Days had passed since she and her friend had discovered the stranger on the beach, and only twenty-four hours had gone by since Cymbelina found the mutilated body of that same friend. Coupling her closest ally's death with her expulsion from the Glenrolk clan left the woman with a shattered sense of reality. So, no matter how pleasant the autumn night appeared, her thoughts refused to stray from her reflections on recent events and her worries about the future.

"Yeah, it's fine, but it would be even better if Idal were here to share it with the rest of the group."

"Wow," the male sputtered, flustered by his forgetfulness, "how absent-minded of me. With our journey to the Wilds on my mind, Idal's death seems to have slipped it. My apologies."

"It's alright, Kayven," Cymbelina replied, the glow of the fire reflecting in her green eyes as she looked at her ally. "I know you meant no harm."

The male álf nodded, his high cheekbones accentuated by the warm glow of the fire. His stare wandered about the makeshift camp, desperately searching for an item to which he could shift the conversation. Sensing his uneasiness, Cymbelina brought up a topic from the Eldenfield Festival.

"So, you said you rejoined the Glenrolk clan. What made you decide to do that?"

The male stiffened. It was clear to the brunette that she had brought up a discussion he wasn't quite ready for. She had assumed that his previous comment about continuing their conversation later was his way of communicating that he would be prepared to talk about it whenever, but Cymbelina had clearly been wrong. Before she could apologize, the tense male spoke.

"I was just...ready to come home. Nothing too interesting. But enough about that," Kayven paused, gesturing toward the sack leaning against the female's leg. "That's an interesting backpack, Cymbelina. I can't say I've seen one like it before. Did you get it at the Eldenfield Festival?"

His yellow-orange eyes landed on Cymbelina's bag. The silver buckle bore many strange symbols on it, none of which the brunette had ever been able to decipher. The peculiar marks formed a circle around an red eye, which looked similar to those of the many lizards that dotted the island of Florella. The eye in the center of the buckle glimmered in the light of the autumnal fire, causing a ray of light to reflect off the surface of Cymbelina's light brown skin.

The brunette smiled, her fingers gently brushing against the old, supple fabric of the bag. "This old thing? It actually belonged to my biological father. Before he vanished years ago, he left behind three things: a snapdragon, this backpack, and one more item."

"Do you not recall the third item?"

"It's not that I don't remember it; I've never been told what the gift is. According to my mom, my father left it behind and she just assumes it's for me."

"I see," the male hummed, his gaze glued to the scintillating buckle.

Speaking about the unknown present summoned a feeling of regret in the she-álf's chest as she recalled that her revoked Glenrolk status prevented her from ever receiving the last of her father's possessions.

Oh well, the brunette thought, her eyes turning to the full moon above. *Hopefully, Mom will give the gift to Una so she can get some use out of it.*

A clump of grass feet away from the campfire rustled as Master Arvel and Malaveen returned with their haul. The teacher dangled two bass from either hand as the blonde carried a small cup of berries. Malaveen proudly held the bowl in her hands, gazing at the fruit with hunger.

"Wow," Kayven admired, "you two were able to reel in some decently sized fish."

Master Arvel nodded. "I was impressed by that as well. Although I've traveled to this region multiple times in my life, I never grasped how big the fish could get in Laufeia's Sorrow."

"I was more shocked by the number of berries I was able to find on the bushes surrounding the lake," the blonde said. "In fact, if we're hungry enough, there's plenty more to gather should we find the number in the bowl lacking."

The blonde grasped a shiny, rose-colored berry between her right forefinger and thumb, momentarily eyeing the fruit before popping it into her mouth.

Kayven grinned, looking between Malaveen and Master Arvel before speaking up. "I'll pass on eating those berries. I would also advise you to not eat any more of those, Malaveen."

The female scoffed, rolling her eyes as she consumed another one. "If you're not eating any, why do you care? There's plenty to go around."

Realizing what Kayven was getting at, the brunette smirked, content with remaining silent and letting the blonde figure things out the hard way.

Master Arvel leaned over to take a better look at the gathered fruit. He raised his eyebrows before leaning back. "Yes, I advise you to cease your consumption of the berries as well."

Malaveen scooped up a handful of fruit, shoveling it into her mouth before mumbling, "I already said I wouldn't eat them all."

"For someone who claims to be so resourceful, you sure

know little about the vegetation of Terralynia's Folly."

"Is there a point to what you're saying, Kayven? If so, spit it out!"

Kayven skewered one of the fish on the sharpened stick he had prepared, his eyes flicking back to the blonde. "I'm saying that unless you want to spend the rest of the night behind the bushes you found those berries on, I suggest you stop eating them while you're ahead. The specimen you've gathered there is what all Sylvanrolk cooks have affectionately named '*cacas berricus*': aka, 'shit berries.'"

The blonde's face paled even in the warmth of the flames, her cheeks bulging. She dropped the cup and ran to a nearby bush, expelling bits of undigested berry. The other three álves heard Malaveen retching as they sat around the campfire, looks varying from amusement to disappointment painting their faces.

Malaveen soon returned with a sickened but furious expression on her face. "How could you guys sit there and let me eat that?"

"We tried to warn you," Kayven said with a wry smile. "What were we supposed to do? Snatch the bowl from your hands or force our fingers down your throat to make you vomit?" He chuckled, shaking his head in disbelief.

The disgusted álf's hazel eyes glared at her three companions. "We shall never speak of this again, do you hear me?"

"None of us would dream of it," Master Arvel said, stifling a laugh. "Now, come and sit with us. We all need to eat and go to bed: we have a long day ahead of us tomorrow."

Into The Wilds
21st of Red Moon, 1300 AC

The sun began to rise on the eastern horizon, its soft rays bathing the travelers' campsite in a subtle golden glow. The cattails planted along the edges of Laufeia's Sorrow waved in time with the lake's rippling surface, the quacking of ducks floating in the air. On the northern edge of the body of water sat a shabby dock, on which Master Arvel and Cymbelina were seated. It creaked and groaned as the wind swept across the valley. The two álves ignored the sounds as they sat cross-legged across from each other as the teacher initiated a patron lesson with his pupil.

"Breathe in…breathe out. Breathe in…breathe out."

Master Arvel repeated the mantra several times, hoping to coax the brunette into the meditative state required for their lesson. Her teacher's soothing whispers and the pre-lesson potion the half-álf consumed were supposed to guide her into the dream-like state that allowed her to experience visions from her inner self. This practice was officially called '*anas tusinca*,' or soul reading, and all Wood Álves were supposed to participate in it daily until they mastered the abilities of their patron. Cymbelina always had difficulty reaching the meditative state required for a soul reading, and her distracted thoughts about recent events made the process even more difficult than usual.

"Breathe in…breathe out. Breathe in…breathe out."

Cymbelina squeezed her green eyes shut, trying her hardest to reach the vision she was meant to see.

"Breathe in…"

Dense fog shrouded her mind's eye. Cymbelina focused all her mental strength on penetrating the smoky clouds, which swirled around the mental scene she was destined to see.

Dissipate, dammit, dissipate, the brunette willed the mist away, intertwining her fingers in a prayer-like gesture.

"And breathe out."

The Half-Sylvanrolk cut through the clouds on her next exhale, her energy concentrating on the revealed mental image. Behind the fading curtain of smoke was a dark wooden door, which the female was all too accustomed to seeing. Unlike her fellow Sylvanrolk, who usually experienced at least slightly different visions each day, Cymbelina had seen the door's image every day since she turned five when her patron lessons first began. She had hoped today's vision might be different, but, of course, it wasn't.

"Are you witnessing your vision?" The patron guide probed, his distant voice echoing throughout the bleak chamber of the she-álf's mind.

"Yes, Master Arvel."

"What do you see?"

Cymbelina looked around. She was bathed in a pool of shadows, everything around her obscured beside the door, which was aglow in the fiery light of a nearby torch. Bolted padlocks adorned the wooden structure, along with chains that zig-zagged across its deteriorating surface. At the top of the door was a rusted, barred window. Peering through the bars, the green-eyed woman gazed into another room shrouded in darkness.

"I see the locked door. Again."

"Can you see anything else?"

"No, Master Arvel. The room is pitch-black."

"Hmm. Well, I know you've tried to force the door open in previous sessions, but have you tried to this time?"

"Not yet, but I will now."

Cymbelina took phantom steps across the room, approaching the decaying apparatus. Her light brown fingers traced over the worn surface, encountering jutting splinters here and there. Although her vision's overall composition of items was the same as usual, the door appeared different. She was used to a smooth surface that felt strong and sturdy—the wood now felt worn, as if it could be cleaved under three swings of an axe. Cymbelina's nimble joints shifted from the wood to the iron locks. They appeared weak and rusted as she jiggled them side to side, a faint jingling noise echoing in her mind. Shaking her head, she let go of them and pushed against the door. It didn't budge.

"It won't open, Master Arvel. However, there's something different about the door."

"What do you mean?"

"Well, the wood doesn't appear as strong as it usually is. It feels old and pliable."

"Interesting. We should investigate further. Is there still a window at the top of the door like in your previous visions?"

"Yes, sir."

"Good. Tell me what you see when you gaze through it."

Following her instructor's advice, the brunette glanced through the dark aperture once more. Although Cymbelina unsurprisingly saw nothing, she heard a faint noise emitting from the room on the other side of the window. Pressing one of her pointed ears up to the hole, the woman held her breath, focusing all her energy on the room.

What is that sound?

The door subtly vibrated, causing her body to tremble as it leaned against the wooden structure.

"Cymbelina? What do you see?"

The brunette ignored her teacher's distant question, focusing on the quivering of the door. The humming from the other room appeared to crescendo, the sound akin to a vibrating chuckle.

What could that be? The she-álf pondered, backing away from the window. *I've never heard anything like that during my visions before.*

"Cymbelina? Can you hear me?"

The student never had the chance to answer her teacher, for as soon as the brunette began to form a response, she was ripped out of her vision by a pair of cold hands, which dug into the fabric covering her relaxed shoulders.

"Gotcha!" Malaveen exclaimed, her giddy voice echoing across the field. The ducks calmly floating on the pond nearby quacked in fright as they flew away, some of their feathers floating in the breeze. The brunette's shoulders tensed as she instinctually flung her right arm back to elbow the sneak in the face. Cymbelina's head followed her arm in the turn, her green eyes wide in shock as she looked at the blonde, who had a wicked grin spread across her countenance.

"Are you insane?" Cymbelina gasped, halting her swing inches from the other she-álf's face.

"Malaveen," the teacher grunted, glaring at the blonde, "you know it's highly inappropriate to interrupt a patron lesson."

The woman feigned ignorance, raising her hands in a defensive stance as she backed away. "I didn't know you guys were in a lesson. I thought you two were praying to Mother Terralynia."

Cymbelina scoffed. "Would that make your disturbance any better?"

"Whatever the case may be, you've ruined any chance of further exploring Cymbelina's vision today. We'll continue tomorrow, Cymbelina—WITHOUT any interruptions. Is that clear, Malaveen?"

The blonde smiled cheekily, nodding her head. "Crystal clear, Master Arvel."

The male dusted off his periwinkle robes and stood up, tying his long umber locks into a tight bun as he glanced at Malaveen. "Where's Kayven?"

"He's still sleeping."

"Then would you please do me a favor and wake him up? Gently, though, nothing like what you just did to the two of us. Cymbelina and I will join you at the camp momentarily."

As the blonde she-álf nodded and skipped away, Master Arvel turned toward his pupil, offering the brunette a hand as she attempted to stand up.

"Don't let her get a rise out of you, Cymbelina," the teacher began, helping the half-álf to her feet. "You're giving her what she wants."

"That's easier said than done, Master Arvel. She can be a real pain in the ass sometimes."

"Ha, don't I know it. However, you're stronger than you give yourself credit for. I know you can reign in your reactions a bit if you put effort into it."

Cymbelina remained silent, unsure how to respond to her patron teacher's guidance as she brushed off some dirt that had gotten onto her sleeping clothes.

Feeling her hesitance, Master Arvel continued. "Let me clarify that I'm not telling you this to scold you. You're a twenty-two-year-old álf, for Goddess's sake. I'm giving you this advice for your own sanity, not for anyone else's." Master Arvel bent over and picked up the fur mats the two álves had been meditating on, handing Cymbelina hers. "Now, what do you say? Should we head back?"

Cymbelina nodded, following her patron guide as they walked off the pier and towards the campsite. Kayven was now up and about, his disheveled locks framing his face as he mashed various ingredients together with his mortar and pestle. Malaveen was sitting off to the side, meticulously combing her fair hair.

"What're you making, Kayven?"

The marigold-eyed male smiled, looking up at the brunette as the morning sun bathed his frame in heavenly light. "A light breakfast. I figured we'd be in a rush to venture into the Wilds this morning, so I'm using some hawthorn berries I brought on the trip to make hawthorn paste."

Malaveen groaned, clutching her stomach in exaggerated disgust. "The thought of eating berries any time soon makes my stomach churn. Got anything else in your pack?"

"I do, but not for today." Kayven's eyes followed Cymbelina and Master Arvel as they swiftly packed their belongings. "Would you like some hawthorn paste,

Cymbelina?"

"I'd love some. Thank you."

"How about you, Master Arvel?"

"Of course. Thank you, Kayven."

By the time the travelers finished packing up and eating, the sun was high in the sky. The brilliant star shone upon the green hills from its celestial throne, under which the travelers walked as they followed the northern path. The party banter was minimal until the álves reached the border of the Glimmering Wilds. The hilly grasslands of Terralynia's Folly sunk into a leveled glade bordering the forest. The entrance to the Wilds was marked by a wall of tall trees, which bore lush foliage that came in shades of emerald and moss, defying nature's autumnal kiss.

"How come the leaves don't change during fall in the Glimmering Wilds like they do in the Sunshade Forest?" The blonde inquired, turning toward the patron guide.

"Great question, Malaveen. I don't know the answer, but it is probably due to the forest's magical properties."

"What sort of magic are we talking about, Master Arvel?" Kayven questioned.

The teacher smiled, scanning his three allies in amusement. "You'll soon see."

The group continued their march forward, eventually breaching the wall of trees. Maneuvering through a small gap, Cymbelina and her fellow Sylvanrolk followed the path into the strange woodland. Unknown critters chirped and chittered as they jumped from branch to branch above the travelers' heads, their noises filling the cool, crisp air. Small beams of sunlight filtered through the dense leafy canopy and scattered off the myriad of branches overhead, creating floating specks of light. The glowing particles resembled tiny sparkles as they fell around Cymbelina and her kin.

It seems like the Glimmering Wilds was aptly named, the Half-Sylvanrolk thought, staring at the world around her in wonder.

Vibrant mushrooms appearing in shades from the brightest chartreuse to the deepest vermillion bordered the edges of the forest trail, some crunching under the wary feet of the distracted álves as they continued onward. The group exchanged very few words as they crept along the trail for hours on end. Eventually, the adventurers found themselves in a dark spot deep within the Wilds, where the air was still, and the scenery was dim. Master Arvel squinted from the map the kinlord had given him to the path ahead, his indecisiveness becoming more evident to his companions with each passing second.

"I thought you've traveled into the Wilds before?" Cymbelina asked, an inkling of worry perverting her inquisitive demeanor.

"I have. I just don't remember the trail looking quite like this."

Malaveen scoffed. "So, we're lost?"

"I didn't say that. I have a map on hand, after all. I'm simply shocked by the differences between the road before me and the road from my memories.

Cymbelina and her fellow group members tried to remain calm as they watched the teacher study the map, the sound of distant crows disturbing the formerly quiet atmosphere.

"Why don't we stop and take a second to study the map?" Cymbelina suggested. "We will never get to where we need to be if we don't take a moment to regain our bearings."

Kayven and Arvel agreed with the sentiment while Malaveen stared at the group in disbelief, placing her hands on her hips. "Am I the only one who sees what Cymbelina's doing? She clearly wants us to stop so she can avoid finding a new home for herself while simultaneously slowing our mission down. This is all a ploy so she can get back at her grandfather for casting her out of the Glenrolk!"

Cymbelina emitted an exasperated sigh, turning her weary eyes to the blonde. "You have a warped sense of reality, Malaveen."

"Do I, Cymbelina? Because my theory seems to make a lot of sense to me, considering the circumstances."

"How exactly does it make sense? The damage has been

done; I am no longer a member of the Glenrolk clan. Why on Sacarnia would I risk the safety of all Sylvanrolk in order to get back at one specific person?"

"You just...I don't know. I would be mad if I were in your shoes, so I imagine you're pretty frustrated about your situation. I bet you're even irritated enough to get revenge on Kinlord Emyr. It just makes sense."

While Cymbelina tried to figure out how to respond to Malaveen, Master Arvel and Kayven found a small sheltered clearing adjacent to the confounding path the álves had been following. In the center of the small glade sat a rock, on which the two males placed the kinlord's map before crouching to take a closer look at it.

"Listen. Even though I disagree with my grandfather's decision to expel me from the clan, I wouldn't take out my disappointment on the rest of my kin. The very idea is cruel and childish, so drop it."

"No," the blonde sputtered, her face turning red, "I won't drop it. Unlike you, I have an undying loyalty to the Glenrolk. Unlike you, I..."

Malaveen droned on with her inane accusations, Cymbelina's attention rapidly decreasing with each syllable that exited the blonde's lips. The brunette's green eyes drifted to her male companions, choosing instead to focus on what they were discussing. Even that conversation was tiresome to pay attention to until Kayven said something that caught the she-álf's attention.

"There's something odd about this map, Master Arvel. See how the trail bends and swirls on the parchment? I'm positive we've made no such movements while traversing the trail thus far. The drawn path and the actual one seem to be different."

With Kayven's comments piquing her interest, Cymbelina walked away from Malaveen, who was still prattling on with her ill-conceived notions.

"Hey! You can't just walk away from me! I'm talking to you, Cymbelina!"

Cymbelina didn't respond, opting to crouch between the

males and glance at the crinkled map they were studying. "What were you saying about the trail being different from the one on the map?"

"Oh, don't dwell on that notion, Cymbelina. Like I was about to tell Kayven, the path on the map is a crude replica of the real one. It's supposed to give us a general idea of where the road will take us, not be an exact model."

Kayven shook his head. "Then, with all due respect, Master Arvel, how're we supposed to follow it? What if the real road branches off into another one? What will we do then?"

"I can assure you, that's very unlikely to happen. All recorded instances of Sylvanrolk venturing into the Glimmering Wilds indicate that only one path leads throughout the forest. The one that brought us into the Wilds is the only one there is."

"But how can you be so sure, Master Arvel? Based on your initial reaction, the road appears to have changed. Is there a possibility that an unknown group of individuals has taken up residence within the Glimmering Wilds and decided to form new roads?"

Cymbelina remained silent as the two males discussed the situation at hand, unconsciously leaning forward as she studied the chart. *The drawn trail seems pretty straightforward to me,* the brunette thought, her eyes scanning the document before her, her body ever so slightly tilting forward with each passing second. *Many moons have passed since Master Arvel visited the Wilds. Perhaps it's just a matter of his memory failing him?*

Cymbelina was so enraptured by her thoughts that she didn't realize how far forward she had been leaning, eventually losing her balance and stumbling. Her hand shot out to support her weight, her dirty palm landing in a dip in the stone's surface. Pulling her arm back, the brunette noticed a soft turquoise glow emanating from a series of engravings in the middle of the rock's surface. The swirls etched into the side of the stone began to glow as the light from the center drawing began to spread. The light pulsated, a soft humming noise arising from the impressions.

Master Arvel snatched the map before the trio stood up, none of their eyes peeling away from the luminous formation. They watched in amazement as the entire rock began to glow, the humming noise getting progressively louder.

"Have you seen anything like this before during your travels in the Wilds, Master Arvel?" The she-álf whispered, the radiant light from the rock casting a bluish-green gleam across her face.

"I can't say that I have, Cymbelina, but I can tell you that it wasn't doing that before you touched it."

"What do you think it means?"

"It means," Malaveen began, stomping over to her companions, "that we need to find a place to camp. In case you three hadn't noticed, the light filtering through the trees has lessened substantially. If we lose the light of day, we'll never be able to navigate through the forest."

Cymbelina looked toward the patron teacher for guidance. "What should we do, Master Arvel? Should we head back down the trail and figure out what all of this means before venturing deeper into the forest?"

The umber-haired man was silent for a moment, his eyes moving from his younger companions to the map in front of him. Sighing, he rolled the parchment up and attached it to his belt. "Let's take the trail back to Terralynia's Folly. That way, there's no chance of us getting lost. We'll camp on the edge of the Wilds and be ready to enter the forest again tomorrow morning."

"But Master Arvel," Malaveen objected, "why don't we just camp in the Wilds? Wouldn't that be easier than leaving just to come back tomorrow?"

"In theory, yes. But I think making a plan for navigating the forest from our point of entry would be easier than making a plan from within the depths of the Wilds." The patron teacher rolled his shoulders and walked back toward the trail. "Now hurry along, everyone; the sooner we leave the forest, the better."

"Please, Your Lordship. Don't let Mistress Tihana inject that vile liquid into me. She told me about it before you arrived, and I-I don't want to take it."

The man was silent as he looked at Petiča, who was sweating profusely in her restraints. Her lavender eyes were wide with fear, the tears pricking at the inner corners of her eyes shining in the light of the incinerator's fire. She had been locked in the depths of the alchemist's lab since she returned from Florella, and her recent isolation led to the realization that she would most likely not leave the testing site alive.

"Please," the yellowish-gray fairy whined, yanking on her restraints in a fruitless effort to tug at the monarch's heartstrings.

Although Vukasino's eyes remained fixed on the struggling woman's frame, his thoughts were elsewhere, his captive's pleas falling on distracted ears. *Hopefully, Tihana's newest batch of the Elixir of Annihilmon will prove to be successful. If not, we'll have to keep trying. I'll submit every fae on this island to testing if I have to, just so I can find the right mixture. That'll be the only way to eliminate the scum littering my homeland.*

The wooden door leading into the basement laboratory banged against the stone walls of the warm room, causing Vukasino's eyes to flick to the side. The source of the noise was Mistress Tihana, who had a confident smirk plastered on her face as she sauntered around the slab Petiča was tied to. The alchemist had a vial clutched in her right hand, the orchid-colored contents of the tube contrasting with her grayish-blue skin. In her left hand sat a syringe.

The items in the scientist's hands increased Petiča's struggling tenfold, whereas a smile spread across Vukasino's gray lips.

"Do you have everything you need, Mistress Tihana?"

"I certainly do, Monarch Vukasino," the alchemist responded. Her bobbed, white hair swayed as she placed her equipment onto a wooden trolley, rolling it toward the rack the fairy was strapped to. The wheels of the cart squeaked as it moved across the uneven stone floor, the nearby fire crackling.

The purple-eyed woman shook her head vigorously, her eyes lighting up with fear as she gazed at the unusual tube of liquid. "Please, Monarch Vukasino, don't subject me to this unorthodox testing! I'll do whatever you want if you let me go."

"Tsk, tsk, tsk...but my dear, this *is* what I want."

"Well, I...I...I won't tell anyone what you and Mistress Tihana have going on down here!"

"Don't be silly. You won't be telling anyone regardless."

The ruler's top alchemist shook the tube of liquid, watching the glowing bubbles rise and fall within the container. Sticking the syringe's tip into the vessel, the three vilek watched as the pinkish-purple liquid filled the barrel.

"If it's any consolation," the man said, kneeling so that he was at eye level with the bound fae, "your participation in this experiment helps your kin in more ways than you can imagine. Without your assistance, we would never know how the chemistry of a living vilek reacts to this potion."

Sniffling, the woman briefly stopped her pleading. Turning her watery gaze toward the glowing, pinkish liquid, she asked, "And what, exactly, is that potion called?"

Mistress Tihana shot the leader a wary look, but he quickly shooed her unsure glance away. Coughing into his fist, he answered, "I suppose there's no harm in telling you, as you won't leave this room alive. About a month ago, Mistress Tihana acquired the elusive recipe for The Elixir of Annihilmon." The man paused, his black eyes flicking from the captive to the scientist. "I'm not sure how she acquired such a treasure, but I try my best not to look a gift horse in the mouth."

Ignoring the ruler's admission that she would die soon, Petiča stuttered, "D-Did you say Annihilmon?"

"The one and only," Tihana responded, flicking a finger against the syringe.

The bound fairy's panicked expression quickly morphed

into one of rage. "*Ka ravoyja!*" the woman snapped before spitting in the ruler's face. "How dare you bring a product of that defiler into the Dark Vilek kingdom. Your mother would be ashamed."

Moments of restless silence passed until the warm air of the lab filled with the unsettling sound of Vukasino's angered chuckle. "That," the visi-vilek began, bringing up his hands to wipe his face clean of saliva, "was one of the worst things you could've done for yourself at this point in time."

Pulling his arm back, the leader of Elderfell slapped the detained woman, eliciting a string of pained cries from her parched lips as her eyes squeezed shut. Rising to his feet with a frustrated groan, he shoved one of his slate-gray hands into a pocket inside his robe. Fishing out a handkerchief, the man balled the square of fabric in his hands before pushing it into the sniveling woman's mouth.

"That's much better," the ruler sighed, ambling away from the operation table. Taking a seat on the other side of the lab, the malicious male watched as Petiča cried through her gag. "As I previously stated, your involvement in this test greatly benefits our people. In fact, it will mean more to the Dark Vilek than your life ever could. After all, this potion will help me to reclaim our rightful place on Florella. However, before I administer it to the rest of the troops, we need to research the possible side effects it may cause. That's where you come in."

The alchemist allowed Vukasino to talk as she set down the syringe. She then grabbed a swab and cleaned the skin protecting one of Petiča's jugular veins.

"Before your sister was tossed into the incinerator, she helped our dear Tihana discover things about the potion we never thought possible. I mean, who would have thought the Elixir of Annihilmon would affect the muscle mass of a corpse? However, with this finding came a slew of new questions."

The prisoner's muffled whimpers became progressively louder as Tihana adjusted her grayish-yellow neck.

"I know I speak for both Mistress Tihana and myself when

I say that we hope you can answer our remaining inquiries. After all, the sooner our questions are answered, the sooner Florella will belong to the Dark Vilek."

With one grayish-blue hand on the subject's neck and another holding the syringe, the alchemist looked at the visivilek for permission to proceed.

"And once the war is won, I'll make sure to include your name as well as Urskana's in my victory speech." The cocky man crossed his left leg over his right, placing his folded hands on his left bent knee. "You may begin, Mistress Tihana."

The tip of the syringe penetrated the woman's jugular vein. Petiča's face contorted in anguish as the needle sank deeper and deeper into her neck, unmercifully pumping the glowing liquid into her bloodstream. Once the barrel had been emptied of its contents, Tihana set the tool down and joined Vukasino on the other side of the room to watch the prisoner's reaction to the elixir.

There were no apparent changes to the grayish-yellow woman's frame at first. She continued to tremble in fear, just as she had before. Her purple eyes darted back and forth, her teeth grinding against the cloth in her mouth.

This has to work, dammit. I have neither the time nor patience to search for another test subject.

It wasn't long before the monarch's wish was granted. Soon, erratic gasps erupted from the test subject's throat, the handkerchief doing nothing to contain the prisoner's strangled cries. The frightened fairy's eyes repeatedly twitched before they rolled to the back of her skull. Her bound body violently seized up and down, creating an echo of skin slapping stone throughout the torrid chamber. Foam poured out of either side of her stretched lips. She rhythmically clenched and unclenched her hands, her head bobbing back and forth with each sudden movement she made.

Vukasino's eyes flicked to various parts of Petiča's body, studying it until he found what he had been searching for: signs of muscle growth. The restrained woman's forearms slowly swelled with each passing second, the veins on each arm bulging underneath the pressure. Her leg muscles soon followed suit. Enraptured by the sight, the monarch leaned forward in his seat, his black eyes gleaming with wonder.

"How remarkable," the ruler muttered, his gaze transferring to the alchemist beside him. "I have never seen a Dark Vilek react to a potion in this fashion. You truly are a genius, Mistress Tihana. Where on Sacarnia did you receive the recipe for this elixir?"

The alchemist was silent, ignoring her ruler's prying question, one she had refused to answer many other times. Her stony stare was set on the convulsing test subject, whom she eyed with great interest. Her right hand fiddled with the amulet dangling from her neck, a smile slowly spreading across her concentrated face. "Thank you, Your Lordship."

The prisoner continued her shuddering movements for several moments until the potion had sufficiently traveled throughout her body, her frame becoming as still as a corpse. Petiča's eyes landed on the ruler, a sense of newfound strength and fury emanating from her gaze. Tearing one of her arms out from underneath its restraint, the grayish-yellow fairy pulled the wadded cloth out of her mouth.

With lips coated in spittle, the test subject whispered venomously, "*Jetav ka.*"

Tihana tensed after witnessing the woman's strength, her hands instinctively drifting to the sword at her side. Before she could act, Vukasino raised his hand to cease her movement. "Don't act hastily, Mistress Tihana. We must observe the side effects of the elixir."

Petiča analyzed her muscular frame, which was cloaked in a mysterious black aura. Staring at the tips of her throbbing fingers, her eyes worked their way up her pulsating biceps. With a sense of mournful disgust, the vilek screeched, her lavender eyes returning to the leader of Elderfell. "You'll pay for this!"

The monarch grinned as gusts of dust began to stir from nearby bookshelves and the stone floor below. Drawing together, the particles of dirt and dead skin formed thin streams that turbulently swirled around the sitting ruler and his scientist. The controlled flames from the incinerator started to sway violently, their crackling noises crescendoing into a deafening roar.

Unfazed by the windy conditions, Vukasino stared at Petiča in delight. *It seems like the Elixir of Annihilmon impacts the user's elemental abilities as well as their muscle mass. This just keeps getting better and better.*

"Did you hear me, you contemptuous cretin? I'll kill you!"

The male chuckled, his white hair whipping in the wind. "Oh really?"

Petiča pried her left arm out of its restraint before doing the same for her feet, giving the ruler ample time to stand up and hide a dagger behind his back. Understanding that the deranged woman had no intention of stopping, he dismissed Mistress Tihana so she could fetch some of his guards in case things went south. He doubted he would need the support, but it was better to be safe than sorry.

"This is for my sister and the rest of the Dark Vilek!"

The prisoner lunged forward in the blink of an eye, her potion-enhanced wind abilities allowing her to travel to the leader faster than usual. She attempted to punch Vukasino, but he moved to the side, his abilities assisting him in a speedy dodge. He could've killed his subject right then and there, but he wanted to see the limits of the concoction.

Vukasino tauntingly yawned as Petiča attempted to strike him again, her sharpened nails inches away from his unscathed face.

"You're wasting time and energy, my dear," the male said, adjusting his regalia as he slid to the right. The prisoner missed him again. "We both know how this is going to end."

Regardless of what he said, the woman refused to stop attacking him, which he found to be excessively irksome yet a bit amusing. *Either the potion sends subjects into a blind rage, or Petiča is so overwhelmed by anger from her imprisonment that she fails to see how reckless she's being.*

Dodging another one of the fae's strikes, the monarch

laughed. "You still have time to call it quits, Petiča. You can either die a peaceful death after the potion wears off, or you can die a painful one at the end of my blade."

"Never!" The female spat, swinging at the male with her taloned fists. "I refuse to allow my sisters-in-arms to be poisoned by some abomination and his scientist creator!" The female paused, directing a gust of wind at the monarch. He was unfazed. "You're not a true vilek, Vukasino. If you have any shred of decency, you'd give up the throne to someone who is!"

Vukasino saw red, all mirth evaporating from his being. *Abomination? ABOMINATION?!*

The leader sent a blast of warm air toward the enraged fairy, a blast stronger than any Petiča could dream to muster. Her muscular body flew backward as she slammed against the wall, which trembled upon impact.

"You want to call me an 'abomination'?!" Vukasino questioned, his voice shrill. "I am a being perfected by science," the leader declared, approaching the fairy as she began to stand up. "It took Tihana years to create me, using the best DNA from Matriarch Zlatana and the best DNA of countless beings across the face of Sacarnia. What did it take to create you?" The male questioned, delivering a sharp kick to the downed woman's ribcage. Petiča cried out in agony. "Soul bonding? Love? Pah, you're just like every other damn vilek on this blasted world." The man kicked again, his gray complexion slowly turning red. "I am the only unique fae on the face of this planet. I was created using magic and logic. I am the pinnacle of our race."

The woman clutched her ribcage but continued to try and stand up to face the monarch. Her muscular arms and legs slowly began to shrink, the black aura that once cloaked her frame petering out. Scoffing, the male stepped away, a fireball forming in his palm. His angered face was a similar shade to the flames in his hand, which swirled wildly.

Aiming the fireball at the woman near his feet, he whispered, "You are a reminder of why we need to evolve."

Vukasino tossed the produced flames like they were nothing, watching as they engulfed Petiča's aching form. The woman's cries of anguish echoed throughout the lab as she was bathed in fire, the light from which caused Vukasino's dagger to shine before it plunged into her gut. He repeatedly stabbed the fairy, ignoring the heat from the fire licking at his skin. The ferocity in each motion stemmed from the woman's blasphemous words, which repeated in his head like an undying mantra.

By the time Mistress Tihana returned to the room with the monarch's three bodyguards, the flames had already eaten away at the grayish-yellow woman's corpse, her body nothing more than an unrecognizable crisp. Vukasino was still crouched above the fae's deceased frame, stabbing areas of her body he hadn't gotten to yet as the inferno began to die.

"I.AM.NOT.AN.ABOMINATION.YOU.WORTHLESS. WENCH."

The male stopped his assault as he felt the eyes of his closest allies on him. Standing up from his crouched position on the blood-soaked floor, the monarch attempted to brush the dust off his robes but accidentally smeared the cobalt-hued lifeforce on his clothes instead. Tihana doused the flaming body with her water abilities as the leader adjusted himself, grunting in disgust at his mistake.

Turning his gaze away from his stained garments, the ruler declared, "I've seen enough of this elixir, Tihana. We need to start distributing it to the troops immediately. Conceal the deaths of Urskana and Petiča however you must. The last thing I need is an uprising on my hands right now."

"But...Your Lordship, one test is hardly enough to determine the efficacy of the elixir. I strongly suggest—"

The male wagged his finger, silencing the alchemist. Spitting out some blood that had gotten into his mouth, he said, "And I suggest you cease your objections. We need to get this show on the road. I'm sick of minor assaults on the Snøthorn Mountains and Eldenfield. I want big, history-making battles across all of Florella. I want to wipe the filth off our homeland.

So when I say we're ready to start supplying the elixir to the soldiers, I want to hear zero protests. Do you understand?"

All three women nodded, even though Vukasino was mainly addressing the scientist.

"Good. Now, start making larger batches of the Elixir of Annihilmon tomorrow. Also," the male paused, stepping over Petiča and motioning to her corpse, "take this filth out of my sight. I would hate the stench in here to get any worse."

* * *

"Any chance those mushrooms we ate back there were hallucinogenic? Because I swear, this was the way back."

The confused travelers squinted at the path they had taken into the forest, a route now bathed in a muted glow thanks to the colorful, luminous mushrooms that lined it. The light from the mushrooms was the only source of illumination around, as the sunlight from above had long since vanished, leaving the rest of the forest cloaked in a blanket of midnight.

The blonde huffed. "This is no time for jokes, Kayven. Plus, you're the son of the clan's chef; you would be the one to know."

"I didn't see any other paths on the way back," Cymbelina spoke, her eyes scanning the dark forest surrounding the adventurers. "Is there any possibility we could've gotten turned around and somehow delved deeper into the Wilds?"

"We must've! Forests don't change on their own!"

"Well, Malaveen, Mother Terralynia has always had a bad sense of humor, hasn't she? Maybe she came out of hiding just to tease our little band of adventurers."

"Stop it, Kayven!" the blonde hissed. "We may never see our home again! At least Cymbelina doesn't have to worry about that; she's already been cast out of the Glenrolk."

Cymbelina's right eye twitched as she withheld the retort that threatened to pass her lips.

The road, which should've led back into Terralynia's Folly, wound through a dense group of trees, even thicker than the groups the companions had seen in the forest previously. Stray specks of light danced around the luminescent fungi, the cawing of mysterious birds echoing in the canopy of leaves above.

The three younger álves turned their attention away from the road, opting to stare at the patron guide instead. The male was silently studying the way ahead, ignoring the worried glances of his kin.

"What should we do, Master Arvel?" Cymbelina questioned. "Should we continue moving ahead?"

The male shook his head. "No, we're not going to move any further until we discover one thing." Master Arvel's eyes flicked to the blonde. "Malaveen, since you're the only álf here that possesses a patron animal that can fly, can you take to the sky and discern how deep we are in the forest and how far we are from Terralynia's Folly?"

Malaveen glanced at the trees above. Their boughs formed a thick curtain of foliage, with only traces of shadow hidden beyond. An unknown animal chittered here and there.

The blonde cocked an eyebrow in astonishment. "Me, through those trees?" Malaveen looked around the group in astonishment. "You're right, Kayven; there must be something *special* in those mushrooms."

"Please, Malaveen, we could be lost in here for Goddess knows how long unless we get a feel for where we are."

The blonde smirked. "Begging suits you, Cymbelina."

"Will you do it or what?" Master Arvel uncharacteristically snapped.

"Ok, ok, I'll see what I can do."

The she-álf changed into her swan form. Twisting and twirling, she made her way through the sinuous limbs of the surrounding trees, emitting a large honk as she accidentally flew into one of them. Cymbelina stifled a laugh, watching Malaveen amble her way up.

Kayven smiled at Cymbelina, teasing, "Laughing at the expense of others? I didn't know you had it in you."

Cymbelina chuckled, shaking her head.

"Shush, you two," Master Arvel admonished. "Do you see anything up there, Malaveen?!"

There were a few moments of silence before the she-álf honked twice, branches rustling as she made her way to the ground again. Once she transformed out of her swan form, the blonde glanced at her companions in a worried fashion.

"As we all surmised, the sun has fallen below the horizon, and the moon is high. Even in the moonlight, however, Terralynia's Folly is nowhere in sight."

"That's impossible! Are you sure you didn't miss it?"

"'Miss it'? All I can see is a sea of trees when I'm flying above the Wilds!" The blonde sighed, pinching either side of her nose. "I'm positive, Master Arvel. I don't know where we are."

A heavy silence fell upon the group of travelers as the eyes of the younger Sylvanrolk looked to Master Arvel for guidance once more. However, the male was at a loss for words; his amber eyes were wide before he shut them, drawing in a deep breath.

"Get ready to unpack your bags, you three. I guess we're sleeping in the Wilds tonight."

Gradgate
22nd of Red Moon, 1300 AC

The sun was high in the sky, its chilled, autumnal beams filtering through the trees of the Glimmering Wilds. Floating particles of sunlight danced in the chilly air, which swirled around the teacher and his pupil. The duo sat in a clearing off to the side of the makeshift camp, where Kayven and Malaveen were just beginning to stir in their sleeping mats. The morning birds sang their infrequent tunes as Cymbelina and Master Arvel wrapped up their soul reading session for the day, as they were both desperate to get on with their journey through the confounding forest.

The Half-Sylvanrolk watched her teacher as he stood up and retrieved his mat, neatly rolling it up. She silently followed the man with her green eyes until she asked, "Do you want to talk about it, Master Arvel?"

The man puffed a stray strand of hair out of his face. "I'm not sure what you mean, Cymbelina."

The she-álf had never seen Master Arvel so anxious before. The patron teacher's nervousness carried over from the night before into the soul reading he had shared with the brunette this morning. Even though the man was trying his best to hide his emotions from the brunette, he was utterly failing.

"I know you're trying to hide your dismay about our current predicament, but it's not working very well. You're the leader of this group, and if you're feeling apprehensive about something, please feel free to share it with the rest of us."

The male shrugged. "I'd rather dive deeper into the vision

you experienced during today's lesson."

"There's nothing new to explore; it was the same as yesterday. So please, Master Arvel, share your thoughts."

The man let out an amused sigh. "You've always been stubborn; I don't know why I even try to hide anything from you." Shaking his head in defeat, he continued. "Look, it's not that I'm overly worried about what lies ahead; I'm just perplexed about the road situation. Did the path we were following magically change, or did we just get turned around? And if the trail did alter, who or what caused it?"

"Looking back, I don't see how it's possible that we got turned around; it seemed like we were following the trail back in the direction we came from." Cymbelina's face lit up as a thought dawned on her. "Do you think that glowing stone we encountered yesterday has anything to do with the shifting path? After all, you did say the forest was magical."

"Ha, that was more of a reference to how beautiful the forest is than anything else. However, I'm starting to suspect my joke wasn't far from the truth." The male paused, helping Cymbelina as she attempted to collect her things. "As for the stone, well... anything's possible, but I'm unsure how it could have altered the environment. Either way, let's avoid touching any other rocks we come across, just in case."

"That's a good idea," Cymbelina murmured as she turned her eyes toward the camp nearby. Kayven and Malaveen were still in their bedrolls, which sat beside the long-dead campfire.

Master Arvel's gaze traveled in the direction of where Cymbelina was staring. He chuckled. "It's about time we got the other two out of bed. The sooner we find our way through the forest, the better."

Shaking her head in agreement, the brunette accompanied her teacher as he returned to the campsite.

Rousing their sleepy companions, the adventurers began their day, hitting the perplexing path they were all growing to detest. The route was seemingly unchanged from the previous night, so the álves journeyed north on the trail to venture deeper into the woods. Each step the travelers made through the labyrinthine forest was slow and deliberate, each of them wary of what lay in wait around them.

"I might've done a few things differently if I had known last week that I would be stuck in some damned forest for eternity with the lot of you."

"Don't be dramatic, Malaveen. We'll figure something out."

"That's easy for you to say, Cymbelina. You were essentially sentenced to death in the Wilds, so the amount of time the three of us spend here is inconsequential to you."

The wandering álves eventually reached a fork in the trail, which not only cleaved through the woods but through the group's steadily rising hope of finding a way out.

"What in the—Master Arvel, you said there was only one path through the Glimmering Wilds!"

"I know what I said, Malaveen. Clearly, I was wrong. As were all the Sylvanrolk scholars who came before me."

"Ughhhh," the blonde groaned, rolling her eyes, "now, what are we going to do?"

Unvexed by the group's discovery, Kayven suggested, "Why don't we split up?"

"You're either joking, or you've lost your mind."

"I'm not joking, and I haven't lost my mind, Blondie. I'm not saying we go our separate ways permanently, but going halfway down the paths to get a quick look ahead isn't a bad idea."

"It wouldn't hurt to try," Cymbelina agreed, voicing her opinion for the first time in minutes.

The blonde blinked rapidly. "Master Arvel, surely you don't agree with this *tarbalcacas*."

"It's not bullshit, Malaveen. What other choice do we have?"

"Enough!" The patron guide intervened, grabbing his bow and two arrows from the quiver. "We'll split up, but don't go farther than where the arrows are. Malaveen and I will go down the right path while you two go down the left one. Make a note of anything you see."

Engraving an 'X' into the soil where the travelers would

reconvene, the older male shot two arrows at a tree on either side of each path, marking where each group should stop. With their orders apparent, both groups set out to explore their assigned routes.

Kayven and Cymbelina approached the arrow-embedded tree with caution. As they trudged along, the male's gaze drifted to the left side of the path while the female's wandered to the right. The brunette's eyes scanned over a row of trees, all of which seemed unremarkable compared to the hundreds of others the group had seen thus far. For a few minutes, Cymbelina could spot Master Arvel and Malaveen between the evergreens. The brunette kept her eyes trained on her two companions for as long as possible until their forms were swallowed by the dense wall of trees separating the paths.

"Thank Mother Terralynia, we're not going to be away from Malaveen and Master Arvel for too long," the she-álf whispered. "We could easily get lost in this damn forest."

"I'll say," the male paused, his marigold eyes turning away from the leafy abyss and toward the tree ahead of the duo. "Let's hope we can find some information about the vilek soon and then get out of the Wilds."

At this point, I'm starting to think there's no information to be found, the brunette thought dejectedly. *Wouldn't we have found a trace of the fairies at this point if they lived here? I mean, come on. How large can the Glimmering Wilds be?*

The two álves looked at each other as they arrived at the tree bearing the arrow. Nothing noteworthy seemed to be on the path ahead or on either side of them, just a bunch of trees similar to the countless ones they'd already passed. However, something felt off about this patch of the woods: something that raised the hairs on the back of Cymbelina's neck.

The area was silent. All sounds of life had faded into an eerie void, a stillness so quiet Cymbelina could hear the beating of her own heart.

"Cymbelina," the male álf murmured, his eyes flicking every which way, "is it my imagination, or has everything suddenly become silent?"

"It's not just you," the brunette paused, her eyes scanning the surrounding forest. "I noticed it, too."

"Shit. Let me grab the arrow, and then we can head back."

As Kayven pried the projectile from the tree's hardened bark, the snapping of nearby twigs caught the she-álf's attention. Turning to the right, Cymbelina heard low, rumbling growls emanating from a nearby thicket. The bushes shook, leaves falling to reveal multiple drooling maws, all of which trembled with primal hunger. The dripping mouths belonged to a small pack of woodland wolves, all of whom stalked out of the undergrowth. Strings of dribble dangled from their bloodstained chops before falling onto their burr-filled paws. Their ears were drawn back, their stances firm as they lowered their bodies into a pouncing position.

The female grabbed the steel daggers attached to her waist, stepping back to distance herself from the pack. "Kayven, we have company."

Instead of hearing a response from her álven companion, she saw the wolves' countenances change in the blink of an eye. Most of the gathering predators slowly backed away from the duo. An affronted snarl originating from behind the brunette masked the whimpers of the fleeing pack. The source of the noise was an enormous wolf bathed in an indigo aura. His dark brown fur stood on end, his yellow-orange eyes glistening in the thin ray of sunlight that filtered through the leafy canopy above. Dropping the arrow in his mouth, Kayven, who was in the form of his patron, Toryn, took a defensive stance and snarled, urging the creatures to stalk other prey. Most of the animals heeded the larger wolf's message, departing with their tails tucked between their legs. All except one, whose starved frame remained steadfast in Kayven's presence. Its ravenous eyes remained on the patronless brunette, its growl slowly increasing in volume by the second.

"Kayven, that wolf is going to—"

Before Cymbelina could finish, the wolf lunged forward, its hungry gaze glued on the she-álf. Sensing the ravenous animal's intention, the patron-possessed male interrupted the wolf's attack, Kayven's wolven jaws biting into the other wolf's neck. The duo somersaulted into a nearby bush, the foliage shaking as yelps and snarls emerged from within.

"Kayven?!" The brunette yelled out to her companion as she approached the undergrowth, the sounds of a struggle still filling the air.

A scared but understanding yelp was the only response Cymbelina received, the frightened woodland wolf scurrying out of the bushes and into the trees. Sighing in relief, Cymbelina tucked her daggers back into their sheaths, watching the male transform into his álven form as he emerged from the bush.

"You saved me a lot of trouble just now. Thank you."

The male smiled, plucking out the leaves stuck in between his dark locks. "Don't mention it."

The she-álf picked up the dart Kayven had dropped, handing it to him before wiping her slobber-covered hands on her trousers. "Are you ready to head back? There doesn't appear to be anything of interest around us."

"Of course," the male answered. "After all, we don't need any more animals sneaking up on us."

The two travelers walked down the path toward the 'X,' where Malaveen and Master Arvel were waiting for them. The teacher bore a relieved expression on his face as he watched the two álves approach.

"There you two are; we were beginning to worry. What did you find?"

"Nothing noteworthy besides a pack of hungry wolves, but Kayven was able to take care of them. However, I believe it would be in our best interest to move on before their hunger gets the best of them and they return. What about you two?"

Malaveen adopted an arrogant air about her, flipping her short blonde hair over her shoulder. "I managed to spot what appears to be a small village in the distance."

"A village?" The younger male asked, a perplexed look crossing his chiseled features. "Did you see it too, Master Arvel?"

"I did. I know it seems a bit odd, but investigating it might provide clues into what's going on with the forest or may lead us to find information about the vilek and whether or not they're behind the recent attacks. So, since the two of you didn't find anything worth exploring on your path, I think it would be best if we went down ours."

"I concur," Kayven said, adjusting his travel bag. "After you, Master Arvel."

The three younger álves took the rightmost path, following Master Arvel as he retraced his and Malaveen's footsteps. With the wolves gone, the sounds of tiny forest critters filled the midday air once more, much to the traveling party's delight. Cymbelina discerned faint outlines of structures through the thick wall of trees the chattering animals inhabited. The silhouettes of the buildings were taller than anything álf-made she had seen in her lifetime. With each step the group took toward the mysterious buildings, Cymbelina felt drawn to them more. The desire she possessed to discover what lay within each structure's walls gnawed on her mind, distracting her from all of her worries.

I wonder if the vilek live in that strange town. If so, maybe we can talk to them and then get the hell out of here.

The travelers arrived a few minutes later. Instead of makeshift tents surrounded by a few buildings like Cymbelina surmised, the settlement was full of stone towers. These towers were connected by a series of walls, which helped them form a circle around a large oak tree. Even from where the álves were standing, Cymbelina could see thick green vines swirling up and down the oak's bark, a ring of mushrooms surrounding its expansive roots. However, the area's most notable feature was the stones adorning the town's outer wall. The swirls on the surface of the rocks bore a striking resemblance to the stone the brunette had touched the day before.

I wonder if the rocks atop the walls act the same way as the stone we came across yesterday?

The group halted near the entrance of the village, their four pairs of eyes flicking every which way. Cymbelina's gaze landed under the stone arch at the mouth of the town. She could see a handful of citizens off in the distance, their blurry frames hanging back and observing the outsiders.

"Would you look at that! It's magnificent."

"Could it be the work of Sylvanrolk outcasts?"

Master Arvel continued to look around in amazement as he responded to Malaveen's inquiry. "Our clans have always preferred tents to buildings; it makes it easier to travel when no stone foundations are holding us back. So, I doubt these structures are the work of any Wood Álf nomads."

"Since we're not sure," Kayven began, motioning towards the leader of an approaching group of strangers, "why don't we ask him?"

An armored male with slicked-back garnet hair sauntered away from the village and toward the travelers with two heavily armored guards in tow. Bright rays of sunlight bounced off the leader's steel-plated armor and silver circlet, the purple stone in the center of the headband gleaming. A friendly smile spread across his ivory visage, and his brown eyes emanated a welcoming energy as he approached the Sylvanrolk.

"Welcome to our humble settlement, travelers! What business do you have with the people of Gradgate?"

"None, actually," Master Arvel spoke, his eyes warily assessing the three strangers before him. "We stumbled upon your town by accident."

"Ha! Nonsense, my good man. The Mother of Fate makes no mistakes—you are here for a reason, whether you know it yet or not. I'm Knight Commander Emerik, or, as my kin call me, *Vatez* Emerik. To my right is Officer Grigor, also known as *Casni* Grigor." The blonde male standing beside the leader nodded. "And to my left is Officer Hana, also known as *Casna* Hana." The blue-eyed woman smiled.

Cymbelina cocked her left eyebrow. *I've never heard such titles in the Sylvan or Hominan lexicon. Maybe these nomads have started their own language?*

"Happy to make your acquaintance, Knight Commander Emerik. I'm Master Arvel, and these are my companions:

Malaveen, Kayven, and Cymbelina."

The younger Wood Álves bowed.

"It's nice to meet the four of you," Emerik said with a smile.

"So," Malaveen started, staring at the trio of strangers in interest, "you three are Sylvanrolk outcasts, right?"

"Malaveen!"

"What?!" The blonde shrieked, "I was just asking because maybe they'll allow Cymbelina to move into their town. After all, she is an outcast now."

The brunette scoffed.

Emerik was silent for a moment as if he was deciding on how he should respond. After a few tense seconds, his grin returned. "Yes, as are the rest of the inhabitants of Gradgate."

The teacher crossed his hands over his chest. "Fascinating. According to our clan's intel, most nomads head south to the Jungle of Solitude. What made you and your kin come to the Glimmering Wilds?"

"Let's just say we wanted to deviate from the norm. After all, the founders of this village didn't want to fight over resources with the other outcasts. But I digress. What brings you four to our corner of the Wilds?"

"We're looking for the vilek," Master Arvel said confidently. "We would like to discuss a few things of the utmost importance with the fairy women, and legends say they inhabit this forest. Have you or any of the other residents of Gradgate encountered the vilek before?"

"Out here in the middle of nowhere? No, I can't say my people have encountered fairies before. We don't get many visitors out here. In fact, you and your merry band are the first outsiders we've seen in quite some time."

Cymbelina smirked. *Merry band, huh? If only he knew.*

Officer Grigor, who was still standing behind Emerik, shifted, a look of discomfort passing his youthful face. "What about the álves that came from the north, sir?"

The leader's light brown eyes narrowed, his head turning toward the forthright guard. "Besides them, of course."

A look of interest passed the patron guide's face. "Álves from the north? Do you mean you've received Dokkalrolk visitors recently or another group of Sylvanrolk nomads?"

"A group of Dokkalrolk. They came to the Glimmering Wilds searching for the vilek too."

Cymbelina tilted her head, her gaze shifting to her teacher. "Could you remind me who the Dokkalrolk are again?"

"More descendants of the ancient álfrolk who currently reside in the Snøthorn Mountains. But I'll tell you three more about them some other time. Are the group of Dark Álves still here?"

"Luckily for the four of you, yes."

"May we speak with them?"

Knight Commander Emerik's cheerful expression had slowly faded as the conversation progressed, and now his smile had descended into a tight, thin line. A look of unease shone in his eyes, his eyebrows slightly furrowing. "I don't see why not," Emerik answered, the apprehension in his voice betraying his seemingly blasé words. "Follow me; I'll take you to where they're staying."

Knight Commander Emerik guided the companions along a stony path that hugged the town's walls and bent around the central oak tree. The towering walls loomed over the Sylvanrolk outsiders, who marveled at the settlement with wide-eyed wonder. Cymbelina gazed upward, noticing a small group of guards patrolling the ramparts. They looked down at the travelers in interest, their metallic armor glimmering in the light filtering through the trees. Shifting her gaze back to the path, the brunette passed a handful of citizens, all of whom looked just as shocked by the outsiders' presence as the guards. The Half-Sylvanrolk found the pervasive sense of unease deeply unsettling.

These outcasts act as if they've never seen a fellow Sylvanrolk before. What gives? Were some of them born outside a clan to begin with? Dismissing the contemplations from her mind, Cymbelina focused on the task at hand.

As they rounded the bend, Emerik guided the adventurers

to the largest tower in the circle, positioned across from the town's entrance. A wooden sign, which read 'The Hammered Swallow,' was stationed outside of the building. An intricate design depicting a woozy bird bathing in a beer mug was etched underneath the establishment's title.

"What a name," Kayven humorously whispered.

Loud tavern music erupted from within the stone structure as the red-haired male opened the door. The music and the boisterous noises of the pub's patrons consumed the five álves as they stepped into the establishment. On either side of the front door sat two gatherings of laughing outcasts, both of which seemed too consumed in their jokes to notice the arrival of the adventurers. While those by the door were busy drunkenly chortling, there were other revelers who danced on the opposite side of the pub. These dancers wore flower crowns and flowing clothes, their gaiety being laughed at by those at the bar nursing a drink.

"Some of the Dokkalrolk appear to be at the bar!" Emerik shouted, pointing at a rambunctious group of customers bothering the barkeep. "I'd love to stay and introduce you, but I have other matters to attend to. I'll check on the four of you in a bit, so just hang tight."

"Thank you!" Master Arvel yelled at the knight commander, his voice barely audible over the hubbub of the tavern.

The garnet-haired male waved goodbye to the new arrivals before swiftly exiting the building, leaving the four Wood Álves alone to gather their wits.

"I guess we better catch up with the Dokkalrolk visitors and see if they're reaching out to the fairies for the same reason we are."

"You three go ahead," Malaveen said, her hazel eyes glued to the merrymaking álves dancing in circles around one another on the dancefloor. "I have a bit of my own investigating to do."

"I'll go with her," Kayven said, his eyes also locked on the boisterous scene. "Just so she doesn't get lost."

"Hey! I'm perfectly capable of—"

"Just go," the male interrupted, playfully pushing the blonde toward the frolicking alves.

While Kayven and Malaveen were busy immersing themselves in the merry atmosphere of the tavern, Master Arvel and Cymbelina headed to the bar. A gaggle of laughing Dark Álves was sitting on barstools, gulping down copious amounts of frothy beer between their drunken laughs.

"Let's split up," the patron guide suggested. "I'll talk to the drunkards on the right; you talk to the loner on the left."

"Sounds good."

Cymbelina approached the sullen álf, who sat alone at the edge of the bar. He had a dark brown hood concealing his face from the side, with only a sliver of a white braid peeking out. The man didn't utter a single word between his furtive sips of alcohol as the brunette approached.

"Excuse me, sir, do you mind if I ask you a few questions?"

The álf burped, looking up at the brunette. The male's sunken gray eyes were surrounded by dark circles, and his mouth slackened from inebriation. He gulped the rest of his drink down in a matter of seconds, waiting until the last drop had been drained from his mug before responding.

"Do I look like I'm in the mood to talk?"

"I'm sorry to interrupt, but it's really important. I promise I'll be quick."

"And who are you to decide what's important or not, eh?" The male slurred, sweeping his greasy white bangs out of his face before turning away from the she-álf. "Hey, barkeep!"

The woman tending the bar quickly glanced the patron's way but ultimately didn't respond. This angered the drunken man, who began to bang his wooden flagon on the counter. When that didn't give the Dokkalrolk the results he wanted, he growled, turning back toward the brunette. A look of drunken shock shone in his eyes as he jumped.

"What in the name of the Supreme Mother are you still standing around here for?"

"I wanted to ask you a question, sir. Remember?"

"Well? Spit it out!"

Deciding it was best not to prod the man any further, the brunette resigned to asking him a single inquiry. "Who is in charge of your group of Dokkalrolk?"

The man rolled his eyes before almost falling off of his chair. "Scoutmaster Estrasta. She's upstairs in the loft. Now piss off, you blasted Wood Álf."

Well, at least he had something helpful to say, Cymbelina thought, walking away from the male patron and calling Master Arvel over. Saying goodbye to the laughing customers, the patron guide rushed to his pupil.

"Did you learn anything useful?"

"Sort of. The man wasn't in the mood to answer many questions, but he said the leader of the band of Dokkalrolk goes by Scoutmaster Estrasta. She's hanging out in the loft upstairs. Maybe she might be able to help us out?"

"Great. Let's seek this scoutmaster out."

Maneuvering through the ever-growing crowd, the two álves approached a shabby ladder on the far side of the tavern. Carefully climbing the ladder rung by rung, the Sylvanrolk ascended into the loft above. The small space was filled with rows of bookshelves and a small reading area, which included a few cushions and a table for customers to rest their drinks on. How anyone could read in this environment was beyond Cymbelina's knowledge, but the area looked comfy enough. In the center of the floor sat an ash-gray she-álf, whose tousled pearl-colored locks framed her scarred, downcast face. She was sitting cross-legged on the floor in front of the low table, examining a faded map.

"Are you Scoutmaster Estrasta?"

The woman looked up, her right artic-blue eye shining in the candlelight, as did the row of piercings on her pointed ears. Her other eye was covered by a black eyepatch.

"What's it to you?" The woman questioned defensively

"A man downstairs said you might be able to answer a few questions for us."

The Dark Álf sat up straight, crossing her arms over her chest. "In that case, I am. I can also answer your questions depending on what you want to know. And why you wish to know."

"Knight Commander Emerik said you and your Dokkalrolk companions stumbled upon Gradgate while searching for the vilek. The same thing happened to our group, so we're curious as to why you were searching for the fairy women in the first place."

The woman's eye squinted as she assessed the teacher. "I might be more inclined to share my kin's reasoning behind our search if you share yours first. You approached me, after all. It's only fair if you share what's on your mind."

"Several attacks have occurred against the Sylvanrolk clans to the south, and we have reason to suspect the vilek might be connected to them," Cymbelina said, drawing the attention of the scoutmaster.

"When did the attacks first start?"

"A few days ago."

Scoutmaster Estrasta's gaze drifted to the map as she dabbed her quill in an inkwell and scribbled a note on the map. "You Sylvanrolk are lucky. Over the past couple of weeks, we've experienced multiple raids on our patrol camps surrounding the Snøthorn Mountains."

"How do you know fairies are involved?"

Estrasta laughed, shaking her head before she set her quill down. "Do either of you know any other creatures that come in shades of pink, yellow, blue, and green and possess various elemental abilities?" The two Sylvanrolk were silent. "No? I didn't think so."

"Well...do you have any idea why the fairy women—if they truly are the ones behind these attacks—are targeting álves?"

"If I knew that, why...wait. I never caught your name."

"You can call me Master Arvel. And this is Cymbelina."

"I see. Well, Master Arvel, if I knew that, the Dokkalrolk wouldn't just be searching for the vilek; we would be killing them." Estrasta rubbed her forehead, her gloved fingers combing through her hair. "But that doesn't matter right now. The damned forest changed around us, so who knows if we'll ever be able to get home."

"So you've experienced it too?" Cymbelina noted. "We thought we were hallucinating the changes."

"Oh no, the woods actually change. I'm not sure how, but they do. If I wasn't afraid that the Wilds would close in on my group as we left, we would've left Gradgate days ago. There's no certainty of finding food or water out in the woods. But here, I know my men and I have food, water, and, most importantly, beer." The scoutmaster stood up from her seat and approached the balcony, gazing down at her fellow Dokkalrolk. "I'm shit out of ideas, to be honest. And I know our kin need us back home."

There was a moment of silence as both Sylvanrolk studied the Dokkalrolk leader. It was clear to the brunette that the woman was as desperate for solutions as the band of travelers was. Because of that fact, a thought blossomed in Cymbelina's mind. "What if our groups worked together to find the vilek?"

Master Arvel and Scoutmaster Estrasta glanced at one another before looking at the Half-Sylvanrolk.

"That's not a terrible idea."

"If I could convince Knight Commander Emerik to give my troops and me some supplies before we leave, I wouldn't be opposed to it."

Cybelina felt a sense of hope grow in her chest. *Maybe this is precisely what we needed to get our search for the vilek going.*

The creaking noises of someone ascending the ladder caught the trio's attention as the garnet-haired outcast lifted his head over the edge of the loft. Hoisting himself onto the platform, he stood up, beaming at the three outsiders.

"I see you two have become acquainted with Scoutmaster Estrasta. So, how are things going?"

"Things are going great," Scoutmaster Estrasta said, backing away from the balcony to address Emerik and the Sylvanrolk. "In fact, I think we have a plan."

"That's it? That's our grand plan?"

"Do you have a better idea, Malaveen?"

"No, but give me some time, and I'll think of one."

"We don't have time, Blondie. That's part of the problem."

The four Wood Álves were camped outside of Gradgate since no rooms were available at the Hammered Sparrow. The lack of vacancy was acceptable to Cymbelina, as their private campsite allowed the travelers to discuss the plans Master Arvel and Scoutmaster Estrasta had formulated without the incessant noise that accompanies revelry.

The two older álves decided they would take their groups northwest, as neither believed Estrasta or Arvel's group had been in that area of the Wilds. Knight Commander Emerik agreed to give the two groups provisions for their journey, so the álves had nothing to worry about regarding food or water during their trip. Although the plan to work together seemed the best option for most people present, Malaveen wasn't a massive fan of it.

"Tch. My name is Malaveen, not 'Blondie'."

"I don't know, Mal…Blondie kinda suits your personality more."

"Mal-a-veen, Kayven. Not 'Mal', not 'Blondie'—Malaveen."

"So when are we leaving with the Dark Álves tomorrow?" Cymbelina asked her teacher, hoping to get the conversation back on track.

"At sunrise, so we'll need to go to bed here shortly."

Malaveen snorted. "I still think it would be better if we traveled alone."

"Why?" Cymbelina questioned, shooting an agitated look toward the blonde. "What could possibly be wrong with receiving outside help?"

Malaveen shook her head in bewilderment. "Um, hello? Were you not there during the attack during the Eldenfield Festival? Did you not see the massacre awaiting us when we returned home from said outing? How do we know we can trust these Dokkalrolk anyway? What if they're working with the vilek, or whoever is behind the attack, and are just trying to lure us out of the Wilds so the fairies can slaughter us!"

"And what would they gain out of such an abhorrent agreement?"

"I don't know, Kayven. Maybe the Dark Álves want to get back at the clans since Laufeia the Kind never assisted Snaerr's followers when they tried to take back Snøvern? Or Maybe the Dokkalrolk hope to claim the southern reaches of Florella for themselves? Only Mother Terralynia knows. Either way, I don't like the idea of working with them."

As much as I hate to even think it, Malaveen is right, the brunette thought, her eyes glued to the crackling campfire blazing between the four álves, the remains of their dinner sitting off to the side. *There really is no way of knowing if the Dark Álves are working with the enemy or not. I'm not sure I agree with Malaveen's reasoning behind why they may be assisting our attackers, but the suggestion isn't entirely out of the realm of possibility.*

"We don't know their allegiance for sure, Malaveen," Kayven stressed, "but it's a chance we'll have to take. What other plausible option do we have? Wait around until the enemy appears?"

"I was going to say we should go home and submit a report to Kinlord Emyr, but since we're stuck in this forest…sure."

"No!" The three other álves exclaimed simultaneously.

The night air was still as the four Sylvanrolk companions avoided each other's glances. The unattended campfire crackled and hissed in the night air, dying with each passing second. Nightjars churred in the trees above, their calls piercing the eerily quiet air. Having had enough of the silence, Malaveen stood up from her spot near the fire, tossing her platter on the ground.

"I'll pray to Mother Terralynia for you three to regain some semblance of sanity, if that's even possible. After that, I'll be going to bed." The blonde marched over to her bedroll, dragging it away from the other three mats belonging to her companions. "So please, keep your incessant chatter to a minimum, yeah? Goodnight."

The brunette and her two male companions were left alone by the waning fire, unaware of what to say after Malaveen's outburst. Their gazes were focused in different directions. Cymbelina's green eyes remained on the dying flames, thoughts of her family flashing through her mind.

Dear Goddess, I hope Mom, Dad, Una, and Grandpa are safe, as well as the rest of the clan. Mother Terralynia knows Florella's soil doesn't need to absorb any more blood of her citizens. The brunette's gaze turned toward Gradgate. A brilliant glow emanated from within the walled village, the light turning the green leaves of the central oak a bright shade of orange. Cymbelina heard the villagers' cries of jubilation as they danced around the tree, causing a brief smile to cross her face. *Hopefully, these outcasts and Dokkalrolk will end up being the key we need to defeat our attackers.*

Strange Dreams And False Hope

23rd of Red Moon, 1300 AC

By the Goddess, what is happening? Am I dreaming? The brunette thought worriedly glancing from side to side. *I must be. I don't recall waking up, but why am I seeing the room from my visions? What is going on?*

Cymbelina stared intently at the wooden padlocked door she had seen in her visions every day since she was five. Its appearance was worn, just like it had been two days ago when she first noticed the change in its appearance. There was nothing glaringly unique about the scene before her besides the fact that the brunette had never experienced her vision in her dreams before.

My dreams are supposed to be my escape from the waking world, not a grim reminder of what I must deal with while awake. I have to find a way to wake up. I can't deal with this right now.

As if her mind sensed her desire to depart from the dream world, something unusual happened. The torch on the wall beside the rotting door suddenly blazed, revealing a string of scintillating text scrawled on top of the doorframe Cymbelina had never noticed before. All notions of fleeing her nightmare dissipated as she approached the door with trepidation, peering at the sentence in curiosity. At first glance, the Half-Sylvanrolk could tell that the words were not written in Common (also known as Terralynian), Wood Álven, or Hominan (the language of the human mages the Sylvanrolk descended from).

Is this a normal extension of my vision, or is my mind concocting some silly fantasy language for this insane nightmare?

The she-álf's pine-green eyes traced back and forth over the text, trying her best to make some sense of the unknown dialect.

"Te draco...a containeo...dun te animus...somnullis?"

As the last word left her mouth, an echoing bang reverberated throughout the chamber of her mind. The door handle trembled as the door vigorously shook, causing the she-álf to jump. With each violent shake of the door, Cymbelina backed away, creating distance between herself and the structure.

"H-Hello?!" She cried out as her back slammed into the cold, unyielding stone wall. Her trembling hands fumbled over the rough surface, desperately searching for something— anything—to use as a weapon. But there was nothing.

The door continued to rattle, the padlocks banging against the wooden surface of the apparatus. There was no response from whatever was causing the door to move, leaving a pool of anxiety to stir in Cymbelina's gut.

"Who's there?!"

More shaking was accompanied by a hot wind, which poured forth from the barred window at the top of the door and permeated the small chamber of the Sylvanrolk's mind. Before she could say anything else, some mysterious force pried her away from the wall, teleporting her right in front of the door.

She blinked rapidly. Even though she was dreaming, she could feel her heart racing. *This isn't real,* she told herself, staring through the opening at the top of the door. *This is all a figment of my imagination, a reflection of my inner self. I am in complete control of this experience. There's no reason to be afraid.*

Offering sufficient self-consolation, the brunette allowed her curiosity to guide her closer to the trembling door. Delicately placing a hand on the wooden apparatus, it stopped moving. Cymbelina cringed, swallowing the lump in her throat before gazing into the window again. Using her pointed ears and watchful eyes, the Wood Álf scanned the room on the other side of the door for any signs of life. What she found was an empty void, lacking both light and noise, giving the illusion of emptiness. But the brunette wasn't fooled—there was definitely something on the other side of the door, and she needed to know what it was.

"I know you're in there," the she-álf announced, not as convincingly as she would've liked. "Come toward the door and reveal yourself."

A deep humming filled the other room, the noise akin to a low chuckle. The sound was soon followed by that of a rattling chain, which rang in the Sylvanrolk's ears.

"I'll reveal myself when I please," the entity in the other room murmured, its low voice as smooth as silk. "After all, you have no control over me."

Cymbelina was shocked. She suspected something was in the other room, but she never expected it to respond to her in any capacity.

Of all the things I could possibly dream of, my brain chooses an unknown being that won't even cooperate with my demands.

"You're not dreaming," the deep voice said. "And I'm certainly not something *your* brain has created."

"I refuse to play these games with myself," the brunette chuckled. Trying to force herself awake, Cymbelina resorted to a tactic that usually worked; pinching herself mid-dream. This time, however, nothing happened.

"Just as you have no control over me, you have no say in when you can leave. So why even bother trying to flee?"

Regardless of what the presence said, the half-álf continued to pinch her arm. She even resorted to slapping herself. In response to the self-harm, the creature simply laughed.

"Oh my, you are an amusing sight, *animus hospi*. But please, stop. We are connected, you and I. And I cannot fathom being connected to someone so... embarrassing."

The brunette stopped her pinching, instead turning her attention to the unknown voice. What it said piqued her interest. "We're 'connected'? What does that mean?"

The being sighed, as if it was ashamed it even had to explain. "It means you can see the words. Well…you can, can't you? If you can, that means it's only a matter of time."

The female uneasily looked at the unknown phrase once more. It continued to glow and occasionally flicker, the letters resembling those of a hellish pact. Looking back at the window, she inquired, "It's only a matter of time until what?"

The voice snickered, gleeful at the Sylvanrolk's inquisitiveness. "That shall be revealed in due time."

Cymbelina scowled, her patience coming to an end. "This is my dream, creature. You must answer my questions!"

The creature hissed before releasing a hearty laugh, which shook the door. Cymbelina squinted her eyes, trying her best to search for the mysterious being in the darkness.

"How many times must we go over this? You are not in control here, *animus hospi.* But I, too, grow weary of this game."

"Cymbelina."

A faint whisper penetrated the thick walls of Cymbelina's mental prison, her head swiveling away from the door, trying to find the direction of the voice.

"Who is it? Who is out there!" The brunette meekly called out. Her throat was surprisingly hoarse.

"Cymbelina, wake up!"

The room rattled, the sound of distant slapping bouncing off the walls.

"Whoever's there, please, help! Argh!" The she-álf's head began to pound, the woman falling to her knees in agonizing pain as the door in front of her began to tremble. Her green eyes watered as she stared at it in horror, the noise from each shake sending shockwaves throughout her mind.

"Please, Lina, WAKE UP!"

"Don't cry," the being on the other side cooed. "The sight is unbecoming of one such as you."

"Master Arvel, is there a way to wake her up?"

Is that Kayven's voice? The brunette thought, her heart fluttering in false hope. Turning her eyes toward the ceiling,

Cymbelina screamed, "Kayven, help me!" The brunette's voice bounced off the stone walls, her head throbbing from the vibrations. Regardless of her discomfort, she yelled again, her scream two octaves higher than the last.

Sensing her unending dedication to be freed from her vision, the voice behind the door chuckled, twisted amusement filling its tone. "We'll meet again soon, *animus hospi*. Hopefully, you'll prove to be a more gracious companion next time we meet."

"Wake up, Cymbelina. Wake up!"

The brunette blinked wearily, the world around her blurrier than usual. The only thing the woman could see was Kayven's worry-stricken face. The male's yellow-brown eyes were blown wide in terror as he shook Cymbelina's sweaty frame awake.

"K-Kayven?" The she-álf mumbled weakly with a slight quiver in her voice.

The male's face softened slightly upon hearing the female's voice, releasing her shoulders and sitting back on his heels. As Cymbelina's eyes began to focus, she perceived Master Arvel, who was standing over Kayven's shoulder.

"Thank the Goddess, you're awake."

"Where-where am I?"

"We're still at our camp near Gradgate." Master Arvel answered. "Kayven came over to your bedroll to wake you up, but you began to thrash about when he called out your name. Are you alright?"

The brunette gasped in pain as she sat up, rubbing the back of one of her trembling hands across her throbbing forehead. Her entire body ached. Blinking rapidly, she looked back and forth between the two men. "I think I will be once I wake up a bit more."

Kayven gave her a doubtful look. "Are you sure?"

"We can delay our departure if you need time to regain your bearings," Master Arvel added.

"Thank you, guys, but I'll be fine. I just need to be alone for a few minutes to think about the nightmare I just had."

The black-haired male nodded before standing to walk away, heading in the direction in which Malaveen was waiting impatiently. Master Arvel lingered, his amber eyes full of worry.

"Cymbelina, what did you dream about? I've never seen you like this before." Holding out his hand, the teacher offered to help the she-álf up. "Come, let us talk about your nightmare together. It might be related to—"

"I'm fine, Master Arvel, really," Cymbelina interrupted, forming as much of a convincing smile on her face as she could muster. Her lips twitched as she shooed the man's hand away. "I'll get up in a second. I...I just need to be alone for a minute, ok?"

The male smiled in defeat. "If you say so. Just know I'm here to talk about it if you change your mind, ok?"

The brunette nodded, the fake smile still lingering on her tired face.

"Alright. Well, I'll be waiting with the other two outside of the Hammered Swallow. We're all packed up to leave, so whenever you're ready, join us."

"Gotcha. I'll join you three in a few minutes."

What was that nightmare about? The female wondered, staring at Master Arvel as he left her side. *I've never experienced anything like that before. Did I begin a soul reading session while I slept? Is that even possible?*

The faint orange glow of the rising sun filtered through the leafy boughs of the towering trees, the canopy of branches quivering in the autumn wind. Cymbelina's green eyes analyzed the trees as she inhaled and exhaled slowly, trying desperately to calm her racing mind. As she stared at the evergreens around her, a thought penetrated her mind. *Maybe it wouldn't be a bad idea to talk to Master Arvel about what I just went through. Perhaps this is something Wood Álves experience when they're getting close to discovering their patron animal.*

Or, at least, that's what the brunette hoped it meant. The alternatives that crossed her mind were not nearly as exciting or comforting. With a heavy sigh, Cymbelina snapped out of her reverie and returned to the present. Shaking her head, the brunette peeled the damp covers from her sweat-soaked skin and crawled out of her bedroll to start packing her belongings.

The murmuring of the Dokkalrolk and Sylvanrolk filled the air as Cymbelina headed to the local tavern. The outsiders gathered in a large group outside of the Hammered Swallow, the brunette's Glenrolk allies standing out amongst the sea of Dark Álves. Making her way through the crowd, Cymbelina stood beside Kayven and Malaveen, her green eyes flicking to the front of the group and landing on Master Arvel, who stood beside Scoutmaster Estrasta in front of Knight Commander Emerik.

"You've received waterskins, a sack of potions, and a bag of nonperishables. Is there anything else the people of Gradgate or I can do for you all before your departure?"

"While my Dokkalrolk kin and I are very thankful for the help you've shown us so far," Estrasta began, "there is one piece of information we would appreciate if you divulged to us. You've been reluctant to share any information about the Glimmering Wilds with my men and me, especially regarding why and how the landscape can change. I hope your secrecy on the subject has changed since I last asked, considering two groups have wound up in Gradgate due to the changing environment surrounding it."

"So if you know anything," Master Arvel added politely, "we would appreciate any knowledge you have to share. The more our group knows, the sooner we can leave the Wilds."

Emerik's amber eyes warily gazed at Arvel and Estrasta. His lips formed a subtle frown, his displeasure at the outlanders' inquiry palpable. Glancing away from the álven leaders, his brown eyes flicked to Cymbelina. She hadn't moved from her spot in the crowd, yet Emerik decided to distract himself with her presence.

"Good morning, Cymbelina! I hope you slept alright."

All eyes turned to the brunette, who faintly blushed from all the attention. "Good morning to you, too, Knight Commander Emerik!" The brunette coughed before lying, "I slept fine; how did you sleep?"

"I slept fine too, thanks for asking!"

"Please, Knight Commander," Master Arvel urged, "do not evade the question."

"My apologies, Master Arvel. The truth is that I don't have anything else to say on the matter. My final answer is the same as the one I gave Scoutmaster Estrasta the other day: the Glimmering Wilds is an ever-changing enigma that is not easily solved."

The pearl-haired Dokkalrolk frowned. "So, you have no tips that might be useful to our group as we find a way out of the woods?"

"The best advice I can give the lot of you is to stick to the road." Emerik pointed to the rightmost path leading out of Gradgate. "Don't stray even a moment from the road, and it should lead you out of the Glimmering Wilds—eventually." Before the outsiders could question him further, the Knight Commander turned around, waving to the travelers. "Now, I really must be attending a meeting of the guards, so I have to say farewell to you all. Safe travels, my friends! May the ancestors guide you down the path you seek."

"Well, how do you like that?" The Dokkalrolk leader remarked, placing her gloved hands on her hips as she watched the garnet-haired male waltz away. "We're on our own. Let's hope our group can find some way out of this magical labyrinth."

"All we can do is try!"

Master Arvel nodded, agreeing with one of the Dark Álf scouts. "Indeed. So, who wants to lead?"

"I'll split my scouts up," Scoutmaster Estrasta offered, turning toward the teacher. "Half will travel in the front and half in the back. Master Arvel, you and your compatriots will walk in the middle of the group. Does that sound good?"

"It works for me. Are you three ready to leave Gradgate?" the patron guide asked, his gaze turning toward his three younger companions situated within the depths of the throng of álves. The trio nodded in agreement.

"Excellent!" Scoutmaster Estrasta said. "Then let us be off."

Gathering in the agreed formation, the two groups of álves began their journey down the rightmost path, marching under the tall stone archway leading out of Gradgate. They followed the dirt trail through an array of trees, a scene mimicking one they had seen many times over the past few days. Once the group traversed the road for about an hour, Malaveen began to whine in displeasure, catching Kayven's attention.

"What's wrong with you, eh?"

"Oh, nothing. I'm just thinking about how we're going to regret this," Malaveen grumbled, low enough so that none of the Dokkalrolk around her could hear.

"To be fair, you think any idea you didn't come up with is a bad idea right off the bat."

The blonde laughed. "While that may be true, Kayven, that's not why I'm saying that. We're squished between two walls of Dark Álves. Do you know what that means?"

"That we're safe if anything tries to attack us?"

"Only you would come up with such an asinine answer, Cymbelina. What it truly means is that if the scouts decide to turn on us at a moment's notice, we're screwed."

"You're too paranoid," Kayven chastised. "We share a common goal with the Dokkalrolk, so I doubt that'll happen. I'm more concerned about Knight Commander Emerik and the outcasts from Gradgate."

"Why is that?" The brunette questioned.

"Think about it. Don't you find it slightly suspicious that Emerik was reluctant to share information regarding the Wilds? Also, he neglected to mention the Dokkalrolk when we first arrived. That's another red flag."

"Why are these things significant to you, Kayven? Maybe he's just a tight-lipped person," Malaveen chimed in.

"Perhaps you're right; who is to say? I'm just pointing out that you should be more concerned about him than the Dark Álves, Malaveen."

I never even thought about that before, Cymbelina thought. *Emerik was acting a bit strangely. Of course, the four of us don't know him that well, so we can't compare his recent behavior to his usual mood, but he did seem odd to me.*

"Pfft. Whatever you say, Kayven."

"In any case," Master Arvel began, turning around while walking to address his fellow group members. "We could wind up stuck in these woods if we ignore our surroundings. So please, keep the chatting to a minimum and focus on the forest, alright?"

The younger Sylvanrolk did as they were told, ceasing their conversation and focusing on the woods surrounding either side of the path. As Cymbelina's green eyes glossed over every shrub the travelers passed, her mind wandered back to the dream she had experienced earlier in the day.

Is now the right time to ask Master Arvel about my dream? My heart is telling me it revealed something important to me, and I would hate to keep the information inside when it could be vital to my progression toward mastering my patron animal.

The she-álf flicked her gaze toward the teacher. After seeing the determined look on his face, she decided it was better to drop the subject until they reached their destination.

Hopefully, we'll be out of the Wilds soon.

* * *

"Where are they? The sun is high in the sky. They should've returned home by now."

"The scouts sent a message last night saying they would leave Florella by dawn, Monarch Vukasino. So they should arrive any time now."

"They better, Kazimiera. They better."

The lord of Elderfell had tasked one of his knights, Kazimiera, to send a dispatch of her best scouts to study a region of Florella. The region was known as Tundrana, where one subrace of álfrolk, known as the Dokkalrolk, dwelled. A slew of Dark Vilek had been sent to the area in the past, and some had even successfully destroyed some Dark Álf camps set up along the outskirts of the snowy land. However, Monarch Vukasino now had his eyes set on the jewel of

Tundrana; the Snøthorn Mountains. If he could get his spies into the mountain range to study the habits of the álves living within, he would be able to obtain priceless information for his takeover of Florella.

If the scouts value their lives, they'll return with helpful information.

Vukasino shifted in his seat, gazing out of the doors that led onto his balcony. From his seat at his desk, the ruler heard the tumultuous sea and cawing seabirds, all the while getting a brilliant view of the sun as it shone upon Elderfell's crags. Beyond the rocky ridges that jutted out of his homeland, the monarch saw the faint outline of the isle he strove for his people to reclaim as their own.

"What do you think Florella is like, Kazimiera?"

The grayish-green woman was silent, her red eyes widening in shock at the ruler's uncharacteristically friendly question. "I don't know, Your Lordship. My scouts always praise its diversity in terms of terrain and biomes, as well as the lush vegetation and wildlife most regions host."

"Hmm, yes, it does sound lovely. But one can expect nothing less from a land that housed our ancestors, eh?"

"You're right, sire."

"Well, we won't have to wonder what it's like for long. We can take back our rightful homeland as soon as we wipe out the álves polluting the island."

A knock pounded against the doors of the monarch's quarters, the male swiftly swiveling in his seat to look back at the wooden structures.

"You may enter."

The doors swung open to reveal three women: one of the lord's servants and two of the scouts Kazimiera sent to Tundrana.

"The scouts have returned from Florella, Your Lordship. Here are the leaders of the trip, Wavoda and Jadah. The other scouts have returned to the barracks."

"Excellent. You're dismissed."

After the servant ushered the two women into the room, she bowed before scurrying away.

135

"Welcome back to Elderfell. Please, take a seat." Vukasino motioned to the two empty chairs beside Kazimiera on the other side of his desk. The leader didn't give the women any time to relax as they sat down, instead throwing a barrage of questions in their direction. "So, what was the region like? Did you find any suitable locations for future encampments? Were you able to find any entrances into the Snøthorn Mountains? Oh, and did you discover any creatures we should keep an eye on—besides the álves, of course."

Wavoda coughed, thrown by the lord's intense line of questioning. "We were able to draw up plans for camp schematics for future expeditions and encountered some lower lifeforms, but they weren't anything we couldn't handle. However, we did meet someone you might find beneficial to our cause."

The monarch sat back in his seat, running his thin, gray fingers through his hair. "Fascinating. Was it a runaway Light Vilek?"

"No. A power-thirsty local of Dokkalrolk origin."

"Huh. And how did you stumble upon this individual?"

"We found the álf walking around the base of the Snøthorn Mountains while we were scouting the region for future camps," Jadah explained. "The individual was alone and appeared agitated, so some of our scouts asked why he was upset. The man was startled at first, but once we used one of Tihana's beguiling sprays on him, he opened up like a flower. After he spilled his deepest desires, we informed him that the interests of the Dark Vilek are similar to his. So, through alchemy and charisma, we obtained information about the cities inside the mountains."

A wicked smile spread across the ruler's lips, his eyes closing in delight. *A power-hungry álf with loose lips? Yes, this is just the sort of advantage I've been waiting for.*

"This is certainly a fortuitous find you two have acquired. Show me the map of the camps you two have planned."

"Certainly."

Wavoda fished her hand into one of her pockets, taking out

a yellow piece of parchment before handing it to the monarch. Unrolling it, the gleeful man gazed upon the weathered map in excitement, his black eyes darting to and fro across the paper.

The two women had plotted four camps along the western coast of Tundrana. The campsites were strategically spread throughout dense areas of wintery forest near the mountain range, allowing the lord's troops to remain hidden near the Dokkalrolk capital.

"Marvelous," Vukasino whispered, his gray fingers swirling around each planned makeshift settlement. "You two have served me well. Due to your excellent job in scouting the region, you may take two days off. You'll certainly need the rest for the plans I have in store for our troops."

Wavoda and Jadah thanked their ruler before swiftly leaving the room, ready to make the most out of their allotted days off.

The days of the Dark Vilek reclaiming Florella draw nearer; I can feel it, the visi-vilek thought. *With each successful step I take, the more I prove how much of a fool Mother was for doubting my abilities to lead our people.*

"May I approach?" Kazimiera asked the monarch, distracting him from his smug inner musings.

"You may."

The knight sat at the man's desk, her eyes flicking from Vukasino to the map he was caressing. "If you don't mind me asking, my lord, what's our next move?"

The man hummed, mulling over the options available to him. *Is now the time to send soldiers to other regions of Florella to continue hunting for the Light Vilek? Should I send another dispatch of warriors to scour the island's southern reaches to seek vengeance for the fairies the Sylvanrolk killed? Or should I send scouts to the areas marked on the map to establish tents and prepare an official attack?* His black eyes looked at Kazimiera's red ones as he reached his final decision.

"Gather more of your best scouts and tell the other two knights to meet me up here. We have campsites to plan in Tundrana."

***

"We can't stop now! We have to keep going."

Kayven, Cymbelina, and Master Arvel were preparing dinner while Malaveen paced back and forth in front of the glowing campfire. Her eyes drifted from the ground to the Dokkalrolk a few feet away, who were having their own hushed conversations near another campfire.

The teacher sighed, shaking his head. "We've been traveling all day, and the lack of sunlight makes the Wilds dangerous to navigate at night. It's safer to set up camp and get moving again first thing tomorrow morning."

"The Dokkalrolk gave us a spare lantern, remember? We should use it to get the hell out of here!"

"They gave us the lantern for the expedition, Malaveen. It's not ours to keep."

The blonde ignored Kayven's comment, her hazel eyes glued on the patron guide. "I know you mean well, Master Arvel, but the sooner we get away from the Dark Álves and leave the woods, the safer we'll be. Speaking of which, they're planning to continue heading northwest while we should be traveling south towards Terralynia's Folly. So...when exactly are we going to head home?"

"We're not going back to the Glenrolk camp anytime soon," Master Arvel responded, adding another twig to the campfire. "If you three recall, I said we were going northwest with Scoutmaster Estrasta and her kin. I didn't mean that we'd be traveling with them in that direction for a short period of time; I was implying that we'd be accompanying them out of the forest."

The three younger álves looked at the patron guide, all wearing a mask of perplexity on their faces.

"Are you sure that's wise? Didn't Kinlord Emyr say he wanted us to return to camp if we couldn't find the vilek during our travels through the Wilds?"

"Not only what Kayven said," Malaveen added, frustration tinging her tone, "but we don't even know where they're going, so why should we follow them?"

"Where else would they be heading? They're going back to the Snøthorn Mountains," Master Arvel answered. "Scoutmaster Estrasta told me that she and her scouts came into the Wilds to find the vilek in the hopes of reasoning with the fairy women if they turned out to be the creatures behind the attacks at the Dark Álf patrol camps. So, because they were unsuccessful in their mission, they're returning home to check on their kin."

"Isn't that what we should be doing?" The blonde inquired, plopping down near the fire and grabbing a kabob of roasted mushrooms. "Our camp has been attacked by those strange creatures, and we live out in the open. The Dark Álves live in the mountains. Who do you think is in more jeopardy, our kin or theirs?"

Cymbelina shook her head in annoyance. "It doesn't matter. If we follow the Dokkalrolk out of the forest, not only will we find a way out of the woods, but we'll be able to investigate their home and confirm whether or not the creatures attacking their settlement are the same as those that have been attacking us. If they are, maybe we can join forces."

The blonde rolled her eyes and scowled, slouching as she finished chewing a mushroom she had popped into her mouth. *"Day'm milnier vala caas."*

"You know the old adage," Kayven smiled, taking his food away from the fire to examine it. "It takes one to know one."

"Except I'm not an idiot. However, I'm thoroughly convinced the three of you are."

Pivoting the conversation away from the blonde's petty remarks, Cymbelina spoke. "Master Arvel, there's something I'd like to talk to you about after dinner if you don't mind."

"Of course. We'll talk about it before our lesson."

"Why not now, Cymbelina?" The blonde hissed. "Are you afraid Kayven and I will hear what you have to say?"

"No," Cymbelina responded, tossing the stick she used to roast her food into the campfire. "It's related to my patron animal, so it's simply a matter of it not being any of your business."

"How are your lessons coming along?" Kayven asked, swallowing the bits of fungi he had left in his mouth. "I know our situation hasn't provided a ton of time for you and Master Arvel to spend soul reading, but I hope the little time you have had has proven sufficient enough."

"Oh yeah, that's right." Malaveen sniggered, tossing her hair back. "Any luck discovering your patron animal, Cymbelina? What is it? A frog? A minnow? Perhaps a fly?"

"No, Malaveen, it's none of those. However, I would hate to verbally put you and Flora to shame, so you'll need to wait and see it in action before you find out what it is."

"Yeah, right. The swan is an elusive patron most Sylvanrolk only dream of having."

"You're right about it being rare," the patron guide confirmed with raised eyebrows, "but I'm not sure about that last part."

"Whatever."

And with that, Malaveen got in the last comment before dinner was finished. Malaveen and Kayven retreated to their bedrolls on either side of the campsite while Cymbelina and Master Arvel retrieved the items both álves would need for their lesson. Dragging their sleeping mats over to the far side of the camp, the teacher and student waited until most of their traveling companions were asleep before initiating Cymbelina's lesson. Once the night patrols were the only ones left awake, the two Sylvanrolk sat cross-legged on their bedrolls.

The dying fire cast muted shadows across Master Arvel's face, his amber eyes twinkling in the faint firelight. "Before we begin, what was the question you wanted to ask me?"

"About that...is it normal for a Wood Álf to experience a vision from their soul reading sessions while they sleep?"

"Well, I wouldn't say it's 'normal,' per se, but it is possible. Possible but rare. An interesting question, though—why do you ask?"

"I'm asking because I saw the door from my daily visions in my dream last night. It didn't feel like I was truly sleeping, though. It was as if I was meditating and interacting with the scene from my visions."

"It sounds like you experienced a lucid dream surrounding your patron lessons, Cymbelina. You've always been worried about your visions, so I wouldn't be surprised if the stress from recent events has caused you to think about *anas tusinca* more than ever before."

"You don't understand," the she-álf paused, her green eyes drifting from Master Arvel to the nearby fire. She searched the flames as if they would help her verbalize her thoughts properly. "The emotions I experienced were...palpable. I've never felt so scared in my entire life. Hell, you saw how Kayven had to shake me awake this morning. Now that I'm thinking about it, I heard his voice in my vision, too." After a few seconds of silence, the brunette shook her head, her eyes returning to the teacher. "No, Master Arvel. I'm convinced I wasn't dreaming last night. It all felt too real."

The older álf gave his protégée a doubtful look. His brown eyes bore into the brunette's green ones as if he were searching for any hints of overexaggeration. Sighing, he said, "You were just dreaming, Cymbelina. I'm sure of it. However, maybe today's vision will shed some light on your predicament. Let's find out, shall we?"

I'm almost convinced I wasn't dreaming, Cymbelina thought as she watched Master Arvel reach for the bowl containing a Sip of Tranquility, the cider-colored potion some Wood Álves drank before soul reading. The liquid sloshed in the dish as the male brought it to his lips, swallowing a hearty gulp before giving it to his pupil.

"Drink the potion, and then we'll begin."

The brunette did as she was told, allowing the elixir to relax her mind. With each passing second, the Glimmering Wilds faded away, the dark forest slowly being replaced by the oppressive walls of the dungeon from her daily visions. The torches flickered, enveloping Cymbelina's mental form in a faint warmth.

"All right, I'm in," the woman breathed, relaxing her

shoulders.

"Tell me, does the environment look how it did in your dreams?"

The she-álf cautiously approached the door, looking to see if the text she had seen above the doorframe this morning was still there. To her shock, the message was no longer there.

How is this possible? How could I have dreamed of a language I know nothing about? Was it merely an invention of my restless mind?

She looked through the glassless window towards the top of the door. Although she was afraid of confronting the entity that possibly awaited her on the other side, she had to know if what she experienced this morning was truly a dream. Much to her chagrin, there were no signs of life in the empty void of the dark room.

A wave of confusion washed over the Wood Álf's body. How was this possible? She could have sworn she entered her vision this morning, but she would be experiencing the same thing again if that were the case.

I guess Master Arvel's right; it was all just a dream.

"No, Master Arvel. My vision does not look the same as it did this morning."

"Pity. Does anything look different at all? Or is it the same as usual?"

"It's all the same as it was the other day when I first noticed changes in the appearance of the door," the she-álf responded, her voice dripping with self-directed shame.

Cymbelina forced herself out of her meditative state. Fury welled in her core. She simply couldn't wrap her mind around the fact that everything she had imagined earlier in the day was fictitious.

"I don't understand, Master Arvel. How is this possible? I've never experienced lucid dreams involving my daily visions before, so why now?"

"I'm almost positive that it's because the stress of recent events is finally catching up to you. You don't have access to an outlet to release the stress you're experiencing, so it's beginning to take a toll on your mental health."

"Almost positive?" The brunette questioned, ignoring most of what her teacher had said. "You mean there might be another explanation as to what I experienced this morning?"

"There is another possibility," the male trailed on, clearly regretting mentioning it, "but it's much more unlikely. So unlikely that I don't even feel compelled to share it with you."

"Now that you've brought it up, you might as well tell me, Master Arvel."

"That's not how it works," the teacher said. Although he shook his head, the brunette could tell his defenses were slowly crumbling.

"Please. I'll be worried about the alternative if you don't tell me about it."

The male looked at the shadowy tree branches above. Sighing something about the Supreme Mother under his breath, he responded, "Well...the second option has to do with your father."

Cymbelina narrowed her eyes, her heart leaping into her throat. Taken aback by the patron guide's comment, she leaned back, whispering, "What's that supposed to mean?"

"Tell me, Cymbelina, what has Deirdre told you about your father?"

"Next to nothing."

The male's gaze quickly averted from the female, a sense of sorrow penetrating through the depths of his dark eyes. "Well, if she hasn't told you much, it's not my place to explain. Let's just say the alternative to your predicament involves your father."

"What? And leave it at that? You can't be serious."

The man stood up, tucking his bedroll under his arm. "Since your vision didn't reveal anything new to us, it's best that we call it a night. We have an early start tomorrow."

"Please, Master Arvel," the Half-Sylvanrolk pleaded, rising on her knees, "you know I won't be able to go to bed with the ominous statement you've just planted in my head. Can you please elaborate a little bit more?"

"I don't think that would be wise, Cymbelina. I apologize. I

143

shouldn't have brought it up."

"But Master Arvel!"

The man just shook his head, not wanting to hear any more of her pleas. "I'll think it over, alright? I can't promise anything more than that. Goodnight, Cymbelina."

"…Goodnight, Master Arvel."

The male left the she-álf alone on her bedroll, her fists clenched and eyes teary at the news she had received. Looking into the depths of the nearby campfire, the brunette thought, *why do most of the things involving my patron seem to go back to my father?*

Revelations
27th of Red Moon, 1300 AC

The dawn of the fourth day of the Sylvanrolk travelers' journey began tumultuously. The four álves awoke to the news that the second set of Dokkalrolk that were supposed to be patrolling the camp while everyone slept had missed their rotation. Their absence left the food rations open for pillaging, which the local raccoon population took advantage of. Not only had the thieving mammals stolen a good portion of the food the álves needed for the journey ahead, but they also helped themselves to Malaveen's backpack: a fact the blonde would not allow anyone to forget.

Now, three days later, the absence of food was starting to take a significant toll on the travelers. The álves hit dead end after dead end on their quest to find a way out of the Glimmering Wilds, and their hope of salvation seemed to be dwindling with every passing hour. No matter how bleak the situation appeared to be, the hope that the travelers would eventually find an exit kept their feet moving, even though they were famished and weary.

"Those damn raccoons must have nabbed my comb. It couldn't have just vanished."

"Why are you still going on about your comb, Malaveen? We haven't eaten much in four days, and one silly little accessory is your biggest concern? Are you for real?"

The blonde snorted. "You wouldn't understand, Kayven. It's a female thing."

The male shook his head emphatically. "No, no, it's not a

female thing. It's an ego thing."

"Whatever."

Normally, Cymbelina would be chuckling at the blonde's dramatic arguments, but her mind was elsewhere at the moment. The dream she had experienced four days ago was still fresh in her mind, and the patron lessons she had taken with Master Arvel since then had not provided any further insight into the situation.

Cymbelina's eyes were glued on the lean patron guide, who was at the front of the crowd of travelers talking to Scoutmaster Estrasta. Besides their daily soul reading, the brunette hadn't conversed with the older Wood Álf much, leaving the many questions she still yearned to ask him floating around in her mind.

What did Master Arvel mean when he said my dad might have something to do with what I dreamt the other day? How is it even possible for him to influence my mind when I've never met him before?

"Watch out for the tree roots, Cymbelina; you almost tripped over one."

The woman continued to eye the path ahead, instinctively responding, "Thanks, Kayven, but I can handle myself."

And even if my father could influence my thoughts, how could that involve the entity behind the door or the text I saw on the doorframe? He wasn't Sylvanrolk, so what does he have to do with my patron animal? If that's what the source of the voice is, of course.

Despite what she had told Kayven, the brunette still tripped over a root after her right boot got stuck underneath it. Tumbling forward, Cymbelina emitted an uncharacteristic squeak.

"Cymbelina!"

Noticing the Half-Sylvanrolk's descent to the ground out of the corner of his eye, Kayven swiftly leaned to the side. Snatching Cymbelina's tan left arm in his firm grip, the ebony-haired male prevented the distracted woman from falling flat on her face. Laughing, the male helped the brunette regain her balance.

"You can handle yourself, eh?"

Cymbelina blushed, scratching her head as an embarrassed grin spread across her face. "I guess I wasn't paying as much attention as I thought."

"I'd say," Malaveen chimed in. "For Mother Terralynia's sake, Cymbelina. I knew you couldn't transform into your patron form, but you can't walk either?"

"Will you hush? Now, are you alright, Cymbelina?"

"Yeah, I'll be fine," the brunette mumbled, her green eyes turning toward Kayven's marigold ones. "I got wrapped up in my thoughts for a second there. Thanks for looking out for me."

"Don't mention it," he responded, releasing her toned arm. "The best way to repay me is by watching where you step."

"Ha," the she-álf chuckled, tucking a stray strand of hair behind one of her pointed ears, "that's fair."

The trio fell back in step with the rest of the álves, marching on for hours. The mid-afternoon sun soon shone through the perennial emerald leaves that formed a canopy above the forest path, allowing the slightest bit of warmth to fill the chilly air of the forest. With each passing day, the month of Red Moon came closer to an end, as did its accompanying season, fall. It was almost wintertime, and because of the group's proximity to Snowy Hollow, the wandering álves were in for cold days ahead, leaving them to huddle together as they grumbled about their empty stomachs.

Cymbelina shivered, holding her golden cloak close to her shivering frame. "Master Arvel said that Snowy Hollow borders the Glimmering Wilds to the north. Since the air is frigid in this neck of the woods, hopefully, that means we're getting close to finding a way out."

"We should be so lucky as to find a way out now," the blonde whined, her hands shivering in the pockets of her trousers. "The four of us should've left the forest while we could. Well, at least Master Arvel, Kayven, and I. Cymbelina's stuck here either way."

"You're such a quitter," Kayven sighed, tugging the hood of his cloak up. "We'll find a way out of the Wilds, I'm sure of it."

147

Before Malaveen could respond to Kayven's comment, the Dokkalrolk male walking in front of her abruptly stopped, causing the blonde to ram into his back.

"Hey, watch it! I—"

"Stop!" Scoutmaster Estrasta and Master Arvel yelled simultaneously, silencing the blonde and thawing her and her fellow Sylvanrolk from their chilled daze.

The brunette turned her gaze to the throng of scouts ahead. They stood shoulder to shoulder, their different colored cloaks forming a sea of rainbow hoods across the forest path. Standing on the tips of her toes, she peered above the mass of people, unable to see what the commotion was about.

"I wonder why we're stopping?" The brunette questioned as she remained en pointe.

"I don't know," Kayven spoke, motioning for his kin to follow him, "but we should find out."

Cymbelina and her allies pushed their way through the confused Dokkalrolk. The brunette muttered apologies to each álf she passed, her eagerness guiding her and her companions to the front of the crowd.

Please tell me Scoutmaster Estrasta and Master Arvel found a way out of this infernal forest, the Half-Sylvanrolk prayed.

Squeezing past the remaining álves that shielded the three Sylvanrolk from the patron guide and the scoutmaster, Cymbelina was taken aback by the sight of a mauled deer. The buck's lifeless eyes gazed up at the brunette as she examined the animal's body, an unholy scent infiltrating her dry nose. Scanning the creature, she noticed its body was ripped in half, its festering entrails the home of hundreds of maggots. Claw marks marred either half of the deer, indicating it was hastily torn apart. The scoutmaster crouched next to half of the corpse, muttering words to another Dokkalrolk standing nearby as her single eye gazed upon the strewn guts.

The sight was putrid enough to make Malaveen retch repeatedly before running to a group of nearby bushes. The other two Wood Álves stared at the mangled carcass in silent horror before Cymbelina inquired, "What in the world could have done that?"

"A Florellan troll, no doubt. Look at the claw and teeth marks. No other creature that I know could've done something like this."

"What in the Supreme Mother's name is that?"

"Florellan trolls are ferocious monsters that inhabit the northern reaches of Florella, such as the wooded areas in Snowy Hollow and Tundrana. The fact that we came across the remains of a troll's prey spells good and bad news."

"G-good news?" Malaveen gagged, wiping her mouth with the back of her right hand as she returned to the group. "I fail to see any good news that could accompany a corpse!"

"I suppose it means that we're getting closer to an exit out of the Glimmering Wilds," Cymbelina said weakly, prying her gaze away from the lifeless buck. "The bad news is that we have to watch our backs for any trolls that might be lingering nearby."

"Exactly," Estrasta agreed, her artic blue eye turning to the brunette. "You were right, Master Arvel. She is a bright one."

Cymbelina eyed her patron teacher suspiciously. "You were talking about me?"

"Only good things, I promise."

The leader of the Dark Álf scouts stood up from her crouched position near the corpse, dusting the dirt off her pants. "Shall we move on, Master Arvel? The day is slipping away, and now that we know some trolls could be lurking in the trees, I think it's essential that we get a move on and try to find a way into Snowy Hollow as soon as possible."

"By all means."

"Let's go, men! Home awaits!"

"Now, wait just a damn moment," a Dokkalrolk male hidden amongst the crowd called out, his demanding voice scratchy as he made his way to the front. "The break you promised us, Scoutmaster."

"What about it, Dagver?"

"When are we taking it? We've been walking all day, and our bellies haven't seen much more than a crumb of mushroom in

149

four days. I can't speak for these Wood Álves here, but I know the men and I are famished."

The pearl-haired woman took a deep breath, approaching the objecting male. Placing one gloved hand on his shoulder, she used her other hand to point at the dead deer.

"You see that right there, Dagver?"

"Yes."

"Well, unless you or any of our companions wish to end up like that, we need to keep moving. Going a few more hours without food won't kill you."

"It might," another man spoke up, stepping forward from the crowd. "Food gives us energy. Without energy, we have no chance against the foul beasts that might be skulking in the bushes ahead."

"Yeah, what Inar said!" Another scout yelled.

Murmurs of agreement flooded the gaggle of male scouts, who debated what to do about the situation in hushed whispers.

The scoutmaster lifted her hand off Dagver's shoulder and brought it toward her thin nose, squeezing either side of it. "Listen, men, if we don't keep going, we might never make it out of the Glimmering Wilds. You talk about being hungry? Well, I am, too, and this forest provides little food besides the mushrooms that line the forest trail or the occasional bird we're able to hunt. The sooner we get out of the Wilds, the sooner we'll be able to consume something a bit more substantial."

"Not only that," Master Arvel added, stepping forward to stand beside the female Dokkalrolk. "If we don't keep going, the more likely it is that we'll run into any trolls that could still be in the woods."

The two Dark Álves who had spoken out against Estrasta, as well as the men who had rallied around them, looked at each other and huddled together, deliberating on whether they should stay behind or accompany the scoutmaster onward.

This is not what we need right now, the brunette thought, crossing her arms over her chest. *The longer we stand around and*

debate on what our next move is, the hungrier we'll all get, and the more
likely it is that we'll make an excellent snack for a Florellan troll.

After much discussion, the instigator of the rebellion, Dagver, spoke out: "We'll accompany you for a while, but if we don't have food by the end of the day, we're staying put."

"Disobeying the orders that have been given to us by our king?" The scoutmaster spat, adjusting her eyepatch. "That's treasonous, but we'll cross that bridge if the time comes. For now, come along; we've wasted enough time discussing this matter."

The álves continued their journey deeper into the Wilds, the mid-afternoon sun slowly falling toward the horizon. The nip in the air had morphed into a blistery breeze, making the impatient travelers speed up in an effort to depart the forest.

"Hey, Scoutmaster Estrasta!" One of the Dokkalrolk scouts urgently cried, stirring some of the birds in a nearby tree as the group stopped again. "You'll want to take a look at this!"

"Must we stop?" Malaveen whined, her shoulders slumping forward as she watched Estrasta approach the yelling male.

"It could be important," Master Arvel said, his eyes following Malaveen's. "I better accompany her to see what the fuss is all about."

"I'll go too," Cymbelina and Kayven said simultaneously.

"You three go ahead. When it turns out all the commotion was about another dead deer, I'll be here to say I told you so."

"That's fine," the patron guide sighed dismissively. "Cymbelina, Kayven, let's go."

The three Wood Álves walked around the dense vegetation lining the forest trail, following the Dark Álf's footsteps. Cymbelina could hear the she-álf talking to a scout through the verdurous foliage, her green eyes closing as she concentrated on the scoutmaster's displeased whispers.

"Kivi, what are you doing over here? You were specifically instructed to remain on the trail. How did you end up here?"

"I'm sorry, Scoutmaster," the male stuttered, his voice filled with curiosity. "As we walked past this section of the woods, I saw this strange stone through the bushes. I...I felt drawn to it.

151

I couldn't help myself, I needed to take a closer look at it."

"What kind of rock is that anyways?"

Parting the final bush that separated the Sylvanrolk from the Dokkalrolk, Cymbelina caught a glimpse of the stone in question. Although most of the rock was concealed by the álves surrounding it, the brunette could make out familiar swirls on the stone's smooth surface from where she was standing. The details of the rock didn't go unnoticed by Arvel or Kayven either.

"Don't touch that!" Master Arvel warned. "My kin and I discovered a stone similar to that one when we first entered the Glimmering Wilds. Soon after Cymbelina touched it, we noticed the forest around us seemed different than it had been originally."

"So?"

"So, Kivi," Kayven continued, "if someone touches the stone, it might close whatever exit is currently open. And if that happens, there'll be no way out, and the lot of us might be stuck in the woods with a troll."

"Or the opposite might happen," Cymbelina countered after a few brief moments of silence.

Master Arvel raised an eyebrow, stunned by the brunette's theory. "Oh? How do you figure?"

"It's just a thought. Scoutmaster Estrasta's men are on the verge of rebellion. They're tired, hungry, and ready to hunker down if they don't get their way. If there's even a chance that touching the stone will reveal another way out of the forest, it might be worth our while to try it.

The scoutmaster nodded her head. "Cymbelina's right. My men are out of practice. This is our first assignment outside of Tundrana since Sowing Sun, and we've been trapped in the Glimmering Wilds for longer than you Sylvanrolk have. At this point, I think the men will do anything to find relief...even if that means disobeying our king. I'll do whatever it takes to prevent that from happening."

The four álves went back and forth, debating their course of action. Unbeknownst to them, Kivi was getting more anxious by the second. His brown eyes flicked from his superior to the three Wood Álves, his body thrumming with nervous energy. Unable to control himself, the rookie slapped his hand on the stone. The swirls on the rock began to glow instantaneously, and an overwhelmingly loud humming sound reverberated from within the rock.

"Kivi!"

"I'm sorry, I-I couldn't help it."

Seconds later, a discordant symphony of shouts of Estrasta's name and rank came from the forest path. With her single eye blowing wide with shock, the she-álf quickly turned on her heels to run back to the group. The other four álves soon followed.

"What is it, men? What's happened?"

"Just look for yourself," Dagver stated, pointing to the north.

Estrasta, Kivi, and the three Sylvanrolk turned their attention toward where the muscular dark álf was pointing. Where there once was a sinuous path weaving through the thick forest now stood an opening, allowing every traveler to get a perfect view of Snowy Hollow.

A vast glade sat ahead of the álves, snow flurries dancing in the frigid air. A thick blanket of snow rested atop the coarse grass and covered the thousands of stones jutting out of the ground, some small and some larger than the travelers. The taller rocks competed with the nearby spruces in height, which dotted the land surrounding the clearing. Their needles shook as a blistery breeze swept across the land, leaving Cymbelina grasping for her golden cloak. The difference between the Glimmering Wilds and Snowy Hollow was night and day, causing a sense of awe to well in the brunette's core.

"How...how is that possible?" Kayven stuttered dumbfoundedly, a small snowflake landing on his head. "A path through the Wilds was there, and now it's not."

"Now is not the time to wonder the hows and whys of the situation. We need to leave before the opening has a chance to close!" Estrasta cupped her hands around her mouth, scrunching her eye as she yelled, "Move, everyone, move!"

The scoutmaster's orders did not need to be repeated. The thunderous noise of shoes hitting dirt echoed as the álves scrambled into the frozen meadow, none of them chancing a glance back into the Wilds from which they were fleeing. The travelers didn't stop until they were far away from the magical forest, ensuring its trees would not swallow them if the exit closed.

Famished and exhausted, the group's dash quickly ceased. The álves struggled to catch their breath as the cold air burned their lungs, their noses and cheeks slowly turning pink.

"There was a moment there when I thought we would never escape the woods," Kayven huffed, turning his head to look back at the Glimmering Wilds.

"I was thinking the same thing for a while," the brunette said, her gaze wandering as she analyzed the snowy region, "but look where we ended up. This place is beautiful."

"It's also freezing," the blonde panted, standing up from her bent position. "How well do you know this region, Master Arvel?"

"I know nothing of this area, Malaveen. The scouting party I took into the Glimmering Wilds years ago never traversed farther north than the magical forest itself, so the only information I know about Snowy Hollow is from legends."

"Great, so we're screwed?"

"Why would you be in trouble when you're accompanying natives of this region?" Scoutmaster Estrasta questioned, approaching the group of Wood Álves after tending to her men. "You four have proven valuable these past several days, and neither my men nor I would object if you decided to come with us to the mountains tomorrow. After all, you mentioned something about dealing with the fairies as well, right? We could surely use your help to get to the bottom of these attacks."

"Oh no," Malaveen said, raising her hands. "We just got done traipsing about one unfamiliar area, and now you're asking us to do it again? I don't think so."

154

"The decision to accompany our fellow travelers isn't up to you, Malaveen. I'm the leader of this group, and I'm telling you that we'll be accompanying the Dokkalrolk to their homeland."

"But Master Arvel, we'll disobey Kinlord Emyr's order by going to the Snøthorn Mountains! Our original task was to find the vilek in the Wilds and, if that failed, return home. By going farther north, we'll defy the Glenrolk leader's command."

"But Kinlord Emyr had no way of knowing that the vilek have been attacking the Dark Álves, too, Malaveen. He wouldn't have made that decree if he did."

"You have no right to assume that, Kayven. You're not the clan leader."

"But I'm the kinlord's granddaughter," Cymbelina spoke up, "and I know him well enough to say that what Kayven said rings true. If he knew about the similarities between what the Sylvanrolk and Dokkalrolk have experienced, he would want us to collaborate with the Dark Álves to get to know more about these mysterious beings."

"Shut it, Cymbelina." The blonde spat. "You're a Glenrolk outcast and have no say in what any member of the clan does anymore."

"But I do," The umber-haired teacher interjected, turning his attention away from his quarreling allies and toward the female Dokkalrolk. "We'll take you up on your gracious offer, Scoutmaster Estrasta. Hopefully, we'll get to the bottom of the attacks our people have experienced after we reach the mountains."

Malaveen glared at the patron teacher, mumbling a curse under her breath.

The one-eyed female smiled. "So it's settled. Excellent."

Kivi approached the group, standing beside Estrasta and looking at her pleadingly. "I'm sorry to interrupt, Scoutmaster Estrasta, but may we take a break now? There are plenty of cranberry bushes nearby that contain plenty of fruit. We could always have some of the men harvest the berries while the rest of us set up the campsite for tonight."

A troubled look passed the female Dark Alf's face. It was

clear to Cymbelina that Estrasta wanted to keep going to check in on the rest of her kin, but she knew that wasn't the best option for the rest of her scouting party.

"We still have a day's worth of traveling to do before we arrive at the Snøthorn Mountains," the female began, placing one of her hands on Kivi's shoulder. "But I don't see why we can't settle down here for the night."

The inexperienced scout let out a victorious holler, running off while yelling that he would tell the others what the scoutmaster said.

"Well, that's my cue to help prepare the camp for the night. I'm sure my men could use some help if any of you were so inclined."

"I'll help," Kayven volunteered.

"Malaveen will assist your men as well, Scoutmaster Estrasta."

"What?! Master Arvel, I—"

"Please, Malaveen, you'll be doing me a favor. We don't need four people to set up our campsite, so you two might as well help the others while Cymbelina and I set up the bedrolls. We wouldn't have gotten out of the forest without the help of the Dokkalrolk, after all."

"Fine," the blonde huffed. "I'll help out."

"Thanks, you two. I know the men will appreciate it. Now, follow me."

Kayven and Malaveen followed Estrasta toward the heart of the snowy glade, leaving Cymbelina and Arvel alone. The two Sylvanrolk immediately set up the bedrolls and the campfire, working away as the sun began to set on the horizon. Excited chatter from the Dokkalrolk camps danced on the crisp gusts of wind that repeatedly swept through the region, the campfires doing little to warm the exhausted travelers.

By nightfall, Cymbelina and Arvel were still alone at the campsite as they waited for their fellow Wood Álves to return. Master Arvel and Cymbelina hadn't talked much outside of their soul readings since the day of the she-álf's nightmare. Now that the duo was alone, they knew little of what to say to one another. After hours of silence, Master Arvel was the first one to speak.

"Tomorrow's the last day of fall, you know."

"I guess you're right," the brunette began, calculating the days spent on the road in her head. "I've been so focused on our journey that I haven't been paying attention to the days that have passed by."

"Understandably so. We've been through a lot." The man spoke, poking at the campfire to stir the flames.

Cymbelina's pine-green eyes flicked between the campfire and the patron guide as she studied his form. He was unusually tense; his shoulders were close to his ears, and his eyebrows were nearly stitched together. Although the brunette couldn't see herself, she assumed her own appearance was akin to her nervous teacher. Taking a deep breath, the brunette annunciated the question that had been plaguing her mind. "So, are we ever going to discuss what you said the other night?"

"What I said about what? I've said many things about many subjects these past few days."

"Please, Master Arvel, you know what I mean. Are you ever going to explain to me why you believe my father could be connected to the nightmare I had the other night?"

The male sighed, his eyes drifting to the crackling fire. "Believe me, Cymbelina, I want to; it's just…complicated."

"It can't be that complicated."

"Believe me," the male paused, the flickering flames shining in his brown eyes. "It is."

The brunette slowly exhaled. "Look. If you're afraid that you'll upset my mother by telling me certain information about my father, don't worry. It's not like I'll ever have the chance to tell her you shared certain secrets with me. Everything you say here will never reach my mother's ears."

The teacher was silent.

"Please, Master Arvel," the brunette pleaded. "I'm an outcast now. When will I ever get the chance to know more about my father now that I've been expelled from the clan?"

The male gazed contemplatively into the depths of the fire, its flames dancing in the reflection of his amber eyes. It was evident that each of the she-álf's pleas acted as a battering ram into the walls of Arvel's defenses, his will to remain silent slowly deteriorating. Although Cymbelina wasn't proud of the tactics she employed to pry the information out of her teacher, this was one of the last chances she would have to learn more about her father and his possible involvement with the dream she experienced.

"Ancestors, forgive me for going back on my word," the man sighed, settling his eyes on his pupil. "I'll tell you the little I know about your father and his possible connection to what you experienced the other day, but that's it."

"Every little bit helps. Thank you."

"Just ask what you wish to know before I realize what kind of mistake I'm making."

"What was my father's name?" Cymbelina began earnestly.

"His name was Ignatius."

"That's an unusual name. Well, I've always heard he was from outside the clan, so maybe the name is more common among one of the other álven races. Speaking of which, what was his race?"

The male's eyes quickly averted to the side.

"Master Arvel?" The she-álf said nervously, wary of her mentor's expression. "What type of álf was he?"

"Well," the patron guide said, a slight tone of unease in his voice, "he wasn't an álf at all."

A wave of confusion washed over the she-álf's brain. Although the Sylvan Tenets recognized those born to at least one Wood Álf parent a member of the collective kin, it was still rare for there to be a half-álf living amongst one of the clans. It was so infrequent that no living member of the Sylvanrolk clans was a half-álf. So, although Cymbelina had never known her father's race before this moment, she never would've assumed he was something other than an álf.

Why would Mom hide something like this from me? The brunette pondered, her eyebrows scrunching in frustrated confusion.

Having a non-álf parent can be life-changing. In fact, that might explain why my patron animal has taken so long to show itself.

"If he wasn't an álf, then what was he?"

"That's where things become confusing. Ignatius said he was a human, and since our records don't tell tales of non-magical humans, we had to take his word for it."

"Who is 'we'?"

"Everyone in the Glenrolk clan. He shared many features with our magical human ancestors, such as rounded ears, so his word seemed reliable."

"How and when did he arrive on Florella?"

"Cymbelina, I hardly call that pertinent information regarding your nightmare."

"Please, Master Arvel. I need to know this."

The male pursed his lips momentarily before answering his pupil's question. "One of the Glenrolk hunting parties found him washed up on our shore after a night of summer storms twenty-four years ago. Seeing as he was alone and badly injured, they brought him back to our camp. After a few days of recovery, he finally confessed to Kinlord Emyr and me that he was an exile from the mainland."

"Why...why was he in exile?"

"I don't know, and that's hardly the point."

Kayven and Malaveen's voices floated on the night wind as they approached the campsite, their footfalls heavy with exhaustion and their arms full of bowls of cranberries. Knowing that the other two had no business in the brunette's affairs, Master Arvel began to wrap up the conversation.

"Look," the man jabbered, "the reason I said your father might be connected to what you dreamt the other day is that, during one of my conversations with Ignatius, he said his nightmares were partially to blame for his departure from the mainland." The teacher paused to catch his breath. "Now, I understand how much learning about your biological father means to you, but I'm afraid that's all I can tell you. I'm sorry."

"You must know more. Please, Master Arvel, don't stop now."

159

"I've already noted that I cannot say anything else, Cymbelina. Now hush, lest the other two know what we were discussing."

Cymbelina's eyes bore into Arvel as a thousand entreaties died on her tongue. Her stare bordered on a glare as her two Sylvanrolk companions sat by her and Master Arvel's side around the campfire. The brunette clenched her fists as anger and sadness battled for dominance in the deepest parts of her soul.

Why does everyone feel the need to hide information about my father from me? The Half-Sylvanrolk thought, her eyes unwavering from the anxious Master Arvel. *There's little time left for me to learn about Ignatius now that I'm an outcast, so why am I still being deprived of the details surrounding his life?*

"So," Kayven began, stirring the she-álf out of her thoughts as he passed around the cranberries he and Malaveen had brought back for the group. "What were you two talking about before we arrived?"

"We were discussing how easy it was to forget that tomorrow marks the last day of fall. Isn't that right, Cymbelina?"

"Yes," the brunette agreed, forcing a smile that barely concealed the frustration and grief swirling in her mind. "We were discussing the end of fall."

"Well, don't let me stand in the way of that riveting discussion," Malaveen teased. "I'm starving. I have to eat."

"I think that's an excellent idea; Cymbelina, Kayven, you two should do the same. We have a long journey tomorrow, and every little bit of energy is necessary for venturing into unknown territory.

"Do you plan on eating, Master Arvel?"

"Not right now, Kayven," the man said, pushing himself up off of his bedroll. Wiping away some of the snow that had gathered on his robes, he continued, "I need to talk to Scoutmaster Estrasta about a few things, but I'll be back for some food shortly."

"Suit yourself."

The black-haired man dished out three servings of fresh berries for himself, his marigold eyes landing on Cymbelina as she gazed after Master Arvel.

I wonder what he needs to talk to Estrasta about.

"Are you alright, Cymbelina?"

"Sort of," she muttered, looking away from the patron guide as he approached the Dokkalrolk campsite. "I'll feel much better when we reach the Snøthorn Mountains."

"I'll feel better, too," the blonde added, shoveling a handful of berries into her mouth. "Now, let's eat so we can go to bed. The sooner we sleep, the sooner tomorrow will come."

The Snøthorn Mountains
28th of Red Moon, 1300 AC

"Is that…is that what I think it is?" Malaveen stuttered in awe, her chin slack in astonishment.

"If you think those are the Snøthorn Mountains," Estrasta began with a hint of pride, "you'd be correct."

Cymbelina and her fellow Sylvanrolk companions absorbed the magnificence of the distant mountain range. Dividing the region of Florella known as Tundrana in half horizontally, the snow-covered peaks scintillated under the morning sun. Even from miles away, the travelers noticed the thin clouds floating above the craggy summit, the occasional bird soaring high above the intimidating mounts. If the álven travelers hadn't left their campsite when they did, they would never have seen the breathtaking scene before them.

"I'm not one for sentimentality, but I'm glad we had the opportunity to see the mountains in this light."

"Going soft on us, Malaveen?"

The blonde scoffed. "Not in a million years, Kayven."

"Well, enjoy the scenery while you can," Scoutmaster Estrasta said. "I don't know what the foot of the mountains will be like or whether or not any trolls or vilek-like creatures will be prowling around the entrance to the Dokkalrolk kingdom."

Malaveen rolled her eyes. "You thought trolls would attack us yesterday, Scoutmaster, but none ever did. I think we'll be fine. You're just overreacting."

The Dark Álf, who was walking in front of the rest of the

travelers, stopped, turning to face the argumentative blonde. "I don't know the hierarchy of command amongst the Sylvanrolk clans," Estrasta spat, "but I can assure you I would never allow someone under my leadership to talk to me in such a fashion. So I expect the same from you. I know this region more than you do, and I'm telling you that we must keep our eyes open for trolls."

"What about the attempted rebellion back in the Glimmering Wilds?" Malaveen rebutted, ignoring the last part of Estrasa's spiel, "That was insubordination, was it not?"

Cymbelina glared at her fellow Wood Álf. "But neither the Dokkalrolk scouts nor we had eaten in days, Malaveen. At least they had a reason to be cross. You're captious even when you're full."

"Pfft, you're one to talk."

"I assume we'll arrive at the mountains within an hour or so," Master Arvel said, his gaze shifting to the female Dark Álf ahead of him as he prompted her to move onward. "We should all keep our mouths shut and look out for any sort of trouble, as Scoutmaster Estrasta suggested."

The explorers continued to move forward without incident, slowly maneuvering through the sparsely scattered trees that dotted the boreal biome. Cardinals flitted above the large hills of snow that towered on either side of the group's path. These mounds glittered in the morning sun and were breathtakingly monumental, leaving the álves vulnerable to a surprise ambush. The travelers proceeded carefully, following a zig-zagged path between the hills, keeping their eyes on either side of the trail for both trolls and other magical creatures.

The whistling wind brought twinkling snow flurries down on the crowns of the adventurers' heads. Some shook them off and pulled their cloaks up; others left the frozen bits of water alone. Cymbelina fell into the first category, shaking the snowflakes off her head as she shivered and pulled her golden hood up. The Wood Álf was still in the process of mentally digesting what Master Arvel had told her about her father. Although she was grateful that she knew more about him now, the slivers of information provided to her were nowhere near large enough to satiate her hunger for knowledge about him.

His name was Ignatius, and he was a non-álf exile from the mainland. But why was he sent to Florella, and where did he go when he left Mom? There has to be more to the story...someone must know something!

"It's hard to believe that it's still technically fall. It feels like we're experiencing one of the coldest days of winter right now."

The brunette flinched, stopping in her tracks as she snapped out of her thoughts. "Kayven! You scared me!"

"Lost in thought again, eh?"

The half-álf chucked. "Yeah, you could say that."

The male grinned, his obsidian locks falling to the side as he tilted his head to look at his shorter companion. "So, what were you and Master Arvel chatting about last night?"

"We were discussing the ending of fall, remember? You asked both of us that question yesterday."

"No, no, I meant, what were you two *really* talking about?"

The female gulped. "I'm... I'm not sure I follow?"

"Ha. Come on now, Cymbelina. You're too honest to be a good liar."

"Oh really, now?" the female said, trying to play it cool. "Is that what you think?"

"And now you're deflecting."

"How did you get so good at reading people, Kayven? You should teach me your ways sometime in the future."

"You didn't think my only talent was cooking, did you?" The man teased, cocking his eyebrow. "Also, you're doing it again."

The she-álf sighed, looking ahead at the group members as they passed by the duo. She and Kayven were toward the back of the crowd now and out of earshot of most of their companions. Because of their relative aloneness, Cymbelina decided to answer her friend's inquiry.

"Master Arvel and I were talking about my biological father."

"Your dad? Why, if you don't mind me asking?"

"Well," the brunette began, her eyes drifting to the snowy ground, "I experienced a horrific nightmare the other day. Once I went over it with Master Arvel, he suggested one of the possible reasons I experienced it is somehow connected to Ignatius."

"Ignatius? Was that your father's name?"

The brunette weakly nodded, her eyes unwavering from the snow-covered ground underneath her boot-clad feet.

"That's odd. Well, I hope Master Arvel didn't tell you anything unsavory about your father."

"Unsavory? The jury is still out on that one. But unexpected? Yes."

"Huh. Regardless of what was told to you, I'm here if you ever feel like discussing the situation with someone else."

Cymbelina smiled, looking away from the ground and to the man beside her. "Thanks, Kayven, I appreciate it."

The male grinned back before coughing into his curled fist. "Since we're being open with one other, I must confess that I wasn't exactly honest the day you and I talked at camp before we entered the Glimmering Wilds."

"Oh? What weren't you thoroughly honest about?"

As the male opened his mouth to answer, a high-pitched scream rang out across the edge of Snowy Hollow, catching the attention of both stationary Sylvanrolk.

"Trolls ahead, everyone! Trolls!"

A ferocious roar rang in the freezing air of the snowy clearing, the ground quaking underneath the adventurers' feet. The walls of towering conifers surrounding the álves quivered as three Florellan trolls barreled their way through the sea of travelers. The hulking beasts toppled over every álf in their path, their fisted claws striking anyone on their right and left sides. Luckily, Kayven and Cymbelina were in the back of the quickly parting crowd, giving both Wood Álves time to prepare for a counterattack.

"Probably best to attack from a distance," Cymbelina said, retrieving her bow from her back and an arrow from her quiver.

Kayven mirrored her actions. "I couldn't agree more," he replied, his collected demeanor contrasting the chaos around them.

The duo let arrow after arrow loose, watching as some of the projectiles hit their mark and others missed. The trolls seemed to shrug off most of their attacks, much to the álves' dismay, treating the arrows like flies surrounding food.

The monsters mashed their sharp incisors together, drool pouring from either side of their trembling maws. Infuriated hunger radiated from the primal beings, their rumbles terrifying the brunette as she fired at the twelve-foot-tall monsters. Cymbelina had never seen anything like these trolls before.

Some of the Dokkalrolk that were cast aside began to stir, some attacking the offending trolls while others checked on their trodden allies. These new assaults from the Dark Álves distracted two of the encroaching beasts, but one was still focused on the archers. The creature's beady red eyes glimmered in the sun, causing mixed feelings of fright and desperation to stir in the hearts of the Wood Álves.

The barrage of arrows Kayven and Cymbelina continued to send the troll's way did little harm besides a few nicks to the creature's flesh, which was littered with warts and pockmarks.

What does it take to kill these things? The she-álf wondered, firing her projectiles with increasing vigor as the troll swiftly sped toward Kayven and her.

The enraged creature stretched its muscular arms above its head, lacing its chubby digits to form a fist. Taking five more strides forward, the troll went in for an overhead attack.

With eyes blown wide, the Half-Sylvanrolk screamed, "Roll!"

Kayven and Cymbelina rolled in opposite directions. The monster continued to pursue Kayven, causing the male álf to roll again. The brunette fired a plethora of arrows into the monster's exposed back, causing enough vexation to make the troll divert its attention away from the male. Hitting an extremely sensitive nerve drove the beast to yowl, flipping its stance to face the female archer as it reached for the arrows lodged in its back. Unable to grasp any of them, the beast howled. Stomping its hair-covered feet, the ground quaked as the being charged toward Cymbelina. The brunette stumbled as she reached for another arrow, only to discover that the quiver was empty.

Mother Terralynia has a sick sense of humor.

Tossing the bow to the side, the she-álf dodged the troll's series of desperate swings. Reaching for the steel daggers fastened at her waist, the female prepared for the melee battle she had tried her best to avoid.

Kayven's arrows flew at and past the troll, whose eyes never faltered from the she-álf. Shaking its head and roaring, it continued its dash toward the brunette, who returned the gesture instead of avoiding the troll's advances entirely. Her gaze was glued to the space between the monster's wide-set legs.

"Cymbelina, what are you doing?!"

The female warrior didn't answer, allowing her actions to speak for themselves.

Somersaulting underneath the troll's towering frame, she barely avoided the creature's hammer fist. After landing on her back, she speedily turned to the left. In the blink of an eye, she raised her right hand and brought the dagger down upon the beast's right heel, leaving a grisly, weeping gash in her wake.

The monster released a staggered cry, throwing its arm back in an attempt to thwart any more attacks on its right foot.

"Aim for it, Kayven!" Cymbelina yelled, her voice filled with determination as she nodded toward the injured heel. "We need to take it down!"

The creature ignored the black blood oozing from its wounded appendage, trying its best to strike at the quick she-álf with its left foot. Ducking, the half-álf rolled away from the foot to strike the damaged heel again. Howling, the beast tried once more and missed. The pattern of hits and misses between the two continued as the male ran around the troll, who was too distracted by Cymbelina to notice Kayven's advance.

Finally, after reaching a vantage point where he could clearly see the monster's right heel, Kayven launched multiple arrows at the creature's bleeding foot. Soon, five projectiles were protruding from the wound, with a sixth one joining shortly after the fifth one.

The seventh arrow launched at the creature's heel was the final straw, as the troll's right leg gave out and sent it reeling to the ground. The monster's ginormous frame hit the snow-covered earth with a ground-shaking thud, leaving a gaggle of nearby álves to surround its flailing frame in awe. The Dokkalrolk whispered as they stared at Cymbelina, who dusted the snow off her armor. She gazed at the struggling creature, her mind racing with thoughts of what she should do next. Her heart pounded in her chest, adrenaline rushing through her veins.

"Kill it," Kayven exclaimed, "before it has time to stand up again!"

Leaping on the troll's back, Cymbelina ran up its bony spine, skillfully avoiding the dozens of projectiles protruding from its back and stopping once she was perched on the base of the colossal being's neck. The troll, however, was not ready to give up. It tirelessly fought back against the female's grip on its greasy, yellow-stained tresses, its arrow-filled hands swatting at the woman as if she were a gnat. Its red eyes roamed the pale sky, its neck craned back and open for a quick slice. But as soon as Cymbelina lifted her dagger to make the final cut, a vision flashed before her battle-tired mind.

The hallucination pulsed as it took over her vision, the words on the doorframe from her patron lessons repeating in her distracted brain.

'Te draco a containeo dun te animus somnullis.'

"What are you waiting for, Cymbelina?!" One of the scouts called out. "Kill it!"

Cymbelina's grip on the being's hair loosened, her pine-green eyes rolling to the back of her head as she repeated the phrase aloud.

"Te draco a containeo dun te animus somnullis."

"Cymbelina!" Kayven screamed, slinging his bow over his back and approaching the female Sylvanrolk. His walk toward his companion was halted by Scoutmaster Estrasta, who jumped directly in front of him.

"Allow me," Estrasta said, turning away from the male álf with her metallic crossbow poised and ready. She aligned the weapon to focus on the trembling troll, her eyes narrowing with focus. Releasing the poison-coated bolt with a smooth, practiced motion, she watched as it streaked through the air and buried itself precisely between the troll's eyes. The creature's head fell forward, its face falling forward and sinking into the thick snow.

With the troll's demise, something snapped inside of the she-álf's mind, the door fading from her vision as her thoughts and vision cleared.

"Are you alright?" Kayven asked, staring at his Sylvanrolk companion dumbfoundedly.

Cymbelina rubbed her forehead, staring in disbelief at the dead being underneath her. The sight of black blood pooling from the troll's wound caused a disconcerting feeling of satisfaction to dwell in the brunette's core, a post-battle emotion foreign to her.

Keeping her twisted feelings to herself, the half-álf muttered, "I-I'm not sure what just happened."

"You could've gotten yourself killed, that's what." The scoutmaster snapped, attaching her crossbow to the harness on her back. "Now get off the troll. The other two monsters have already been slain, so we need to regroup with the others right away. But know this; you and I will chat with Master Arvel about what just happened once we reach the mountains. Is that clear?"

Stunned by the Dark Álf's shift in demeanor, the brunette agreed without a second thought, her mental fatigue too significant to articulate a rebuttal. Jumping off the troll's corpse, Cymbelina and Kayven followed Estrasta as she herded the travelers back toward the rest of the álves.

Most of the adventurers were reveling in their collective

victory. Some álves looted rare crafting supplies from the fallen creatures, such as troll teeth, while others babbled on about the combat tactics used in the fight. Neither occurrence distracted Master Arvel, who paced back and forth while worrying about his companions. Malaveen stopped his anxious pacing by pointing out that their fellow Wood Álves had returned with Scoutmaster Estrasta.

"There you two are," Master Arvel exhaled, relief flooding his voice. "Are you two alright? Have either of you sustained serious injuries?"

"No," Estrasta curtly answered for the pair. "But there is something that I would like to discuss with you and Cymbelina."

The umber-haired man looked confusedly between his pupil and the scoutmaster.

Before the teacher could ask any questions, Estrasta elaborated, "We'll talk about it more once we reach the Snøthorn Mountains."

"If that's what you think is best, Cymbelina."

"I recommended it, actually." The female Dark Álf said. "The smell of dead trolls is sure to attract unwanted attention, and we don't need to waste any more time than necessary in Snowy Hollow."

"Well then, Scoutmaster Estrasta, after you."

The female smiled at the four Sylvanrolk before cupping her hands around her mouth to call out to her scouts. "Alright, men, let's get a move on! Home awaits!"

The journey out of Snowy Hollow and into Tundrana was stressful yet exciting. The prospect of Florellan trolls ambushing the álves as they wove their way through the mounds of snow kept the travelers on their toes, some more than others. Unlike her fellow Sylvanrolk companions, Cymbelina felt a conflicting sense of fear and hunger for a battle duel in her gut. She had felt a bit off when she first woke up this morning, but the unusual feelings had all but vanished once she and her allies gazed upon the mountains. However, her lust for violence soon reared its ugly head after she helped take down the troll.

The unusual feelings stirring within the she-álf were potently repulsive enough to stimulate the rise of bile in the brunette's gullet. The sensation increased tenfold when Cymbelina dwelled on how mentally incapacitated she had become in the blink of an eye on the battlefield.

Why is this happening to me? Is my weariness from traveling getting the best of me, or is something else occurring? Maybe the hallucination from earlier is connected to my father as well?

The sun had all but fallen in the west, the ending of fall drawing near as the day came to a close. The looming shadow of the nearby mountain range bathed the travelers in ravenous darkness, which Cymbelina overlooked until she was immersed in its depths. Standing alongside her allies at the base of the summits, the she-álf averted her gaze from the gigantic peaks to the Dokkalrolk scoutmaster, who stood at the front of the crowd with her arms raised.

"We did it, everyone! Welcome home!"

A clamorous wave of hoots and hollers erupted from the gathering as the Dark Álves cheered. With an affirmative nod from their leader, the scouts formed a line and rushed into the mouth of a jagged cave, which led inside the towering mountains. The Wood Álves stayed in their places, staring at the formation in relief and wonder.

Malaveen shook herself out of her wonderment, turning her hazel eyes toward the patron guide. "It's not too late to go home."

"Yes, it is, Malaveen," Master Arvel mused, adjusting his robes in the chilly Tundrana air. "Scoutmaster Estrasta, what is our next course of action?"

Patting the last few scouts on the back, the scoutmaster waved the Sylvanrolk over, her happy expression turning serious. "Our first action must be to journey to the main gate so your names can go down in our record books. Besides that, I also need to check on someone before we visit the king. Are you four ready?"

"The King?" Malaveen sneered, "Why are we—"

The flaxen-haired she-álf was swiftly silenced by Master Arvel, who shot her a glare. "We're ready to proceed into the mountains whenever you are, Scoutmaster Estrasta."

Nodding, the Dark Álf led the outsiders through the entrance to the drafty cave system. Although the mountain range appeared large on the outside, Cymbelina would never have guessed just how much room there was within the peaks until Estrasta began to explain how the Kingdom of Snøthorn was structured. The Dokkalrolk domain was composed of four cities: Krigdor, which the group was currently approaching; Jordstand; Sølvcast; and Gullhum, the kingdom's capital. All of the towns besides Gullhum were ruled by a jarl, who enforced the king's laws. Instead of a jarl, Gullhum was watched over by the king.

"It's fascinating how different our civilizations are," Cymbelina remarked, her voice bouncing off the towering walls of the rocky passageway.

"It truly is. Maybe you and your kin will be gracious enough to share information about Sylvanrolk culture once we deal with the vilek-like creatures."

"Pfft, I won't be," the blonde muttered.

The rank scent of mildew pervaded the foreigners' nostrils as they traversed further into the winding tunnel, the temperature of the tight space drastically increasing. As the álves reached the end of the walkway, they encountered a massive stone wall. The partition spanned from the rocky floor underneath Cymbelina's feet to the jagged roof of the mountainous room. The torches adorning the structure cast an orange glow on the iron gate in the center of the wall, which slowly rose as two well-armored troops approached the adventurers. Their golden armor glimmered in the dim light, the shine of their attire mirroring the brightness in the wearers' eyes.

"Scoutmaster Estrasta, it's so nice to see you again!" The female warrior exclaimed.

The male Dokkalrolk smiled. "Especially because you came back in one piece."

"Satula, Lufor," the scoutmaster began, grinning, "How splendid it is to see you two again. I see that both of you have been promoted to gate duty in my absence."

Satula flipped her long white tresses over her shoulder, beaming with pride. "Yes, ma'am, and what a privilege it is."

"Indeed," Lufor agreed, his welcoming aura fading as he set eyes upon the Wood Álves. "But we digress. Who are these álves that have accompanied you home?"

"These four are Sylvanrolk from the Glenrolk clan to the south, near the western coast of Terralynia's Folly. The oldest one is Master Arvel, the blonde is Malaveen, and the other two are Cymbelina and Kayven, respectively."

Lufor peered up from his stone tablet, on which he was carving the outsiders' details. "Last names?"

The patron guide smiled. "We have none, Ser Lufor. We only go by our first names; when necessary, we state our clan name after our first name. For example, you may call me Master Arvel of the Glenrolk."

"Well, you can mark down most of us in that fashion," Malaveen sneered, her eyes landing on Cymbelina. "You don't have to address her in that fashion: she's been kicked out of our clan."

The brunette rolled her eyes.

"It doesn't matter," the male warrior responded, finishing his inscription before looking at the Wood Álves. "You four won't be in the mountains for long, so Cymbelina's current entry will suffice."

The scoutmaster's eye narrowed. "Why do you say that?"

"To be truthful, Scoutmaster, Ser Satula and I aren't supposed to be letting any visitors inside the kingdom. However, since you're a city official and the newcomers arrived in your presence, they're allowed limited access to the city until you speak with King Ragnar."

"Why has our king reached this decision? Has there been another attack on our patrol camps?"

"Unfortunately, yes. However, the most recent attack proved to be more alarming to the king than the past few. This time, Jarl Orsala was involved."

For the first time ever, Cymbelina noticed the scoutmaster's ash-gray face blanch, exposing a look of anxiety that seemed foreign to the fearless Dark Álf. "Where is Jarl Orsala?"

"In the Krigdor *lovhuss*, but—"

"That's all I need to know," Estrasta said, cutting Ser Satula off. "Please, open the gate. I need to check in with her at once."

The Dark Álf patiently waited for the gate to rise, and once it did, she was off. Sprinting through the gateway with a speed that Cymbelina never would've expected from the shorter álf, she watched as the leader kicked up bits of rock as she sped off. Looking at her kin in shock, the brunette quickly charged after the Dokkalrolk, who was their only guide for navigating the foreign city.

"Scoutmaster Estrasta, wait up!"

The group's desperate pleas were met with indifference as Scoutmaster Estrasta surged forward, her booted feet pounding against the winding stone path that wound through a bustling marketplace. The locals, sensing the urgency in the leader's stride, hastily backed up against the row of stalls on either side of the streets, creating a narrow path for the restless scoutmaster. She uncharacteristically barked at them to clear the way. The four outsiders were on Estrasta's heels, their bewildered expressions mirroring those of the nearby Dokkalrolk.

"Scoutmaster Estrasta!" Malaveen yelled, struggling to summon enough air to call out to the anxious she-álf, "Please wait up!"

"We're almost to the *lovhuss*," the pearl-haired woman huffed over her shoulder. "You can survive at this pace for a few more minutes."

The scoutmaster's trail led the outsiders to the base of a looming estate perched upon a stone landing. Dozens of steps cascaded down the slope leading up to the building, the Dark

Álf leader running up the incline with ease. The Sylvanrolk followed Estrasta up, their pace nowhere near as swift as the Dokkalrolk's. The fire from the nearby torches flickered as the five álves ran through a set of gigantic, silver-plated doors and into the elaborate main hall of the edifice.

The travelers' boots came to a squeaking halt on the smooth, gleaming marble floor, their gaze immediately drawn to the two Dark Álves standing regally in the center of the ornate chamber. The room was illuminated by the soft, flickering light of a grand chandelier, its crystal droplets casting a kaleidoscope of colors across the space. One álf was dressed in elaborate black and gray regalia. Beside him stood another álf, clad in striking gold-plated armor that gleamed with a burnished luster.

The scoutmaster knelt before the two Dokkalrolk, her Sylvanrolk companions following suit.

"King Ragnar," Estrasta whispered, almost all of the fear present before leaving her tone, "Jarl Orsala."

The king gave the scoutmaster a warm smile and a nod, his black braided bun bobbing atop his head. "You've returned, Scoutmaster Estrasta. And with *utelanders* in tow."

"I have, Your Majesty," the Dokkalrolk responded, her light eye lingering on the jarl as she spoke. "May I approach?"

"You may, Scoutmaster Estrasta. Your guests, however, must stay where they are. I would like an explanation for their presence."

"Yes, sir."

The scoutmaster stood up and approached her superiors, the scintillating light from the chandelier shining down on the trio of Dokkalrolk. Her shoulders relaxed as she looked upon the jarl, her eye lingering on the woman until the king spoke.

"Your report, Scoutmaster."

"The scouts' task to find the fairy women was a failure, King Ragnar. However, during our journey, my men and I found a small settlement called Gradgate in the Glimmering Wilds. Not only did the inhabitants prove to be most hospitable, but they also provided us with the opportunity to

175

meet these four Wood Álves." The Dark Alf paused, motioning toward the umber-haired alf. "The leader of their group, Master Arvel, shared his kin's reasoning behind their adventure into the Wilds. It turns out their motive for seeking out the vilek was the same as ours."

The king cocked a thin eyebrow, his gray forehead scrunching. Looking away from the scoutmaster, the king turned to the bowing teacher.

"Is that so, Master Arvel?"

"It is, Your Excellency." The teacher replied. "Our peoples share a common objective regarding the elusive woodland fairies."

The king smiled, pointing at the kneeling teacher. "You may approach, *Utelander*. Your kin, however, must stay put."

Master Arvel did as instructed, his long hair framing his thin physique as he approached the king. Cymbelina's gaze turned from the marble floor beneath her palms to the patron guide.

"It's a pleasure to make your acquaintance, King Ragnar."

"And yours as well, Master Arvel. If only it were under better circumstances. Please tell me what you told Scoutmaster Estrasta about your group's journey into the Glimmering Wilds."

"The Sylvanrolk have experienced multiple attacks from creatures that the clan leaders perceive to be similar to the vilek. So my group and I entered the Wilds hoping to converse with the fairies to see if the clan leaders' predictions were accurate and, if so, reach a compromise and eliminate the notion of any future disagreements."

King Ragnar hummed, his light gray eyes scanning the kneeling Sylvanrolk behind the teacher, his lips pursed in reflection. "And you truly believe these Wood Álves are trustworthy, Scoutmaster?"

"I do, Your Majesty."

"I see. Yulla!"

A sprite-like Dark Álf briskly entered the room, curtseying as she approached the king. "Yes, King Ragnar?"

"I would like you to pen two letters to Jarl Wray and Jarl

Yngraham and have messengers send them out immediately once we return to the palace. Write down that I'll be holding a meeting in the Gullhum *lovhuss* at the sixth blow of the horn tomorrow morning. Make sure they know that Jarl Orsala will be there as well."

"What is the topic of discussion?"

Ragnar's gaze bore into Cymbelina, who he caught staring at Master Arvel. His cool, assertive eyes pierced through the confident shell the she-álf constructed, causing her gaze to falter from her teacher. "The topic is the *utelanders* and their presence in our cities."

"Will that be all, King Ragnar?" Yulla asked after she finished engraving the king's task onto the stone tablet in her hands.

"For the letter, but bring my carriage around from the stables. I'll be ready to leave momentarily."

After the king's assistant left the room, he turned his gaze towards the scoutmaster and the jarl of Krigdor. "I would love to stay and chat, but there are some things I must attend to. The Sylvanrolk are free to stay in the city for tonight until the court decides what to do with them tomorrow morning. I'll see you in court, Jarl Orsala. Oh, and Scoutmaster," the king continued, "make sure you escort your companions to my *lovhuss* tomorrow morning. We can't talk about the Wood Álves if they're not there to witness our discussion."

"Will do, Your Majesty," Scoutmaster Estrasta spoke, bowing for the leader of her kin, "we'll see you tomorrow."

The king nodded, his gaze flicking back and forth between his kin and the outsiders as he exited the entryway to the courthouse, his shoes clacking against the marbled flooring.

All forms of royal etiquette went out the door with the king as he left. Beaming with relief, Scoutmaster Estrasta brought Jarl Orsala in for a back-breaking embrace. The scout leader kissed the head of Krigdor's forehead before burying her face in the jarl's bobbed, gray locks.

"I'm so glad you're safe, Orsala! When Ser Satula and Ser Lufor told me you had been involved in the most recent attack,

I began to panic."

The jarl chuckled, breaking the hug to clasp the scoutmaster's gloved hands. "You know me better than that, Estrasta. I'm your wife, after all. You've seen me in battle. I might acquire a few minor scrapes and bruises, but I won't go down easily."

"Of course, how foolish of me. But where are my manners." Estrasta let go of her wife's hands, gesturing toward the four Sylvanrolk. "Jarl Orsala, meet Master Arvel, Cymbelina, Kayven, and Malaveen. You four, meet the esteemed ruler of Krigdor."

"Secondary ruler of Krigdor, that is," the gray-haired woman playfully added. "I'm second in command to King Ragnar when it comes to business involving fine city."

"Charmed, truly," Malaveen huffed, aiming a sardonic grin in the jarl's direction, "but I'm exhausted. Today's been a dreadfully long day, and based on what King Ragnar just said, we'll be thrown out of the mountains tomorrow if the court doesn't approve of our presence. In case that happens, I want a hot meal and a place to sleep. So if either of you could show me to the nearest inn, I'd be grateful."

Estrasta's eye twitched; Jarl Orsala raised an eyebrow in stupefied confusion. The three Wood Álves standing beside Malaveen glared at the ungrateful woman.

Malaveen has the social graces of a pig.

"What Malaveen meant to say," Master Arvel began, his eyes turning away from the blonde to look at the jarl, "is that we'd be delighted if either you or Scoutmaster Estrasta could show us to the nearest inn. We are truly exhausted and would appreciate any little bit of rest we can get before the long day tomorrow."

"I'd be delighted," Estrasta said, her voice thick with distaste at the flaxen-haired álf's decorum. "Just make sure to keep up this time."

* * *

178

"Come on, everyone, let's get those tents set up! We don't have all night."

A chilly wind swept through the dense gathering of trees lining the western edge of Tundrana, whipping the leaves on the rustling branches. Clumps of snow fell from the evergreens to the frigid ground, crowning the hills of snow that formed towers across the frozen tundra. Above such a hill stood Knight Kazimiera, her gray mane lashing against the wintry night wind. A pool of shadows lingered underneath the slab of rock she had magically stretched from the ground, the stone now standing ten feet tall. Her merciless red eyes flicked between the parchment in her scarred hands and the busy spies setting up the campsites below, a hideous smirk spreading across her grayish-green face.

Hopefully, the recent attack on the Dokkalrolk has convinced them to cease their nightly patrols. If not, however, the towering trees should mask our troops from the occasional patrolman who might meander this way. Or any of those pesky trolls.

The green-skinned fairy turned toward the mountains. Bathed in the blood-red light of the final moon of the month, its white snow-capped peaks took on a pink hue as they scratched against the sapphire sky.

If Monarch Vukasino's plan doesn't pan out as expected, Bojana and I will be as good as dead. Not only that but our people's quest to reclaim Florella will be set back exponentially.

Delicate snow flurries began to fall from the sky. The female knight followed one of the snowflakes with her gaze, which was as cold as the falling snow. Her eyes eventually landed on an approaching figure, which she discerned to be her fellow knight, Bojana. A sly smile formed on Kazimiera's chapped lips as she stared at her sister-in-arms.

And just like that, Bojana appears.

The knight lowered the crumbling pillar of rock beneath her, returning it to its rightful spot upon the earth. Shaking off the bit of snow that had fallen on her head, Kazimiera approached her fellow sister-in-arms with renewed vigor.

"Did you do it? Did you speak to the contact?"

Bojana nodded in confirmation, her wolf-fang earrings glistening in the sanguinous moonlight. "I did. And he confirmed that he can secure a passageway into the mountains for our troops when the time comes. He'll meet us at the northern edge of the woods tomorrow."

"At what time?"

"An hour before sunrise," Bojana smirked, her eyes glistening with anticipation as she turned from Kazimiera to look at her agents. "This plan is going much smoother than I anticipated."

"It truly is. If only Morana were here with us to smell the sweetness that permeates the air after a fierce battle."

"Or Tihana. It would be nice for her to see the efficiency of her concoction."

Kazimiera sneered at the mention of the alchemist's name. "I could do without her presence."

"Why is that?"

"What do you mean, 'why is that'?!" Kazimiera unconsciously exclaimed, attracting the attention of the nearby workers. Sensing her error, she turned to her subordinates and explained, "This is a private conversation between Knight Bojana and me. Should I discover that anyone has listened to our conversation, I'll send them to the dungeons to become one of Mistress Tihana's test subjects. Is that clear?"

Heeding the knight's warning, the scouts quickly returned to their tasks. The green-skinned woman only returned her fellow knight's gaze when she was sure nobody was still staring. "Tihana's been acting strangely these past couple of months."

"How so?"

"Have her absences from council meetings gone unnoticed by you? Or the inexplicable nights she's gone missing from the Monarch's castle without a trace? Have you not seen that ugly amulet she started wearing around her neck a few months ago? I mean, by Mother Terralynia's tears, that thing is hideous."

"I can't explain the jewelry, but maybe her disappearances signify that she needs a break from Vukasino?"

Kazimiera chuckled. "Don't we all. But no, Tihana helped

to create him; the least she can do is follow our beloved Matriarch Zlatana's final wishes and watch over her son. Especially when Vukasino's goal is to reclaim Florella for the fairies."

"Never mention that to the Monarch," Bojana hissed, shaking her head. "He already despises Zlatana for making him constantly feel like a 'petulant sapling'; he'll kill anyone who mentions her name if you ever tell him her final wish."

"We wouldn't have to worry about it if Matriarch Zlatana was alive. Oh, how I miss her."

"I do, too, but let us not dwell on the past. Tomorrow is a big day, after all."

Another brisk breeze swept through the forest, sprinkling snow on the gathering of Dark Vilek. Bojana's eyes were glued to the full moon, its red hue mirroring the álven blood she craved to spill.

"Indeed it is, Kazimiera: indeed it is."

* * *

Scoutmaster Estrasta gave the visiting Wood Álves a tour of Krigdor. Past the imposing city gates lay a city bathed in gold and silver. Even as the smallest of the four Snøthorn cities, Krigdor offered a variety of accommodations, including an inn, a pub, and a variety of stores and stalls strewn about the metallic town square, which lay in the heart of the bustling megalopolis underneath the shadow of Jarl Orsala's *lovhuss*.

"I've never seen so much gold and silver in my life," Malaveen murmured, her eyes darting back and forth greedily between the golden and silver pillars that lined either side of the main path, which wound throughout the dying market plaza. "How have the Dark Álves been able to create cities such as this?"

The outsiders fell in step behind the scoutmaster, who traversed over a small bridge arching above a stream of lava. The liquid gurgled and hissed underneath their feet, hellish heat radiating from its molten surface.

Estrasta smirked, turning to face the Sylvanrolk as they approached a two-storied building made of stone and lined with gold. "We have our ways. But here we are, the Golden Pillow Inn. This is where you four will be staying for the night."

Cymbelina eyed the establishment, whose walls were connected to those of two neighboring stores. Even from where the álves were standing, the brunette could hear wild shrieks of laughter and mayhem emanating from within. "Are you sure there's a vacancy?"

The Dokkalrolk smirked. "We haven't had any outsiders within the Snøthorn Mountains for many moons, and whenever we do receive visitors, they typically stay in the capital. The most you'll have to deal with tonight are a handful of drunkards who have been cast out for the night by their wives." Estrasta swung the door open and beckoned the Sylvanrolk inside. "Hurry, I'm sure there's room for you here."

And sure enough, there was. The source of the clamorous hoots and hollers had been five drunken men who clambered up the creaky stairs within the inn. The innkeeper, nestled behind the desk, watched the sight with amusement until his eyes shifted to Scoutmaster Estrasta. Dropping a sack of clinking coins on the greedy proprietor's desk, the female Dark Álf inquired about a room the outsiders could rent for the night.

"Yeah, I have some rooms the lot of ya can rest in for the evening," the owner spoke, his eyes unable to hide the curiosity that welled in his core at the sight of the foreigners. Tucking the bag of currency on a shelf underneath the countertop, the man said, "Follow me; I have two vacancies upstairs."

The stout álf led the group up the steps and down a carpeted hallway, ornate paintings adorning either wall. At the end of the corridor sat two doors, both of which appeared unoccupied.

"Here we are," the male gasped, reclaiming his breath after his traversal down the long hallway. Swiping his greasy black hair off his gray face, the male continued, "The men can stay in

182

the room on the left, and the women can stay in the room on the right. Checkout time is at the eighth blow of the horn."

"Thanks, Brynnor. I'll ensure the *utelanders* are out of your establishment before then."

The male nodded, wobbling back down the stairs and to his seat behind the desk in the inn's entryway.

Master Arvel smiled at the female Dokkalrolk. "Thank you, Scoutmaster Estrasta. I don't know what we would do without you."

The woman flashed a brief smile before an overwhelmingly serious expression overtook her features. "On a more serious note, Master Arvel, there is something that I need to discuss with you and Cymbelina."

A lump rose in the brunette's throat, the troll's death from earlier in the day flashing before her eyes.

"Ok," the blonde said, placing her hands on her hips. "We're all ears."

"I meant there's something I must discuss with them alone."

The teacher cocked an inquisitive brow. "Is that so? Well, if you insist." The umber-haired male turned to Kayven and Malaveen. "Why don't you two begin to unpack your belongings? We'll figure out what to eat tonight when Cymbelina and I return."

"Sounds good to me," Kayven shrugged, heading into the room he would share with the patron guide without further comments. Malaveen stared at the duo in distaste before heading into the chambers intended for her and Cymbelina.

When the three álves were alone, Scoutmaster Estrasta led the outsiders out of the entryway to the inn and around the back of the building, with the trio ending up in a dark alleyway. Nestled between the Golden Pillow Inn and a neighboring store, the street was illuminated by the glow of a singular torch, which flickered as Estrasta and the Sylvanrolk passed by it. Gazing all around her to make sure there wasn't anyone around, Estrasta turned to address Master Arvel, but the teacher cut her off.

"I think a side room in the inn would've sufficed."

"Brynnor loves to eavesdrop, Master Arvel, so I figured I would spare you two of that nonsense. Anyways, Cymbelina, do you want to tell Master Arvel about what happened today, or should I?"

"What do you mean?" The male questioned, looking curiously between the two women. "Tell me what?"

The younger she-álf blushed in frustration and embarrassment. "I don't think this is the place for such a revelation. It's not that serious."

"Oh yes, it is, Cymbelina."

"Will someone please just tell me what's going on?"

The scoutmaster looked at the brunette knowingly. Sighing in defeat, Cymbelina admitted, "I...I became entranced by a vision during the battle today, Master Arvel. I saw the same things I did in my nightmare I told you about the other night."

"While on top of a troll, I might add," Estrasta continued.

The male was silent for a moment, thinking of the best way to respond to what he had just heard. "That is...unusual."

"More than unusual, Master Arvel. She was so invested in the daydream that she even began to chant something in a language that certainly wasn't Common or any Álvish dialect I've ever studied before."

"What did you say, Cymbelina? Do you remember?"

The half-álf gazed at her feet. "I do remember, Master Arvel; I just don't quite know what it means."

"So it wasn't Hominan either?"

"No, sir."

The patron teacher's eyebrows furrowed. "Can you at least repeat the phrase?"

A sense of nausea washed over the she-álf's frame as she struggled to annunciate the familiar sentence. Thinking about the fiery text sent an overbearing surge of bloodlust straight to her core, her mouth unable to expel the words engraved into her mind: *'te draco a containeo dun te animus somnullis.'*

"I don't think I can, Master Arvel," Cymbelina shakily announced, her stomach convulsing at the thought of the sentence.

"What do you mean, Cymbelina? Master Arvel is your patron guide, and from what I've gathered over the past few days, he's supposed to help you with this sort of dilemma."

"That's not what I meant," the brunette spoke weakly, "I just don't think that—"

"I'm always there to help my students, whether former or present. But I will never force any pupil of mine to do something they feel they ought not to do."

Surprised by her teacher's interruption, Cymbelina tried to speak again. "It's not that I don't feel like sharing the phrase; I just feel like I'm—"

The scoutmaster scoffed. "Even when the student in question is zoning out while on top of a foe during battle?"

Cymbelina frustratedly sighed, looking at Estrasta and Arvel in astonishment. *Why did they pull me outside if they planned to bar me from speaking?*

A flash of irritation crossed the umber-haired man's face, but his voice remained passive. "My rules remain the same, regardless of the circumstances."

Scoutmaster Estrasta hissed. "Well, that's a damn good way to get your kin killed."

"In my experience, it's quite the opposite."

Cymbelina shuddered, the arguing between her two companions becoming more irksome by the moment. However, with the rise and fall of the acid in her stomach, she kept her mouth shut.

"How do you figure? Are Wood Álves immune to damage when they're daydreaming?"

"That's not what I meant."

"Then what did you mean, Master Arvel? Because life is full of pain and uncomfortable circumstances, and if you give your students a free pass in times of inconvenience, they're doomed to fail when situations truly get tough, such as the fight with the trolls this morning."

"You know nothing of which you speak, Scoutmaster Estrasta. Giving people time and space to open up about their issues makes them more receptive to help and guidance. If we just give Cymbelina the time she needs, I'm sure she'll be able to tell us what she saw in her hallucination."

"Stop!" The brunette screamed, unable to hold back her irritation any longer. The ferocity in her voice startled the álves beside her. "I'm sick of this conversation. I said the situation wasn't serious, and I stand by those words, especially when you two won't stop bickering long enough for me to say what's on my mind."

"But Cymbelina, we just—"

"With all due respect, Scoutmaster Estrasta, I'm not finished speaking," the female Half-Sylvanrolk said, her voice strained with agitation. Her light brown cheeks were flushed as she struggled to catch her breath through her rant. "We have an enemy lurking behind us: a viper poised to strike at any moment. The last thing we need to do is dwell on my hallucination. After all, we have a bigger problem to deal with."

Master Arvel placed a delicate hand on the she-álf's shoulder, but she simply shook it off. "I'm not a child, Master Arvel. In fact," the female paused, her eyes blowing wide, "I think I'm through with my patron lessons."

"W-what? Cymbelina, you haven't discovered your patron animal yet. If we stop now—"

"I might never learn it. At this point, I'm quite content with that," Cymbelina said, her voice steady and resolute. "Especially if it means I won't have anyone speaking for me or over me as if I'm a child."

The brunette's eyes flicked between Arvel and Estrasta, their expressions a mix of astonishment and discomfort. Arvel's brows furrowed in surprise, his mouth slightly agape, while Estrasta's eyes widened, her usual composure momentarily slipping as she grappled with the brunette's bold demeanor. The air between the three warriors seemed to crackle with the tension of Cymbelina's unyielding stance.

Neither one of them is used to me sticking up for myself. I've been stubborn before, but I've never outright called them out on how poorly they address me sometimes, the brunette thought, looking between the two leaders standing beside her. *And it feels good. From this moment on, I'll never allow someone to treat me like an álfling again. Never.*

After moments of silence, the female snorted as she turned to leave the alleyway. "You two can remain here to debate the situation all you like, but I'm returning to my room. We have an audience with King Ragnar tomorrow, and I would like to be able to convince him that our presence here is important."

The she-álf left the alley without another word; the feeling of two sets of shocked eyes resting on her back followed her all the way back into the building. A sense of pride welled in her chest as she realized how well she had stood up for herself. It was from that moment forward that she decided she would chase that feeling. She would never allow herself to be spoken for again.

The Uninvited
1st of Winter's Breath, 1300 AC

Gullhum, the capital of the Snøthorn Mountains, was much larger than Cymbelina could've ever imagined. The she-álf, who had been taken aback by the sheer size of the first city in the kingdom, Krigdor, found herself dumbstruck in the looming shadow of the colossal metropolis before her.

A large moat filled with lava surrounded the bulk of the capital, smoldering waves of heat emanating from its glowing surface, blanketing the álves that sat at the mouth of the city. The light from molten liquid shone off the nearby metallic statues, which sat atop the arched bridge that provided passage over the stifling fosse. On the other side of the walkway sat a long cobblestone path, which weaved throughout the town. Thousands of Dark Álves waltzed down the path, minding their business until the outsiders passed by. The locals, unaccustomed to the southern álves, stared at the Sylvanrolk in both wonder and fright as they crossed the bridge. Their eyes traveled from their neighbors to Estrasta and the outsiders, their gazes filled with curiosity and a hint of fear.

"Have your people never heard of the concept of beauty sleep, Scoutmaster? It's super early, and your kin are already flooding the streets to go about their day."

"Who needs beauty sleep when there's work to be done, Malaveen?"

The blonde scrunched her nose. "Ah. Forget I asked."

The álves entered the throng of Gullhum inhabitants packing the marketplace. Situated in the center of the city, the bazaar featured stalls that lined the plaza in densely packed rows, allowing little room for individuals to filter through. Some merchants yelled about sales and various once-in-a-lifetime promotions, while others were too busy thrusting their products into prospective customers' faces.

Shoving a shoe that a merchant was showing him out of his face, Kayven's eyes wandered to the staggeringly massive constructions that bordered the plaza. "All I can say is that the Dark Álves do wonders with architecture. I mean, look at the size of these buildings. Some seem to be scraping the top of the cave!"

"Thank you, Kayven. My people settled in the Snøthorn Mountains over a millennium ago, so we had to find some way to rebuild an álven society. Luckily for our ancestors, the mountains have always been filled to the brim with stone and rich ore veins."

"Quite lucky indeed."

The group members' shoes clacked against the stony path as they exited the shopping plaza. The main street eventually bled into a massive stone courtyard, divided into five streets that mimicked the shape of a star. Each course was divided by long pools of lava on either side, all of which were lined by titanium fencing. Following one of the paths, Cymbelina heard the fountains on either side of her burble and spew out streams of lava.

Cymbelina felt Kayven's stare shift from Estrasta to Master Arvel and herself as the group continued on the path. His marigold eyes swept over their figures, a mixture of curiosity and confusion playing across his face. The patron teacher and the brunette had been unusually silent since the night before, and it was evident by the look on the young male's face that he was intrigued by the duo's unusual demeanor. Ignoring his probing look, Cymbelina looked ahead, her eyes remaining on the *lovhuss*, which sat on an elevated terrace three flights of steps above her and her allies.

"So," Kayven began, breaking the silence the half-alf attempted to maintain. "What do you think of the city so far,

Cymbelina? Isn't it magnificent?"

The brunette flashed a pleasant but fake smile in the obsidian-haired male's direction. "It's certainly incomparable to anything I've seen before."

"What about you, Master Arvel? What do you think of Gullhum?"

"It's breathtaking, Kayven, but we should focus on the task at hand," the teacher replied in an uncharacteristically curt manner. "The four of us must put on a confident face for the Dokkalrolk Court to convince them that we deserve to stay here. We can discuss the brilliance of the architecture at a later time."

"I agree with your patron guide," the scoutmaster spoke. "Although I'm flattered by the praise you're offering my people's handiwork, now is not the time to gawk. We must present a convincing case to the court if you four wish to stay within the mountains. King Ragnar isn't keen on allowing visitors into the cities during a shutdown."

"If that's the case, why did he even allow us to stay? Was it simply because he trusted your verdict, Scoutmaster Estrasta?"

"Yes, Malaveen: I'm one of his most trusted military personnel, and he knows how hard it is for people to gain my confidence. Since you four have earned it, that speaks volumes about your characters." The Dark Álf side-eyed the blonde. "Well, most of your characters, that is."

Reaching the end of the northernmost path, the allies arrived at the base of the first staircase. Quickly ascending three flights of steps, the álves stepped foot on the stony terrace. Braziers lined the short street leading to the *lovhuss*, bathing the group in a warm glow as they approached the courthouse. Two armored guards stood on either side of the entryway, nodding to the scoutmaster as she led the outsiders into the building.

Three elegant chandeliers dangled from the tall ceiling of the law house, casting a golden hue upon the dark marbled walls and floors. Stone furniture was scattered across the main hall, the minuscule crystals embedded within each piece glittering under the heavenly light. A set of tall, cream curtains covered an opening on the other side of the room, creating a partition between the entryway and the hall that led to the courtroom.

As the Sylvanrolk adjusted to their surroundings, a booming voice resounded off the room's marble walls. A withered gray hand snuck between a part in the drapes, forcing either one to each side. The loud, raspy voice appeared to belong to an older male álf.

"Scoutmaster Estrasta, what a pleasure it is to see you!"

"Jarl Yngraham! It's been a while."

"Indeed it has."

The Dokkalrolk official ambled over to the group of álves on the opposite side of the room, his wooden staff clacking against the floor. His dark gray features had seen many moons, as each of his wrinkles was accentuated under the flames from the chandeliers. His weary, deep blue eyes scanned the outsiders, a smile slowly spreading across his face.

"You four must be the visitors that King Ragnar mentioned in his letter. I'm Jarl Yngraham Steineyes, leader of the city of Jordstand and a member of the Dokkalrolk Court. It's a pleasure to meet the four of you."

Master Arvel smiled, bowing his head. "It's a pleasure to meet you as well, Jarl Yngraham. I'm Master Arvel, and my three companions are Cymbelina, Malaveen, and Kayven."

"Well met," Cymbelina said, earning another smile from the aged leader.

Yngraham chuckled. "It seems like you've brought some fine visitors to our kingdom, Estrasta. They're even more polite than some of the locals!"

"Speaking of being more polite than the locals, where is Jarl Wray? I haven't seen him since I arrived, and it certainly isn't like him to be tardy to a hearing."

The older Dokkalrolk chuckled once more, his laugh lines creasing. "I must admit, I'm surprised I didn't find him here when I arrived. I'm usually the one who arrives either just in time for a hearing to begin or I'm tardy. Who knows, maybe he'll be the one running late this time. Either way, Jarl Orsala and King Ragnar are wrapping up preparations for the hearing, so we can begin just as soon as Jarl Wray shows his face."

"Well, hopefully, he arrives soon."

"I hope so too, Scoutmaster Estrasta." The Dark Álf paused, wiping away the sweat that lingered on his forehead. "Well, I should get going; I'm sure you younglings need to get your wits about you before the hearing, yes? I'll see you five shortly."

"Of course, Jarl Yngraham. We'll see you shortly."

The man nodded, his wooden staff pounding against the floor as he meandered his way back to the set of tall curtains.

"Well, he seemed pleasant enough. Hopefully, the disposition of the rest of the assembly will be the same."

"Jarl Yngraham isn't the álf we'll have to worry about today, Kayven," the scoutmaster commented, her smile fading into a snarl. "The only Dokkalrolk we'll have to watch out for is Wray Volsen."

"Why do you say that?" Malaveen asked, sitting down on a nearby bench.

"Because," Estrasta began, her voice dripping with malice, "he's everything I despise. He's xenophobic, finicky, and has a knack for convincing folks to see his point of view even though it's tainted with falsehoods."

"But not you?"

"No," Estrasta said bitingly, glaring at the blonde for the mere suggestion. "He's never convinced me of anything."

The room trembled as a brassy note of a horn rang out from atop the *lovhuss*, signaling to the álves that the sixth hour of the day had arrived.

"Well, it appears that the Jarl Wray now has a knack for being late, too. Let us enter the hearing chamber and—"

"Not so fast," a sleek voice called out from behind the curtains. Parting the fabric, the álves saw a slender man swaggering toward them, his long, cloud-white braid swishing back and forth behind him. His cold silver eyes scanned the group, the corner of his mouth tilting upward in a condescending smirk.

"Jarl Wray," Scoutmaster Estrasta murmured, "I see you found another way into the *lovhuss*."

The male looked at the scoutmaster confusedly before he sneered. "I have no idea what you mean. I entered through the front door, just as I usually do."

"But Jarl Yngraham said you hadn't arrived yet."

"Pfft. Why are you trusting the words of that old codger? It's his last season as a member of the Dokkalrolk Court, you know. And it's for a good reason."

Cymbelina's eyes narrowed, scrutinizing the jarl. Although the man was dressed for the part, the brunette could quickly discern that he was not fit to be a caring leader in any way, shape, or form.

I can tell why Estrasta dislikes him already.

"Yes, well, are the leaders ready for the Sylvanrolk yet or not?"

"Of course we are. Follow me."

The group followed the cocky man as he parted the portière, ushering the álves through the grand hallways of the law house. Following the ivory strip of carpet lining the marble-floored corridors, Cymbelina and her allies arrived at the end of a long hallway. Two silver doors, engraved with a myriad of pictographs, sat wide open, allowing the outsiders to gaze into the courtroom for the first time.

The enormous hearing room was filled with stone pew after stone pew, all of which remained empty in front of the four thrones that sat at the northernmost point of the room. Three of the thrones, made of silver, sat upon raised platforms, which Cymbelina estimated to be fifteen feet above the floor. Elaborate spiral staircases descended from the three stages, all of which bore the emblem of one of the three minor cities in the Snøthorn Mountains. The final throne, made of gold and embossed with a swirling design, sat upon a platform positioned about twenty feet above the ground. This stage also had a spiral staircase leading up to it, except it had the emblem of the Kingdom of Snøthorn on it. Each throne was adorned with luxurious jewels, which sparkled in the well-lit room.

The young jarl continued to move into the room while the scoutmaster stopped her Wood Álf allies in their tracks and whispered, "Do exactly what I do and not a movement more. Understand?"

The Sylvanrolk nodded, following Estrasta into the heart of the courtroom. Kneeling in front of the marbled dais situated in the center of the floor, the álves bowed before the seated jarls and King Ragnar as Jarl Wray found his way up to his throne. Once the youngest ruler was sitting in his seat, Ragnar spoke.

"Court is now in session. My first act as king is to call upon you to speak, Scoutmaster Estrasta Gundblad. Set foot upon the podium."

Rising, the woman wordlessly acceded as she approached the small platform. "Thank you, Your Lordships, for allowing us to seek counsel with the Dokkalrolk Court this morning."

The king nodded. "Of course. Before we begin the proceedings, I request that your Sylvanrolk kin take a seat at the pew to their right."

Master Arvel assented, leading his fellow Sylvanrolk to their designated seats. Once the Wood Álves were settled on the bench, King Ragnar spoke to Estrasta.

"As I'm sure you were informed about at the gate to Krigdor, Scoutmaster, the Snøthorn Mountains have been placed under a lockdown due to recent attacks. With such a period of isolation comes restrictions to visitors who seek entry into our beloved kingdom. What makes you think the four visitors in your party deserve to be exceptions to such a rule?"

"I brought these *utelanders* to the mountains because they have encountered the same creatures who have been terrorizing our homeland, Your Majesty. I reasoned that if our cousins to the south have been dealing with these creatures, they might be able to help us in our fight against them as well."

Jarl Yngraham, who was seated on the throne to the far right, hummed, picked up the bell on the table in front of him, and rang it.

"You may say your piece, Jarl Yngraham Stineyes."

"Thank you, King Ragnar. I have a question for you, Scoutmaster Estrasta. Where exactly did you meet these *utelanders*?"

"I met them during the investigation my scouts and I launched in the Glimmering Wilds. They sought me out in the local tavern, and that's where our acquaintanceship began."

Jarl Wray chuckled from the leftmost throne before he rang his bell. After he was given permission by the king to speak, he inquired, "And what makes you so sure that these Wood Álves are telling the truth, eh? They could've spouted some random drivel to you, and you ate it all up."

"Based on how they explained the creatures to me, there's no way they fabricated their experiences."

A wave of tremors shook the ground, causing Cymbelina and her fellow Sylvanrolk to clutch the bench seat underneath them. None of the Dokkalrolk seemed to notice.

"What was that?" Malaveen hissed at the patron guide.

"Just a small earthquake. While we were traveling through the Wilds, the Scoutmaster told me that they're frequent in the mountains."

Jarl Orsala rang her bell. "Now, Scoutmaster Estrasta, explain how you think these Sylvanrolk might be useful to us here in the mountains?"

"Through an exchange of observations about the fae-like creatures: the travelers would tell us about their findings, and we would tell them ours."

Jarl Wray shook his bell again. "And what would the purpose of that be? Do you underestimate the intelligence of your own kin, Scoutmaster?" His words hung in the air, heavy with accusation and challenge.

"No, I do not, Jarl Wray Volsen. I simply believe that seeking outside information will not only strengthen our chances of winning any future battles but also lessen our troops' casualties."

"Well, did the possibility that these outsiders could be working with the fae ever cross your mind, Scoutmaster? Or were you too desperate to bring Sylvanrolk into our homeland that you neglected to see that they could pose a threat?"

"That's enough, Jarl Wray," the king announced, trying to calm the agitated male. "This is a courtroom, not a battlefield. There is no reason to be so hostile."

The male's face flushed with anger, his cold eyes glaring hatefully at the outsiders in the pew. After a tense moment, the youngest Dokkalrolk exhaled, his voice laced with resentment. "Of course, Your Majesty. I apologize for my brutishness."

Jarl Wray is really hammering home the fact that he doesn't trust outsiders, the brunette thought, her gaze lingering on the arrogant male. *I hope we won't have to rely on him for any sort of help in the future because I doubt he would be willing to lend a hand.*

Jarl Wray's eyes roved over Estrasta and her Sylvanrolk companions. When his gaze fell on Cymbelina, it locked onto her, as if he could sense the unease churning in her stomach. The she-álf shivered inwardly, his leer lingering in her mind even as she turned her gaze to one of the other jarls.

"Are there any lingering questions the Court would like to ask?" the king queried, looking down at the three jarls below him.

"No, Your Majesty," uttered Jarl Orsala.

"Not presently," announced Jarl Yngraham.

Jarl Wray continued to look at the brunette, not uttering a word. Noticing his unapproving look, King Ragnar spoke out to the jarl.

"Jarl Wray, do you have anything you would like to ask Cymbelina?"

"Nothing that I would like to ask her, but something that I would like to ask my fellow members of the Dokkalrolk Court."

"I'll allow it. Estrasta, you may be seated with your allies. Jarl Wray, please approach the podium."

Another rumble shook the earth, this time stronger than the last. Assured that it was an everyday occurrence, the jarl descended the staircase and ascended the stage in the center of the courtroom.

"My fellow members of the Court, please listen without judgment to the information I discovered before the meeting this morning. According to one of my contacts at the gates of Krigdor, one of the *utelanders* that have accompanied Scoutmaster Estrasta into the mountains, the she-álf known as Cymbelina," the male said, pointing to the brunette, "has been cast out of her clan. Do we really think it's wise to welcome one such as her into our cities with open arms? After all, if her own kin rejected her, who are we to offer her a warm reception into our kingdom?"

The Sylvanrolk outsiders glared at Malaveen, who had been the one to share that fact with the guards at the gate. Unshaken, the blonde whispered, "He has a point. I would feel the same way if I were in his shoes."

Shaking his bell, Yngraham said, "We don't know the circumstances of the situation, Jarl Wray. To judge the girl based on that alone is tantamount to—"

"King Ragnar, King Ragnar!" a squealing voice rang out, interrupting the jarl. The voice belonged to the king's assistant, Yulla, who ran through the open doors of the courtroom. Halting feet away from the platform, the girl was hyperventilating, her pale white face coated in sweat. She had a glowing saber clutched in her right fist.

"What is the meaning of this interruption, Yulla?" The king asked, standing up from his throne.

"I would not intrude on a hearing unless it weren't-weren't dire, Your Majesty." The woman took a deep, shuddering breath, her tone shaky. Fear shone in her eyes. "Those vilek-like creatures...they're attacking the capital."

Another tremor rocked the *lovhuss*, this time strong enough to shake the foundations of the building. The sound of distant screams permeated the inner chamber, rousing all the álves within to action.

"To arms!" Cried the king without hesitation, his voice far less audible due to the incessant rumbling.

King Ragnar descended the flight of stairs leading down from his stage, issuing orders to the people in the room. "Jarls, return to your cities with your guards and restore your defenses. Yulla, Estrasta, and the Wood Álves: I would greatly appreciate it if you accompanied me back to the palace."

"Yes, sir," the scoutmaster spoke for the group, "lead on."

"What!" Malaveen squealed, looking toward the patron teacher. "So the scoutmaster speaks for us too, now?"

"What else do you propose we do?!" Master Arvel questioned incredulously. "Follow the king!"

King Ragnar led the álves out of the courtroom and down one of the many hallways that filled the gigantic *lovhuss*. Taking a sharp right down one of the corridors, the leader of the Snøthorn Mountains guided the allies to a painting beside a stone statue of a Dokkalrolk warrior. The king's gray fingers caressed the chin of the figurine. Seconds later, a loud click was heard, followed by the wall with the painting on it sliding into a slit in the floor. A dimly lit passageway was revealed. Within said hallway was a flickering torch, which shone down upon the surface of a silver hatch that led to a crawlspace underneath the floor. Rushing forward, Ragnar threw it open.

"Scoutmaster Estrasta!" The king yelled, his eyes flicking from the woman he was addressing to the trapdoor, "I want you to lead the way down. I want the *utelanders* to be between you, Yulla, and me. Quickly now, we don't have much time."

"Yes, Your Majesty. You three," the scoutmaster paused, motioning toward the Wood Álves before she descended the ladder leading into the trapdoor, "follow me."

The Sylvanrolk, King Ragnar, and Yulla quickly followed Estrasta down the ladder, the wooden structure shaking under Cymbelina's sweating palms. The steps descended into a cold tunnel lit with sparse light. Rats squeaked under the álves hands and knees as they swiftly crawled toward the exit. The scoutmaster kicked off the grate at the end of the tunnel, leading the álves to exit the claustrophobic quarters and enter a dilapidated slum.

The shacks that lined the alleyway were painted with the remains of the fallen, their fresh corpses decorating the potholed streets in gore. Like breadcrumbs left by a starving child, the bodies made a trail leading to a group of Dokkalrolk warriors who were battling the elemental foes. The Dark Álven blades sparkled as they clanged against those of the vilek-like creatures, the bloodcurdling screams of both teams floating in the hot air.

"Listen to me and listen to me carefully," the king hissed to his allies, his voice filled with distress. "We need to round up any surviving civilians and direct them to the castle as soon as possible. Let's start here. Yulla, Kayven, and Master Arvel: you will accompany me to take care of those vermin," the leader paused, motioning toward the enemies the warriors on the other side of the alley were fighting. "Then we'll round up any survivors we encounter. Scoutmaster Estrasta, Malaveen, and Cymbelina: kill any creatures you see and send any surviving Dokkalrolk to my estate. Do not stop searching until you hear the royal bell toll. Are your orders clear?"

"Of course, Your Highness. Let's go, you two."

Taking a sharp left, the trio of she-álves ran into a slim alley separating two rows of shanties. The foul smell of blood infiltrated the álves' noses as they dashed toward the end of the back street. Their journey was cut short by three vilek-like beings, who were bathed in the sanguine lifeforce of the nearby fallen Dokkalrolk. A black aura surrounded the three fairy-like beings, each gleefully stomping on the álven remains surrounding them.

I've never seen one of the fairy creatures surrounded in that black cloud before, the brunette thought, her hands hovering above the hilts of her daggers. *What on Sacarnia could be causing that?*

One of the creatures let out a twisted chortle, her laughter echoing in the air. She wore a grotesque expression on her gaunt face as one thin, clawed hand smeared a streak of blood across her cheek. Her eyes glinted with a malevolent sparkle as she spoke in a harsh, guttural tone. "*Vasa ova na slanava.*"

"What did she just say?" Malaveen whispered, raising her iron sword above her shoulder.

"I don't think it matters," Estrasta replied, her voice steady despite the impending danger as she grabbed the silver rapier at her hip. A soft, white glow emanated from the blade as a shower of sparkles cascaded down the handle. "The end result will be the same even if she hadn't said a word. Attack!"

The trio of creatures released shrill cries before splitting apart, each targeting one of the she-álves. The yellowish-gray woman turned her fierce gaze toward the brunette, her deep purple eyes bloodshot and her pupils dilated. Lifting a talon-like finger, she beckoned Cymbelina forward, her thin lips parting to reveal two rows of sharp teeth.

"Do you truly think you stand a chance against me with those puny blades?" The being brandished her broadsword, showing the dried blood coating the edges of the weapon as she and Cymbelina walked in a slow circle, neither one of the women letting their eyes drift from their opponent.

"Based on my past experiences with your kind," the brunette paused, the familiar sensation of bloodlust bubbling in her core, "it won't take long to bring you down."

The being's eyes narrowed, her smile bending into a frown. "You foolish little *nak-vilek*, I'll end you where you stand!"

Vilek? Did she just say vilek?!

The monstrous woman appeared before the brunette in the blink of an eye, her quick form leaving a hazy white trail behind. Jumping in the air, the creature's white locks flicked behind her pointed ears as she lifted her broadsword above her head, the black aura rippling around her frame. Somersaulting, Cymbelina avoided the overhead attack, the being's sword clanging against the pavement. Quickly rising, the brunette was taken aback by the fairy-like woman, who swiftly recovered from her missed blow and sprinted toward the she-álf.

Spinning to the right, Cymbelina agilely avoided the woman's sword, but she wasn't fast enough to circumvent her enemy's grasp. Grabbing a fistful of the Half-Sylvanrolk's long brown hair, the creature threw the young woman on the ground, knocking the breath out of her. Stunned by the motion, Cymbelina's daggers left her grasp and clattered against the street. Ignoring her scraped elbows, the she-álf's eyes affixed to the blood-soaked sword as it sliced through the sultry air, the creature aiming for her throat. Rolling over, the Wood Álf retrieved one of her weapons as she rose to her feet, eyeing her foe.

The veins in the magical female's arms pulsated, the dark cloud surrounding her muscular frame thickening. Her breaths came out in laborious pants, her purple eyes filled with loathing as she looked from the ground to the álf. Lunging, the yellowish woman dashed, her form becoming a blur until she appeared inches away from Cymbelina, swinging her sword above her head once more.

She might be fast, but she doesn't have many tricks up her sleeve, the brunette thought, quickly sliding out of the way. As soon as the woman's broadsword clanked against the street, Cymbelina jabbed a dagger into the fairy-like being's side, a look of excruciating pain painting her opponent's face.

"AHHHHHHHHHHH!" The woman shrieked, her voice ricocheting off the walls of the nearby huts.

Sparkly blue fluid gushed out of the wound on the right side of the being's abdomen as Cymbelina unsheathed her dagger from the woman's body. The brunette flicked the blade, cobalt gore splattering against the ground. Letting out a scream, the fairy-like creature threw her right elbow backward, hitting the Half-Sylvanrolk in the center of her chest. Pain blossomed from the point of contact as Cymbelina staggered back and clutched her chest.

"*Fokashel.*"

The creature bared her sharp fangs, twisted delight twinkling in her eyes as she drank in her enemy's pain. Attempting another attack on the brunette, the duo resumed their violent waltz, their strife continuously ringing in the air. Cymbelina's allies fared the same, the trio of elemental beings holding out strong as their auras grew darker with each attack.

What will it take to end these things?!

It wasn't until the brunette's adversary slipped in a puddle of blood that the Half-Sylvanrolk gained a fortuitous advantage. The fairy-like being cried in agony when her head slammed against the stony street. Sensing her chance to end the quarrel, Cymbelina quickly straddled the supine woman. The fairy-like being clawed at the air, thrashing about underneath the panting half-álf. Not giving her actions a second thought, the brunette buried her blade into the center of her opponent's chest. The creature wheezed in defeat, its lavender eyes rolling to the back of its head as Cymbelina watched the being die.

With her warped thirst for violence satiated, Cymbelina unceremoniously stood up, her green eyes flicking toward her two álven allies.

Estrasta was nearly finished battling her magical opponent, but Malaveen appeared to be struggling. Both women, covered in dirt and scratches, had abandoned their weapons, leaving the blonde and her rival enraptured in a duel of fisticuffs. After a swift blow to the cheek, the grayish-blue-skinned woman pinned the Wood Álf to the ground, prompting Cymbelina to jump into action.

Retrieving her second dagger from the ground, the brunette ran and jumped on the woman's back, taking the creature by surprise. Quickly standing from her bent position, the enemy tried to buck the Half-Sylvanrolk off, but her grip remained firm. With the dirty fingernails of her left hand digging into the dull skin of her mount, Cymbelina drove the blade in her right hand into the back of the woman's skull. Sputtering, the vilek-like being wobbled back and forth before collapsing, the two women colliding with the ground with a thump.

At first, the downed blonde was silent, her breath caught in her throat. Her eyes, wide with disbelief, gazed at the brunette in a fashion Cymbelina had never seen before, an amalgam of fright and awe.

"You-you saved me," Malaveen gasped, her chest heaving as she stared at her kinswoman in shock, her voice trembling with relief.

Dusting the dirt off her armor, Cymbelina walked toward her fellow Wood Álf, who was sitting upright on the blood-stained street. With the final scream of Estrasta's opponent filling the air, the brunette extended a hand to the shocked woman.

"Regardless of our feelings for one another, you're still my kin. And as the elders say…"

"'No Sylvanrolk gets left behind,'" Malaveen finished with a feeble smirk, clasping Cymbelina's hand as she was hoisted up. "Now you sound exactly like Kinlord Emyr."

"Enough of the chit-chat!" The Dark Álf bellowed, her voice resembling a whisper compared to the raging pandemonium engulfing Gullhum. Scowling at the blue blood coating her rapier, the Dokkalrolk turned her eyes to the Sylvanrolk. "We must move forward, stamp out the rest of those elemental freaks, and save any civilians we encounter along the way."

"And how do you suppose we do that? The three of us alone had a hard time defeating three of those beings; what will happen if we run into a large coterie of them?"

"Why don't we try searching for King Ragnar and the rest of the kin we split from?" Cymbelina offered. "With a few pairs of helping hands, we could defeat a small group of those things."

Scoutmaster Estrasta shook her head fervently. "Not a chance. The king gave us orders, and I intend to see us follow through."

"But what if the others need our help?" The blonde uncharacteristically implored.

"The less time we spend gabbing, the more likely it will be that our allies will turn out to be unscathed. Plus, they're strong: I'm sure they've encountered little trouble."

* * *

A squelching noise followed the movement of Kayven's iron shortsword as he sliced through one of the vilek-like creatures, gore coating his hands and weapon as his attacker crumpled to the floor. Dozens more lined up for the slaughter ahead of Kayven and his two companions, blocking the group's path to the king's castle.

203

"Do you think the women are alright?!" Kayven yelled to the patron teacher, pirouetting away from one of the aggressors.

"They'll live, I'm sure of it."

"That—ugh—doesn't answer my question."

"We need to worry more about the civilians," the king cried, slashing one of the creature's arms off with his glowing golden longsword before kicking it to the ground. "Yulla is waiting for us to clear a path to the castle so she can guide them there, so that should be our priority."

"Then we better pick up the pace," Kayven responded, dropping his weapon and shaking his head. Transforming into his wolven patron form, the male álf went on a frenzy, attacking the aggressors with all the strength he could muster.

The enemies took forever to take down under the trio's combined efforts. Their stamina in battle was incomparable to the ones the Sylvanrolk had faced at the Eldenfield Festival, which sent pangs of doubt to the young Wood Álf's core.

Why are these beings so much stronger than last time? What gives?

"Kayven, behind you!"

The patron-possessed male jumped, narrowly missing one of the creatures' attacks. He chomped onto the arm swinging toward him, penetrating the thick aura surrounding the fairy-like woman and breaking through flesh and bone. The female flailed about as Kayven gave the being's other arm the same treatment, flames pouring forth from her unhinged jaws before she fell to the ground in shock.

The other invaders soon shared the same fate, leaving the male álves alone in the desecrated plaza. Red and blue blood painted the cobblestone paths, forming a circle at the base of the staircase leading to King Ragnar's estate. Bodies lined the streets, the smell of death mingling with the smoke from the shanties in the slums below, most of which had caught fire.

Turning back into his álven form, Kayven approached Master Arvel and King Ragnar, who gathered on the bottom step of the towering flight of steps.

"What is our next move, Your Majesty?"

"Well, Master Arvel, this is where we part ways. I will assess the situation in the royal palace and then send a dispatch of scouts to discern the status of the cities. If all is clear, I will ring the royal bell, which alerts the guards that they need not search for the vermin anymore. If the bell does not ring, well... you two shall continue to search Gullhum, executing any of those women who dare to desecrate my kingdom with their presence. Maybe you'll reunite with your allies in the process."

"Are you sure you don't want the two of us to accompany you?" The younger male questioned. "What if enemies are waiting for you inside the castle?"

The Dark Álf smiled grimly, his gray eyes drifting to the corpses adorning the gore-stained steps. "Whatever violence has transpired here seems to have passed. Now go! I need to find my wife and gather some scouts. Terralynia willing, I'll see everyone safe and sound inside."

Assenting, Kayven and Master Arvel sprinted down the path and into the depths of Gullhum. The putrid stench of sanguinary corpses intensified the further the duo traveled into the bowels of the capital, the smell accentuated by the smokiness of the nearby huts, which were engulfed in flames. Dokkalrolk lined the streets in droves now that the action had subsided, some mourning their fallen loved ones and others gathering water from the nearby wells to extinguish the flames.

Following Master Arvel down a swerving dirt path, the two Sylvanrolk ascended an incline, leading to another series of shanties on the outskirts of the Gullhum main square. The stone stores and houses of the city's heart remained intact, while the shoddy domiciles outside were burning. Following the trail of huts with his marigold eyes, Kayven spotted three familiar figures.

"Look, Master Arvel! Cymbelina and the others!"

"I see them!" the amber-eyed male yelled, his gaze glued to the fighting she-álves as they were battling a gaggle of elemental beings. "We need to catch up to them."

Four of the vilek-like creatures lay lifeless around them as the three she-álves clashed swords with a yellow one. Its movements were fast, but it was easy to see that each subsequent swing was draining the being's stamina.

As Kayven caught up to the women and prepared to transform into his wolf form to help, a strangled battle cry came from Cymbelina as she buried her daggers up to the hilt in the magical being. The lack of remorse the female displayed in her attacks was foreign to her usual demeanor, and it took both Kayven and Master Arvel's breath away in astonishment.

The yellow being dropped to the ground lifelessly, its eyes blown wide in shock.

"Well, that's the last of them," Scoutmaster Estrasta huffed, looking down at the dead creature.

"Seems like the three of you did fine without us," Kayven spoke, the feeling of shock slowly ebbing away. "Especially Cymbelina."

"Fine is a bit of a stretch," Cymbelina admitted. "But we are all still alive."

"Barely," Malaveen muttered.

"*Inferdon-an,*" Estrasta groaned, her eyes clenched in exhaustion. "Cease the chatter. We have more important things to worry about," the scoutmaster said, gesturing to the flame-ridden buildings around her. "Our next task is to put out the fires and extinguish the threat of lingering outsiders if any are left. Follow me to the wells, and keep an eye out for any stragglers."

"Alright, lead on," Cymbelina said, following the Dokkalrolk scoutmaster toward the wells.

Kayven eyed the female cautiously, wave after wave of concern washing over him.

What's gotten into Cymbelina?

Expulsion
1st of Winter's Breath, 1300 AC

After hours of working to eradicate the flames engulfing the capital, the álves eventually heard the tolling of the royal bell. Traversing the corpse-littered streets, Estrasta and the outsiders headed toward King Ragnar's palace, their heads downcast and their footsteps swift.

What was supposed to be a peaceful day fit for a debate had become a bloodbath in a matter of minutes. Now, after the raging battle had ceased, the remains of the fallen lined the cobblestone streets. The air reeked of smoke and spilled blood, the most horrific combination the half-álf had smelled. Besides the day Cymbelina lost Idal, this day was shaping up to become one of the worst days of her life.

I'm glad Idal wasn't around to see this. Mother Terralynia knows how he would be dealing with this situation.

Ascending the stone stairs leading to the palace, the companions arrived at a pair of wide-open, ornate golden doors. Through the opening, the álves laid their eyes upon a crowded throne room. Sorrowful wails and pain-filled whimpers echoed out of the cramped space, the smell of sweat and blood pungent in the air. Bodies lay huddled together; some Dokkalrolk held their loved ones close, while others wept while curled up in a ball. Crossing the threshold, Cymbelina spotted King Ragnar, who was assisting a woman as she helped an álfling find her mother.

The resounding thuds of the warriors' heavy boots against the marble flooring caught the monarch's attention. Stepping away from the unknown woman's side, the male approached his guests.

"I'm glad you five made it out alright," the ruler said, his face bearing an expression that reflected both melancholy and relief. Looking over Scoutmaster Estrasta's shoulder, he gazed into the city below. His lips quivered wearily as if he attempted to smile but couldn't muster the strength to do so. "I can see from here that you've dealt with some of the fires in the alleyways, which I greatly appreciate."

"It was our honor, Your Majesty."

The woman who had been helping the king approached the group. Her billowing indigo dress trailed across the cream-colored floor behind her as her hands protectively covered her swollen belly. Her plaited black hair bobbed against her back.

"Greetings, Scoutmaster Estrasta. I suppose I have you and your friends to thank for safely escorting my husband out of the courtroom."

"Hello, Queen Norsla. There is no need for thanks; we were doing what was just."

A warm grin spread across the ruler's frost-toned skin, betraying the perturbation in her gray eyes. "I'm glad to hear it. We may require more assistance in the future, after all. But first, introduce me to your friends: they did help save the kingdom, after all."

Thunderous footfalls of an angered approach echoed throughout the crowded hall. Cymbelina's eyes darted to the entrance of the palace, where five imposing soldiers trailed behind a disheveled Jarl Wray. His usually light gray skin was now a canvas of reds and pinks, reflecting his anger and a series of scrapes and bruises.

"I wouldn't be so sure of that, Your Highness."

"Jarl Wray," the king said, "I'm relieved to see you. Tell me, how does Sølvcast fare after the attack? I've heard mixed rumors from the patrolmen."

"Not well, King Ragnar, not well at all. Hundreds of Dokkalrolk line the streets, and some of our prized buildings lay in ruins. The size of today's incursion was greater than any of the attacks from the fairies thus far, and I think," the male paused, his cold, silver eyes drifting toward the Wood Álves, "the *utelanders* are to blame."

Ignoring etiquette, Cymbelina reflexively replied, "I'm sorry for what happened in your city today, Jarl Wray, but we had—"

"Do NOT address me, you filthy mongrel. You and your allies have brought great evil upon this kingdom. Your Majesty," the male huffed, sweeping a stray strand of hair out of his face, "I sincerely beg you to expel these rats from this fine city before any more of those vile creatures attack us again."

"Rats?!" The blonde she-álf spat, "why you—"

Master Arvel held up his hand, effectively stopping the young woman before she could say anything regrettable.

The sobs of the nearby citizens quieted as they drank in the sight of the outburst, their eyes attentive to the actions of their kingdom's leaders.

"Jarl Wray," the king curtly whispered, "now is not the time to discuss expulsions. Not only are we outside the *lovhuss* at this point in time, but hundreds of Dark Álves across the Snøthorn Mountains are wounded and need our help. They are our top priority right now, not expelling the *utelanders*."

"If you don't mind me saying so, Your Majesty, I think Jarl Wray has a point," Jarl Orsala said, entering the room with a small group of guards in tow.

"My love," Estrasta gasped, throwing etiquette to the wind as well, "you're not truly siding with Jarl Wray on this matter, are you?"

Orsala gravely nodded her head. "Krigdor is a mess. The few civilian homes in my city have been toppled, leaving my people homeless and scared. I suggest we expel all visitors from the cities in case they're drawing more attention to our kingdom."

Master Arvel coughed, looking at the king for permission to speak. "I know it's not my place, nor is it the place of my peers to suggest what's best for the Snøthorn Mountains, but I think

209

having us stay here might bolster Dokkalrolk defenses for any future assaults."

Jarl Wray laughed. "Bolster our defenses? You and your companions are a bunch of random Wood Álves that were erroneously allowed to enter our homeland. Our resources aren't so petty that four random warriors would help turn the tide in the future."

"I wouldn't bet on that," Jarl Yngraham said, joining the group of quarreling álves. "I feel as if these four *utelanders* saved many lives today. Without them, many more Dark Álves could be lying face down in the streets."

"Oh? And how did Jordstand fare in the battle, Jarl Yngraham? Do you mean to suggest these foreigners helped defend your city and Gullhum?"

"I'm suggesting no such thing, Jarl Wray. I'm merely saying that these Sylvanrolk did more help than they did harm in today's battle."

"Pfft," Jarl Wray scoffed, "you give these dogs more credit than is due."

From that moment on, the throne room erupted into a disharmonious song of outrageous accusations and oversimplifications. The jarls were at each other's throats, their anger so potent that a few nearby citizens were roused from their sombrous stupor, joining the fray and screeching their ideas on the matter.

"Silence!" King Ragnar roared, his voice bouncing off the intricate walls. With clenched fists so tight that his knuckles turned white, he glared around the room, looking from Dokkalrolk to Sylvanrolk alike. His subjects and the outsiders remained silent.

"This fighting must cease. These *utelanders* are not our enemies, but it is clear that their presence is sowing an amount of discord that is unhealthy for our people at this time. Due to this, I've come to a decision." King Ragnar paused, his voice slightly wavering. His fear-filled eyes swept over each of the Wood Álves as he continued, "Master Arvel, Cymbelina, Malaveen, Kayven, you may stay in the Snøthorn Mountains for one more night as long as you promise to depart at some point tomorrow."

"But my lord," Scoutmaster Estrasta protested, "they might hold the key to—"

"Hush, Scoutmaster Estrasta. My decision is final. Thank you for the help you have bestowed upon my people on this terrible day, *utelanders*, but this is how it needs to be."

Jarl Wray smirked as Master Arvel gravely nodded. "We understand, Your Majesty."

"Thank you. Now, Jarl Orsala, is your inn in suitable condition for visitors?"

"No, King Ragnar: it was destroyed in the attack."

"They may stay at the inn in my city, Your Majesty," Jarl Yngraham offered. "I'll even guide them there myself after we're done here."

"Then that settles it," the king declared. "Jarl Wray, Jarl Orsala, and Scoutmaster Estrasta: stay here so the four of us can make relocation efforts for the citizens. Jarl Yngraham, please lead the *utelanders* to the inn they'll be staying in for the night and then return here."

"Of course, sire."

The scoutmaster's crestfallen gaze fell on the Wood Álves, who were promptly escorted out of the king's throne room along with Jarl Yngraham. All Cymbelina could think about as she exited the elaborate building was where her group had gone wrong and how they were supposed to deal with the threat those creatures posed now that they had no allies to lean on.

What are we supposed to do now? Is now my time to leave the group and find my own home in the wilderness? Is this where my former kin go back to the Glenrolk camp? The female shook her head, her green eyes closing to trap the tears behind her eyelids. *No, there's got to be another way to solve the situation. We can't back down.*

The brunette kept her contemplations locked within her mind as she and her fellow álves left the city of Gullhum.

Traversing one of the many winding tunnels burrowed within the mountains, the álves approached Jordstand, their disappointed footsteps echoing off the jagged grayish-black rocks that composed the tunnel walls. The passageway bled into a narrow street, which wove between a series of stone homes. Unlike the capital, which had statues and fountains spewing lava, Jarl Yngraham's city was much more austere.

Cymbelina's thoughts wandered as she looked upon a gathering of Dark Álflings, which quickly dispersed once they noticed the brunette's foreign gaze. They hid behind the ruins of a nearby house, the tops of their shaking heads visible amongst the wreckage.

The Half-Sylvanrolk's heart ached as she stared at the frightened children, her gaze drifting forward. She then saw the remains of countless álves, both old and young alike.

These poor people. I can't imagine how many lives have been lost in the torment the Dokkalrolk have continuously suffered recently. This turmoil must come to an end.

Although the wheel in the brunette's head was ceaselessly turning, the silence amongst her peers was stifling and remained so until they were outside of the Iron Heart Inn.

"You know," Jarl Yngraham began, stopping in front of the faded hotel sign to face the Sylvanrolk behind him, "I just might have an idea about how the five of us can change the king's mind."

"Change the king's mind?" Malaveen questioned, her voice laced with curiosity. "Why would you want to do that? Isn't your duty as jarl to follow all of King Ragnar's commands?"

The older álf chuckled. "Yes, that is one of my duties as jarl. However, I'm also tasked with keeping the kingdom safe, and I think the decision the king has arrived at puts the Snøthorn Mountains in jeopardy, which is why I propose a plan to win back his trust."

"And how do you suppose we do that?"

"It's simple, Master Arvel, but it's not safe to talk about it here. Plus, it's been a long day, and you four should take some time to rest. I'll send some of my guards to fetch you tomorrow morning at the seventh horn blow."

"But we're supposed to leave tomorrow," Kayven

212

protested. "I would love to stay and change the king's mind, but not if it puts our group in danger."

"Trust me, it won't take up the entire day. We should be able to convince him before nightfall."

If the jarl's plan gets us back in the king's good graces, we might just be able to deal with the vilek-like creatures once and for all.

"We have a deal," Master Arvel declared, shaking hands with the jarl.

"Excellent. Let's hope the king will come to his senses by then. But for now, I must depart. I will see you four tomorrow morning. Farewell."

"Good night, Jarl Yngraham," the Sylvanrolk said in unison, watching the older man walk up the steep incline back toward the capital.

"Do you really think we have a shot at making this work, Master Arvel?" Kayven asked, his voice tinged with doubt.

"I don't know, Kayven," the teacher said, his eyes lingering on the jarl as he traversed the crest of the slope. "But we must try. Now, let's get checked in and settle down for the night."

Entering the desolate establishment and haggling with the innkeeper, the four álves were directed to a modest side room. The room, akin to a storage closet, was starkly bare, with only two flickering candles, a myriad of nearly empty shelves, and a broom that leaned against the far wall.

Setting up her bedroll and adjusting to her surroundings, Cymbelina attempted to fall asleep.

"Psst, Cymbelina. Are you awake?"

The brunette's bloodshot eyes flew open, eyeing the mat across from hers. Kayven occupied the bedroll, his recumbent frame bathed in a shroud of darkness. The candle hanging above him did little to highlight his striking features, which formed harsh edges in the inky shadows.

"Barely. What can I help you with, Kayven?"

"I wanted to talk about your behavior during today's battle."

The she-álf sighed as the sound of Master Arvel's snoring filled the air. "What's there to talk about? I fought to protect the people around me."

"You and I both know there was more to it than that."

"No, Kayven, there wasn't."

"The more honest you are with yourself, the more likely you are to get to the root of what's bothering you—because it's clear something is."

Cymbelina remained silent, prompting the male to continue.

"If Idal's death is starting to weigh you down, and you need a shoulder to lean on, I'm here for you, Cymbelina. I know all too well the toll a death of a loved one has on an álf."

The she-álf felt herself stiffen. Kayven was right; she hadn't felt like herself these past few days, ever since she heard that voice behind the door in her nightmare. Idal's death certainly wasn't helping her psyche, either. But she didn't know she was making her instability so damn obvious.

Trying to shrug off the male álf's observations, she closed her eyes and snuggled into the blankets.

"I appreciate your concern, Kayven, but please drop it."

"Not unless you tell me what your problem is."

"You wanna know what my 'problem' is?" The brunette loudly hissed, her green eyes opening wide to stare at Kayven's shadowy figure. "My 'problem' is people assuming they know everything about my situation and trying to make me do things I don't want to do."

Malaveen halfheartedly groaned, interrupting the Half-Sylvanrolk's spiel. "Shh. I'm trying to sleep."

The brunette paused, regaining her composure so as to not lash out at the blonde. After taking a deep breath, she continued in a much quieter but harsh tone. "I'm asking you to drop it, yet you still pester me as if there is an issue. Yes, I acted somewhat out of character during the skirmish today, but what do you expect? The four of us are on a suicide mission, for Mother Terralynia's sake." The female feigned a sound of surprise. "Oh, that's right. I have no home to return to now that I'm a Sylvanrolk outcast."

The blonde slammed one of her fists against the floor. "SHHHHH!"

Cymbelina exhaled, her eyes narrowing as she whispered her final thoughts, ignoring her female companion's pleas for silence. "And that's only half of it, Kayven. Don't even get me started on the rest."

The rumbling of distant snoring of the inn inhabitants bled into the room underneath the wooden doorway, adding to Master Arvel's snorting melody. The crackling of the flickering flames above the sleeping mats filled the fusty room with a faint ashy smell. The silence was uncomfortable. Cymbelina shifted on her mat, her mind wandering. She pondered on whether she had been too harsh on her caring ally or if she had been stern enough to cease his endless probing. Either way, it was too late to take back her words; this much she knew.

"I see," the male began slowly after a period of agonizing quietness. "Well, I apologize for worrying, Cymbelina. I'll be here when you're ready to talk about it. Good night."

"Good night, Kayven," the female said, flipping onto her left side to face away from the man next to her. Ignoring the sense of guilt collecting in her core after her outburst, she summoned the strength to murmur a final "good night."

* * *

Wave after wave of ecstasy washed over the ruler of Elderfell as he basked in the news of his army's victory at the Snøthorn Mountains. The announcement of the glorious battle arrived thirty minutes ago, yet Vukasino acted as if the information had been shared with him only moments earlier.

If only Mother could see me now, Vukasino thought, his half-open eyes resting on Tajni as he slumbered upon his perch. *Under my guidance, the Dark Vilek struck a massive blow against the scum inhabiting the mountains of our homeland. She never accomplished such a feat under her leadership.*

The man was stirred out of his reverie as the wooden doors to the throne room opened, issuing a brisk breeze throughout the drafty chambers. Tajni squawked and flapped his shiny midnight wings at the suddenness of the intrusion. Tihana entered the hall through the open doors; a heinous grin spread across her sickly grayish-blue features.

"I just received the best of news, Monarch Vukasino."

The male grunted, marked disinterest permeating his tone. "You're becoming much too informal when entering my throne room, Mistress Tihana."

"I apologize, my lord. May I approach your throne?"

The male sat upright in his stone seat, his hands clutching at the armrests. Tajni fled his perch and landed upon the monarch's shoulder, nesting in the long white locks that draped over half of his body. The bird released an indignant screech.

"You may."

The alchemist quickly but respectfully approached the smug ruler, whose guards watched the kneeling woman with great interest. After the grayish-blue woman had finished genuflecting before him, Vukasino spoke out to her.

"What *amazing* news do you wish to present to me, Mistress Tihana?"

"Do you remember the individual who helped our troops infiltrate the mountains?"

"Yes, go on."

"Well, Kazimiera has made contact with the individual once again. However, this time, the álf has proposed an offer we simply can't refuse."

The leader cocked a thin white eyebrow in response to the woman's wording. The base of his wings twitched at the sound. *First, she approaches my throne, ignoring all established protocols, and now she's equating the power she has as my royal scientist to my authority as monarch. Hmm, something will need to change.*

"'We,' is it?"

"I meant 'you,' my lord."

"Hmm. What sort of offer is the contact proposing?"

"According to Kazimiera, the insider mentioned something about a band of promising young warriors wandering into the Snøthorn Mountains recently. In fact, one of the warriors caught the contact's attention so much that they suggested that if the warrior were captured, she would make a good test subject. The individual has offered to catch her for us."

The ruler frowned. "Test subject? Have we not already passed the point of testing our concoction on people? We've already distributed it to a few of the troops on the front line, so there's no need to conduct further testing."

"But sire, we've only used citizens of Elderfell as lab rats so far. Don't you think we should test how members of other races react to the substance?"

Vukasino scoffed, waving his hand in dismissal. Tajni squawked. "Why would we need to? We're using the serum so our troops can win, not to sell to other civilizations so their armies can prosper."

"That's correct, Your Majesty, but what if we used the serum for other purposes?"

"Such as?" The male replied, vexation lacing his tone.

"Such as abducting some of the locals across Florella, indoctrinating them with our magic, and injecting them with the serum to make them our strong undercover agents across the island?"

The monarch's eyebrows stitched together as he sat back on his throne, looking at the scientist in disbelief. "It's clear you've been thinking about this for some time now, Mistress Tihana. Why are you just now coming to me with this idea?"

The woman's cold, twisted smirk grew wider. "I had to wait for a realistic opportunity to implement the plan. Our contact has offered to kidnap the warriors if we agree to give him a vial of the Elixir of Annihilmon, so—"

"Absolutely not!" Vukasino barked, slamming one of his slate-gray fists down on the throne. "While the álf has been loyal so far, who's to say that the vial we give him ends up in the wrong hands or he uses it and turns on us? No, his deal is unacceptable."

"But Monarch Vukasino, we can kill him after the exchange has been made to ensure the serum never truly gets out of our hands. If we time it right, we can—"

"My decision is final. I will not budge. My goal remains firmly on reclaiming Florella, not continuously spreading mischief throughout the land using underhanded tactics."

The woman was silent for a moment, her short white hair framing her downcast face. After seconds of silence, she nodded her head, her orange eyes meeting the coal-black ones of her ruler.

"Yes…Your Majesty."

"Now that we're on the same page, you may see yourself out, Mistress Tihana. You're sullying the mirth that follows a successful battle."

"Of course, my lord. Have a good night."

The scientist left without uttering another word, her pointed ears acutely aware of the grumbling spilling from between the leader's thin lips. However, through all of his murmuring and jokes he shared with his two royal guards, Vukasino remained blissfully unaware of Tihana's complete indifference to his commands.

Tihana stomped down one of the castle's cold corridors, the purple rug lining the floor scrunching underneath her feet. Passing innumerable paintings of previous rulers of Elderfell, the woman sighed in frustration, shaking her head.

"What a pompous fool," she maliciously whispered under her breath. "I intend to get ahold of those warriors, and I won't let his ignorant demands stop me. Not anymore."

Rounding a corner, the alchemist arrived at the laboratory. Ushering her aide, Jelkaza, to the side, the female entered the room, faking an air of happiness to fool the young fairy.

"Welcome back, Mistress Tihana. Is there anything I can do to help you with your studies this evening?"

The alchemist stood above the vat of the orchid-colored solution that sat off to the side of the fireplace. Her fiery eyes bore into the still surface of the liquid, her grayish-blue fingers toying with the amulet around her neck. The blood-red jewel twinkled in the light of the nearby fire, as did the swirling golden thorns that clung to it.

"Yes, Jelkaza, there is. I need you to have a message delivered to Kazimiera and Bojana."

"What do you want the message to say, Mistress Tihana?"

"Tell Kazimiera that we accept the contact's deal," the alchemist said, her orange eyes drifting to her aide. "Bring those álven warriors to Elderfell Spire."

* * *

"Your time is almost up, *animus hospi*. Soon we shall be together on the material plane."

Cymbelina stood before the dilapidated door again, her body separated from the unknown voice on the other side by a weak slab of wood only a few inches thick. Her heart pounded, her thoughts raced, and the thrill of curiosity rushed through her veins like a stampede of angered buffalo. Unable to suppress the emotions welling within herself, the she-álf threw herself against the barrier. The chains clinked and rattled against the wooden surface, the metallic din falling under the cacophony of Cymbelina's exclamations.

"Who are you?! What are you?! What do you want?!"

The torch beside the door flickered in the wind produced by the woman's erratic movements. Although Cymbelina went to great lengths to stir a genuine reaction out of the being, all she got in return for her efforts was a familiar rush of hot air through the barred opening in the door, followed by a rumbling chuckle.

"I believed that you would be a better host after our last visit with one another. I was clearly mistaken."

"This isn't a visit, and neither was the last time we spoke," the female spat, wrapping her hands around the bars. "I don't even know the person...or thing...that I'm talking to."

The voice hummed darkly. "I suppose you have a point. But I think it's better that way for the time being."

Something snapped inside the Half-Sylvanrolk upon hearing the voice's words. Rapidly tugging against the bars, the woman braced one foot against the door, trying her best to pull the structure open.

"Let...me...in!"

The being chuckled. "In due time."

219

"No," the brunette snarled, continuing her efforts in vain, "I want you to reveal yourself. Now."

Although the being was quiet for a time, the delight it received from hearing the she-álf's predicament was palpable through the wooden apparatus. The air rang with rattling chains as the woman let her attention drift from the bars to the padlocks adorning the door, giving them all a quick tug in her frustration-fueled haze.

Why is this happening to me? The brunette wondered, tears of agitation brimming in her eyes.

Sighing, the woman turned her back to the door, slowly sliding down until her backside collided with the cool stone floor. Her head fell back against the wooden surface.

"I can taste your desperation. Hatred and sorrow burble and spill from the well of your soul. Hmm...yes, our joining won't be long from now."

"Joining?" Cymbelina sobbed, rapping her fists against the door, "What joining? I-I demand to know, creature."

"You will demand nothing of me, *servanus*. What you seek to know will be revealed to you in due time."

Cymbelina gave up on her fruitless banging by pushing away from the door and standing up. Her green eyes turned from the structure inches away to her swollen hands. Staring at her reddened fists aroused a memory of something Master Arvel had previously said.

Master Arvel said that my father experienced horrendous nightmares. Since he was a human, maybe that means I'm susceptible to more frequent nightmares, too, even though I've never really experienced any until recently.

"Ignatius? A human?" The deep voice questioned, its voice cracking in amusement. "Young one, that is...that is..."

The being trailed off before breaking out into a booming song of laughter. The vocalization caused the door to shake for minutes, its guffaw seemingly neverending. Startled by the voice's knowledge, she called out a series of questions, her shrill voice piercing through the racket the entity created.

"How do you know that name? What in the Goddess' name

do you know about my father?!"

"Enough to say with confidence that he wasn't a human!" The being said, before breaking out into another bout of laughter.

The brunette glared through the window and into the inky abyss, her eyes scanning for the beast who taunted her, even though she knew she wouldn't find it.

"I know what I am. You cannot fool me."

The mirthful noises came to a discordant halt, their cheerful echoes dissolving into an unsettling silence. The room was suddenly enveloped in an eerie quiet, lasting only a few brief seconds but enough to make the she-álf instinctively recoil from the door. Her green eyes narrowed in focused scrutiny as she observed the door, its surface emitting a soft, rhythmic thrumming that vibrated faintly beneath her fingertips. The words carved above the door burned brightly, their brilliance etching the ominous phrase deeply into the brunette's memory.

'Te draco a containeo dun te animus somnullis.'

"Your knowledge of the human race is flawed, *animus-hospi*. If you had non-magical human blood flowing through your veins, we would not be having this conversation right now. In fact, my very presence would tear your body asunder." The being chuckled, trying to compose itself after its mirth-filled outburst. "So, let's try this again, Cymbelina. What. Are. You?"

The brunette remained firm in her stance, trying to convince herself that her mind was trying to mess with her through a delusional nightmare. "I'm half-álf and half-human."

"Human!" The unseen creature's thunderous humor-filled baritone cackled, shaking the room around the Half-Sylvanrolk.

The lettering above the door pulsated and hummed unpleasantly, crescendoing into a violent beat that caused the woman to screw her eyes shut and cover her pointed ears from the discordance. Thousands of different voices, all of which varied in pitch and tone, repeated the phrase that was inscribed on the wall. A single, hellish mantra broke through the written

221

sentence, a saying that the being behind the door blithely repeated.

"She still thinks she's half-human! She still thinks she's half-human!"

"Cymbelina, are you awake?"

The brunette opened her eyes at the sound of the patron teacher's voice. His amber eyes shone dimly in the candlelight, as did the forms of Kayven and Malaveen. Sitting up in her bedroll, she looked around, noticing that her companions were packing their things.

"I'm assuming that it's time to leave?"

"You'd be correct," Master Arvel murmured. "Jarl Yngraham's men are waiting outside to escort us to his estate."

"So hurry up," Malaveen chimed in, "we have a king to persuade."

Bait and Switch
2nd of Winter's Breath, 1300 AC

Cymbelina and her fellow Sylvanrolk hastily followed Jarl Yngraham's guards while trying their best to seem inconspicuous. However, the task proved arduous in a kingdom filled with Dokkalrolk, especially since King Ragnar's verdict about the Wood Álves leaving by nightfall had spread like wildfire around the cities.

The glares of nearby villagers followed the outsiders as they passed a series of demolished homes. Some were missing doors, while others were missing roofs, two situations that led the inhabitants to spend their time scouring the streets for materials to repair their domiciles. Their displeased whispers floated in the warm air, Cymbelina's eyes faltering to the ground to avoid the disgusted glances she received from some of the dirt-caked Dokkalrolk.

It seems like we've overstayed our welcome, Cymbelina thought, slowly lifting her gaze to the winding stone path ahead. *Hopefully, whatever plan Jarl Yngraham and Master Arvel concoct to win back the king's trust will help us gain allies amongst the citizens of the Snøthorn Mountains. After all, if the Sylvanrolk cannot acquire the confidence of the Dokkalrolk, defeating those creatures will prove to be nigh impossible.*

"This plan needs to work, or else we'll be in a world of trouble," Cymbelina accidentally muttered aloud.

"I agree," Kayven chimed in, walking beside the she-álf. "A lot is riding on our success today."

Cymbelina flushed in embarrassment, flashes from her

outburst the night before invading her mind. "I'm surprised you even want to talk to me after how I reacted to your questions last night. I'm sorry about that, by the way. I know you were just trying to help, but I wasn't in the right mindset for the sort of conversation you were trying to initiate."

"Please don't apologize," the male interrupted. "You tried telling me you weren't interested in talking about it, yet I pushed anyway. I should be the one apologizing, not you."

Cymbelina smiled at Kayven. "Thanks for understanding."

"We're almost there," one of the guards muttered, his helmeted head turning to face the foreigners as they stood before a humongous flight of stone stairs. "Prepare to address Jarl Yngraham."

The guards quickly ushered the group up the stairs, their boots thudding against stone as they arrived in front of the jarl's estate.

A set of towering bronze doors inlaid with various drawings depicting the island of Florella sat wide open. Through the metallic entryway sat an ornate room with marble flooring resembling that of the *lovhuss* in Gullhum. A long strip of narrow crimson carpet ran vertically down the center of the vestibule, a series of chandeliers casting a golden glow upon its surface. Various statues depicting acts of heroism committed by the Dark Álves lined either wall, which met in a semicircular fashion at the northernmost area of the room. In front of one of the many archways that adorned the northern wall stood Jarl Yngraham, who was harshly addressing an elderly she-álf.

The two bickered away until the footfalls of the outsiders and those of the jarl's guards echoed throughout the elaborate chambers. The leader of Jordstand coughed as the Sylvanrolk proceeded toward him and the female, a smile quickly replacing his scowl. However, the facial expression of the woman standing next to him did not morph so swiftly.

"Welcome to my home, *utelanders*. Quendol, Hjaldar, you may be dismissed." Once the guards departed, the male continued. "I don't believe you four have had the chance to meet my lovely wife, Helda."

The four Wood Álves bowed as Master Arvel replied, "We have not. It's an honor to meet you, Lady Helda."

The frail, gray-haired woman was silent, her frightened eyes similar in color to her hair. Her thin hands clasped together as she forcibly smiled, her fear and discomfort palpable. "It's a pleasure to meet the four of you as well. However," the woman continued, her eyes drifting to her husband, "I have things that must be attended to this morning. Perhaps I'll see you four after the meal."

"The meal?" Master Arvel questioned, his gaze shifting to Yngraham as Helda departed. "While we appreciate the gesture, Jarl Yngraham, isn't regaining the king's favor our utmost priority? After all, my companions and I are expected to depart the Snøthorn Mountains by day's end."

"Of course, getting on the king's good side is imperative, but my servants spent all morning preparing a meal for you four. It would be a grave insult to ignore their hard work," the jarl spoke with a glint of irritation in his blue eyes. "So please, follow me to the dining hall. We'll discuss our plan there."

Although I appreciate the sentiment, I'm nowhere near in the right state of mind to consume a feast, the brunette thought, following Master Arvel and the others into the dining room. *There's too much work to be done.*

No matter how abnormal the situation appeared to be to the brunette, any notions of hesitation fell to the wayside once her green eyes feasted upon the delectable spread set out by the jarl's staff.

A myriad of silver platters was placed neatly across the satin tablecloth that covered the stone table next to a grand fireplace. The silver tableware glittered in the glow of the nearby fire, highlighting the delicious foods on display. In the center of the table sat a plate full of venison, with multiple servings of honey-smothered carrots and brightly colored berries in bowls on either side of the meat. A pitcher of water and a steaming teapot sat on either end of the table, next to two throne-like seats.

Cymbelina's heart soared as she sat at one of the two

benches flush to the long sides of the table, her two younger Sylvanrolk companions sitting beside her. Master Arvel and Jarl Yngraham occupied the grand chairs on the shorter ends.

"Wow, Jarl Yngraham, this all looks delicious. Thank you for your hospitality."

The three younger Wood Álves nodded in agreement with the teacher.

"It is my pleasure. Now, please, have some tea."

The outsiders did as instructed and passed around the hot teapot, filling each ornate teacup with the warm reddish-orange liquid. As the jarl poured water for himself, the servants doled out food to the Wood Álves, who didn't realize how hungry they were until they took the first bite of their meal. Cymbelina found it painful to stick to decorum as she indulged in the feast, elated to consume something other than random mushrooms and fruit.

The álves ate in silence until half of the food was devoured; when Master Arvel broached the topic the Sylvanrolk were desperate to discuss.

"So, Jarl Yngraham," the patron guide asked, stabbing his fork into a juicy slab of meat, "what plan have you formulated for us to regain the king's trust?"

"There's a group of trolls located in a patch of woods outside of one of the entrances to the mountains. I believe dispatching those vile beasts is the key to regaining King Ragnar's trust."

"Trolls?!" The blonde choked on a berry, breaking out into a string of coughs before regaining her composure. "We could barely kill three of those things when we first arrived at the mountains with Estrasta and her scouts; what leads you to believe the four of us can take down multiple trolls ourselves?"

"Well," Jarl Yngraham said, placing his knife and fork down on the table, "you wouldn't be alone. I would accompany the four of you to the woods. Also, I have an assembly of my guards waiting outside the mountains to assist us with the trolls."

The group of Wood Álves looked at each other, exchanging looks varying from trepidation to doubt. The older Dokkalrolk chuckled, an underlying sense of annoyance lingering in his tone.

"This is truly the only plan I could think of that would allow you four to regain some semblance of the king's confidence. Whether or not you decide to execute the plan is up to you."

Cymbelina blotted either corner of her mouth with her handkerchief before placing it on her dirty plate. *I don't like this. But we can't afford to leave the kingdom empty-handed. It's essential that we get on King Ragnar's good side. Álfkind depends on it.*

"You have a point," Master Arvel spoke, stirring the brunette from her inner musings. "We appreciate your plan, and we'll gladly accept any help you're willing to provide when it comes time to deal with the trolls."

"Very well," Yngraham smiled, his laugh lines creasing. "Let us finish our meal, and then we'll be on our way."

After the four adventurers had cleaned their plates of every scrap of food presented to them, the older Dokkalrolk did as he promised. Leading the anxious outsiders out of the estate through a secret tunnel, the álves traveled onward until they reached a cavernous hall. Mineralized columns stretched from the ceiling to the floor, a pool of gurgling lava bathing the area in a scalding glow. An armored guard sat in front of one of the three passageways that led out of the chamber, his shiny golden armor clinking together as he approached Jarl Yngraham and the Sylvanrolk.

"Jarl Yngraham, what a pleasant surprise. What're you doing traversing the outer tunnels with the *utelanders*? Are you showing them a way out of the mountains?"

"Of course, Ser Calmar," the leader lied with ease. "It wouldn't be right for me to send these fine visitors out of our kingdom without giving them tips on how to get out of it easily."

"An excellent idea. Shall I accompany you?"

"That won't be necessary. In fact…isn't it almost time for you to change patrol shifts with Ser Ulfric?"

"Indeed it is."

"Then why don't you take the rest of the day off, Ser Calmar? Your wife is probably trying her best to restore the house to its former glory. Go home and help her. Your brother-in-arms will take your place shortly."

"But Jarl Yngraham, what if those creatures sneak in through the caves while I'm gone? We're still unsure how they were able to get into the cities. What if it was through this group of passageways?"

"Don't argue with me, Ser Calmar. Take the gift I've bestowed upon you with grace and depart."

The young Dark Álf looked between the leader of Jordstand and the outsiders with uncertainty before nodding. "As you command. I'll see you later, Jarl Yngraham."

"Farewell, Ser Calmar."

The soldier stomped off with his spear in hand, never looking back.

"If you don't mind me asking, Jarl Yngraham, why did you turn him away? He could've helped us kill the trolls."

"The fewer people that know about our plans, the better. After all, it wouldn't look good if someone found out I left the Snøthorn Mountains during these trying times. Now come along; the guards outside are waiting."

Delving into one of the twisting passageways, the álves marched forward, leaving the warmth of the lava pool behind. The cave walls seemed to close in on the travelers as they continued onward, causing them to fall into a single-file line. The flickering flames of the torches lining the walls danced as chilly winds swept through the earthen hall, prompting Cymbelina to pull her golden hood up. The continuous flow of air forced the conversation between Yngraham and Arvel to increase in volume, which Cymbelina could audibly hear through the fabric covering her ears.

"So, when did you find out about the trolls?" Master Arvel

asked, his voice filled with curiosity and concern.

"Not until recently. A scouting party I had sent for a daily tour of the mountainside discovered them. Seven álves were sent out, but only two returned to tell the tale."

"Have you ever alerted the king to their presence?"

"Of course. But with the constant invasions from those magical creatures, King Ragnar has more important things to worry about than a few monstrous brutes squatting outside our cities. Besides, the beasts typically keep to themselves unless they spot you in their territory."

"If the king cares so little about the trolls, why are we trying to eliminate them? There has to be another task we can deal with that proves to be more important to him," Kayven interjected.

"There's a common saying amongst my people," the male paused, the knocking of his cane echoing throughout the cave." "'The only good troll is a dead one.' Helping to get rid of trolls will bring a smile to King Ragnar's face, I'm sure of it."

Master Arvel and Jarl Yngraham continued to blather on as the other three Wood Álves followed closely behind. Cymbelina stood on her toes, her gaze flickering between her chatting companions and the tunnel ahead. She kept her eyes peeled for an opening as the strong winds blowing through the cave assured her that one must be nearby.

A sense of unease slowly bubbled in her gut as her search for the exit continued, but she couldn't summon the words required to describe how the situation made her feel.

Something about this doesn't feel right. But then again...what if everything is completely fine, and I'm overreacting? What if my unease is just a byproduct of my recent nightmares and yesterday's battle? Cymbelina sighed, closing her eyes and shaking her head. *No, I can't say anything. We can't afford to lose this opportunity to regain King Ragnar's trust.*

"Is something the matter?" Malaveen asked from behind the brunette. Although the fabric covering Cymbelina's ears slightly muffled the blonde's voice, she still detected an uncharacteristic softness in her tone.

"I'm alright, Malaveen. Thanks?" The Half-Sylvanrolk answered, turning around to face her blonde companion. She eyed the female in a worried manner before inquiring, "Are you ok?"

"Me? Pfft, yeah, I'm fine. This place just gives me the heebie-jeebies. I just wanted to see if I was alone in the sentiment."

"Oh. Well, yeah, this place is kind of eerie, but I'm trying not to think about it."

"Yeah, yeah," Malaveen responded, shaking her head in agreement and looking away. "Thanks for saving me yesterday."

Cymbelina smiled as she turned forward, not responding to the blonde. It was rare to hear Malaveen say thank you, and she didn't want to ruin the moment by saying anything snide.

"What was that?" Kayven inquired playfully, a smile evident in his voice as he intruded on the conversation between the two women.

"None of your business, Wolfy."

"Oh, so we're going back to nicknames, eh? If you say so, Blondie."

"I can see the light from the exit ahead, everyone," the jarl spoke out. "Keep your eyes peeled for any trolls that might be lingering nearby."

The wintry breeze increased tenfold as the álves exited the passageway, the frosty air chilling the tips of their noses. Thick snow flurries swept the tundra as the blinding sunlight of the rising sun penetrated through the rippling, sheer blanket of clouds the flakes created. Cymeblina blinked rapidly; her days spent in the mountains had clearly taken a toll on her ability to withstand the sun's rays.

If I'm struggling to withstand the light of day, I can't imagine how Jarl Yngraham must be feeling.

"Do you need to pause momentarily to adjust to the sunlight, Jarl Yngraham? My companions and I have most likely been outside more recently than you, so I'm sure your eyes are suffering."

"That won't be necessary, Master Arvel, but I appreciate it. In fact, the sooner we get this over with, the sooner we'll be able to return to the mountains, and that will do me much more good than any momentary rest could."

"Where are the guards you said would be waiting for us outside the mountains?" Malaveen asked, looking around. "There doesn't appear to be any signs of life nearby."

"They probably moved in the direction of Snowy Hollow since that's where this particular clan of trolls dwell. Now hurry along, everyone."

The group of álves slowly trudged through the thick snow, some of which clung to their boots as they followed the jarl out of Tundrana and into Snowy Hollow. Cymbelina's eyes darted from side to side, straining to pierce through the blizzard's whirling veil as she examined her surroundings. From what she could tell, no trolls were lurking nearby, yet that did nothing to dissuade the sense of malaise that had been consuming the she-álf since she had eaten at Yngraham's estate. She wasn't alone in feeling fatigued, as her fellow Sylvanrolk seemed to falter in step as they journeyed further into the trees.

I hope the guards aren't too far from here because I don't know what's happening to us. Are the four of us allergic to something that the Dokkalrolk are accustomed to eating or drinking?

"How deep into these dense woods do these trolls dwell?!" The teacher called out, his voice a mere whisper in the roaring winds. "I thought you said they were settled outside one of the entrances to the mountains, Jarl Yngraham!"

"Fret not, Master Arvel. We're almost there!"

Although the howling wind caused Cymbelina's ears to ring, she could still hear the hushed grunts of Kayven, who was trying to mask his discomfort from the rest of the group. With each step he took, the male winced, his right hand coming up to clutch his abdomen. Noticing his distress, the brunette hurried to the male's side and called out to the rest of the group to stop where they were. Malaveen and Arvel were quick to join her.

231

"Are you alright?" Cymbelina asked the slumping male.

"Tch—I'll be fine. I'm just feeling a bit tired…and sick. But I'll be ok. We need to get those trolls, after all."

The patron guide shook his head, his hands clutching the younger male's shoulders. "No, you need to rest here. I'll tell Jarl Yngraham we must momentarily stop and regather our bearings."

"No! We can't afford to stop. We must deal with the trolls swiftly so that we can...can," Kayven trailed off before descending into a coughing fit.

"The lad is right," Jarl Yngraham agreed, standing beside the hacking male. "Time is of the essence. So come, he can stand aside for the battle: I'll ensure my guards keep a close eye on him."

A harsh wind swept through the gathering of trees, their needles sprinkling snow down upon the hooded heads of the álves. The boughs of the trees creaked and groaned, but Cymbelina thought nothing of it; she was too busy attending to Kayven and trying her best to ignore the fatigue clouding her brain.

"What sense does that make?!" Malaveen argued as she crouched beside her fellow Sylvanrolk, her legs shaking with weariness. "He's staying here."

A group of armored warriors emerged from the dense wall of trees, their golden armor scintillating in the sunlight that breached the canopy of conifers. Elation rose in the brunette's core as they approached the group and stood beside the jarl of Jordstand.

Jarl Yngraham's guards! Maybe they'll be able to help us out.

Before Cymbelina could request anything from the guards, the aged Dokkalrolk uncharacteristically sighed, causing her green eyes to drift from the soldiers to the older male.

Using his thumb and forefinger to rub the space between his brows, the leader said, "I really didn't want to do this here."

A wave of uncertainty washed over the Half-Sylvanrolk, whose slowly began to shake as she looked up at the older man. "W-what do you mean, Jarl Yngraham?"

Instead of responding, the male Dark Álf turned to face the guards resting beside him, gesturing toward the outsiders and whistling. The warriors nodded in agreement, approaching the Wood Álves and forming a circle around them. As they did that, another set of hazy figures emerged between the trees, two of which were operating a cart.

"Jarl Yngraham," Master Arvel spoke cautiously, his voice weak. "What's happening?"

"What's happening is what I like to call 'a change of plans.' Or 'bait-and-switch,' if you will. You see, you four were supposed to follow me deeper into the woods, allowing the paralysis potion I slipped into the tea plenty of time to settle in before receiving the news that the trolls I told you four about are fictional. In actuality, no group of trolls has been spotted in this neck of the woods. The real threat is them."

The jarl motioned to the armor-clad troops standing around the weakened Sylvanrolk, who bore a look of confusion on their countenances.

"The Dokkalrolk soldiers? But why?"

The jarl chuckled, shaking his head. "Oh, foolish Malaveen, they're not Dark Álves. Ladies, please, reveal yourselves."

Demented trills reverberated from the women dressed in gold, all of whom took off their helmets to display faces colored in various shades of gray infused with either blue, yellow, pink, or green. Their skin faintly glittered in the sunlight. Their mouths twisted into malicious grins, revealing rows of sharpened teeth.

"T-the vilek creatures," Master Arvel muttered, sinking to the snowy ground in shock and lethargy.

"Not 'vilek creatures,' you *mamlazan*," one of the women spat, her grayish-pink frame swaggering up to the downed male and yanking on his umber hair. "We're Dark Vilek, and it's about time you álves got the name right."

"Let go of him!" Cymbelina shouted, her voice raw with desperation as she lunged toward the woman gripping the patron guide's tresses. Her resolve quickly faltered as she stumbled, her legs collapsing beneath her. She fell to her knees, the impact shooting jolts of pain through her weakened body. The elixir's effects began to take a toll as her limbs grew stiff as if they were encased in lead. An icy chill spread through her veins, leaving her body trembling uncontrollably. Cymbelina's vision blurred, her breath coming out in shallow, ragged gasps.

Throwing the teacher to the side, the fairy advanced toward Cymbelina, grabbing her in the same fashion she had held Arvel. Her piercing, blue-green eyes bore into the brunette's, a look of utter disgust etched into her harsh features.

"Brown hair…green eyes…light brown skin. Oh, Jarl Yngraham," the woman began, turning her bald head toward the leader, her wolf fang earring moving from side to side. "Please don't tell me this was the special warrior you had me to tell Monarch Vukasino about."

Special warrior? The dazed half-álf thought, her eyesight becoming blurrier with each passing second.

"It is, but she's only weak due to the potion I slipped into their drinks. She'll prove to be stronger in your studies."

"She better be, or I'll make sure you regret meeting our kind."

The jarl nodded. "Yes, Knight Bojana. Give your monarch my thanks when you return to Elderfell."

"Of course," the woman replied, letting go of Cymbelina's hair and watching her teeter over. The fairy leered down at the weakened Sylvanrolk in triumph before turning to her fellow Dark Vilek. "Our work here is done. Load the prisoners on the wagon. We'll take them to the central camp to prepare them for Mistress Tihana's testing on Elderfell."

"And what about our promise?" the Jarl spoke, watching some of the vilek carry the paralyzed Kayven to the cart. "Will you give me a vial of the elixir you gave your troops during yesterday's battle so that I might try it for myself?"

An elixir? Maybe that's what caused the fairies to be cloaked in that black mist I noticed during the fight. That must've enhanced their powers!

"Of course, Jarl Ynhgraham. We had a deal, after all."

"And what about Dark Vilek warriors? You intend to send

more disguised guards into the mountains with me for the uprising, correct?"

Uprising? Oh, ancestors, what does Yngraham have planned?

The bald woman scoffed as Cymbelina was hoisted up, two fairies carrying her underneath the armpits and knees.

"Yes, you'll receive assistance from the Dark Vilek once the time comes to attack."

"Excellent."

Cymbelina's torpefied frame was tossed carelessly into the back of the wagon, landing beside Malaveen as her head thumped against the wooden floor. Jarl Yngraham departed the scene accompanied by a few disguised Dark Vilek as the Sylvanrolk were being tied down. Those who did not follow the Dokkalrolk attended to the fairy-drawn cart as it traveled toward the secret Dark Vilek camp.

How could we let this happen? Oh, Mother Terralynia, how could we have been so foolish?

The tumbling of wheels and shaking of the cart caused Cymbelina's ears to rattle, a headache budding in the depths of her bewildered mind. Her body, along with the bodies of her companions, was snugly secured to the floor of the cart, her head facing the rear of the vehicle. From her current position, the she-álf barely discerned that they were being taken down a path that had been magically raised off the snowy ground, no doubt the work of one of the earth-controlling Dark Fairies. The longer the group traversed down the trail, the more Cymbelina's eyes fluttered open and closed as she fought off the side effects of the potion the jarl had given to her.

I should've gone with my gut feeling. But even if I did, who would've believed me? Not Malaveen or Master Arvel: they would've attributed my nervousness to a side effect of my nightmares and overall stress. And Kayven? No, he would've trusted Master Arvel's judgment over my own.

A blanket of snow flurries covered Cymeblina's supine frame as the wagon passed tree after tree, the chill of the snowflakes seeping into the woman's frozen bones. She could guarantee that her teeth would chatter if she wasn't paralyzed.

Must get out, the brunette thought, squeezing her eyes shut and willing her fingers to move in an impossible battle against the strength of the paralysis potion. *I don't care where the movement starts: my little fingers, my little toes; all I know is I need to help us get out of here.*

The she-álf's efforts led to a string of inarticulate noises to pour forth from her icy lips, catching the attention of one of the grayish-green vilek walking beside the cart.

"You hear that, Jara?" She yelled at the grayish-blue fairy walking on the side closest to Kayven. "The 'special warrior' is grunting like a disgruntled piglet."

"Hush, Ilmava, and focus on the task at hand."

"Jara's right. You're the only one of the four of us who can keep the path raised so that Zhikavza and I can keep tugging along the cart, so shut up and keep working."

The green vilek sighed in contempt. "I can multitask, Pajana."

"Well, don't."

After crossing over an extremely thick expanse of snow, Ilmava lowered the ground back to its normal height as the cart continued trailing along. It wasn't until the group penetrated a deep copse that the fairies halted, surprised by a couple of rustling bushes.

"Did you three hear that?"

"Hear what, Pajana?" Questioned the youngest fairy, Ilmava.

"Well, that answers my question. Ilmava, go investigate the bushes. We can't afford to have anyone follow us back to our camp."

"You can't be serious. It's probably just—"

"GO!"

"Ok, ok," Ilmava exhaled, traipsing over to the foliage in question.

Although she remained on the cusp of slumber, Cymbelina forced herself to stay awake, waiting with bated breath as she listened to see who or what could be lurking in the bushes.

Please let it be someone who can help us out of this situation.

The whooshing of the ever-dwindling snowstorm became

increasingly quiet with each passing second, leaving an unnatural stillness along the trail. The she-álf put an extreme amount of effort into listening for something, anything that would give away the presence of a friendly being. Her green eyes looked every which way as she tried to ascertain her surroundings, the thick cloud masking her vision making it nearly impossible to achieve. However, she didn't have to look for long as a shocked bellow arched overhead, as did the woman the sound was emitting from.

The blueish-gray skinned being yelled as the driver named Pajana demanded, "Who's there?! Show yourself!"

A deafening thud landed upon Cymbelina's pointed ears before another shriek of a fairy being thrown echoed throughout the snowy forest. The sound of swords clashing soon followed before another scream was heard.

Please let the source of the action be friendly, the brunette prayed, squeezing her eyelids shut.

Soon, six hooded figures took the places of the Dark Vilek. The silhouettes were muttering something unintelligible, yet the tone of one of the voices sounded oddly familiar. The reason was unbeknownst to Cymbelina until the cloaked person turned around, their slick garnet hair and silver circlet visible in the shadows of his hood.

It's Knight Commander Emerik from Gradgate!

He looked across the still figures of the Wood Álves, his gaze softening in relief. Digging through a pouch attached to his hip, he produced a handful of sparkles. Throwing them over the paralyzed Sylvanrolk, he uttered a single word before Cymbelina fell asleep.

"Spatazi!"

The Court Of Mothers
3rd of Winter's Breath, 1300 AC

The tinkling of bells floated into Cymbelina's pointed ears. As irresistible as fervent whispers from a lover, the bells slowly coaxed the Wood Álf from her deep slumber, her head aching from her enforced rest. Rubbing her right palm over her forehead, Cymbelina's vision steadily returned, allowing her to examine the foreign room she was in.

Floating Orbs of muted shades of purple and blue cast an ethereal glow throughout the room, illuminating the unfamiliar space. They danced upon the viridescent vines clinging to the walls, sparkling against the glistening dew drops that adorned the surface of the vines. The bells, although distant, still rang loud enough for the woman to hear, but her mind was too focused on the scenery to search for the source.

Where am I? The she-álf wondered, hopping off her leafy cot and turning every which way to analyze the room.

The walls were covered in tapestries of roots and vines, some of which intertwined to form various vague symbols. Some resembled hearts, and some resembled eyes; all of them had flowers sprouting from their surfaces. Approaching the wall to the left of the cot, Cymbelina dragged her right forefinger across a row of flower buds. Sounds similar to the chords of a harp emitted from the blooms as they revealed their inner colors to the inquisitive woman, spanning from the deepest cobalt to the brightest vermillion.

She backed away from the flowers, her eyes darting every which way in profound curiosity. *How is such a place possible? It's beautiful! I wish the others were here to see this.*

Only then did memories flood the she-álf's mind, reminding her of the events that led her to this foreign room. Turning around, the brunette saw three other leafy cots sitting beside the one she had slept on. The surfaces of the beds were bedecked in blankets of chrysanthemums and pansies, which had been tossed aside as if someone had gotten off of the cots recently.

They must've been here!

The Half-Sylvanrolk rushed to the archway on the right. A thick curtain of undulating creepers covered the exit, their trunks rolling in a rhythmic flow. Shoving two fingers between the narrow spaces the vines allotted, the brunette tried to pull them apart to no avail, no matter how hard she tugged.

"L-let me out of here!" the she-álf grunted, pulling so hard that she fell back onto the soft, grassy floor. "I need to leave!"

The obstruction blocking the brunette's way shriveled into the floor, revealing a figure shrouded in a silk cloak the color of frost. Cymbelina backed away in wariness, her fingers digging into the soil as she scrambled for purchase. All attempts to retreat were forgotten once the person lowered their hood.

The cloaked individual was Knight Commander Emerik.

"Knight Commander Emerik," the brunette breathily murmured, her heart pounding against her ribcage. "You scared me half to death!"

"I apologize. I heard your cries to be released, so I came immediately."

"I appreciate it," Cymbelina sternly remarked as she stood up. "Now, where are my friends?"

"They're in the other room waiting for you."

"Ok," the she-álf paused, her heart slowly returning to its natural rhythm. "Care to explain why I've been separated from them?"

"It's not like that. As your friends woke up, they were guided out of the room one by one. Once they were where they needed to be, my kin briefed them on the situation."

"Hmm."

The female glanced around the verdurous chambers, her curiosity piqued by the sight of the unfamiliar flora. The hushed harmonies of stringed instruments traveled into Cymbelina's pointed ears as flowers opened and closed. Lightning bugs flitted in the damp air, alighting atop the buds. One landed in the brunette's outstretched palm, the bug's abdomen glowing like an evening star. After examining it for a few moments, the Half-Sylvanrolk shooed it away, her eyes locking onto Emerik's.

"I must confess that I still feel a bit...unsettled that you left me locked away in an unknown location away from my friends. And these strange plants and bugs are doing little to dissuade my worry." The Half-Sylvanrolk paused as another lighting bug flew on her arm, its wings fluttering. "However, now that you've graciously unlocked the door, I'd like to leave and see my allies."

"Of course. I came here to guide you to them, after all. But first…"

The man clapped, causing light green pods on the ceiling to open. Golden, sparkly pollen rained down from within the leaves and landed on Emerik and Cymbelina, their skin absorbing the glittery specks.

"What was that?" The brunette asked, following up on her question with a sneeze.

"It's *spratsina*, also known as calming dust. My fellow villagers and I use it as a sedative."

"I've never heard of it. And considering the situation I've been placed in, I would say I'm acting extraordinarily calm as it is, no?"

"You have, but it's a part of the local protocol, nothing more. Now, please, follow me."

The Wood Álf agreed wordlessly, desperation to see her companions guiding her footsteps out of the verdant chambers as she followed Knight Commander Emerik down the hall.

Like the room the álves had just departed, the hall was like something out of Cymbelina's wildest fantasies. The stone walls were covered in verdant vines, between which hung luminescent bulbs that flickered on and off as the duo passed by them.

I don't recall seeing anything like this during our last visit to Gradgate, Cymbelina thought, continuing to follow the knight down the hall.

A mat composed of flowers emitted melodious tunes with each step the álves made, their footsteps composing a unique symphony until they arrived at a large foyer. The large, rectangular room was filled with rows of stone benches, all adorned with leaves and flowers. Three familiar figures sat hunched over on a seat situated toward the middle of the room, one figure turning toward the hallway from which the duo emerged.

"*Ma brethanna!*" Master Arvel greeted, his voice filled with relief. Rising from his seat, he approached the pair. "I'm so glad you're alright, Cymbelina."

"I am as well," Kayven added, smiling as he quickly joined the others.

"I knew she would be alright. But now that everyone is here, we can get down to business." Malaveen turned her attention to Emerik as she remained on the bench, "How did you and your pals know how to rescue us from the Dark Vilek? And where are we now?"

"I think a little patience is in order, Malaveen."

"I think a little *explanation* is in order, Kayven. Don't get me wrong, Knight Commander Emerik, I'm glad you and your friends saved us, but I don't like how you're still keeping us in the dark about so many things."

"I thought you said they were briefed?"

"Oh, we were, Cymbelina," the blonde answered, "if by 'briefed' you mean we were told to remain calm so as to not wake the other sleeping patients, as this is a healer's sanctum. But with all those magical plants in the other room, I'm not inclined to believe that their healer is a Sylvanrolk outcast like Emerik implied the citizens of Gradgate were."

Malaveen finally stood up from her place, slowly joining the huddle of álves surrounding the knight commander. Her hazel eyes narrowly assessed the leader, a frown forming on her countenance.

"In the end, I don't think Emerik has been as forthcoming about Gradgate as he should've been."

The red-haired male chuckled, clearly unphased by Malaveen's rambling. "Well, Miss Malaveen, you are right about one thing: I haven't been as open with you four as you have been with me."

"Ha! I knew you couldn't be trusted."

"Well, I wouldn't exactly say that."

"And why not?" Kayven sneered, crossing his arms over his chest. "Lying by omission isn't the best tactic for winning someone's trust."

"I understand that, but I assure you I had sound reasons for doing so."

"Such as?"

A female attendant standing beside a nearby vine-covered door spoke out in an unknown language, prompting Emerik to turn his head and nod. After receiving his acknowledgment, the woman left the room.

"I will admit," Master Arvel said, his piercing eyes flicking between the door and Emerik, "speaking in a foreign language doesn't help your case."

"I apologize for the discretion. However, if you follow me, you'll receive all the answers you could possibly seek."

"Oh no," Malaveen argued, "the last time we followed someone, we ended up paralyzed on the back of a cart."

"I have no intention of harming the four of you."

"What about the sparkly dust in the room we stayed in? What if—"

"He said it was to help keep us relaxed, although it doesn't seem to be working," Cymbelina answered, her eyes never faltering from the Gradgate local. His face was stoic and reassuring, his light brown eyes emanating a sense of warmth. "Think about it: if Knight Commander Emerik really planned on hurting us, why wouldn't he have maimed us while we slept?"

"Cymbelina has a valid point," Master Arvel agreed.

The blonde exhaled, slapping a palm over her face. "You can't truly be taking his side right now."

"What choice do we have?" Kayven conceded. "He's willing to supply answers to any questions we have."

"Indeed I am, as are my superiors," Emerik smiled. "Your caution is indeed warranted due to your recent experiences, but if you could trust me a little further, I'm sure you'd be happy with what I have to tell you."

The four Sylvanrolk looked at each other, each individual wearing an expression of anxiousness and intrigue.

"We accept your offer," the patron guide responded, his eyes reflecting his inner trepidation. "Lead on."

The Knight Commander nodded, leading the group toward the door the attendant had been standing near and opening it. With a resounding creak, the construction opened, causing a rush of crisp air to sweep throughout the room, along with the scent of fresh soil and flowers.

What lay before the outsiders' eyes was not the familiar settlement of Gradgate, but a fantastical, botanical haven. Hundreds of different types of flowers lined the mossy stone walkway that twisted and turned throughout a series of buildings. Towers made of stone stood high above the bewildered travelers, their creeper-covered pinnacles scraping against a dense canopy of trees. Luminescent orbs floated on the cool breeze, the chirping of distant songbirds and chattering citizens filling the air. In the center of the settlement sat a tall tree with mushrooms surrounding its roots, a tree reminiscent of the one located in the center of Gradgate.

"Welcome to Nebesati! Or, as your people call it, The Whispering Grove," Emerik shouted, his voice filled with excitement as he introduced the Sylvanrolk to the exotic paradise.

"Where on Sacarnia are we?" The blonde alf excitedly inquired, her eyes darting back and forth. "Are we near Gradgate? Why have you brought us here? What purpose does this place serve for the outcasts?"

Emerik laughed. "You'll know all about it soon, Malaveen. For now, follow me."

The redhead led the outsiders down a mossy stone path, which was paved with magical stones that lit up once the travelers set foot upon them. The area surrounding the settlement was dim: the only light source nearby was the floating orbs and glowing leaves of the tall trees, which came in shades of blue, pink, and purple.

I wonder why Emerik never mentioned anything about this place before, Cymbelina pondered. *Surely he didn't keep it a secret because of its beauty?*

After reaching the end of the path, the group was quickly ushered into a vast stone edifice. Parting the doors, the outsiders were greeted by a sight that was nothing short of amazing. Flower-studded vines cascaded down the tall walls, their blossoms glowing softly in the ambient light. Blue flames danced in the sconces mounted along the sides of the room, casting an otherworldly glow that painted the room in shifting shades of blue. Plant-crafted tables and chairs, intricately woven with creeping ivy and vibrant flora, were scattered across the polished stone floor.

The door closed behind the visitors with a vibrating thud, alerting a nearby álf to their presence. Standing up, the woman approached the arrivals, her billowing white dress trailing behind her. Her jeweled headband, identical to Emerik's, glimmered in the faint glow permeating the room.

"Hello, *Vatez* Emerik. It's lovely to see you again."

"It is lovely to see you too, Milena."

"Are you here to see the Mothers?"

"The who?" Kayven whispered to his Sylvanrolk brethren incredulously.

"Yes, we are. Please tell their excellencies that their guests are ready to speak to them."

The woman nodded, walking toward a long corridor at the opposite end of the room.

"Are the Mothers the superiors you mentioned earlier?"

"Yes, Master Arvel."

"That's an odd name for a group of people in power."

Emerik's eyes momentarily narrowed at Malaveen's comment before promptly correcting himself. He turned to face the blonde. "Do you make a habit of insulting the cultures of others when you're welcomed with open arms within their cities?"

The hazel-eyed twenty-four-year-old paled while her younger male compatriot chuckled. "She does, but she's getting better."

Milena returned moments later, a pleased expression plastered on her delicate features.

"The Mothers are ready to see you if you'd be so kind as to follow me."

The group readily followed the woman toward the hallway from which she had just returned, only to find that the passageway was much more mysterious than ever expected. Instead of a pristine corridor leading toward the Mothers' chambers, Emerik and the Sylvanrolk were met with a chasmic, elongated pit.

"Is this some kind of joke?" Malaveen hissed, her brownish-green eyes assessing the water-filled hole below. "Because now is really not the time for—"

"*Espon!*" Milena chanted, raising her arms in the air and interrupting Malaveen.

From within the pit's watery abyss rose a series of large rocks, which floated in the air as water poured off their slippery surfaces. The levitating slabs formed a straight line above the trench, creating a path for the visitors to traverse.

"You're free to pass," the woman said, bowing before the commander and the outsiders.

"Thank you, Milena," Emerik spoke before his light brown eyes turned toward the others, one of his hands gesturing to the hovering, glistening stones. "Come along, everyone."

One by one, the álves hopped from rock to rock with carefree ease, leaving Cymbelina alone with Milena under the archway leading into the hallway. Sighing, the brunette gazed into the hole.

Not this again. I can't handle another incident like the one on the bridge over Terralynia's Gorge.

Noticing the brunette's palpable unease, Milena whispered, "Don't worry. If you slip, I can use the same magic I used to raise the stones to arrest your fall."

"Ha. Thanks," Cymbelina responded, slightly more uneasy than before.

"Hurry along, Cymbelina!" The garnet-haired male shouted, his voice echoing off the stone passageway walls. He was so far ahead of the brunette that his cloaked figure resembled a speck in the distance. "The Court of Mothers is waiting for us!"

After swallowing the lump that had settled in her throat, the Half-Sylvanrolk followed in the footsteps of her allies, her heart beating a chaotic rhythm in her chest. Whispering hushed prayers under her breath, the brunette leaped from stone to stone until she stood beside her allies on the other side of the rift. Taking a deep breath and recollecting her bearings, Cymbelina followed Emerik and the others down the magical corridor.

Glowing pictographs moved along the stone walls. Some drawings depicted the frothy waves of the Albastra Abyss, the sea that lay on the eastern coast of Florella. Others showed sprouting flowers in various stages of life, their petals moving in the wind. Another featured an álf being embraced by a fairy. Such drawings were scribbled across the entire expanse of the walls, Cymbelina's green eyes following each pictograph until she and her allies arrived at a pair of elegant doors.

"On the other side of this door lies the hearing room for the Court of Mothers. In terms of etiquette, it is custom to—"

The knight commander was in the midst of his speech when the doors began to open. He let out an exasperated sigh, his brows furrowing, before he summarized with a curt, "Don't speak unless you're spoken to."

Entering the octagonal room, the visiting Sylvanrolk were bathed in a dispersive teal glow originating from a blue sphere floating at the pinnacle of the tall space. The delicate light that shone upon the room highlighted trees drawn in white powder, which covered four of the walls composing the eight-walled chamber. Each tree depicted the four seasons known to the inhabitants of Sacarnia. Below the trees sat row upon row of leafy benches, each row progressively sinking deeper into the room, akin to a stadium. At the base of the chamber sat a swirling rainbow pond, by which sat four elegant thrones bedecked in flowers and vines. Veiled figures occupied each seat, the glow from the nearby pool causing their gossamer gowns to glimmer.

"*Dobay dana*, sweet Mothers!" The knight commander exclaimed, his eyes glued to the thrones fifty feet below where he and the outsiders were standing. "May the outsiders and I approach?"

The orb floating twenty feet above the álves flickered twice.

"That's our cue to descend. Hurry along now; we have important matters to discuss."

The Sylvanrolk outsiders followed Knight Commander Emerik down the long staircase. Butterflies and dragonflies danced in the air around them, and the luminescent glow of nearby flowers shone on the álves' boots as they thudded against the stone steps. Working their way around the rainbow pool in the center of the room, the five individuals knelt before the veiled women.

"*Dobay dana*, Emerik Vesnavin," replied the figure sitting on the far right. Although her facial features were undiscernible under the glittering veil, the brunette perceived a pastel pink face underneath the shroud. "I see you have brought the Sylvanrolk travelers to our hearing room today."

"Indeed I have."

"Fine work," spoke another woman from her place on the throne to the far left. "It is nice to finally meet you, Master Arvel, Malaveen, Kayven, and Cymbelina."

I suppose Knight Commander Emerik told them our names.

"He did no such thing," a third woman spoke.

Stunned, the brunette looked up, a confused expression plastered on her face. *Did she just read my mind?*

"All four of us can sense your thoughts, Cymbelina," the final female stated. "But that will be explained momentarily. For now, it is only fair for us to introduce ourselves." The woman paused, lowering the fabric away from her face to reveal a pastel yellow visage with hooded purple eyes and a pair of plump lips. A set of black wings tinged with blue specks slowly flapped behind her back as she stood up. "I am Mother Danica."

"I'm Mother Jasmina," the individual on the far right spoke, revealing her almond-shaped, blue-green eyes and flowing white hair to the outsiders. Her periwinkle wings remained still.

"I'm Mother Vesna," the ruler on the far left announced, sharing her pastel green face and red eyes with the outsiders. Her yellow wings beat rapidly.

"And I'm Nadasha," the last figure announced, joining the others standing up. Her pastel blue skin glimmered in the light of the rainbow pool, as did her orange eyes. Her lilac wings rhythmically fluttered. "And we make up the Court of Mothers."

"And now that we've revealed ourselves," Vesna continued, her red eyes turning toward the knight commander of Gradgate, "you can dispose of your disguise, my son."

Cymbelina blinked rapidly. *Son?!*

"Of course, Mother Vesna," Emerik replied, taking his hand off his heart to slide the silver circlet off his head. As soon as the jeweled accessory left the man's scalp, Emerik's natural form came to light. His pastel green skin, similar to that of Vesna's, glittered in the glow of the rainbow pond, his garnet locks turning a bright shade of white. Once the transformation was complete, he opened his eyes, revealing them to be a deep shade of red.

"So you're not a Sylvanrolk outcast after all," Cymbelina said, still kneeling on the stone floor alongside her companions. "That explains a lot."

"Nobody in Gradgate or Nebesati is," Vesna began, folding her hands in front of herself.

"Why lie about it?" The blonde spat, her voice sharp as her

lips pulled into a tight frown. "Pretending to be something you're not is outrageous."

"I apologize for lying, but we had our reasons," Emerik explained, an apologetic look covering his face.

"Of course we did. In fact, Knight Commander Emerik brought you to the Whispering Grove so we, members of the Court of Mothers, could explain why we had our citizens lie to you in the first place."

"We share a common goal, after all," Nadasha added.

Master Arvel blankly stared at the members of the court. "And what would that be, Your Majesties?"

"We'll be happy to explain that, Master Arvel, but for now," Vesna spoke, snapping her fingers. The flowers composing the floral rug blanketing the stone floor suddenly grew, forming seats for the outsiders to sit on. "Make yourselves comfortable. We'll be here for a while."

* * *

"And from the information Knight Kazimiera and Knight Bojana's scouts gathered, we can conclude that the forces of the Snøthorn Mountains will crumble if you give orders for your troops to attack soon," Knight Morana explained to Monarch Vukasino, rolling up the parchment in her hands.

"A *resounding* victory," Mistress Tihana reinforced, a sly smile creeping across her grayish-blue face.

Vukasino sat at his desk across from the duo, who made up half of his war council. With two of his knights leading covert operations on Florella, the third knight and the alchemist were the only two people the ruler had to consult.

I yearn for victory more than anyone else in this room, but is now truly the time to strike? Although the troops were victorious in the last battle, I am blind in terms of just how victorious they were. How many of the Dokkalrolk were slaughtered? How many of the cities were sacked? What if the element of surprise in the next battle doesn't work like it did in the previous one?

The leader of Elderfell sighed, closing his eyes as he clasped his hands behind his back. "Read the battle report from the last attack on the mountains to me again."

"But sire, the report has already been filed in the vaults. It might take hours for me to retrieve it."

"Just do it, Morana."

"Your Lordship, I truly feel that it's an unnecessary venture—"

"You dare question my whims? JUST DO IT!"

"O-of course, Monarch Vukasino," the knight stammered, her voice trembling. She hastily rose from her seat at the ruler's desk and fled down the hallway. Her hurried footsteps reverberated through the empty corridor, the only sound in the ruler's chambers.

The gray-skinned male stared at the doorway as if in a trance.

Why am I faltering so close to my first major victory? Vukasino pondered, biting his lower lip. *If I stop now, everything Mother said about me will be right, and I cannot allow that.*

With clenched fists, the ruler pushed away from his desk, cursing under his breath. Walking toward the balcony, he gazed out onto the horizon, which was cloaked in the blanket of night. Seabirds cawed their nocturnal songs, the sloshing of the tide against the rocky walls of the isle echoing in the cold breeze.

Tajni flew on the visi-vilek's shoulder. Vukasino began to tremble. *I can't allow Zlatana to be right; I can't allow Zlatana to be right.*

Noticing the male's fragile state, the scientist spoke out, her voice coated in feigned concern. "Your Majesty, are you alright?"

"Yes, Mistress Tihana."

The woman hummed. "May I approach?"

"Why?"

"Because I care about your wellbeing, Your Lordship."

Monarch Vukasino stared at the bird on his shoulder. The rook emitted a pleased chirp as the male pet its silky black feathers, its dark eyes closing in delight. After moments of calming silence, the male acquiesced, nodding in affirmation. The woman got up from her seat, rounded the table, and stood beside the male at the edge of the porch.

"Why do you question your chance of victory, my lord?"

"It is better to be safe than sorry."

"That's true, but with the Elixir of Annihilmon and the hordes of loyal subjects ready and able to do your bidding, why pause? We defeated the heathens once, and we shall do so again. Especially if we can get the Florellan Trolls under our control."

She's right. If my troops were able to put a dent in the Dokkalrolk forces once, surely they will be able to do so again. Especially if they receive assistance from those hideous monsters that call the northern reaches home.

"That's a fair point," the monarch agreed, his coal-black eyes turning towards the woman beside him. "Go on."

"Why, Your Excellency, what more is there to say? You are not only the first visi-vilek to rule Elderfell but the first one to successfully mature past adolescence. If anyone was to lead our people in reclaiming our homeland, it would be you. The overwhelming victory of the most recent battle thoroughly proves this."

"I suppose that's accurate," the male agreed, his ego stroked and his nerves calmed.

"So what do you say, Monarch Vukasino? Shall we make plans for another attack on the mountains?"

A ferocious grin spread across the man's face, his eyes narrowing with hunger as he gazed upon Florella.

"Let the planning begin."

* * *

"So let us run through the situation again, just to ensure I understand your words correctly, Your Majesties," Master Arvel began, his amber eyes resting on the Court of Mothers. "There was a division in the vilek race hundreds of years ago due to the creation of the Magijarolk with our álfrolk ancestors," the patron guide paused, his eyes flickering to

Emerik before resting on the Light Vilek once more. "Out of this division came the Light and Dark Vilek, and you four are the only Light Fairies left alive. The Dark Fairies sailed to an island off the coast of Florella and have remained in isolation until now."

"That is correct," Mother Danica agreed, "and we believe their return has to do with their vengeful vow, which they uttered hundreds of years ago."

"And what would that be?"

"They would return to Florella and claim it as their own."

"But the island wasn't theirs to begin with. Mother Terralynia dedicated this land to our álfrolk ancestors and the vilek."

"It matters little to our fallen sisters. They've always believed the álves were beneath fairies. The fact that they're attacking Sylvanrolk and Dokkalrolk settlements demonstrates this."

"Are you worried Gradgate and Nebesati will be next?" Malaveen inquired, her eyes narrowing. "Is that why you care? Because your descendants, the Magijarolk, might be on the chopping block next due to their álven heritage?"

"That's not it at all, Malaveen. It's because the situation has only recently been brought to our attention."

"What about the pond?" The blonde questioned, pointing at the pool filled to the brim with rainbow water. "The four of you stated that you could see anywhere on the island with that thing."

"The Well of Observation," Mother Vesna corrected, glancing from Malaveen to the pool, "doesn't direct us to any anomalies or battles. We have to direct it to specific locations. So, without knowing where to look, we didn't know about the Dark Vilek attacks until you and your Dokkalrolk kin arrived and told Knight Commander Emerik about what was happening at various álven settlements."

"Why not offer assistance after we told Knight Commander Emerik of our plight?"

"Because we didn't know if we could trust the lot of you,

and we cannot read minds unless we look into the thinker's eyes. For all we knew, you could've been Dark Vilek in disguise. To ascertain whether that was the case, we watched your group as you traveled into the Snøthorn Mountains. Our decision to watch you is the reason my son was able to gather troops and rescue your group."

"Why not send reinforcements once you witnessed the surprise attack in the mountains? Why not—"

"It doesn't matter," Cymbelina interrupted, her patience wearing thin. "The Court is offering assistance now, so let's take them up on their offer."

"Cymbelina's right," Master Arvel agreed. "Anything to end the Dark Vilek threat."

"Thank you for your understanding. We promise to do our best to defeat our misguided sisters."

"In fact," Nadasha said, following up on Jasmina's sentence, "I believe I have a plan."

Returning To The Mountains
6th of Winter's Breath, 1300 AC

The Court of Mothers described the main objective of their plan concisely: to unite the descendants of the álfrolk and stop the incursions of the Dark Vilek across Florella. The ploy, which the women went to great lengths to explain, would unfold as such: first, the Sylvanrolk travelers would split up to perform two major tasks. Once these tasks were completed, phase two would occur, when the united álfrolk would come together to assail the Dark Fairies on their island, Elderfell.

The plan was sound, but the first step made Cymbelina and her companions a bit nervous, so they reluctantly agreed to it upon hearing the court's reasoning behind such a maneuver. The four Wood Álves would split into two groups: Kayven and Malaveen and Master Arvel and Cymbelina. Kayven and Malaveen were instructed to guide a group of earth-controlling Magijarolk toward the Glenrolk clan's camp. Once at the settlement, they would meet with Kinlord Emyr and discuss the gravity of the situation in the hopes he could gather the forces of the other clans, the Forrolk and the Durolk. While those two were playing politics, Cymbelina and Master Arvel were instructed to stay behind and help prepare the soldiers of Nebesati and Gradgate. Once assembled, the two Wood Álves would accompany the troops to the Snøthorn Mountains, expose the traitorous Yngraham, and gain Dokkalrolk support. If both teams were successful, then phase two of the court's plan could be initiated.

The Mother's precise manner of speaking, along with the

subsequent planning, initially gave Cymbelina a glimmer of hope that the Dark Vilek threat would soon be over. But now, three days after the travelers' first meeting with the Light Fairies, the brunette was not so sure. Even after days of helping the Magijarolk prepare, there was a sense of unease in the air and, coupled with the fact that Kayven and Malaveen were no longer by her and Master Arvel's side, Cymbelina found her mind riddled with anxious thoughts.

What if we're too late? What if Malaveen and Kayven arrived at the Glenrolk camp just to find it torn to bits, along with the bodies of our brethren? What about my family? Are they still alive? Oh, dear Goddess, I hope they still live.

Finished with the last project she was assigned to work on, the brunette returned to the local inn for the night. As she entered the threshold of the establishment's entrance, she was greeted by a melody composed of guitars and flutes, the patrons noisily singing in a foreign language. Their voices were filled with hope and longing for a better tomorrow.

It wasn't long before a familiar voice pierced through the tune, the brunette's head turning toward the source.

"There you are, Cymbelina!" Master Arvel exclaimed. He was seated beside a hearth, smoke wafting from the fire into the flue. The orange glow of the flames bathed the male in warm light as he motioned the she-álf over. "Come over here for a moment!"

Cymbelina was immobile, debating on how she should respond to her former teacher. The duo had barely exchanged words since their argument with Estrasta in the alley of Krigdor, where Cymbelina had denounced the behavior of the older álves and forfeited her patron lessons. Although the brunette was no longer upset with the umber-haired male, she still had little to say to him.

Deciding that a conversation might quell the worries gnawing at her mind, the brunette took the male up on his request, approaching his table and sitting across from him.

"Hello, Master Arvel. What did you want to speak to me about?"

"Nothing in particular. I just figured a quick conversation might be a decent distraction from tomorrow's journey. How did your preparations go today?"

"They went as well as could be expected, I suppose."

"That's good to hear."

The inn's tavern erupted into boisterous applause as the song ended, the customers cheering the bards on. The next tune was marked by the sweet sound of dulcet harps, causing the crowd to calm down and fervently whisper to their neighbors instead of sing. Cymbelina tried her best to tune out the locals, focusing instead on the man in front of her. The patron guide did the same as his former pupil, his soft amber eyes resting on her tense frame.

"Are you nervous about tomorrow?"

"Of course I am, Master Arvel. My main concern is that we're too late. And what, then? What if—"

"You're beginning to sound like Malaveen," the older man chuckled, interrupting the brunette's anxious utterances. "You have ample reason to be concerned, Cymbelina, but the Court of Mothers is watching our brethren now. If there was something to be concerned about, we would already know about it."

The Half-Sylvanrolk playfully groaned, shaking her hickory locks. "You have a point, but please don't compare me to her."

Arvel chuckled, a smile gracing his features. "Alright, alright."

The two sat in silence, both álves looking at opposite corners of the room. The brunette stared at a group of female Magijarolk, all wearing flower crowns and billowing dresses. They danced in a slower circle in front of the musicians, their giggles filling the warm air of the establishment.

As she watched the carefree dancers, the Half-Sylvanrolk couldn't help but envy their freedom. *I wish I could be that carefree right now*, she thought, her green eyes flicking back to the older Sylvanrolk. A joyful grin was plastered on his pale features as he watched the Elemental Álves dance, intensifying the longing Cymbelina felt in her heart. She desperately searched her mind for something to say, but her thoughts were as nonexistent as her words. Fortunately, Master Arvel broke the silence with his next question.

Placing his palms on the smooth table's surface, which was embossed with the image of a grand tree, Master Arvel stood up, his eyes returning to his former pupil. "I feel like I need to turn in for the night. Care to join me for a conversation along the way?"

"Sure, I was just thinking of doing the same. I have a terrible headache."

Following the man up a winding flight of stone steps, Cymbelina and Arvel traveled down a long corridor. The duo passed rows of doors, all of which had vines that rippled and occasionally glowed as the álves passed by.

"Since we haven't talked about it in a few days, I'm curious: are you still experiencing those nightmares? You've been fairly quiet about them recently."

The woman stiffened, stunned by the male's inquiry. Stopping in front of her door, she faced the teacher, her eyes studying the guide's facial expression. "I had one a few days ago, but that's it."

"Has anything changed? Have you been able to decipher what your dreams might mean?"

"I'd rather not talk about it."

"It might ease some of your stress and provide a better night's sleep before tomorrow."

The woman sighed, clasping the shiny silver doorknob to her room's door and twisting it. "Listen, Master Arvel, I appreciate what you're trying to do, but you're no longer my patron guide. I've also learned that discussing the matter of my nightmares just creates intrusive questions and concerns rather than helping to alleviate them. So please, I'd rather not discuss it."

The male smiled, although the concern in his eyes pierced the content façade he tried to construct. "As you wish, Cymbelina. Just remember, my door is always open for you should you change your mind. Good night."

"Good night, Master Arvel," the woman responded, promptly entering her room and closing the door behind her. Leaning her exhausted body against the vine-strewn surface, the she-álf sunk to the floor, stress-fueled tears threatening to spill from her eyes as images of those who had lost their lives flashed through her mind.

When will this all be over.

Cymbelina and Master Arvel woke up early the following day, hitting the trails of the Glimmering Wilds alongside Emerik and a multitude of his Magijarolk kin. Instead of fumbling about through the ever-shifting foliage like the brunette and the patron guide did before, the knight commander demonstrated a way to use the glow stones throughout the forest. Although it was interesting to watch, the she-álf and her former mentor emphasized that such knowledge would have helped them on their last journey to the Snøthorn Mountains.

Their time in the magical forest was brief due to the new trick demonstrated by Emerik, allowing the group to pass through Snowy Hollow and into Tundrana reasonably quickly. With each step the álves took on the snow-covered land, the sun steadily rose in the cold winter sky, its warm rays filtering through the travelers' misty breaths. Chat was kept to a minimum to avoid detection from unwanted adversaries, with the only dialogue exchanged being of a crucial nature. When hushed whispers weren't being exchanged, the only sound dispersed through the wintry landscape was that of the whooshing breeze. The lack of discussion left a void in the atmosphere, which the brunette filled with racing thoughts as she and her allies steadily approached the mountains.

I wonder how Estrasta and her kin are doing. Have they discovered Yngraham's treachery yet? Or did the traitorous bastard start an attack on the Dark Álf cities before they could discern the truth?

The Half-Sylvanrolk's gaze traveled from the ground beneath her feet to the mountain range miles away. Gray clouds swirled around the snow-capped peaks, large hawks dancing in the frosty air. The sight ignited a sense of doom in Cymbelina's core.

The brunette swallowed the lump in her throat. *Are any of our Dokkalrolk allies still alive?*

Passing a cluster of trees, the álves stopped as Knight Commander Emerik motioned to the frozen grove.

"We'll cut through the patch of trees to our left," the leader directed, his voice a whisper compared to the blustery breeze. "It will allow us to get a better look at the main entrance from a safe distance."

Trudging through thick clumps of snow, the group followed the green-skinned Magijarolk commander. With her eyes wandering to and fro and scanning each tree she passed by, Cymbelina followed Emerik until he stopped midway into the forest, turning his attention to the mountains to the north. Instead of observing an abandoned entryway, the travelers spotted a coterie of Dark Vilek, whose presence blocked the entrance into the mountains.

"Why am I not surprised," one of the Magijarolk warriors mumbled.

"Now, how are we supposed to get into the Dokkalrolk kingdom?" another Elemental Álf grumbled.

"Now, now, everyone, don't get sullen on me," Emerik commented, a determined smile plastered on his face. "We didn't come all this way for nothing. Besides, I'm sure this is nothing compared to what we'll find within the mountains."

"You can say that again," the brunette murmured, more to herself than anyone else. *I wish I remembered where the passage Yngraham led us through was. That entrance might be less guarded.*

"What do you suppose we do, Knight Commander Emerik?" Master Arvel inquired, glancing at the leader of the Magijarolk. "The fact that Dark Fairies are so brazenly patrolling the perimeter of the mountains implies that they have more forces inside."

"You're probably right. But I have an idea as to how we can get into the mountains. Notice how the wind is steadily starting to pick up? Well, we can use that to our advantage. Andrzej, Usenia, Saskia, and Bela: come here for a moment."

Four pastel-yellow-skinned Magijarolk, two males and two females, moved swiftly through the crowd toward the commanding officer.

"Yes, Knight Commander Emerik?" The one known as Saskia inquired.

"I summoned the four of you because your wind abilities will be useful momentarily. The way I see it, we can fake a snowstorm in an effort to get close to the group of vilek up ahead. Once they're taken out, we can go into the mountains and deliver any assistance the citizens might need."

"Do you think that will work?" Cymbelina questioned. "Don't the Dark Fairies have wind abilities as well? What if they see through our plan? And how will our other warriors be able to find them in the storm?"

"You can identify a vilek's powers by the color of their skin. If a fairy has blue skin, they can control water; pink-skinned fairies wield fire; green fairies can manipulate the earth; and, finally, fairies with yellow skin can control the wind. It's the same for us Magijarolk, as we descend from the Light Vilek." The male paused, motioning toward the patrol about a mile away. "Did you notice that none of the vilek over there have yellow skin? Because of that, none of them will be able to sense that the winds are being stirred by magic. And as long as I only send out wind-controlling álves, we should be okay."

Done with his explanation, the green-skinned Elemental Álf turned toward his summoned warriors. "Ready to give the plan a shot?"

The four Magijarolk nodded in affirmation, turning their backs toward the group and facing the opposing forces in the distance. Moving their hands in a circular motion, the yellow álves slowly channeled their powers toward the snowy field before them as the wind pouring through the valley became stronger. Cymbelina's eyes were glued to the patrols ahead until the blizzard masked their presence.

As the snowstorm raged in front of them, Emerik called out

to five other yellow Elemental Álves, who were tasked with taking out the Dark Vilek blocking the cave. Stalking through the bushes and invading the flurry of snowflakes, the rogues left, leaving Cymbelina on edge as she crossed her fingers, hoping that the plan would work.

Sensing her unease, the knight commander gently placed a reassuring hand on her shoulder. The brunette gazed up at the tall man, noticing that his eyes were firmly fixed on his Magijarolk kin. "Have faith, Cymbelina. Our warriors will emerge victorious."

"Having faith is easier said than done lately, but I'm trying."

The male smiled warmly. "Well, that's all that counts."

Waiting with bated breath, the brunette watched ahead, tuning her pointed ears to any alarming sounds that might emit from her newfound allies. The minutes she spent waiting for the Elemental Álves to return felt like hours as she worried at her lower lip, blood blossoming from the chapped skin. Before she could voice her concerns to Master Arvel, the silhouettes of crouched figures emerged from the magical gale, their outfits stained with snow and blue blood. They dragged the bodies of the Dark Fairies into the bushes, rejoining their allies with a sense of pride on their yellow faces.

"The women at the entrance have been dispatched," one of the álves remarked, crossing her arms over her chest.

"Excellent," Emerik commented, "now, on to phase two."

Ceasing their wind spells, Andrzej, Usenia, Bela, and Saskia joined the rest of the group as they swiftly ran into the mountains, ready to face any other threats that might come their way.

Charging through the abandoned passageway, the outsiders approached the imposing stone walls of Krigdor. The iron gate to the city was raised, and a mass of scattered armored Dokkalrolk corpses lay underneath it. The once vibrant armor of the deceased warriors was now dull and stained, no longer gleaming in the faint light of the nearby torches. Death lingered in the air, causing the álves to scrunch their noses as they hopped over the fallen citizens of the mountains and moved onward.

The city that Cymbelina and Master Arvel had explored just a week ago was now a scene of utter chaos. The once-familiar cobblestone path was now a river of red and blue lifeforce. The stalls that had once lined the plaza were in ruins, their contents scattered across the street. Among the debris were the bodies of Dark Álves and Dark Vilek, the former outnumbering the latter. The warm air was filled with the cries of the few remaining Dokkalrolk warriors, two of which seemed to stem from sources nearby. It wasn't long after Cymbelina heard these wails that she spotted Scoutmaster Estrasta and Jarl Orsala.

"Look! Estrasta and Orsala are up ahead!"

"We must assist them!" The knight commander shouted. "Hurry!"

The outsiders dashed towards the cacophony of clashing metal, their footsteps trailing through the puddles of blood lining the streets. Adding their weapons to the metallic orchestra, Cymbelina and her companions joined the fray of resistance fighters battling a group of ten vilek.

The clinging and clanging from the repetitive strikes and swings formed a discordant song on the putrid air, along with the war cries echoing from every corner of the sacked city. With each foe she defeated, more sweat beaded on Cymbelina's brow, her heart pounding against her ribcage.

"There's so many of them," Cymbelina huffed, prying one of her daggers out of a deceased fairy's heart, the black aura around its lifeless frame fading.

"Of course," Master Arvel exhaled, sweeping a nearby vilek off her feet and tearing into her stomach with a Dokkalrolk spear. Soaked in cobalt blood, the steel point of the weapon still sparkled as the man flicked the gore off his new weapon. "What else could we have expected? These fairies always seem to be a step ahead of us."

"Well, not anymore. This conflict needs to end today," the brunette said, her eyes landing on an opponent across the battlefield. Readying her daggers, she charged forth, battling another one of the invaders until they fell to the ground in defeat.

Members of the resistance and invading forces fell left and right, their bodies adding to the mound of corpses already piling up on the roads. Even as the Dark Fairies fell, more of them seemed to take their place, creating a neverending cycle of combat.

This is even worse than the last battle, Cymbelina realized, her eyes scanning the ferocious crowd for an oncoming attack. *I dread seeing what the other cities look like at the moment.*

As soon as the thoughts left her mind, a Dokkalrolk warrior to her right let out a death cry as they crumpled to the ground in anguish, leaving the vilek champion to lock eyes with Cymbelina. Crimson stained the fairy's bluish-gray skin, her chest heaving with palpable hunger. The Dark Vilek smirked and licked her lips, causing waves of anger to flood the Wood Álf's mind.

"Kill her, animus hospi," a familiar rumbling voice internally commanded. *"Decorate the ground with the fiend's innards."*

Unusually unperturbed by the strange voice, the she-álf lunged at her opponent, who was taken aback by Cymbelina's boldness. Clicking the pommels of her blades together, the brunette lifted the weapon over her head, swinging downward. The fairy instantly saw through her challenger's maneuver, raising her blood-slicken sword to block the attack. Gritting her teeth, the Dark Vilek pushed the Sylvanrolk backward, creating enough distance between herself and Cymbelina to jump back.

"You're a fierce one," the woman quipped as the half-álf tried to stab her in the gut and missed. "You'll still die, but at least you'll die fighting harder than the rest."

"Don't be so sure about that," the she-álf grunted, launching a barrage of swings in the fairy's direction. The brunette swung and missed multiple times, each time the side of her blade getting closer and closer to the swift fairy as she continuously twirled out of reach. The Sylvanrolk's strenuous and unorganized attacks left her vulnerable, which the blue fairy recognized and took advantage of.

"I am, actually," the vilek proclaimed, summoning a ball of water in her palm and transforming it into a thin stream, aiming the liquid at the álf's green eyes.

"*Dihaal!*" the brunette exclaimed, stumbling and hitting the ground with a thud, her eyes slamming shut. Opening them in the nick of time, the downed woman dodged a stroke of the fairy's sword, causing it to clang against the stony path.

The brunette's chest heaved as she rolled to the side and stood, nimbly dodging another of her opponent's attacks. *I forgot that blue-skinned vilek have water abilities. I'll have to be more careful next time.*

"I can sense your anxiousness," the woman taunted, her voice dripping with malicious delight. She lunged forward, attempting to strike Cymbelina once more. "It seeps through your skin in droplets of sweat and shines in your weary eyes."

"I...I think you're mistaking me for yourself."

The woman chortled, her eyes narrowing. "Am I?"

The Half-Sylvanrolk grunted, swinging her blades toward her opponent. She ended up missing, which resulted in a demented trill from the fairy across from her.

With a self-satisfied leer, the fairy bared her sharp, yellow teeth, her eyes trained on the she-álf. "After all, I don't make a habit of confusing dogs with wolves. Do you?"

"Don't let her talk to you that way, Cymbelina. Show her your fury."

The brunette ground her teeth, her jaw aching from the strain. Her lungs burned as she inhaled the ashy air of the battlefield. Her ears rang, the screams of dying Dokkalrolk multiplying as more warriors fell. Distress bubbled in her gut, pushing her to keep fighting.

Lunging toward the fairy, Cymbelina's double-bladed weapon met the blue woman's long sword, steel against silver. The alf's blood-soaked fingers formed an unsteady grip around the pommels, and she knew she couldn't hold on much longer. Kicking the vilek backward, Cymbelina accidentally dropped her weapon. Blinded by another stream of water before she could retrieve it, the Half-Sylvanrolk ended up on the ground, the cool touch of metal caressing her sweat-drenched chin.

"Don't move, or else your next breath will be your last."

The Wood Álf did as she was commanded, her breath shaky as her vision slowly returned. A carnivorous grin was plastered on the blue fairy's face, her orange, snake-like eyes staring intensely into the brunette's own.

"Where will you go now? What will you do?" The woman facetiously asked, the tip of her blade biting into Cymbelina's chin. Blood trickled from the wound, dripping silently down her neck and armor. "Will you die like a coward? Or will you try to fight back?"

The brunette would've panicked if she hadn't seen a familiar face stalking up on the distracted woman, preparing to aim a crossbow bolt at her.

"Nothing to say? Fine, die like a coward then!" the fairy screamed, raising her blade into the air.

Before her stroke could connect, the blue vilek gasped, her hand uncurling around the sword's hilt. A bolt now breached the walls of her stomach, bits of flesh and sparkly blue tissue caught along the sides of the projectile. Ungodly noises trickled out of the being's mouth as she toppled over, her face twisted into a contorted grimace.

"E-Estrasta," the brunette stuttered, her mind reeling from her brush with death. "You saved me."

"You can thank me later, kid," Scoutmaster Estrasta sighed, ripping the bolt from the fairy's abdomen with a stomach-twisting squelch. "Now get up. We have more vermin to exterminate."

Cymbelina jumped to her feet, joining her companions as they followed Orsala's and Estrasta's group of fighters onward. The combined forces carved their way through the city, leaving both allies and enemies behind them. The sounds of distant screams slowly increased with each passing second, as did the familiar voice inside the brunette's head.

"*Kill them all*," the voice purred demonically. "*Spill their blood so we might meet again.*"

265

With each fairy the she-álf executed, the easier the subsequent slaying seemed. Cymbelina was on a brutal rampage, which both excited and frightened the confused brunette. No matter how many notions about her feelings spawned in her mind, the young woman realized now was not the time to ruminate on them.

Stay focused on the traitor, the Half-Sylvanrolk thought, trying her best to ignore the sonorous voice inside her head. *Stay focused on bringing down that bastard, Yngraham.*

After battling through the various hordes of vilek clogging Krigdor, the exhausted fighters arrived at the edge of the destroyed city, which led to three tunnels branching into opposite directions. Screams poured forth from within the passageways, promising a world of horrors on the other side.

"What's our next course of action?" Cymbelina breathily inquired, tearing her eyes away from the dark, earthen corridors to face the álves beside her.

"We split up," the scoutmaster replied. "That's all we can do at this point. But before we proceed with any plans, I would like to know: Jarl Orsala," Estrasta paused, glancing at the jarl of Krigdor. "Do you plan to stay here?"

"Of course."

"Well then," the scoutmaster continued, "Knight Commander Emerik will lead a group to Sølvcast, and Master Arvel will lead a group to Jordstand. While the two of you do that, I'll lead the remaining troops to the Gullhum."

"Our goal?!" One of the Dark Álves noisily probed, dried vilek blood transforming his gray face into a dark shade of blue.

"To secure Jarl Wray and find any clues as to where that treacherous rat Yngraham has gone. Once your groups have done that and killed as many vilek as possible, we shall regroup in the capital. My kin and I should be at King Ragnar's palace by the time you arrive."

"But how will we know where to go?" the Magijarolk leader asked. "We've never been to—"

"Don't worry about it. I'll ensure some of my scouts join

both your group and Master Arvel's group, and, in return, some of your kin will accompany me to the castle. Sound good?"

"As good as it'll get," Emerik sighed. "I'm ready to leave."

"As am I," Master Arvel added.

The fighters went their separate ways, with Cymbelina following Master Arvel and a few Dark Álf scouts into the tunnel leading to Jordstand. The resounding thuds of their hurried footsteps ricocheted off the cavern walls, blending with the distant screams from the city ahead. None of the warriors uttered a word as they dashed forward, the wind they created causing the flames of the torches on the walls to flicker. As the álves neared the end of the passageway, a thought struck the she-álf, who hurriedly glanced at her former patron guide to share it.

"Our first step should be to search Jarl Yngraham's estate. Not only could we find the jarl there, but we might also find some clues as to why he's working with the Dark Fairies."

"I doubt Yngraham's there," the older álf huffed, jogging alongside the brunette, "but you might be right about finding clues. We'll head there first."

Halting at the threshold of the cave, Master Arvel shared the plan with his fellow companions before splitting the warriors into two groups: one for each trail leading throughout the plundered city. Taking the rightmost path, Cymbelina followed the teacher and a few Dokkalrolk down the stony road. Pools of blood, both wet and dry, covered the trail ahead, she and her group members steadily adding to it as they slew the dwindling fairies blocking their way.

Passing a series of destroyed homes, Cymbelina and her party members finally reached the base of the steps leading to the traitor's manor. Unceremoniously ascending the flight of stairs, the álves pushed the bronze doors in with ten hearty shoves, revealing a seemingly untouched estate.

"Of course, his abode remains untouched," one of the Dokkalrolk scouts muttered, his voice dripping with bitter resentment.

267

"Naturally," Master Arvel sighed disgustedly. "Let's split up and search every room of the manor. There's got to be a clue as to where Yngraham planned on going after the attack."

A ferocious sense of anger gnawed at the brunette's insides as she separated from her fellow álves to scour the abandoned house.

Perfidious mongrel, the brunette seethed, stomping down the leftmost hallway and entering the first door on the right. *When we catch Yngraham, I'm going to make him pay.*

Turning the room over, Cymbelina found nothing. Continuing her dash from room to room, she tossed tables and chairs to the side, toppling bookshelves as she pleased. The Half-Sylvanrolk had little luck finding anything of import until she investigated the tenth room down the hall.

Swinging the door open with a forceful shove, the brunette was taken aback by the sight before her. Lying prone on the floor in a dried crimson stain was Jarl Yngraham's wife, Helda, whose blood had seeped into the white fur of the bear rug underneath her. A look of utter betrayal painted her dead face, her eye makeup smeared by forgotten tears.

This is not something I was expecting. Did Yngraham kill her? And if so, why?

Proceeding to give the drawers in this room the same treatment she had in the chambers, Cymbelina investigated the dead maiden's quarters. Flinging open cabinet after cabinet, the she-álf came up with nothing until she reached the deceased woman's vanity. Concealed within the elaborate desk was a crumpled piece of parchment stuffed into the corner of one of the drawers. Unfurling the paper, Cymbelina scanned the scratchy letters, which composed a series of rushed sentences.

'Yngraham must be stopped. He wants to take the throne, and he is using outsiders as his means of doing so. If someone has found this letter, that means I'm already dead. But please, whoever finds this, kill my husband.'

The sound of approaching footsteps distracted the woman

from the damning note in her grasp. Looking toward the doorway, she saw Master Arvel, a look of relief washing over his face as he stared back at Cymbelina.

"There you are. I'm glad I found you. We must head to Gullhum and rejoin the others as soon as possible."

"I couldn't agree more," the she-álf said, handing over the parchment to the patron guide. "We have a king to save."

Speaking The Words
7th of Winter's Breath, 1300 AC

The turmoil the she-álf experienced in Krigdor and Jordstand compared little to the hellish landscape before her now. The city of Gullhum—the crowning jewel of the Dokkalrolk kingdom—was in shambles. Unlike the other cities, the ground was besmirched with the remains of not only álves and vilek but also trolls, signaling that the fairy's primary goal was overtaking the capital. Cymbelina wasn't sure how the Dark Vilek were able to accomplish sneaking trolls into the empire, but one thing was for sure: the fairies were trying to completely wipe the mountain dwellers out. The ferocity of the vilek on the battlefield was tenfold what it had been during their last attack, the corpses of the resistance fighters tripling those of the fallen fairies, even as the remaining warriors continued to brawl amongst the ruins of Gullhum.

No matter how much assistance we outlanders can supply in the future, this day will forever mar the history books of the Dokkalrolk people, the brunette thought, swiftly backstabbing a fairy blocking her path. *And if we're unsuccessful today, all álves living on Florella will experience the same fate.*

"We must keep moving!" Master Arvel shouted, impaling a fairy on his spear before tossing the limp body aside. "We must reach the others and quickly!"

Cymbelina and her fellow group members did as the patron guide commanded, killing all the fairies in their path along the way.

The heat from the river of lava surrounding the city

permeated the air, making it hard for the brunette to breathe as she traversed into the depths of the capital. The Dark Vilek attacked in endless waves, giving the Half-Sylvanrolk little time to recover between each skirmish. Her muscles cried out in pain with each subsequent stride through the bloody plaza, weary tears threatening to spill from her eyes as her chest rapidly heaved between each stroke of her double-bladed weapon.

I don't know how much more of this I can take.

"The blood of countless warriors flows through your veins," the rumbling voice spoke, its internal vocalization causing the brunette's mind to buzz. *"You can take it. Press on."*

The she-álf and her allies wove around toppled stores and homes as they continued toward King Ragnar's castle, assisting the locals in any way possible. Their journey eventually led them to rejoin Knight Commander Emerik and his kin as they finished off a group of vilek blocking the way forward.

"Have you seen any sign of Scoutmaster Estrasta and the other álves?" Master Arvel questioned the Magijarolk leader, who flicked the blue blood of a deceased fairy off his shiny saber.

"Scoutmaster Estrasta said she would meet us at the king's palace. I'm sure she's already there."

"You're right," the older male Sylvanrolk panted, clanging his staff against the cobblestone underfoot as he wiped away a band of sweat adorning his forehead. "Let us make our way there."

Running across several bridges leading toward the palace, the group repeatedly passed over the moat surrounding the capital. The bodies of deceased álves and fairies floated atop the molten liquid, slowly sinking as the liquid fried their corpses. The pungent scent of burnt flesh grew more potent as the companions traversed further into the city's depths. The king's abode acted as a beacon amongst the ever-growing piles of rubble, pushing the brunette's tired frame forward.

Rushing up the familiar stone steps, the she-álf and her allies spotted Scoutmaster Estrasta, who, along with her fellow group members, hoisted a large stone slab into the air, ramming it against the fortified golden palace doors. Hearing the hurried footsteps of the outlanders sprint up the staircase, the Dark Álf turned, her pearl-colored locks plastered to her sweat-drenched face. Motioning to a scout nearby to take her place, the scoutmaster approached the arrivals, her kin charging at the entrance once more.

"Finally!" Estrasta yelled, her voice barely audible over the commotion from the alleys below. Turning her fatigued, arctic-blue eyes toward the green Magijarolk, she asked, "Did you locate Jarl Wray in Sølvcast and assist him?"

"Yes. Sølvcast itself wasn't in the best condition, but I helped Jarl Wray secure his estate and the streets surrounding it."

The álves slammed against the doors, a reverberating bang cracking through the malodorous air.

"And you, Master Arvel? What were you able to do for Jordstand? What kind of state is it in?"

"Worse than I'd care to admit. However, my companions and I were able to help to the best of our abilities. In fact, Cymbelina found something that might be of interest to you."

"Really? Hand it here."

Ready to be rid of the incriminating note, the brunette frantically passed it to the scoutmaster, who hurriedly unfurled the parchment and scanned its contents. Hoarsely cursing, the woman coughed and scowled, clenching her fists and yelling at the multitude of álves standing behind Cymbelina and her two male allies.

"Help us get into the castle! We need to check on King Ragnar as soon as possible. And if you spot Yngraham," the woman paused, spitting, "do not kill him. He must be apprehended to face justice."

"Justice? In a time like this?!" Cymbelina uncharacteristically shrieked as the other warriors ran past her to assist the other álves with the stone pillar. Heaving it back and pushing it forward, the slab banged against the closed doors as Cymbelina remained motionless. The feeling of insatiable bloodlust crept up her spine, sinking into the base of her neck as she spoke, "Yngraham should be punished for what he's done to your people: what he's attempted to do to my kin and me!"

"And he will be. However, he is a Dark Álf, so it is up to his fellow Dokkalrolk to decide what will become of him. You, nor any other outsider, should strip our people of that right."

"But what if you fail?" The she-álf countered, her eyes still glued on Estrasta as the pillar was smashed against the doors, which were close to giving way. "What if Yngraham escapes?"

"Now is not the time to debate this!" The patron guide yelled, helping the others to plow towards the sealed threshold again. "We need to apprehend the man before we decide what we're going to do with him!"

Although the teacher's words rang true, a sickening hunger gnawed at the brunette's stomach. Flashes of frightening eyes flooded her mind, with pupils like those of a snake and scleras akin to the brightest flame. The eyes formed a haze over her vision, forming an impenetrable fog over the looming castle feet away.

"Speak the words, servanus," the voice murmured, the hellish eyes narrowing. *"So that we may join forces."*

Another bang pierced the blisteringly hot air.

What words? The brunette mentally asked the smooth, baritone voice.

With one final rush at the doors, the structures parted ways, allowing a stream of álves to pour into the entry hall of the palace.

Red and blue blood mixed to form dark purple splats against the ornate marble flooring, the bodies of locals and outsiders creating a mortal rug across the throne room. Across from where Cymbelina and her allies stood sat Jarl Yngraham, who was haughtily perched upon King Ragnar's golden seat. A bloodstained crown sat atop the jarl's cranium, the head of the king resting against his dirtied boots. Queen Norsla screamed in grief as she was hauled down one of the castle's many disorderly corridors, her wails bouncing off the walls. An array of Dark Fairies stood beside the jarl, their evil eyes and spears fixed on the álves.

"So nice of you to join us. I was wondering when the royal entertainment would arrive."

The Scoutmaster trained her icy eyes on the renegade, her mouth curling in disgust. "*Fordaastar*! Get off that throne this instant and submit to punishment."

"Is that any way to speak to your new king, Scoutmaster?"

"You are not the king of the Dokkalrolk, and you never will be!" The female spat, swinging her rapier in the disgraced male's direction. "This is your final warning, Jarl Yngraham. Tell your allies to lay down their arms before it's too late."

The older male chuckled, his head falling forward before gazing at the álves again. His fierce blue eyes scanned the crowd until they landed on Cymbelina, the last álf on the far right. Flashing his pearly canines, he chuckled nonchalantly.

"I guess we're just going to have to solve this debate through battle. Ladies?"

The warriors from Elderfell lept toward the crowd of álves, some of whom fell prey to the surprise attack while others did not. The sudden commencement of battle stirred a fray in the grand entryway of the palace, the sound of clashing swords ringing in the air. A river of lifeforce bathed the flooring, adding to the dried blood already drenching the marble tiling. The fight raged on, enrapturing all of its combatants except for one. Cymbelina, the sole fighter not utterly engrossed in the skirmish, saw the jarl adjusting his robes before sneaking down the same hallway Queen Norsla was hauled down.

I can't let him escape and hurt the queen.

"Charge after him, then!" The deep voice shouted, his tone rattling Cymbelina's brain. *"Strike him down before he can get flee the palace!"*

Not pondering the consequences of her following actions, the she-álf ran around the mass of fighters. Avoiding the swinging swords and bouncing bolts, the brunette trailed the deserter down the corridor, her eyes locked on the male. Pain shot up and down her legs as she sprinted onward, the repetitious exclamations from Master Arvel falling on her deaf, pointed ears.

"Cymbelina, stop! Don't charge ahead! We need to stick together!"

"Don't listen to him, servanus. You and I both know Jarl Yngraham needs to be stopped." The voice paused as the Half-Sylvanrolk jumped over a fallen painting, taking a sharp left down the hallway.

The jarl glanced over his shoulder, a wicked grin spread across his countenance as he took another turn.

"Speak the words, Cymbelina. Speak them now."

The clashing of steel against silver reverberated through the neverending hall, the sharp, metallic clangs resonating off the ornate walls. Cymbelina's green eyes brimmed with unshed tears, the flickering light of nearby torches shining in her glassy eyes. The ache in her limbs intensified as she continued to run forward, her breath coming out in ragged, short pants.

What phrase am I supposed to be saying?!

"The one from your visions. The words above the door."

Cymbelina's body twisted left and right as she followed the man through the maze of corridors, which he seemed to know like the back of his hand. Heat pooled in the brunette's cheeks, sweat beading on her brow.

"He's going to get away if you don't hurry up!"

I know, dammit, I know!

Her sprint ended with a sharp turn to the right, leading Cymbelina into a massive, dimly lit room. Through the faint candlelight permeating the chamber, the she-álf discerned the shapes of Jarl Yngraham and Queen Norsla. The former had a jade dagger held up to the latter's throat, the blade glinting in the weak glow of the nearby candles.

"Take another step forward, and the bitch is dead."

Glistening tears streamed down the queen's frost-toned skin, her face scrunched up in despair. Her hands firmly grasped the jarl's right arm as it held her close to his chest. The man's left arm shook as it hovered the dagger near Norsla's throat, a maniacal look consuming his once-friendly features.

"Let her go," Cymbelina hoarsely pleaded, trying her best to hide the quiver in her voice. "She plays no role in this quarrel."

"Of course she does: she's the queen, after all. If I'm to be king, something must be done about her. I can't have any little brats that aren't my own running amok."

Cymbelina paused, her eyes drifting towards the queen. An entreating glimmer glossed over her gray eyes as she mouthed, "Please, help me. Help my baby."

"Why don't you let her leave the mountains instead? She'll have no power in the wilds."

"Leave her alive so her bastard child can someday seek vengeance for the death of their father? I think not. Now, put your blades down and get on your hands and knees."

There's got to be some way I can help. I can't just sit here and watch the queen die.

"Fight. Don't you dare back down. Say the words."

The brunette searched her brain for the phrase from her patron lessons and her dreams, the foreign words seemingly on the tip of her tongue. They flashed in blurry, fleeting images across her anxious mind, always slightly out of reach.

Why can't you just tell me the words to say?!

"The power to vocalize the words must come from within you, animus hospi. I am forbidden from speaking them."

"I SAID GET ON YOUR KNEES!"

"Cymbelina!" Master Arvel screeched, reaching the threshold of the darkened room with a leap, "to your left!"

A gleam of an unsheathed blade flashed in the corner of the brunette's vision, her breath rushing inward at the suddenness of the maneuver. Before she could lift her weapon in response, Cymbelina was thrown forward and to the ground by the weight of the patron guide's body. A raspy groan pierced the air as the brunette spun around, emitting a shocked gasp as she gazed upon Master Arvel.

A short, silver sword was buried to the hilt in the male Sylvanrolk's abdomen, his spear submerged in his attacker's breast. Both bodies sunk to the tile floor, Master Arvel falling to his knees and then onto his back.

With eyes blown wide, Cymbelina wailed, scrambling to

kneel by the teacher's side in a fit of desperation.

"No, no, no, no, no, no," the female lowly chanted, her palms sliding in the crimson now pooling around her former mentor's silhouette. The male looked at the brunette weakly, his pale hands twitching around the weapon sheathed in his stomach.

"M-Master Arvel?! Master Arvel, stay with me," the she-álf whimpered, her eyes flicking from his face to his wound.

She felt dizzy, waves of nausea bathing the walls of her stomach. Quick breaths left her dry lips, all color fading from her face. The distant words flashed across her vision again, the text slightly more legible than before.

Master Arvel's amber eyes fluttered open and closed as he slowly turned his head toward the brunette, softening as he gazed upon her frantic movements. Tears dripped down the female's dirtied, light brown cheeks, and her body trembled.

"H-hold on, Master Arvel, give me a second to—"

"There's no use," her mentor mumbled before coughing up blood. "The wound is fatal."

"Don't-don't say that," the female sobbed. "Every wound can be healed with the right medicine. T-That's what you told me as a kid, remember?"

The teacher chuckled before hacking up more gore.

The dishonored jarl ordered the remaining Dark Vilek to join the battle in the entryway to the palace, leaving Cymbelina, the patron guide, Jarl Yngraham, and the queen alone in the darkened chambers.

"Pr-promise me something, Cymbelina."

"I won't have to promise anything, Master Arvel; you'll make it out of here alive."

"No, I won't," the man wheezed. "Now, promise me you'll never stop fighting, even when situations seem dire."

The brunette looked over at the older Dokkalrolk. He stared right back at her, a grin spread across his wrinkled face. The queen continued to cry.

The words pulsed over her vision once more, the fiery text burning.

"I…I promise," the female whispered, hopelessness evident in her tone of voice as she gazed back at her former teacher. His skin was paler than usual, his frame nearly void of life.

"Good. I'm… I'm proud of you, Cymbelina." The male paused, coughing, mustering the last of his strength to whisper, *"Day'll sas du dan fairn."*

"No-no," the brunette whimpered, gently shaking the teacher's shoulders. "Master Arvel, please, hold on. Just—"

"HA! He's gone, girl," Jarl Yngraham guffawed, "there's no point in crying over a useless corpse. Now turn around and face me."

Her brain throbbed, a distant humming sound ringing in her ears. Her body began to quake, memories flooding her mind, spanning from her childhood up to the past few days. Images of those who belittled her and those who cared about her flashed in quick succession, her mind threatening to break. The sentence from Cymbelina's patron lessons appeared above them all, forming a blazing phrase.

'Te draco a containeo dun te animus somnullis.'

"Awaken, Cymbelina," the deep voice urged. *"Say the words, so we become one."*

"Face me now! Or I shall kill you where you kneel."

"No," the Half-Sylvranrolk replied, her voice dripping with malice. Her hickory waves shrouded her face, concealing her tear-filled eyes from the jarl. With a slight quiver, the brunette muttered, *"te draco a containeo dun te animus somnullis."*

"Excuse me?" The jarl sneered. "What did you say, you cretinous—"

A fiery silhouette cloaked the she-alf's crouched, shaking frame. Parting the curtain of locks hiding her face, the enraged woman gazed upward. Cymbelina's once green eyes had been replaced with a pair of draconic ones, the color of which mirrored that of the brightest inferno. Her dry lips formed a wolf-like snarl, her canines gleaming in the dim glow of the room.

Stunned by the scene unfolding before him, Yngraham's hold on Queen Norsla loosened, giving the woman the leverage she needed to bite his hand, shimmy free, and dash toward the door.

Grunting, the traitor ignored the fleeing queen. His focus was locked on the deranged Sylvanrolk as he rummaged through one of the pouches on his belt. Fishing out a syringe, the male jammed it into his forearm; the orchid-colored liquid within the barrel then rushed through his veins.

Cymbelina slowly rose from the blood-stained floor, her eyes never faltering from the Dark Álf before her. Her chest rapidly rose and fell.

"If you know what's best for you," Yngraham muttered, wincing as he pulled the syringe out of his arm, "you would remain on your knees."

"And let you get away with all the atrocities you're responsible for? I think not," the brunette replied, her voice emanating at an unusually deep pitch. It was clear the words spilling from her dry lips were not entirely her own.

The Sylvanrolk's muscles screamed as she reached for her discarded weapon, a blood-soaked hand curling around the grip. Something inside of Cymbelina pushed her to rebel against the throbbing aches that spread throughout her body, something that tripled her hunger for the man in front of her to die.

"You're going to die here, Jarl Yngraham. Say your final prayers while you can."

All sense of unease evaporated from the Dokkalrolk's body as his face twisted into an abnormal leer. He tilted his head back and forth, his neck cracking as he rolled his shoulders. Using one of his hands to steady the jade dagger, he unsheathed the scintillating sword clinging to his hip. "Would you like to test that theory?"

The possessed she-álf let out an ear-piercing roar, lunging forward and vaulting over the desk across from her. The male pirouetted in a flash, avoiding the fearsome female's attacks, turning his stance to face his opponent again. A billowing black aura slowly formed around his body, his eyes adopting the color of the darkest shadows.

That's the quickest I've ever seen a Dark Álf move, the brunette thought. *And that glow is similar to the one some of the Dark Vilek possess during battle. Is it due to the substance he injected himself with? Could the fairies be using that to enhance their battle prowess?*

The jarl laughed. "Is that all you have for me? A leap over a worn desk? You're more pathetic than I surmised."

Gritting her teeth, Cymbelina tried to attack the man again. A metallic clang rang out in the air as their blades met. With a hearty grunt, Yngraham used his right leg to kick the she-álf backward.

"You fight tenaciously, I'll give you that," the man praised, dodging another of the she-álf's blows before attempting to return one of his own. "But not enough to avoid your demise."

"We'll see about that," the woman snarled, dodging from side to side to avoid the agile Dokkalrolk.

The jarl's dagger formed a dark green blur as he swung it to and fro, startling the brunette with his speed. Distracted by the shorter blade, the she-álf fell victim to the jarl's other sword. With one perfectly timed swing, the longer blade cut through the orange-yellow glow surrounding Cymbelina's frame, the weapon's edge biting into her skin.

Hissing, the Half-Sylvanrolk glanced at the wound.

What should've been a gaping gash was only a tiny scratch as a faint trickle of crimson trailed down the woman's toned arm.

Yngraham cocked an eyebrow in confusion as his dry lips formed a frown. "What in the—"

The jarl's momentary confusion allowed Cymbelina to return the strike, hitting the male with her double-bladed weapon in the same area he had attacked her.

He howled as his dagger-wielding arm went limp, blood pouring from his laceration. Dropping the blade to the ground, the Dark Álf threw his other arm forward, barely missing the brunette's stomach. Jumping away from the attack, the woman fell onto the surface of a desk, causing the entire table to tumble backward. Cymbelina's weapon clattered to the ground, the wind whooshing out of her lungs as her back hit the hard floor.

The woman inhaled, recollecting her bearings as she looked at Jarl Yngraham, who was sprinting towards her. When he was inches away from her downed form, she kicked him back, rolled to the side, and grabbed her double-ended weapon, slicing it upward and missing. His attempted attack missed the brunette as well.

"I don't know what sort of tricks you have up your sleeve," the male panted, his face turning pink, "but you won't be able to win this fight."

"I wouldn't be so sure of that," Cymbelina growled, preparing herself for her next move.

The two álves fought one another, and neither one was able to get any substantial hits on the other. Yngraham's strikes did little harm to the brunette, and Cymbelina could barely land a blow on the Dokkalrolk due to his enhanced speed. Furniture and decorations were tossed left and right as the duo resorted to other tactics, their luck in battle remaining the same as before.

"Give up," Yngraham wheezed, his face a deep scarlet in the faint candlelight. "The Dokkalrolk kingdom has fallen, and your clans are next."

"Perhaps you should take a look in the mirror, Yngraham," she retorted sharply. "If anyone needs to stop what they're doing, it's you—you're as red as a tomato."

With an irritated grunt, the male rushed toward the woman, his movements more staggered than before.

The concoction is wearing off," the deep voice within the brunette's mind observed. *"Now is your chance to kill the swine. End his reign of terror on this island. Spill his blood!"*

A surge of rage-induced confidence flooded Cymbelina's body, her movements guided by the bravado in the voice's words. Grappling the older álf, the Sylvanrolk forced Yngraham to the floor. Her body thrummed with power as she raised her weapon above her head, the blades coated in sanguine and cobalt. Her serpentine eyes penetrated those of the wiggling man underneath her.

"This is for all your kin you senselessly sent to their deaths!"

Before the Half-Sylvanrolk could use her weapon to end the man's life, a coterie of shadows in the corner of her eye distracted her, along with Scoutmaster Estrasta's voice.

"Cymbelina, no! Leave Yngraham be!"

The familiar face and voice minutely quelled the rage boiling inside Cymbelina's heart, giving her enough restraint to hear her companion out.

"Why should I leave him alive, Estrasta? Have you seen what he and his allies have done here today? The state they've left your homeland in?"

The shadows, which turned out to be a collection of guards, spread out to surround Cymbelina and Yngraham, their spears pointed towards the quarreling álves. Cymbelina's weapon-bound hands remained above her head, ready to swing downwards at the slightest move from Yngraham, whose wiggling was weakening by the second.

"Don't listen to her," the voice within the brunette coaxed. *"The traitorous scum murdered Master Arvel and had zero qualms with targeting the Sylvanrolk homeland next. Kill him where he lays!"*

Before Cymeblina could decide her next course of action, a violent convulsion from the jarl made the brunette turn her attention from Estrasta to the man beneath her. White foam bubbled at the corners of the male álf's mouth, his body heaving beneath her. Crawling off of him, Cymbelina's fiery aura slowly dissolved as her eyes blew wide in terror at the terrifying sight of the heaving Dokkalrolk.

His body rose and fell off the floor, the froth leaking from his mouth tinged with blood. Horrific gurgling accompanied the unsightly spasms, the veins beneath his dark gray skin bulging. The jarl didn't stop his jerking until his black eyes rolled back in his skull, his mouth agape as the white liquid stopped pouring out.

The jarl's death left most of the álves in the room wordlessly stunned except for Scoutmaster Estrasta. The white-haired woman's face showed a potent mixture of anger and confusion toward Cymbelina and the deceased Yngraham, her lips turning downwards into a tight frown.

"Fan out, men. Sweep the city for any lingering threats, and do not stop until you hear the bells toll. And Cymbelina," the scoutmaster growled, her eyes locked on the disheveled Sylvanrolk, "you're coming with me."

* * *

The tumultuous sea crashed against the pillars supporting the loading dock off the northeastern coast of Elderfell. The braisers lining the rocky coastline bathed the gray sand in a fiery glow under the noir, star-tinged sky, the beating ocean waves sending thunderous cracks down the shore. Monarch Vukasino stood proudly on the edge of the wooden boardwalk at the northernmost point of the beach, his coal-black eyes scanning the frothy waves.

It's only a matter of time until Kazimiera and Bojana return to the island with their scouts. I can't wait to hear about all the glorious details of the battle. It's unfortunate that I had to miss it.

"It's quite chilly out here, sire," the ruler's attendant timidly said. "Would you like me to fetch a cloak for you?"

"No, that's quite alright, Latava. The chilly air is nothing I can't handle. Besides, I'm sure it won't be long until our kin return."

"How can you be certain, my lord?"

Vukasino turned to face the petite, pink fairy, a sly smile stretching across his gray features. "A good leader just knows these things. Now, run along and fetch Mistress Tihana and Knight Morana, as well as Zosiana, Rayna, Calina, and some of the other working servants: I'm sure the scouts will need help unloading the supplies."

Nodding, the woman sped away, nimbly ascending one of the sandy footpaths leading up the rocky cliffs surrounding the beach. With the fairy's departure, the ruler of Elderfell turned around to face the moonlit sea.

I hope you saw what a monumental victory my troops achieved today from your seat in Infernus, Zlatana, the male thought, the sly smile

283

still perched on his sharp features. *Oh, Mother, I hope you see that even within the few years you've been gone, I've achieved more than you could in your feeble two hundred years of life. I, a visi-vilek, will return the homeland to the Dark Fairies. I, the child you disavowed on your deathbed, will fulfill the promise you never kept.*

Pulling himself out of his mental ramblings, the monarch discerned the faint outline of incoming ships. The familiar ear-piercing shrieks of his vilek subjects rang out in the murky night, signaling that the boats the man saw were driven by his allies. Letting out an ear-piercing screech of his own, the man called to his messenger rook Tajni, who had accompanied the scouts back after delivering Vukasino's final letter.

The midnight-feathered bird flew onto the leader's shoulder with a caw, his dark eyes glistening in the night as he nuzzled against the ruler's neck.

"Good boy," Vukasino whispered, awarding the bird with praise that his subjects rarely heard.

Members of the monarch's castle staff hurried down the slope as the passenger ship docked. The sails billowed in the salty sea air as the servants hurriedly assisted the new arrivals with unloading the gear. Waves of fairies passed by the nobleman, who stood to the side with his arms crossed over his chest, watching intently as the females did his bidding. Tihana and Morana joined him, greeting the ruler with bows of respect.

"It's about time you two showed up," Vukasino spoke, eyeing the two women up and down before glancing at the crowd of Dark Vilek. Cupping his hands around his mouth, he exclaimed, "Knight Kazimiera, Knight Bojana, where are you?!"

"We're coming, Your Lordship!" the duo called out. Maneuvering their way through the slowly growing crowd, the disheveled knights approached their leader. Their ash-caked frames bowed before Vukasino.

"You two are filthy. That's a sign of a momentous battle."

"Indeed, it was, Lord Vukasino," Kazimiera huffed, her grimy face framed by sweat-slicked gray locks. "You should've seen the number of corpses we left lining the streets."

"And what of the informant inside the mountains? Did you take care of him?"

"We didn't have to," the greenish-gray woman continued, her eyes flicking from Vukasino to Tihana. "One of the scouts who escaped the mountains toward the end of the battle told me that he was killed after he drank the concoction. However, it is with great dishonor that I report that the test subjects Jarl Yngraham handed over to our troops never returned with the dispatch responsible for them."

The elation painting the ruler's face instantly morphed into a look of confusion and budding fury. "What did you just say?"

"We're terribly sorry, Your Majesty," Knight Bojana continued for her sister-in-arms, "we'll accept any punishment you see fit to administer."

"That's not what I meant," the monarch snapped, scowling. "I'm just perplexed as to how the informant got his hands on our potion in the first place."

"What do you mean?" Kazimiera asked. "Mistress Tihana wrote that you approved of the deal our informant proposed about exchanging the test subjects for a vial of the elixir."

Vukasino paused, inhaling deeply, trying his best to keep his composure. Tajni squawked on his shoulder, flittering his wings.

The boardwalk slowly began to empty as the fairies finished unloading all of the contents from the boat. After the leader was sure he was alone with the three women, he released a shuttering exhale, his shoulders tense.

"Knight Kazimiera, Knight Bojana, you may be excused. Go to the castle and draft me a report of the casualties lost during the battle." When his subjects didn't instantly respond, the man added, "NOW!"

The two warriors sped away, quickly following the servants up the side of the rocky cliff and toward the monarch's estate. The waves crashed against the boardwalk, creating a thunderous roar as the male turned toward Tihana, his black eyes glinting with wrath.

"Answer me this: what, in all of Sacarnia, were you thinking?" The leader spat. "And speak quickly before I strike you down where you stand."

"I was doing what I thought was best for the Dark Vilek, Your Majesty." The woman spoke plainly, not a drop of remorse in her voice. "Being able to test our creation on outsiders was an opportunity we couldn't afford to miss. Besides, I instructed Knight Kazimiera to crush a nightshade berry and mix it into the elixir, so Jarl Yngraham would die whenever he decided to drink it. That way, none of the álves would ever know about the ingredients in our little project."

"Well, you see," the monarch began, laughing darkly, "we have missed the opportunity to test the potion on outsiders since they ran away from our troops. And not only that but there's no way of knowing if one of the locals on that damned island knows about the concoction now. So what do you have to say about that, hmm?"

The fairy's unwavering orange eyes looked into the black ones of her ruler, her gaze as cold as ice. "The chance was worth it, my lord."

The monarch shook his head, his lips curled in disgust. "You forget your place in this relationship. You don't get to decide if a chance is worth taking. Also, what you think is best for my subjects means as little to me as an ant under my boot."

Tajni flew off Vukasino's shoulders as the ruler stomped toward the scientist, tucking his wings beneath his rippling cape. The moon cast a delicate glow upon his head, contrasting wildly with the fragmented shadows scattered across his angered face.

"I'll give you one more chance, Tihana. Do anything stupid, and I'll disembowel you myself. Do you understand?"

Vukasino didn't need to hear a single odious word leave the alchemist's mouth to know what she was thinking. Her loathing shone in the fire dwelling behind her orange eyes, which bore a hole through the ruler's soul. He could sense the thousands of thoughts that raced through her head just by looking at her face as she gazed at him. However, no matter how much she wanted to tell him off, he knew she wouldn't. For, in the end, she was a coward, just like the rest of his underlings.

After a few moments of tense silence, the woman whispered, "…Yes, my lord."

"Good. Now go," the male paused, turning toward the horizon. "I need to be alone for a few minutes."

The alchemist sauntered away after a prolonged bow, leaving the enraged leader alone on the boardwalk. His eyes drifted from the raging sea to the shadowy outline of the distant island. Inhaling deeply, he allowed a sense of calm to wash over him as he reminded himself of the battle that happened on Florella.

I will reclaim the homeland for my people, the ruler thought, a devious glint shining in his eyes. *I will be the leader my mother never was and punish any underlings that do not enforce my commands, and I will,* the man paused, the wind whipping his hair as an evil smile spread across his face, *kill every álf that calls Florella home.*

Uniting The Álfrolk
22nd of Winter's Breath, 1300 AC

Two weeks had passed since the attack on the Snøthorn Mountains, and Cymbelina was still unable to fully wrap her mind around all the events that had transpired.

After being interrogated by Scoutmaster Estrasta and her men following Jarl Yngraham's death, Cymbelina was led back to the Glenrolk camp by the scoutmaster and some of her troops. Upon Cymbelina's return, the she-álf discovered that Kayven, Malaveen, and the Magijarolk that had accompanied them convinced Kinlord Emyr to discuss the gravity of the recent attacks with the neighboring Sylvanrolk clans. Through the discussion, the clan leaders had reached a consensus: the threat the Dark Vilek represented was significant enough for the Wood Álf tribes to unite under one banner. Not only did the clans agree to join forces to stop the invading foes, but some Dokkalrolk troops from the mountains also decided to join the army, hellbent on receiving justice for their fallen brethren. Even Knight Commander Emerik and some of his fellow Elemental Álves remained in the Glenrolk camp to join the efforts against the Dark Fairies.

And with that, the descendants of the ancient álfrok were united, a cause that every álf gathered at the Glenrolk clan's camp could get behind. But even the small victory of a united álven populace couldn't rouse Cymbelina from the pervasive thoughts clouding her mind. With the state of her exile temporarily lifted due to the meetings between the various álven leaders, the she-álf spent her time huddled away in the

288

room she used to share with Una, desperately waiting to hear the verdict the superiors had reached.

Cymbelina's pine-green eyes scanned her skin repeatedly as she searched for any glow akin to the one she was cloaked in during the battle in the mountains. Her thoughts screamed out to the internal voice that had communicated with her over the past few weeks. However, no matter how much she pleaded for the rumbling tone to respond, it had remained dormant since Jarl Yngraham's death. She hadn't dreamed about the padlocked door since his demise, either.

What if I imagined it all? The female thought, her head falling forward to rest on her bent knees. *What if everything all of my kin used to say about me is true? After all, Master Arvel would be alive if it weren't for me.* Tears welled at the inner corners of the she-álf's eyes before trailing down her face and plummeting to the floor underneath her. Her fingers dug into the sides of each knee, her knuckles turning white under the force of her grip. Flashbacks to the sorrowful night of the patron guide's passing flickered in and out of her broken mind, images of Master Arvel's dying expression blocking out every thought Cymbelina could conjure to distract herself from the pain.

"'Lina?' Una said timidly, her voice muffled through the cream-colored cloth covering the entryway to the room. "Can I come in?"

The brunette wiped her eyes, her gaze averting to the entryway. She was shocked that her younger sister wanted to see her, considering the vicious rumors about Cymbelina floating around the camp. Utterances about her being a bloodthirsty savage. A killer with voices in her head demanding that she do depraved things to those around her. A loner who sought to take her self-hatred out on the pureblood álves around her. Such vile hearsay had caused most people to stay far away from the Half-Sylvanrolk. Although Cymbelina had been the subject of rumors her entire life, the new ones surrounding her caused her to ponder horrific things about her existence, thoughts she couldn't quite shake no matter how hard she tried.

"I'm not sure why you would want to," Cymbelina sniffled, "but sure."

The young, frizzy-haired álf pushed the fabric covering the room to the side, her navy eyes filled with concern as she stared down at her grieving sister. Una slowly entered the quiet room, kneeling beside her older sibling. After a heavy sigh, she wrapped her arms around Cymbelina, hugging her tightly.

"How are you holding up?" The younger female whispered.

The brunette didn't answer, opting to bury her face in her sister's curly tresses instead.

"Listen. I came to visit you because I'm worried about you, 'Lina. You've spent the past two weeks cooped up in our tent, barely conversing with Mom, me, or anyone else in the clan. It's not healthy to isolate yourself."

The older sibling sat up, wiping her eyes again before looking at her younger sibling. "That's because whenever I leave the house, everyone shies away from me, or they mumble curses under their breath. It's exhausting, Una, and although I've dealt with this sort of behavior as far back as I can recall, it's never been this bad. I'm just sick of it." The brunette sighed, shaking her head as tears formed in her eyes. "I don't know how much more I can take. And every time I think about Master Arvel, I-I…."

Cymbelina trailed off as her head fell forward, a sob escaping her chapped lips as she raised her right hand to cover her mouth. Una hugged her sister tighter as a cold, wintry breeze beat against the walls of the tent. The duo sat silently, the occasional whimper piercing the chilly air until the brunette spoke again.

"It should've been me, Una. I should've been the one to die in the mountains, not Master Arvel. I'm a fatherless Sylvanrolk outcast who doesn't even know her own patron animal. What could I possibly amount to? How could I possibly prove to be of any service to my people?"

Before Una could respond, the fabric covering the entrance into the room flung to the side, revealing the duo's mother, Deirdre. Her chocolate-colored curls were pulled back into a tight ponytail, her dampened, tear-stained face on full display. The older álf's cerulean eyes shone with sorrow.

"I never want to hear you say that again, Cymbelina," the older woman whispered, her voice quivering. She approached her kneeling children with slow, deliberate steps. Extending her arms, she gently guided the two to their feet, looking back and forth between her two daughters.

"Una, your father needs you in the other room; you need to try on your new armor. And Cymbelina," Deirdre said, her gaze fixing on her oldest daughter, "you and I need to talk."

The younger daughter nodded, her eyes drifting between her mother and sister before exiting the bedroom. Once the black-haired álf had left, Deirdre continued with a slight tremble in her voice.

"Do you realize the gravity of what you just said a moment ago?"

Cymbelina's eyes drifted to the floor, her lips pursed and unwilling to part for a response.

"Listen to me," the older brunette whispered, her finger tucking underneath her daughter's chin. "Master Arvel's death is tragic, but it is not your fault. He gave his life for you, and nothing you could've done would've stopped him from doing so."

"But you weren't there, Mom. How do you know that I—"

"Let me finish," Deirdre urged, her hands clutching her daughter's shoulders. "I grew up with Master Arvel by my side. I knew him better than you could possibly imagine, and that's how I know there was nothing you could've done to change his mind. And do you know why that is? Because he saw something in you, Cymbelina," Deirdre paused, one of her hands coming up to wipe the stray tear that escaped one of her daughter's eyes. "You were his favorite pupil. And not because your patron animal situation is unique, although he did find that intriguing. It's because of your refusal to ever give up. Your boundless dedication to getting back up when life has brought you to your knees. Your bravery in the face of adversity. Your curiosity and drive to discover that which is unknown to you. And finally, my sweet daughter," Deirdre took a deep breath, her eyes tearing up, "your father loved you. He might not be around anymore, but that does not mean you are fatherless. And even then, your stepfather loves you very much, even if he does have funny ways of showing it."

Cymbelina laughed, her amused noise breaking up the sob that had tried to escape her mouth. "You are right about that; Séacael can be a bit weird at times."

Deirdre chuckled, her gaze softening as her hands fell from her daughter's shoulders. "Do you understand now, 'Lina? You are very much loved, and I never want to hear you say anything about you dying instead of Master Arvel again. His death was horrendous, and he will always be missed, but he gave up his life for you for a reason. To insist that you should've taken his place does Master Arvel a grave disservice. Do you understand me?"

Cymbelina nodded before hugging her mother, resting her head on the older woman's pale shoulder. Deirdre reciprocated, and the two clutched each other like their lives depended on it. As the two began to separate, Séacael called out to the older brunette from outside the room.

"What is it, darling?" Deirdre called back.

"We received a message from Phalena," the older male responded. "She says the representatives of the álven groups are done deliberating on what to do about the vilek threat. They're about to give a speech in the center of the camp."

Wiping away a stray tear, Cymbelina looked at her mother, pushing the darkest thoughts to the back of her mind to focus on the meeting.

"Well," the brunette mumbled, her voice still hoarse from crying, "we should go see what these plans are all about."

Her mother smiled. "That's my girl."

After Una was done trying on her new gear, Cymbelina's family left the tent, joining the rest of the álves huddled in the center of the camp.

A makeshift platform had been constructed in the center of the town square. The three Sylanrolk clan leaders, Emyr,

Quindlen, and Nairna, were on the wooden stage alongside Knight Commander Emerik of the Magijarolk and Scoutmaster Estrasta of the Dokkalrolk. The five figures looked down upon the huddled crowd surrounding them, waiting for the audience to calm down before attempting to speak. When the hubbub wouldn't cease, Emyr signaled Phalena to blow a horn. With a reverberating hum, the anxious crowd was silenced.

"My fellow álves," Kinlord Emyr began, his voice firm as he gazed upon the crowd, "I know this setting is unknown to most of you and that tensions are high. Because of this, I commend you for your patience during these troubling times. But as of today, each álven leader on this stage has formulated a plan to end the Dark Vilek threat, once and for all."

The crowd around Cymbelina cheered and glowed with elation as she and her family pushed their way through. They stopped midway into the gathering and stared up at the kinlord of the Glenrolk.

"Although we have a plan," Scoutmaster Estrasta continued, "that doesn't mean it'll be an easy one."

"It will take hard work and dedication from everyone," Kinlady Nairna pronounced, her mahogany eyes scanning the sea of álves.

"And a willingness to never back down, regardless of what the odds may look like," Kinlord Quindlen finished, his expression resolute.

"No matter what the odds may look like?!" A Sylvanrolk in the crowd yelled, his voice tinged with fury. "Do you mean to tell us that we should be ready to lay down our lives for a suicide mission? I'd rather just stay here!"

"You'd rather just stay here?!" Another Wood Álf questioned, spitting on the ground. "You'd give up so easily in the face of the enemy? When they think nothing of invading our territories and destroying our homes and livelihoods? Pathetic!"

"Your kinsmen is right!" A Dokkalrolk added. "I lost my home in one of the attacks on the Snøthorn Mountains! Would you like to fight to prevent that from happening to your home, or would you rather stay here like a spineless coward?"

A commotion slowly arose from the tense crowd as each álf began to argue with their neighbor. Cymbelina was one of the only exceptions, as her her attention was glued on Knight Commander Emerik Vesnavin. He was the sole representative who hadn't uttered a word yet, and his irritated expression showed why. In his natural Magijarolk form, the Elemental Álf's pastel green skin glimmered under the winter sun. His red eyes were screwed shut, frustration emanating from his tense frame.

I've never seen Emerik so frustrated before, Cymbelina thought. *I wonder what's going through his head?*

As soon as the thoughts crossed her mind, the ground beneath the she-álf quaked. The horde of álves surrounding the platform lowered their voices to a hushed murmur, turning to and fro to try and find the source of the trembling. However, the brunette didn't need to search; it was clear to her that the knight commander was using his earth-manipulation abilities to quiet the crowd. Noticing his plan had worked, the Magijarolk ceased the shaking and began to speak.

"We'll never get to discussing the plan, much less executing it, if all we do is bicker with one another."

Pulling a scroll off one of the loopholes on his belt, Emerik unrolled it. The ink began to glow a vibrant turquoise blue as the sunlight hit the parchment, revealing a map of Florella and a smaller island off its southwestern coastline.

"This map was created by the four remaining Light Vilek, who currently watch over my people. Our enemies, the Dark Vilek, reside on Elderfell," the knight commander paused, pointing to the tiny landmass. "If every álf present here today puts their best foot forward in the oncoming days, we will be able to reach our enemies and defeat them."

The crowd buzzed with anticipation, whispers of a triumphant victory and the end of the looming threat permeating the gathering of álves. However, a few skeptical bystanders remained, one of whom voiced his doubts openly.

"If the Light Fairies and the Elemental Álves knew where

the Dark Fairies were all this time, why haven't they dealt with them already? Lots of lives would've been spared if they had!"

"There are a multitude of answers to that question," Emerik responded. "The two foremost reasons are that we never had the number of troops required to bring down the Dark Vilek alone and that my people tend to avoid conflict as much as possible."

"If that's the case," another Dokkalrolk questioned, his voice tinged with skepticism, "how can we be sure you and your kin won't abandon us when the battle gets tough? How can we rely on you if your people have a reputation for avoiding combat?"

"Because they've traveled here to fight alongside us," Kinlord Emyr shouted, his voice cracking. "I understand your wariness in these times of doubt, but please, pay attention to the plan. I promise each and every one of us on this stage will be open to questions in the end. Now, Knight Commander Emerik," the Glenrolk leader paused, motioning towards the Magijarolk representative, "you may address your men and women."

"Thank you, Kinlord Emyr," the man nodded, stepping forward and glancing at the huddled group of Magijarolk gathered in the center of the crowd. "Now, listen closely, *mo famija*. For those of you whose powers rely on the wind, your abilities will come in more than you could ever imagine. The yearly snowstorm is set to make landfall in a few weeks, giving us an advantage over the enemy if we can manipulate it in a way that looks natural. When we set for the enemy's island in four weeks," the leader paused, another wave of murmurs floating over the crowd, "the wind-controlling álves will be positioned on each boat. As we sail through the snowstorm, you'll use your abilities to push the storm forward, clearing the way for the rest of the troops while masking our approach. Those of you who can control water will keep the sea as smooth as possible for our journey."

"And then what?" A Magijarolk called out, "Will we be joining the Dokkalrolk and Sylvanrolk in battle?"

"Those of you who haven't used up your strength along the journey, yes."

The gathering of Elemental Álves donned varied expressions, some displaying excitement while others showed fear.

"And they won't be the only ones who help the lot of us navigate our way to the island," Kinlord Emyr added, stepping forward. "My fellow Sylvanrolk with patron animals that can fly will be patrolling the skies, ensuring that we're on the right course and that the enemy isn't catching on to our plan. And once we've successfully landed on the island," the Glenrolk leader paused, motioning towards Scoutmaster Estrasta so she could say her piece.

"We'll combine most of our forces and attack the Dark Vilek fortress head-on. Some of my scouts will break into smaller groups with others álves, searching the isle for hidden entrances to cripple their defenses. The enemy won't know what hit them until it's too late."

The crowd of álves cheered. The apprehension that once filled the air was all but gone. Cymbelina scanned the crowd, taking in the emotions permeating the air. Her heart momentarily filled with joy at the prospect of winning against the Dark Fairies.

If the álves can win the oncoming battle, not only will we secure a future for our brethren, but it will be the first time the álfrolk have been united since 20 AC! Cymbelina thought. A wintry breeze whipped her dark brown hair, her eyes squinting as she gazed into the midafternoon sky. *The defeat of the Dark Vilek will also secure vengeance for Idal, Arvel, and the rest of the álves who have lost their lives in the grueling war.*

Phalena sounded the horn once more, tearing the brunette out of her skyward ruminations.

"Now, before we all start to get excited and riled up," Kinlord Emyr stated, the álves in the crowd calming down, "it's important to note that my fellow representatives and I have taken the liberty of formulating a task list for every álf here. That way, there is no confusion about anyone's assignments before and during the battle. So, once Phalena sounds the horn again, I would like everyone to line up in front of the stage based on the leader representing your group." The Kinlord paused, allowing for his instructions to sink in before elaborating. "For example, all members of the Glenrolk clan will line up in front of me on this side of the stage, and all of the Dokkalrolk will line up in front of Scoutmaster Estrasta. Any questions you may have about your assigned duties may be inquired about later once the crowd has settled down a bit. Does everyone understand?"

The crowd of álves went silent, everyone looking to and fro to see if any of their comrades would raise their hand or their voice. Once nobody made a single sound of unease, the representatives looked at each other and nodded before Emyr signaled to Phalena.

With the reverberating call of the horn, the crowd thinned out into single-file lines, with some extending beyond the town square and circling nearby tents. Unluckily for Cymbelina and her family, they obtained spots toward the back of the queue in front of Kinlord Emyr.

"I wonder what sort of tasks I will be assigned," Una spoke, thrill and wonder reflecting in her dark blue eyes.

"None of us will be flying, that's for sure," Séacael mumbled, relief flooding his voice. "If I'm being honest with the lot of you, I've never been too keen on the idea of flying. Hell, the thought of sailing across the sea to attack our enemies is already making my stomach churn."

"Oh no," Deirdre teased, glancing at her husband with a playful smirk. "What happened to the daring, adventurous man I married? The one who used to lead us on wild hunting expeditions and smiled in the face of danger?"

Séacael laughed, wrapping his right arm around Deirdre's frame. "Let's keep some things in perspective, my love. Your patron animal is a bear, while mine happens to be a badger. Which one of us will fare better in the fight against the vilek, hmm?"

"Surely I will if you go into the fray with that kind of

mindset."

"Ha! You and I both know that's not how it works."

Deirdre smiled, leaning her head on her partner's shoulder.

The line slowly edged forward as the álves left the gathering with a myriad of mixed emotions. Some left the scene feeling a sense of contentment, their expressions calm as they adjusted to their newly assigned tasks. In stark contrast, others gripped their papers tightly, their knuckles white with tension. Their faces were etched with fear and frustration, and they cast anxious glances around as if seeking a way to escape the burden they now faced.

Following one of her kinsmen with eager eyes, Una turned to her sister, who was standing in front of her. "What sorts of tasks do you think you'll receive, 'Lina?"

"I'm not quite sure," the brunette said, her gaze lifting from the ground to look at her sister, "but I have mixed feelings about my chances of getting desirable orders."

"Why's that?"

"Well, I'm technically a Sylvanrolk outcast. I'm lucky I'm even allowed to set foot in camp," the female paused, pushing a strand of hair behind one of her pointed ears, "but I think it's safe to say I proved my mettle in battle during my time outside the camp. Hopefully, I won't be stuck protecting the ships during the final battle."

Una snorted, an amused expression plastered on her face.

"What's so funny?"

"I just think it's comical that you act as if you would follow such orders," the younger sibling remarked, eyeing her sister up and down. "I know how you are. If you receive orders to stay back and protect the ships, you won't follow them. Or, at least, you'll do it in your own fashion. You're too stubborn not to."

Cymbelina grinned, turning her attention toward Kinlord Emyr, who was talking to one of the Glenrolk clan members at the front of the line. "You know me too well."

The line continued to inch forward, Cymbelina and her family trading in idle chatter until it was their turn to receive orders from her grandfather. Cymbelina was the last of her family to obtain her assignments. Unraveling the yellowed parchment in her hands, the she-álf read what was demanded of her.

'Pre-battle tasks: assist in the construction of boats.
Battle assignment: none. Remain at camp and assist in the clean-up after the battle preparations.'

Cymbelina's eyes were blown wide in shock as they darted back and forth between the parchment and her grandfather, who towered above her on the wooden platform. "No battle assignments?! What is the meaning of this?"

"We can discuss this later," the kinlord whispered, his voice filled with warning. "Do not say anything else. Return to my tent after supper, and we'll discuss the situation then."

The litany of protests threatening to spill from the brunette's lips fell flat as she gazed into her grandfather's piercing, mint-green eyes, her mouth reluctantly closing in agreement. Rolling up the parchment, the brunette sauntered toward where her family stood, trying her best to keep her composure.

Keep your cool, Cymbelina urged herself, trying her best to contort her expression into one of contentment. *Grandpa said you could discuss this with him later. Don't get angry here. Maybe you can change his mind later.*

"So, what were you assigned?" Deirdre asked, eyeing her eldest daughter as she took her place beside the rest of the family.

"Shipwright duty."

"Oh, I was, too," Una said, smiling. "See, your task isn't too bad."

"What about your post during the battle?" Séacael inquired.

Cymbelina's eyes drifted to the side. Sensing her daughter's dissatisfaction, Deirdre interjected, "We can discuss this over dinner. Come, let's see what Tadhgmaris is making."

299

A Change Of Plans
22nd of Winter's Breath, 1300 AC

Unlike what Deirdre had said, the subject of Cymbelina's tasks was not brought up at the dinner table. Whenever the she-álf thought the conversation was headed in that direction, she quickly switched topics, doing her best to avoid the subject altogether. All the brunette wanted was to wolf down her food and head to her grandfather's tent, deadset on sorting out the horrendous duties handed down to her.

Avoiding the barrage of queries her parents aimed at her regarding where she was going, the brunette grabbed her golden cloak and slipped out of the tent, half-heartedly reassuring them that she was going for a walk. She wasn't entirely sure they bought her story, but frankly, she didn't care all that much. She was so fixated on finding Kinlord Emyr and sorting out the mess he had put her in that everything else vanished from her mind.

I know that the state of my patron animal is something of a mess, but to be given these childish orders is beyond insulting. It's a slap in the face, Cymbelina reasoned.

The afternoon sun had fallen into the canopy of trees surrounding the Glenrolk campsite, a tapestry of stars adorning the night sky. The frigid air made Cymbelina's extremities tingle as she followed the zig-zag path to her grandfather's tent. The dry, winter grass crunched underneath her feet as she maneuvered through the overcrowded settlement. The brunette let out a refrain of "excuse me" as she worked toward the town center, squeezing through the thick throngs of outsiders. Once she arrived at her desired location, the Half-Sylvanrolk let out a heavy sigh, her shoulders sagging as she saw the long line leading into Kinlord Emyr's tent. At the end of the line stood a familiar figure, Kayven. His eyes were glued to the scroll in his hands, his soft lips drawn out into a straight line.

A sense of unease welled in the brunette's core as she gazed upon her former companion.

Should I say hi to Kayven? Does he even want to see me? The she-álf pondered. *What if he's heard all of the rumors going around and thinks I'm a freak, too? What if he starts asking questions I don't feel comfortable answering?* Cymbelina shook her head, trying to push these unsettling thoughts to the back of her mind as she pulled her hood up. *Reversing these orders is too important to dwell on what Kayven might think of me if he happens to spot me. The best I can do is try to blend in.*

Keeping her wits in check, Cymbelina slowly approached the line, burying her face under her billowing hood to avoid detection by the taller male. Bringing the parchment out of her pocket, she kept her gaze downward, turning her back towards Kayven to avoid his gaze.

Hopefully, the color of my cloak doesn't give me away.

Cymbelina's tactic of hiding in plain sight worked at first, as Kayven continued to mutter his orders to himself as he waited for his turn to enter the tent. As álf after álf entered and exited her grandfather's abode, and Cymbelina remained the last one in line, she became increasingly assured that she could slip into the tent without drawing Kayven's attention. However, her confidence crumbled when a familiar, swearing figure swiftly approached the tent.

"*Dihaal*, I can't believe the kinlord has done this to me," Malaveen swore under her breath, balling up her scroll and shoving it into her pocket. "Hopefully, he'll see reason and—is that you, Cymbelina?"

As Malaveen mentioned the brunette's name, the hooded woman turned to the right, noticing a look of shock crossing the male's warm features.

"Cymbelina? Is it really you?"

"In the flesh," Cymbelina announced, trying her best to sound nonchalant as she lowered her hood and faced Kayven. In an attempt to make herself sound genuine, she released a little laugh. It wasn't until after that she realized how awkward she was being.

"So you've been standing next to me the entire time and didn't think to say something?" Kayven asked with the slightest hint of offense reflected in his voice.

"Yeah, I'm sorry, it's just that—"

"I would never have guessed you survived the attack on the Snøthorn Mountains," Malaveen interjected, crossing her arms over her chest in an exaggerated display of dazzlement. "Color me impressed."

"Haven't you two heard the rumors?" The brunette asked incredulously.

"We've both heard the rumors, Cymbelina, but how much stock do you expect us to place in the ramblings of outsiders? Plus, none of them mentioned you were alive or allowed back into the camp. Either way, I'm surprised you're here. Where have you been?"

"In my tent," the brunette answered, her voice wary from all of the questions Malaveen was directing at her.

A warm hand rested on Cymbelina's covered shoulder, her head jerking toward the right to view the source of the unexpected touch. Her green eyes locked with Kayven's marigold ones as the light of nearby torches danced in the warmth of his gaze. A relieved smile spread across his striking features, revealing two rows of gleaming teeth.

"I'm glad you're alive, Cymbelina. I was worried about you when we left you and Master Arvel behind. My heart grieves for him, but I'm glad you returned home safe."

The brunette smiled wearily. "Thank you, Kayven. I mourn Master Arvel, too. I hope he sleeps peacefully in Mother Terralynia's embrace."

"So," Malaveen muttered, her eyes glued to the male's hand

as it left Cymbelina's shoulder, "what type of orders did you two receive? You're in this line, so there's obviously something you two disagree with."

"I'm content with my assignment," Kayven admitted. "I'm simply waiting here so I can ask Kinlord Emyr if he'll be merciful enough to reassign my father's orders to me."

"And why would you want that? I thought you just said you were content with your duties?"

"I am, Malaveen. I only want to switch with my father because I don't think they're suitable for him."

"Why is that?" The brunette inquired, shooting the male beside her a worried look.

"Well," Kayven began, addressing Cymbelina, "he suffered a leg injury during the fight at the Eldenfield Festival. One of the Dark Fairies ended up scratching him with their long nails, taking a big chunk out of his skin. It looked like it would heal without a hitch by the time we left for the Glimmering Wilds, but when Malaveen and I returned, it appeared to take a turn for the worse. The gash in his leg ended up becoming infected. It's so painful that he can barely walk on it right now." The male paused, averting his gaze to the blonde beside him. "So, the fact that he received orders to attack the frontlines during the battle against the Dark Vilek is perplexing. With luck, the kinlord will allow me to switch orders with my father."

"Does Tadhgmaris know you're attempting to switch his orders?"

"No, he was too busy making dinner for the camp when I snatched them. However, I don't think he'll be mad once he finds out I did."

Mixed emotions rose in the brunette's chest. She was proud to see her friend take a risk and do something for the ones he cared about, but a small part of her was distressed by the thought of the male taking on such dangerous orders. Sure, Kayven is a capable fighter, but so are the Dark Fairies. The pessimist in Cymbelina could easily imagine the male getting overpowered by the vilek if he was backed into a corner.

I couldn't bear losing someone close to me again so soon, not when

Master Arvel and Idal met their graves far earlier than they should have. But I know nothing I could ever say would change Kayven's mind.

"Well," the brunette paused, swallowing the lump in her throat, "I hope you can plead your case to the kinlord."

"Thank you, Cymbelina; I hope I can too."

"And what about you?" the blonde motioned to Cymbelina, the trio inching forward in line as another álf went in to see Emyr. "What assignments are you hoping to change?"

"Well, according to the scroll my grandfather gave me, I'm supposed to help build ships and then stay behind during the battle to help some of the elderly álves clean up."

Malaveen whistled, trying her best to stifle a laugh. "And I thought my assignments were awful. Your grandfather really has it out for you, doesn't he?"

"Not necessarily," Kayven argued, his soft eyes squinting as he considered the situation. "It might be that Kinlord Emyr wants to ensure that Cymbelina's not harmed, especially as the tales of the incident at the Snøthorn Mountains swirl around the camp."

"Sure," the blonde chuckled, waving away Kayven's statement, "but it doesn't make the orders any less insulting."

"Only if she thinks of them in that light," Kayven responded, his eyes turning to Cymbelina. "I think it would be better if you thought of the orders as a sign of love instead of distrust or admonition."

"It's hard to think of it any other way when Una was given an infiltrative role during the battle," Cymbelina sighed, trying her best not to let negative emotions fill her spirit. "But I'll try to think of it that way, Kayven. Anyways, what orders were you given, Malaveen?"

The line moved forward again, the trio moving along with it.

"I've been tasked with shipbuilding leading up to the battle and then as ship guide as we sail towards the island. After we land, I'm supposed to guard the boats." Malaveen groaned, tossing her flaxen locks back. "I'm too well versed in combat to be given such orders."

"But what if you're exhausted after flying through the storm? Surely, you won't be able to fight if you're tired."

"Um, hello? Did you not see my battle prowess during the attack on the Snøthorn Mountains? I doubt I'll be tired after flying if I was able to survive that massacre."

Kayven and Cymbelina simultaneously rolled their eyes, opting to ignore their blonde companion's comment.

Besides the occasional quip or sigh of impatience that would spill out of one of the companion's lips, the three álves sat in relative silence for the rest of the time they stood in line. The álves watched as the people clogging the town square returned to their tents, the torches lining the streets becoming dimmer until they extinguished. The humming of the nocturnal woodland critters filled the air, the winter clouds slowly hiding and revealing the moon hanging in the dark firmament as its heavenly glow bathed the camp in a pale light.

After about an hour of waiting, the trio finally reached the front of the line. Being the only álves left in the town square, they were desperate to see the clan's leader, resolve their issues, and head home.

Anxiously eyeing the kinlord's tent, Cymbelina sighed in relief when the flap leading into Emyr's home opened, the last álf in front of them scurrying away. Reaching out to hold it open for her allies to enter, Cymbelina's motion was swiftly interrupted by Phalena.

"Sorry, you three," the she-álf spoke. A halo of moonlight formed a crown on her scalp, causing her tangerine hair to glow. "Kinlord Emyr isn't taking any more visitors tonight. Preparations begin tomorrow, so he, along with the rest of the álves in the camp, need to get a good night's sleep tonight."

"That's ridiculous," Cymbelina scowled. "He said he would address any questions we might have about our assignments earlier today. In fact, he specifically told me that I could see him after dinner. I'm sorry, Phalena. I know you have your duties, but I need to see my grandfather."

"And so do we," Malaveen added, crossing her arms over her chest. "We've been waiting a little over an hour to see the kinlord, and we're the last people in line. It won't take much time to talk to him."

"I'm sorry," Phalena reiterated, her voice tinged with agitation, "but I have my orders. You need to leave before—"

Shaking her head, the brunette pushed past her grandfather's advisor and entered the tent. Moving swiftly through the entry room and into the hearing room, Cymbelina made her way to Kinlord Emyr. The aged álf knelt beside his throne, his bent, lithe frame bathed in the moonlight seeping through the transparent material comprising the tent's roofing. Blowing out the candle resting snugly in the lantern beside the leader's chair, the male turned his head, his mint-green eyes heavy with fatigue as he gazed upon his granddaughter.

"I told Phalena I wasn't taking any more guests tonight."

"You also told me that I could speak with you after dinner," Cymbelina implored, her dark green eyes filled with urgency. "Please, Kinlord Emyr, we must discuss my instructions."

"As well as ours," Malaveen said, dragging Kayven into the room alongside her. "We've been waiting for an hour to speak to you, sir. I think it's unfair we were allowed to wait that long without any sort of warning that you were done talking to people."

Stunned by the brazenness of the three álves, the older male exhaled, rising from his crouched position to sit on his twig throne. "You make a valid point. Please sit so we can discuss any concerns you might have, beginning with Malaveen."

"Well," the blonde began, kneeling next to her companions on the bear rug, "with all due respect, I believe assigning me to boat duty during battle is a waste of my talents, sir. I would be much more useful on the battlefield fighting alongside my álven brothers and sisters."

"How do you figure?" The leader challenged, lacing his fingers together and leaning back in his seat.

"I have faced the Dark Fairies in battle, sir. That sort of experience is invaluable for the upcoming fight."

"You have a point. However, your first assignment that day

is to guide the boats in the air while assuming your patron form. By the time we reach the island, you'll likely be tired from the amount of energy you exerted flying through a snowstorm. So, no, your task will remain the same. No matter how useful you presume yourself to be."

Exhaling, the older álf turned his attention toward the younger male. "Kayven, tell me what troubles you about your assignment."

"It's not my assignment that troubles me, Kinlord Emyr; it's my father's."

Kinlord Emyr cocked a silver eyebrow, leaning forward on his throne. "Is that so?"

"Yes, sir. With the state of Tadhgmaris' right leg, I think it would be better if he watched the boats during the attack rather than take up arms on the frontlines. I would happily take his place to help my brethren in battle if you allow it, Kinlord Emyr."

"Does Tadhgmaris know you've come to speak with me this evening?" the Kinlord asked in a gravelly tone, his voice tinged with both curiosity and an edge of suspicion.

The male flushed, bowing his head. "No, he does not, sir. I came on his behalf."

"While I appreciate the thought you've given the situation, your father requested his assignment specifically. He said that, with the rate at which his leg is healing, he'll be ready for the battle in four weeks. So, no, his assignment remains the same, as does yours. Now, Cymbelina," the older álf shifted, facing his granddaughter with an expression of intrigue plastered on his face. "What objections could you possibly have about your assignment?"

"What don't I have to object to on this scroll?" the brunette flippantly asked, dismissing etiquette as she unrolled the parchment Kinlord Emyr handed her hours before. "I've been ordered to stay behind during the battle to help the retired warriors clean up? Kinlord Emyr, that seems absurd. With the help I was able to offer during the battles on my journey, I should at least be allowed to sail to Elderfell and defend the boats. I would be much better help there than I will be here."

The kinlord's eyes darkened, his hands unfurling and clasping the armrests with a firm grip. "What is truly absurd is that you dare to approach me in my tent—a place that you have forfeited the right to visit due to your status as an outcast—and try to convince me that you are capable of fighting the Dark Fairies. No matter how much you may dislike these words, they hold true: according to the words of the Sylvan Tenets, you are an álfling. You have not mastered your patron animal; in fact, you don't even know what it is. Due to that reason alone, I find you unfit for combat."

"But please, consider the incidents at the Snøthorn Mountains!" Cymbelina pleaded, her voice filled with desperation. "Look how I was able to fight without knowing my patron animal. Consider—"

"Consider what, Cymbelina? The fact that rumors plague the Glenrolk campsite? Rumors that my granddaughter, my own flesh and blood, lost control and tore apart her enemies like a bloodthirsty, savage beast?" The leader stopped, giving his granddaughter a bewildered look. "What else should I consider? Should I consider the fact that you deliberately disobeyed me—willfully gave up your place among the Sylvanrolk clans—to chase after some adolescent notion of an adventure that resulted in the death of a beloved member of this clan?" Kinlord Emyr paused again, his pale face tinged with pink as he tried to regain his composure. "No, I'd rather not consider any of those things. Your orders will remain the same, Cymbelina. Be thankful that you're even allowed to step foot on the soil of this commune as an outcast and chip in when you're told to."

Her grandfather's words cut through the confident façade the she-álf had meticulously constructed. Emyr was technically correct about everything he had said: there were vile rumors about Cymbelina swirling around camp; she had given up her place among her clan to go on a journey (just not for the same notions the male had ascribed to the situation). Also, Cymbelina fully recognized how fortunate she was to be allowed back in the camp due to how her fellow Wood Álves viewed the Sylvan Tenets. However, as someone who meant a lot to her, her grandfather's continuous dismissal of her ideas based on the status of her patron animal was not just frustrating but deeply hurtful. He couldn't even acknowledge the help the brunette had offered the Dokkalrolk during her time away from the Glenrolk; his mind was too focused on the formalities of the situation. It seemed to Cymbelina that she would never be more than an álfling in her grandfather's eyes.

"Now, are there any more questions you three have?"

The trio of álves was silent, their eyes glued to the cave bear rug underneath their bent knees.

"Alright then," the leader of the Glenrolk announced, standing up from his chair. "I want you three to ensure that you attend to the duties assigned to you by the joint council tomorrow morning. It would be unwise to do anything else," the male paused, eyeing his granddaughter with a look that indicated the previous statement was made directly for her. "Now that the issue has been thoroughly discussed, you three are dismissed. Phalena, lead them out."

An agitated Phalena lifted the fabric leading into the hearing room, ushering the three companions through the entryway and out of the tent. The Sylvanrolk warriors wordlessly walked away from the kinlord's abode, contemplating what Emyr's words meant for them.

"I'll be the first to admit that did not go as I expected," Malaveen said, raising her hands in surprise. "I've never seen Kinlord Emyr that angry before."

"Neither have I."

"It's nothing new to me," Cymbelina said, her eyes glued to the moon hanging in the night sky. "If you're around me and I question any of his wishes, prepare to see him become an angry old codger."

"At least we all tried," Malaveen said, shrugging her shoulders. "I'll guess we'll have to suck it up."

"Ha. You two can, but I won't," the brunette admitted. "I just need to find a way to get to Elderfell on my own."

"Did someone knock you upside the head during the battles in the Snøthorn Mountains?" The blonde sneered. "Because that is about the craziest thing that's come out of your mouth. You heard what your grandfather said: you're lucky to be allowed in the camp as an outcast. Do you really want to press your luck?"

"I've been pushing boundaries my entire life, so why should I stop now?" Cymbelina said, her voice firm and resolute. "Kinlord Emyr's assignments don't sit well with me, so I'm not going to mindlessly follow them, especially in a dire situation such as this."

"I'm with you on this one," Kayven spoke, his voice tinged with a hint of internal struggle. "It's not in my nature to blatantly go against the kinlord's orders, but the fact that he assigned my father orders that clearly go against what is healthiest for him doesn't sit right with me, no matter how much my father requested them."

A smile of relief crossed the brunette's face as she looked at the male beside her. It felt good to know she wasn't alone in terms of distaste for her grandfather's orders.

"Oh, not you, too," Malaveen sighed, shaking her head. "I'm just as disappointed in my posts as you two are, but even I recognize that we can only push so much. It's probably best that we follow Emyr's orders. He did work with the other leaders to come up with them after all, and they've seen the battlefield more times than we will ever care to admit."

"Fighting on the battlefield a certain number of times only provides a certain amount of expertise, Malaveen. It doesn't mean you know what's best for every fighter in your army. To be honest, I'm surprised you're not fighting back against this as well. You're usually the most stubborn of us all."

"While that might be so, Cymbelina, I know my limits. I'd rather not risk my place among the Glenrolk by going against orders that I simply disagree with. It's not worth it to me in the end."

"For what it's worth," Kayven began, standing beside the Half-Sylvanrolk, "I'm willing to help you find a way onto

Elderfell. I refuse to idly sit by and witness my father's death on the battlefield."

The brunette smiled at her male companion.

The blonde grumbled, rolling her eyes before huffing, "Fine, you've convinced me. I want in on the plan, too."

"Oh?" Kayven said, a sly grin crossing his face, "I thought you said abandoning your duties wasn't worth the risk?"

"It's not, but I can't very well stand by and watch you two get killed as you bumble about and try to find a way onto the island by yourselves. You'll need me to get there, after all."

"That all sounds well and good," Kayven continued, "but the three of us alone will never be able to make it to the Elderfell, not with the oncoming snowstorm. We'll have to find other people to help us out."

"People we trust," Malveen emphasized. "If we start recruiting random álves around the camp, they might rat us out to the leaders."

"Well, talking about our plans openly in the town square won't do us any favors, especially since the nightly guards will start patrolling soon," Cymbelina pointed out, her gaze averting to the tents surrounding the trio. "We should meet up tomorrow and discuss any ideas we have from there. That'll give us all some time to think about who we might be able to recruit for our cause while still getting a good night's sleep."

"Where should we meet up tomorrow?"

"I vote the edge of the Sunshade Forest that borders the camp," Malaveen offered, looking back and forth between her two companions. "Since we returned from the mountains, Kayven and I have been assigned patrol duty to that region of the woods. Nobody will think anything of it if we head there tomorrow morning."

"Good thinking."

"That settles it then," Cymbelina said with a determined glint in her eyes. "We'll meet up there tomorrow morning after breakfast. Hopefully, we'll be able to recruit some people before then and get them in on our plans."

The brunette's companions hummed in agreement,

exchanging little in terms of banter before heading their separate ways for the evening.

Upon returning to her family's abode, Cymbelina discovered that her parents were fast asleep. Tiptoeing past their bedroom to avoid disturbing them, the brunette swiftly entered the chambers she shared with her sibling. However, unlike Deirdre and Séacael, Una was wide awake. The black-haired álf eyed her sister eagerly, thousands of questions threatening to spill from her taut lips.

"So, where were you?" Una whispered, sitting upright on her bedroll.

"I went for a walk, just like I said after dinner. I circled the camp a few times and strolled through the town square, which is why it took me so long to return home."

Una chuckled, her gaze following her sister as she got behind the partition the girls used to change clothing. "You might be able to fool Mom and Dad with such a silly fib, but not me. Please, 'Lina, just answer me honestly. Where were you?"

The Half-Sylvanrolk remained silent as her leather armor hit the floor, the ruffling of her nightgown filling the air.

"Please, Sis," the black-haired woman implored. "If you can't trust me, who can you trust?"

"Fine," the brunette hissed lowly, her younger sister's pleas deteriorating her iron will. Popping her head around the screen, Cymbelina whispered, "I went to see Grandfather about reversing his decision about my post."

"I knew it! I knew you didn't go for a walk," Una muttered, a proud smile crossing her face. "So, what did he say?"

"What do you think he said?" Cymbelina answered, moving behind the partition once more. "He declined my request and publicly berated me for it. You know, the usual."

"So, what are you going to do? Are you going to try again tomorrow, or just give up?"

"Neither: I'm going to find a way onto Elderfell myself."

"You're kidding!"

Cymbelina shushed her rowdy sister, pausing in her

movements to listen carefully to the sounds coming from the other room. After seconds of only hearing her stepfather's snoring, the brunette continued, "Do you want to wake up Mom with your shouting? Because you will."

"I'm sorry," Una scoffed, "that was my genuine reaction to hearing your absurd idea. How on Sacarnia do you think you'll get to the island on your own?"

"I'm not going alone, Una. But that's all I'm going to say until you promise not to tell anyone about my plan."

"But 'Lina, you could end up dead if you follow through with this scheme of yours!"

"You should know by now that I don't care about that."

"Well, you should!"

Cymbelina dejectedly sighed, a slightly sad look crossing her face. "Look. I understand you're concerned, and I appreciate that, but I won't go along with some half-baked plans that I think will be detrimental to our people in the long run. So," the brunette paused, moving out from behind the divider with her hands on her hips and eyebrows raised. "Do you promise to keep your mouth shut?"

The sisters sat in silence, listening to the footfalls of a guard circle around the tent and down the street. The brunette approached her bedroll once the footsteps were far enough away, slipping underneath the covers and laying on her side, her eyes set on her sister.

"I'm waiting."

Una groaned, her eyes shutting as she wrestled with the decision that lay before her. After what felt like an eternity, the younger sister acquiesced, understanding that her words held no power over her older sibling's resolve.

"Yes, 'Lina. I promise not to share your plan with anyone."

"Good. Now, here is what Kayven, Malaveen, and I have discussed so far."

An Unexpected Gathering
23rd of Winter's Breath, 1300 AC

"This is where your group plans on meeting up?" Una asked her older sibling, her voice laced with astonishment. "What about any potential guards that might wander by?"

"I told you Kayven and Malaveen are supposed to be patrolling this section of the woods during this time, remember? I doubt we'll encounter any other patrols any time soon."

"Only if you're positive," the younger sister replied cautiously, her dark blue eyes darting between the trees surrounding the clearing. Her curly black hair was pulled back in a loose ponytail, and her cloak, the color of midnight, billowed around her as she shifted in place. "I'm still not so sure this is a good idea."

"Unfortunately, the situation is as good as it's going to get," the brunette reasoned. "Now, keep your voice down. I'm sure the others will arrive shortly."

The two siblings sat under the muted morning sun, its brilliant rays concealed behind a thick curtain of winter clouds. A brisk breeze swept through the dense forest, the fiery leaves of the nearby trees dancing in the chilly wind. Some fell from their branches and waltzed to the ground, forming small piles. It was an hour after breakfast, and most of the álves in the Glenrolk camp had begun toiling away at their assigned posts. All except Cymbelina and her allies, who were set to gather in a small glade located in the Sunshade Forest along the edge of the camp.

I'm curious if Kayven and Malaveen found anyone willing to join our cause, the brunette wondered, her eyes scanning the surrounding woods. *And if they were able to find an álf or two, let's just hope they chose trustworthy ones.*

After about ten minutes of twiddling their thumbs, the sisters finally heard the sound of approaching footsteps crunching on the dead leaves scattered throughout the forest. Their eyes landed on Malaveen as she crawled out of the thick underbrush, brushing away stray foliage stuck in her flaxen locks.

"Couldn't find anyone to bring along, Malaveen?"

"Nope. I would've brought them with me if I had," the blonde answered, shaking her head to rid herself of any remaining leaves she might've missed. Standing up, she crossed her arms over her chest, her eyes falling on the black-haired she-álf. "I see you decided to bring Una. Are you sure that's wise? Are you sure she can be trusted?"

Una grimaced. "Cymbelina can certainly trust me more than she can trust you. You're the one who has relentlessly taunted her as far back as I can remember."

"That's all in the past," the blonde said, waving away the younger woman's concerns. "I'm more concerned about your age. You turned eighteen recently, did you not? I imagine you won't prove to be of much use on the battlefield, especially since your patron animal is a squirrel."

"That's rich coming from the álf who has a swan patron."

"Stop it, you two," Cymbelina chastised. "If we ever plan on reaching Elderfell, we must work together. But to answer your question, Malaveen, yes, we can trust her. She is my sister, after all."

"Blood doesn't prove loyalty."

"My statement still stands."

Malaveen was momentarily silent until she released a heavy sigh. "I hope you're right. After all, it's not your neck on the line alone, Cymbelina. We're all sacrificing our place among the Glenrolk for this mission. So we can't afford to mess up."

The sound of rustling leaves caught the attention of the

three female álves, their eyes flicking to the source of the noise. Two shadows emerged between the trees, revealing themselves as Kayven and another familiar individual. Cymbelina's heart dropped into her stomach, her gaze warily moving between her friend and the male beside him. Swallowing the lump in her throat, her mouth opened to speak as Malaveen blurted out, "Kayven, why you—"

"Why, you seem to have brought Knight Commander Emerik with you," the Half-Sylvanrolk interrupted, forcing a welcoming smile to spread across her face. "To what do we owe the pleasure?"

"You can drop the act," Kayven announced. "He visited my family's tent this morning to speak to me. Apparently, he had visited your tent too, Cymbelina, but you and Una had already left. I was his next stop."

"And what did you wish to speak to us about?" Una asked.

"While I was going to say hello to you, Una, I'll admit I mainly needed to speak to your sister. I stopped by to ask Cymbelina what she planned to do about her assignments," Emerik said, folding his arms behind his back. "Scoutmaster Estrasta and I were the only advisors who weren't keen on the tasks Kinlord Emyr gave you, Cymbelina. Although the Scoutmaster wasn't too pleased about your encounter with Jarl Yngraham, she and I agreed that your battle prowess makes you a invaluable candidate to attack the frontlines during the assault on the Dark Vilek. However, the Sylvanrolk clan leaders disagreed with our sentiment, so we were quickly overruled. Something about the Sylvan Tenets dictating that it wasn't appropriate."

The brunette snorted. *Of course, they would say something along those lines.*

"So he sought me out," Kayven continued. "He asked if I could bring him to you and potentially see if there was anything he could do to help us since he could sense we would not be following the orders handed to us."

"And he thought correctly," Malaveen spoke. "Look, Knight Commander Emerik, you've been a respectable man so far, but how do we know you won't turn us over to Kinlord Emyr after we're done here?"

"What motive would I have for doing so?" the male Magijarolk inquired. "Sure, all of the álves are working together at the moment and trying to be as honest as possible with one another, but nobody would benefit from me sharing what you all plan to do. In fact, I think that you four doing what you believe is best for the álven people is better than the plans the others have assigned for you all. For this reason, I intend to assist you, not rat you out."

The blonde raised her eyebrows. "How do you intend to help us out?"

"In any fashion I can," Emerik answered. "Although I cannot travel with the lot of you to Elderfell, as my absence will surely cause discord amongst the other leaders, I can reassign two of my fellow Elemental Álves to travel with you four to the island if you so approve."

"Thank you, Knight Commander Emerik. We can use all the help we can get, and we would be grateful for any assistance you see fit to provide."

The male smiled. "Anytime, Cymbelina. So, what have the four of you planned, anyway? It would be nice to know what exactly I've agreed to."

"As would I!" a gruff female voice called from the leafy boughs of one of the nearby trees. Jumping down from one of the thick branches, orange foliage rained upon Scoutmaster Estrasta, who adjusted her eyepatch and brushed leaves off her shoulders. Approaching the gathering, the Dokkalrolk stood between Kayven and Emerik, an intrigued look plastered on her gray face. "Hopefully, you didn't get involved in something you can't truly assist with. Wouldn't want to upset the newfound peace between the children of the ancient álfrolk, eh?"

Una chuckled, shaking her head. "So this meeting isn't such a secret after all."

"Don't worry," the scoutmaster reassured the gathering of álves, "I ensured nobody else followed you into the forest. I'm the only unexpected guest you'll receive from the camp."

"Well, that's certainly reassuring," Malaveen said, sarcasm tinging her voice. "How do we know we can trust you?"

"For the same reasons Knight Commander Emerik stated," the Dark Álf said, her eyes scanning the crowd until they landed on the brunette. "Sure, I'm not too pleased with Jarl Yngraham's demise, but I wouldn't expose your plans because of it. It would have no positive impact on the upcoming battle if I did so."

"What do you intend on bringing to the table if we let you in on the plan?"

"As charming as ever, Malaveen," Estrasta joked, a glimmer of light bouncing off her shiny black eyepatch. "I can offer the same thing as Knight Commander Emerik. I can also make sure some of my men keep your Sylvanrolk kin from finding out about your plan by redirecting any curious individuals from whatever place you decide on using as your base of operations."

Kayven nodded in approval. "That would be very helpful. I know it would certainly allow us to work efficiently without any interruptions."

"If we can ever establish what our plans are," Una pointed out.

"It's simple," Kayven began. "We'll build our own boat and mimic the plan of our kin."

"Ha! Simple?" The blonde snorted. "You call building a boat simple?"

"It is when you consider that our vessel will be smaller than those of our kin because it'll be carrying fewer people. With the four extra sets of hands Scoutmaster Estrasta and Knight Commander Emerik intend to supply us with, we can build our boat in no time."

"And then what?" Malaveen questioned, clearly irritated by Kayven's nonchalance. "We're supposed to sail beside our comrades into battle? Surely, they'll spot the extra boat."

"Not with how thick the storm will be if we sail far enough away from them," Cymbelina chipped in. "And with our own special little guide in the air," the brunette paused, motioning towards the blonde, "we'll be able to stay as far away from the rest of the group as we need to until we land ashore."

"That's a solid plan," the male Magijarolk said, his thin, pastel-green fingers resting underneath his chin. "With the size of your boat and the number of people you'll have working on it, you should be able to finish it by the seventeenth of New Star when we attack Elderfell.

"I agree, but I have one condition that needs to be met before I lend my scouts to you," Estrasta said, her gaze unwavering from the brunette. "Although I believe you are talented in combat, Cymbelina, I would like to see you resume your lessons as soon as possible. I'm no Wood Álf, but I believe the unrestrained ferocity you showed in the last battle can be attributed to the fact that your patron animal is coming close to revealing itself, and you don't know how to cope with its power."

Cymbelina froze. She hadn't expected such demands to be made of her, and she was wholly unprepared for how she should respond.

After a brief moment of silence, the brunette swallowed before replying, "Although that's an intriguing suggestion, Master Arvel was the head patron guide of the Glenrolk. If he couldn't draw my patron guardian out, nobody can."

"Nobody you've tried yet," Una said, stepping towards her sister. "Maybe I could help you concentrate your energies and draw it out, especially if it's on the precipice of revealing itself."

"That's not how it works, Una, but—"

"If you want my scouts and me to assist you in your journey to the island, you'll give it a shot," Scoutmaster Estrasta interrupted.

"Oh," the blonde scoffed, "so we're handing out ultimatums now, huh?"

"I'll do it if that's what it takes to receive your help," Cymbelina reasoned, her stomach sinking at the mere suggestion. "No matter how uncomfortable the plan makes me feel."

"So," Kayven began, attempting to wrap his head around the ideas swirling around the group of álves. "We'll meet up every day, work on the boat, and when Cymbelina and Una aren't working with us, they'll be attempting to draw out Cymbelina's patron animal so she can try to control it? That's the general gist of our scheme, correct?"

"Sounds about right to me," Emerik commented.

"Then that settles it," the Dark Álf exclaimed, clapping her hands together. "What say you and I tell our brethren about the change of plans, Knight Commander Emerik? That way, the group can start gathering supplies for the boat."

"Sounds good," the Magijarolk answered. "Where will you four set up shop?"

"Farther south, in the depths of Sunshade and along the shoreline," Una answered, her eyes flicking toward her fellow Sylvanrolk. "If that's alright with the rest of you."

"Sounds like that's as good a place as any."

"Then that settles it," Cymbelina said, her eyes scanning over her allies. "Let the preparations begin."

* * *

"Tell me once more about the deaths in front of the king's palace, Kazimiera. Especially the álves whose bodies you crushed into smithereens," Vukasino whispered, a glimmer of delight reflecting in his abyssal eyes. The ruler was sprawled out on his throne, with his head resting on one of the armrests while his legs dangled over another. He kicked the seat like an excited child, his sharp teeth gleaming in the dim light of the throne room.

Knight Kazimiera's smile faltered slightly, the fairy trying to contain her frustration of having to tell the story again. "Well, Your Majesty, two Dokkalrolk were so busy attempting to kill one of our vilek soldiers that they didn't see me sneaking up behind them. Fortunately, our sister saw me, so she played along. Backing up to put some space between her and the álves, she gave me ample room to bring a rocky overhang down upon the enemy."

"And..." the male goaded his servant on, his eyes full of twisted glee.

"Well... let's just say the path was no longer gray when the ceiling crushed their weak bodies."

The monarch released a demented cackle, which echoed throughout the mostly empty room. The muted sconces adorning either side of the throne room accentuated his delighted chewing as he popped a grape into his mouth. "Oh, my, would I have loved to have seen that."

The wooden doors leading into the expansive room swung open, banging against the stone walls as a steadfast Mistress Tihana approached the throne. Haphazardly bowing before the ruler's seat, the alchemist spoke.

"Your Lordship, there is much we need to discuss."

Vukasino placed another piece of fruit into his mouth. "Such as?"

"Future battle preparations?" Tihana said expectantly, shaking an unrolled parchment in her hand. "I'm here for you to review them. We still have a lot of work to do regarding taking over Florella. We might've experienced a monumental victory a few weeks ago, but that doesn't mean we've won this war."

Masticating the remainder of a berry, he swallowed, his black eyes resting on the female before him. "I will review them posthaste; simply leave them on one of the nightstands in my chambers, and I'll glance them over before I rest for the night."

"With all due respect, Your Lordship, I've known you since the moment you entered this world. I know you'll never read the plans if I put them there. Please, for my sanity, take a look at them now. I'll be able to stop pestering you if you do."

"You'll stop pestering me immediately if I command you to do so," the ruler growled, "but because I'm getting somewhat bored of Kazimiera's storytelling, I'll take a look. You may approach the throne."

Vukasino's bodyguards relaxed as the alchemist approached the royal seat, kneeling before it. Her grayish-blue hands held out the scroll for the leader of Elderfell. Snatching the paper out of her hands, the male glanced over the document, his eyebrows raising as he sat up in his seat.

"You want to send off a hundred troops to the mainland? Whatever for?"

"To patrol the area around the mountains and disperse," the scientist said. "We must ensure those álven dogs stay down before they can gather and bolster their defenses. Who knows, they might even try to attack Elderfell. I say we continue to attack their settlements to prevent that from happening."

The visi-vilek looked from Tihana to the scroll repeatedly, a sense of anger brimming in his core until it came bursting forth. The male fairy tore the parchment to shreds as he stood up. His tall, lanky frame loomed above the kneeling woman, the man's wings fluttering in agitation.

"You need to focus on distributing the potion to the troops, not handing me battle stratagems. I told you to stop doing stupid things last time we talked at length, did I not?"

When the alchemist didn't respond, the male took a deep breath, resting his gray face on his hand and slowly rubbing his forehead. "Oh, Tihana, oh Tihana, oh, Tihana. I keep you employed because I admire your work. Hell, I allow you to live because I feel like I owe it to you since you helped to create me. But you make both of these decisions harder and harder to maintain with each passing day."

The woman remained silent. Her body was still as a corpse, her head bent toward the ground. If she was displeased with how the ruler was addressing her, she did not make it known.

"I order you to return to your lab," the male paused, his voice much more even-tempered than before, "and do what I've told you to do countless times. Work on creating more batches of the Elixir of Annihilmon until you have made enough for every soldier on Elderfell. And, while you're at it, maybe draft some new ideas for other potions that our troops might find useful. Is that assignment clear enough for you?"

The vilek nodded, her eyes drifting from the cold floor to the chilly gaze of the monarch. "Yes, Monarch Vukasino."

"Good. Now leave my throne room."

The scientist stood up, preparing to do what she was told. Reluctantly bowing before the ruler of Elderfell, the female turned away, slowly making her way toward the door.

"You'll regret this decision," the scientist mumbled under her breath, a scowl pulling at her gray lips.

"What did you say?"

"I said that I plan to do exactly what you said, Your Lordship. Good evening."

"'Tis a good evening indeed," the male fairy said, his cocksure grin returning as he watched Tihana leave the room. Returning to his throne, the man turned toward one of his other knights. "Now, Bojana, I want you to repeat the story of the álf you set ablaze during the battle."

* * *

The weeks passed by in an erratic blur. All of Cymbelina's time was either spent building the boat she and her allies planned on taking to Elderfell, participating in unorthodox patron lessons with her sister, or avoiding the inquisitive probing of her parents. Much progress had been made in constructing the vessel, and Cymbelina felt pride well up in her chest whenever she laid eyes on it. She was also pleased that she and Una avoided revealing the truth of their daily whereabouts to their parents. Whether it was because Deirdre and Séacael were too busy dealing with their own projects or too focused on the upcoming battle, Cymbelina did not know; all she knew was that she was glad she and her allies were never caught.

What she was not delighted about, however, was her inability to discover her patron guardian. The brunette believed that although Una's heart was in the right place, she was ultimately wasting her time attempting to help her older sister, that all of the odd lessons they had been going through together had been all for naught. She felt this way down in the depths of her heart. Until Cymbelina closed her eyes on the eve of the battle.

Cymbelina found herself enraptured in a nightmare relating to her patron lessons for the first time in what felt like an eternity. A murky abyss surrounded her rigid frame, the only light source originating from behind the she-álf in the entryway where the padlocked door used to stand. The rhythmic breathing of an unseen being bathed Cymbelina in warmth. A pair of infernal, serpentine eyes gazed down upon her as she glared back. The air was acrid, probably due to the being's breath. Scrunching up her nose, the she-álf confronted the lifeform.

"Are you the being I've been communicating with this entire time? The one that was behind the padlocked door? The one that helped me during the fight against Jarl Yngraham?"

"Of course I am," the creature answered curtly. "What else would I be?"

"Where have you been?" the brunette questioned, a hint of trepidation creeping into her voice. "You haven't made yourself known since the jarl's death."

A guttural rumble emanated from deep within the being's throat, a swishing sound emerging from the shadows to Cymbelina's left. "I don't follow a schedule, *servanus*. I communicate with you as I please."

"You've called me that before, shortly before you insisted that I am not half-human. What does that even mean? Why do you call me that?"

"You'll know the answer to those questions in due time. And once again," the creature's voice dropped to a menacing whisper, "you are not part human. Stop speaking such blasphemy."

"If that's the case, then what am I?"

The creature chuckled, the sound causing the floor to tremble as its eyes closed in twisted mirth. "I have already stated that your answers will come soon."

The brunette's patience was wearing thin, her frustration

akin to a storm threatening to unleash havoc on the world. Here she was, communicating with the obscured creature for the first time in weeks, and it was avoiding everything she asked.

I refuse to be toyed with in my own head, the brunette thought, her lip curling in frustration.

"Why can't you just be straight with me?! Why can't I know the answers that I seek now?! Why Must I wait?!" Cymbelina argued, her piercing eyes boring into the creature's orange ones.

"Your generation lacks patience, young one. It is best that you take this time to learn it."

"It's not patience that I'm lacking, creature. It's my trust in you. After all, how am I supposed to believe anything you say when you refuse to answer my inquiries? How am I supposed to put my faith in you?!"

The ground quaked as the glowing orange eyes suddenly rose up, standing about ten feet above the álf, who could not hide the slight tremble in her frame as she gazed upon the gigantic being towering above her. Still concealed by shadows, Cymbelina was left to guess what the creature looked like.

"Listen to me and listen to me carefully, child. I don't require you to believe anything I say, and frankly, I don't care if you do. The truth of the situation will remain the same. There are a few things I require of you, *animus hospi.* Things that you have not been supplying. Things that when I lack, I do not appear."

"And what would those things be?"

The being paused as its eyes narrowed.

"Bloodshed, hatred, relentlessness: these are the things I seek, Cymbelina," the creature growled, its intense voice sending shivers down the female's spine as she heard it utter her name. "Supply me with these things, and you'll discover that which you crave to know more than anything on this godforsaken planet."

Before the she-álf could question the being further, she was yanked out of her vision by frantic shaking. The brunette's green eyes shot open to lay upon the source of the movement, which happened to be Una.

"Wake up, Cymbelina! Today's the day we give those Dark Fairies what's coming to them."

Assailing The Army Of Elderfell
17th of New Star, 1301 AC

"Is anyone going to help me get this boat into the water? Because there's no way I'll be able to push this into the ocean alone!"

"Patience, Malaveen: the others will be here soon. Plus, we discussed that we would leave shore after our allies had already left for Elderfell. That way, there's even a lesser chance we'll be spotted in the snowstorm."

"We can barely see where we're going now, Kayven!" the blonde yelled, her voice barely audible over the blustery winds. "If we didn't have two Magijarolk with us," the woman paused, motioning towards the Elemental Álves Usenia and Andrzej, "there is no way we'd be able to see where we're going. We must leave soon, and all eight of us are accounted for except Una and Cymbelina. Where the hell are they?!"

The wintry winds howled across the Sunshade Forest, affecting the rebellious álves sequestered in a forested pocket south of the Glenrolk camp. The six warriors huddled together, their fur cloaks doing little to shield them from the frosty onslaught as they awaited Cymbelina and Una's arrival. The only álves unfazed by the Earth Mother's frozen breath were the Dokkalrolk scouts that Scoutmaster Estrasta assigned to Cymbelina and her allies, Kivi and Dagver. Standing beside the clustered rebels, the Dark Álves looked from side to side, scanning the surrounding woods for the sisters.

"*Dihaal*, it's freezing out here. Dagver!" Malaveen shouted, looking over her shoulder as she tried to push the vessel into the freezing waves, shivering beside her fellow álves. "Do you see anything?"

"Not yet, but I'm sure they'll turn up soon."

"They...ugh...better!" The female grunted, her boots sinking into the snow-covered sand as she continued to push. "I swear to Mother Terralynia if they don't turn up any minute now—"

"Look!" Kivi shouted, his shrill vocalization barely discernable over the rapid winds, "here comes Cymbelina and Una now!"

Emerging from the snow-covered undergrowth with cloaks billowing in the high winds, the sisters laggardly approached their allies. With squinted eyes, Cymbelina peered through the white winds rushing along the shore, holding her fur hood close to her face as she gazed at her allies.

"Sorry for our tardiness, but we need to go. Now!"

"You're not kidding!" Malaveen yelled, standing beside the boat and cupping her hands around her mouth. "What took you two so long to begin with?!"

"You mean besides the raging storm sweeping across the land?" Una loudly snorted, standing beside the álves gathered around the boat. "Our mother, that's who. 'Lina and I think she's caught onto our plan. She wouldn't stop talking to us this morning. The boat she's assigned to is destined to leave shore last, so she had all the time in the world."

"Shit," Kayven said, exasperated. "Change of plans, everyone: we need to leave shore immediately. We can't take any chances of getting caught by Deirdre if she's followed Cymbelina and Una here."

Putting their backs into their pushing, all eight warriors pushed against the sturdy vessel, a cacophony of grunts echoing on the freezing gales.

It'll be all my fault if we're caught here today, Cymbelina thought, her face screwing into a look of distress as she gave her all into pushing the ship into the brumal waves. *I'll never forgive myself if any of us get in trouble today.*

"My eyes must deceive me! I know you two are not about to hop into that boat without saying goodbye to me!"

A shiver ran down the brunette's spine, her pointed ears slightly twitching upon hearing the all too familiar voice of her mother, Deirdre. Stopping her pushing, Cymbelina stood up and turned around, her younger sister following suit. The duo's action drew an agitated shriek from Malaveen.

"What are you two doing?! Your mom has already found us; we should leave shore *now* before any reinforcements she might've brought arrive!"

"I doubt she brought anyone else with her, and knowing her, she won't leave until we talk to her. Give us a few moments to drive her off."

"Well, hurry up then!" The blonde scoffed, grunting as she continued her attempts to get the vessel into the water. "We only have a battle to win, nothing major."

Looking around at her other allies and not seeing any signs of disagreement, Cymbelina nodded, motioning to Una to follow her as the older sister approached Deirdre.

Their boots disappeared into the snow with each step they took toward their mother. Deirdre's gray cloak undulated in the storm, her cerulean eyes like ice as she stared through the snow flurries at her disheartened daughters.

"I see you followed us here."

"Of course I did. I had to discover where you two have been sneaking off these past few weeks," the mother answered her eldest daughter.

Cymbelina cocked an eyebrow. "So you know we haven't been reporting to our assigned posts?"

Deirdre barked out a laugh. "I've known for quite a while now that you two haven't been doing as the leaders instructed. Not because someone reported you two for it, but because I'm your mother. I sense these sorts of things."

Unable to contain herself, Una rushed towards her mother, who enveloped her in a giant bear hug. Burying her hooded head into the crux of her mother's neck, the black-haired woman sobbed, "I'm so sorry, Mom. I would've told you, but—"

"But you wanted to help Cymbelina," Deirdre finished, predicting her youngest daughter's words as she held her closer. "Yes, yes, I know, Sweetheart."

"Did you come here to convince us not to take this route to Elderfell? I can't speak for Una, but your persuasion won't work on me...not this time."

"Let's be honest; there have been very few times in your twenty-two years of life that I've convinced you of anything, Cymbelina. So, no, I have not come here to try to sway you from following through on whatever plan the eight of you have devised. All I ask is that you watch over your sister and take care of these."

Deirdre paused, pulling away from Una as her hands drifted to the scabbards situated on either hip. Pulling on the grips of both blades, she unsheathed Cymbelina's prize. Two daggers, the likes of which the brunette had never seen before, were resting in her mother's cold palms. Although both blades were silver, similar to those of some of Cymbelina's companions, the pommels were the most foreign aspect of the weapons. Situated atop a black grip on each sword was a carmine-hued dragon head with orange jeweled eyes the color of the fires of Infernus. Just by quickly glancing at the ornate elements of the weapons, the she-álf could tell they weren't crafted by an álf of any sort: no álven blacksmith would create daggers with the head of a being that destroyed the homeland of their ancestors.

"These weren't made by any álf I know. Were these my father's blades?"

"Indeed they were, Cymbelina. Ignatius always kept them hidden in his trunk, and I'm sure he left them behind as a gift for you. I was going to give them to you after you mastered your patron animal, but I think the circumstances warrant me to give them to you beforehand."

A content look lay behind Cymbelina's pine-green eyes as they darted over the weapons. It was as if a crucial piece of a puzzle had finally clicked into place. Her mind buzzed with a sensation she had never experienced before, her heart

330

pounding at a frenetic pace. A wave of exhilaration washed over her, etching a smile on her frost-kissed features.

"Thank you, Mom. This gift means a lot to me."

"I knew it would. Now, give me the daggers on your hips. I'll need some weapons during the battle, after all."

The brunette nodded, quickly exchanging the steel daggers on her sides for the silver ones in her mother's grasp.

"This is all very touching," Malaveen shouted, "but I think it's time we left!"

"Malaveen's right," Deirdre sighed. "I'm sure my companions will be wondering where I am. We're supposed to sail soon, after all."

"Good luck in the battle, Mother. May the ancestors guide you."

"May the ancestors guide the both of you!" Deirdre shouted as the winds picked up, hugging her daughters before fleeing into the woods. "Make me proud!"

"We will, Mom!" the brunette replied, looking at her sister and then at her awaiting allies. "We will."

"Any day now!" The blonde screamed, her voice barely discernable in the snowy torrent beating against the trees in the forest.

"We're coming!" Una yelled, grabbing her older sister's hand and leading her toward the boat.

After several minutes of strenuous pushing, the eight álves finally sent the vessel into the freezing waves, the wintery waters sloshing against the wooden boat. With oars at the ready, the álves designated to sail began their rowing.

"I guess it's my time to shine," Malaveen said confidently, rolling her head on her shoulders. "I'll check back with frequent updates. All I need from you two," the blonde said, pointing to the Magijarolk, "is to push that snowstorm forward as much as possible. That will allow me to see farther ahead without expending too much energy trying to fly through the blizzard."

"We know our tasks," Andrzej answered. "Just keep an eye on the sea. Usenia and I will figure out the rest."

Malaveen nodded, transforming into her swan form and soaring into the blistery air, leaving the remaining álves on the boat.

We can do this, Cymbelina thought, her eyes shifting from Malaveen's ascending form to the western horizon. *Nothing can stop us from getting to Elderfell now.*

After three hours of vigorous rowing and routine reports from Malaveen, the eight adventurers arrived at the Dark Fairy's island slightly off course, sailing into an uninhabited cove hidden off the side of the main shoreline.

Settled underneath a gigantic stone fortress looming over the coastline, the inlet bled into a cave. Two small, rickety docks branched off the sandy shore, rowboats filled with fishing nets lining either side. Empty weapon racks were scattered around the docking area, but there were no signs of life besides the small, frightened crabs that scurried away as the álves' boat rowed ashore.

A damp stench permeated the air as the adventurers hopped out of their vessel, the cold waves splashing against their boots as they sunk into the coarse sand. The distant sound of swords clashing floated on the frigid winds, making it clear to the outsiders why such a sensitive entrance might be left unguarded.

"Our allies only arrived minutes ago, and the enemy has already redirected some of their troops to the frontlines. Maybe that's a sign that the Dark Vilek are not large in number."

"I wouldn't get your hopes up, Usenia," Kivi stated, his eyes scanning the cave again. "Most of us have seen what these fairies can accomplish with minimal troops. Even if they are small in number, they put up a hell of a fight and should not be underestimated."

Cymbelina nodded in agreement as she did a once-over of her surroundings. Situated on the far side of the cave sat a slight stony incline, which led to a reinforced wooden door.

"Well, sitting here and chatting won't help our allies any.

Look at that door over there," the brunette directed, motioning toward the opening. "I bet that's our way out of this wretched cove. Come on, and keep a sharp eye; the last thing we need is for our enemies to ambush us."

Following the Half-Sylvanrolk's lead, the álves cautiously approached the doorway. Cymbelina stood on the tips of her toes to peek through the barred window at the top of the wooden structure. Squinting, she saw a cavernous, abandoned walkway scarcely lit by a handful of flickering torches. After examining the corridor for a painstaking minute, Cymbelina decided the way forward was clear and ushered her companions into the musty hallway. The chilly, fetid air pierced their nostrils as they raced onward, their ears ringing as the sounds of nearby battle bounced off the corridor's dank walls. Cymbelina kept her hands close to her weapons as her eyes remained fixed on a faint glow of sunlight at the end of the tunnel.

After passing many hallways and rooms, the warriors reached the end of the passageway, which was marked by another wooden door. Standing on her toes again, the brunette gazed through the barred hole at the top of the structure and out onto one of the fortress' many courtyards. She saw fairies rushing to and fro, their voices unintelligible under the uproar of the raging battle and the winds of the dwindling snowstorm.

"Well, our troops obviously caught them by surprise," the brunette whispered, her eyes trained on the dispersing vilek as they scrambled in different directions. Seven of them headed towards the battlement on the closest curtain wall to fire spells down at the álves attacking the fortress gate.

"Do you see any of our men and women on the battlefield?"

"Not yet, Dagver," Cymbelina replied. "But maybe they're around here somewhere. I'm sure we'll need the help."

"Well," Malaveen questioned, "what do you see?"

"I see seven Dark Vilek on the battlements, so if we sneak up on them without being detected, maybe we can take up their positions and help our allies breach the fortress."

Before any of the brunette's companions could voice their opinion on the plan, a door on the opposite end of the fortress's courtyard swung open, distracting the Dark Fairies from their assault on the incoming álven troops. A mountain lion bathed in a coral-hued aura emerged from within the doorway, two Dokkalrolk and a Magijarolk hot on the creature's trail. The lion strategically lept at the closest fairy, its álven companions shooting arrows at the fairies the lion couldn't reach.

"It seems I spoke too soon," Cymbelina remarked, her eyes darting back and forth as she gripped the door handle. "It seems backup has arrived. Get ready for me to open the door so we can help."

Giving her companions a few seconds to prepare, Cymbelina flung the door open, stepping to the side to allow her friends to flow into the courtyard. Dagver and Kivi, who were standing behind the half-álf, shot arrows at two of the vilek while Andrzej used his wind powers to push one of the unsuspecting fairies over the side of the fortress walls.

The enemies were taken down quickly through both groups' combined efforts, leaving the two coteries of álven warriors to stare at each other.

Transforming into her natural form, the mountain lion was revealed to be Kinlady Nairna. Flipping one of her thick onyx braids over her shoulder, the clan leader looked over the brunette and her allies, a mixture of scrutiny and relief filling her gaze.

"Cymbelina of the Glenrolk. What a surprise." The woman took a deep breath, still recovering from the previous fray. The sounds of nearby battle bounced off of the walls of the nearly barren courtyard. "I don't recall Kinlord Emyr drafting you orders to attend today's battle. In fact, I distinctly remember him assigning you cleanup duty back at camp."

"As you can see, Kinlady Nairna, my grandfather's plans fell through," the brunette said, glossing over the implied accusations of disobedience thrown in her direction. "How far have you and your companions traversed into enemy territory?

334

Is this the first batch of fairies you've been able to take down?"

The clan leader smiled, her grin laced with vexation. "You disobeyed the orders of not only your clan leader but every other álven official: I won't forget that. But for now, there's nothing that can be done about it. To answer your question, this is the first area the scouts and I have attacked. While approaching the castle, we spotted several groups of fairies raining arrows down upon the vanguard infantry. Three groups of scouts, including my own, have set out to quell the threat. I'm just hoping their efforts proved to be as successful as ours."

"Where are the other groups of archers that you saw?" Kayven inquired.

"Mainly along the castle walls to the north of here. I planned on dragging my group over there, but since you guys are here, I think you should be the ones to take out the archers. There can't be too many of them."

Malaveen cocked an eyebrow. "And what will you do?"

"Dive deeper into the city, investigate any barracks where these fairies might be coming from, and cut them off before they can regroup with their compatriots. Maybe we'll find a way to open the main gate while we're at it. Now go; the time for useless chatter is over."

The brunette nodded, gathering her allies and heading toward the northeastern section of the curtain walls.

Dark clouds swirled above the fortress as wintry winds pummeled at the outsiders' hoods. The air reeked of charred turf as the fire attacks from the fairies began to spread across the dried grass surrounding the castle, the pungent smell invading the back alleys the álves darted through to sneak past the Dark Vilek. From the group's position in one of the fortress' many alleyways, it was easy for Cymbelina to spot the enemy's castle, which loomed above the rest of the settlement atop a rocky mount. Like a dreadful beacon, the brunette's eyes were glued to the ominous structure, dozens of stone steps cascading down from the stony peak.

I bet whoever is behind this war is situated atop their throne, tucked

335

away in that creepy castle, sending out their mindless hordes to do their bidding. What a coward.

"I think those are the archers Kinlady Nairna was talking about!" shouted Usenia, who had caught up to Cymbelina and the other álves. The Magijarolk pointed north of the warriors' position, past the rows of darkened buildings and up a slight incline.

Following the woman's yellow digit with her eyes, the brunette saw a group of archers near a few homes along the battlements, firing down at unseen warriors.

"Let's take care of them quickly," Cymbelina mumbled. "The sooner we dispatch the archers, the sooner we can get our allies into the castle."

"And the sooner we can end this bloody feud," Malaveen spat.

As the warriors ascended the incline, a loud crack reverberated through the air, followed by distant shouting that clearly belonged to the group's álven brethren.

Our allies were clearly able to get through the gate, Cymbelina thought, her green eyes glued to the enemies ahead. *That happened unexpectedly fast.*

Before any of the álves could even react to the small victory their allies had achieved at the gates, the vilek archers the group had hoped to sneak up on abruptly turned their attention toward them, their fae-made bows now menacingly aimed at the outsiders.

Feeling for the daggers at her hip, the brunette armed herself. All of her brethren followed suit except Kayven, who assumed his wolven form. The álves then lunged at the archers, weaving their way in and out to avoid being hit by one of their arrows, their every move a dance with death.

Cymeblina's gaze was set on a grayish, pink-hued fairy. The vilek dropped her bow, her thin fingers curling inward as flames danced on the palms of her dirty hands. With her hate-filled, bluish-green eyes locked onto the brunette, the woman's dry mouth moved subtly, her head quickly twitching to the side as she pulled back her arm.

"I don't know what you just said," the brunette yelled, gripping her father's daggers tighter as she prepared to dodge a fireball, "but I have a feeling I wouldn't like it if I did."

The fairy screamed, her shriek akin to a banshee, before casting a fireball at the brunette. The flame-made orb grazed past the brunette's leather-clad bicep as she side-stepped out of the way and continued toward the fairy, her heart pounding in her chest. Reaching her target, Cymbelina swiped, her dagger cutting through the air as the fairy dodged the attack. Picking up one of her arrows off the ground, the vilek broke it in two, using a part of the shaft and the arrowhead as a melee weapon to attack the female Sylvanrolk.

The duo attacked each other back and forth, neither giving in to the other's desperate strikes. Scratches and gashes adorned both women's forearms, their eyes never wavering from those of their opponent until the brunette made a well-calculated thrust forward, burying the dagger from her right hand into the fairy's sternum.

The pink vilek emitted a gurgling gasp, blood slowly oozing from around the blade in her chest. Staggering backward, the Dark Vilek collapsed to the cobblestone ground with a thud. Pulling her dagger from the corpse, the she-álf looked down at the sword in awe as she took in an aspect of the blade she hadn't been able to notice before.

A faint glow emanated from underneath the cobalt liquid coating her weapon. Shaking the blood from her knife, the brunette noticed runic text scrawled underneath the blade's fuller, the letters glowing a bright shade of orange. She was ignorant of the message's meaning, as she had never laid eyes on the language before, but whatever it was drew her in.

I wonder if Dad told Mom about this. Maybe she knows what this says.

"Are you going to sit there and gawk at your new weapons all day, or do you plan on helping us?!"

Returning to her senses after Malaveen's outburst, the brunette assisted in executing the remaining fairies that threatened her allies. Once their enemies had been defeated,

337

Cymbelina noticed that the group was an álf short: Kivi. His burnt body lay crumpled in the corner of the battlements, his lifeless brown eyes staring up at the stormy sky. Dagver knelt next to his fellow Dokkalrolk, his hands clasped together in prayer to Mother Terralynia.

Cymbelina stared at the Dark Álf, his pain emanating from his quaking body in waves. Parting her chapped lips, she said, "They'll pay for what happened to Kivi, Dagver. Let us avenge him by moving forward to take down the rest of their army."

"You're right," the grieving male sniffled, his hands balled into fists as he stood up, wiping away a stray tear. "Let's give these monsters what's coming to them. Where to next?"

"I say we hit them where it hurts," Una announced, motioning towards the set of stairs leading up to the gloomy castle, filled with their allies as they ran to the fortress. "It looks like that's what our kin are doing."

"We should join them," Kayven added, transforming out of his wolven state. "I can't even fathom the bloodbath occurring up there."

"If it's anything like the one happening down here, those álves will need help." Grabbing the quiver of arrows and a bow that had belonged to one of the fairies, Cymbelina armed herself with an extra weapon. "Let's take any supplies these fairies no longer need. No telling what sort of danger awaits us at the top of those steps."

Quickly looting the nearby corpses, the group continued their journey to the citadel, fighting any remaining vilek that stood in their path. During the trek up the burdensome steps, the group lost Usenia, who tumbled over the side of the staircase as she was battling a fairy. Andrzej called out in agony for his Magijarolk sister but kept moving forward, knowing full well he was unable to help her now.

Reaching the top of the summit, the group reunited with Knight Commander Emerik, who was directing an assembly of wind-controlling Magijarolk to aim wind streams at the fortified door, determined to batter the door down.

"You couldn't have made it at a better time," the male

huffed, skipping the pleasantries. "Andrzej, assist your kin in opening the door. Where is Usenia? We could definitely use her help right now."

"She-she didn't make it, sir. Neither did the Dokkalrolk named Kivi."

"*Jetav*," the green-skinned álf sighed, his lips pursing and eyes closing. "So many lives have been lost on this day. They shall be given proper burials, but for now, we need to open this blasted door."

Cymbelina stepped forward. "How can we be of assistance?"

"You can help by preventing our enemies from reaching the top of the steps. The fewer interruptions we have up here, the less time it will take us to break into the fortress."

Nodding in agreement, all of the remaining group members besides Andrzej descended a few steps, their eyes peering into the throng of fairies below.

The deranged beings let loose a ballad of disharmonious screeches and wails as they scaled the stone staircase, some of their numbers toppling over the side as they pushed one another to get to the top.

Forming a line along a set of steps, the warriors readied their bows, aiming at the relentless fae that charged their way.

"I guess it's a good thing we grabbed the bows! Everyone, take aim," Cymbelina shouted, naturally guiding her allies. "And fire!"

The álven fighters let loose a torrent of arrows upon the impending vilek forces, some projectiles hitting the fairies between the eyes and others clattering to the ground. Discordant screams echoed in the winter air, the bodies of the fallen fairies tumbling down the steps as those of the living called out for their fallen sisters. Piles formed at the bottom of the stairs, a river of sparkling blue blood flowing through the central courtyard of the fortress.

The deafening sound of the Magijarolks' wind crashing against the wooden doors formed a drum-like rhythm in the background of the onslaught, Cymbelina's gaze flicking to and fro as she adjusted her sights on the next target.

There's no end to them, the brunette thought, firing an arrow into the heart of a fairy and watching her tumble back down the steps. *No matter how many we shoot, more seem to come through.*

Regardless of the number of arrows that rained down upon the enemy, most of the fairy women seemed to pull through. Rising to their feet, the injured vilek aimed fireballs and loose debris at the álven archers, forcing them to ascend the stairs again.

Reaching for the quiver strapped to her back, the brunette found it empty, her heart sinking into the depths of her stomach.

"Fall back!" The Half-Sylvanrolk yelled frantically, tossing her bow to the side and reaching for her daggers, "But keep giving them all you have!"

The allies continued their attacks as more fairies fell down the steps, adding to the pile of ever-growing bodies. The metallic scent of blood assaulted the brunette's nostrils as she backed up behind her friends, waiting to fight any stray fairies that might reach their position.

Luckily for Cymbelina's group, some of their álven allies reached the bottom of the steps and assisted the archers, thinning out their numbers in the courtyard and preventing any more from reaching the summit.

Thank the Goddess for our allies. I don't know how much longer we would've lasted.

A ringing crack echoed through the air as more of the fairies on the steps were picked off. Flipping her stance, Cymbelina saw the wooden doors of the castle slam open, dozens of wind-controlling Elemental Álves flooding into the dark entryway.

That's more like it! Hopefully, the Dark Fairies will fall quickly after we seize the fortress.

Much to her distaste, Cymbelina's elation was short-lived. Although the Magijarolk had broken through the entryway and gained entrance to the castle, the foes within the building seemed to be more formidable than any of the fairies the álves had encountered on the steps. Moving with a speed the Half-Sylvanrolk had not seen from the vilek all day, three silver-armored fairies attacked the Magijarolk that opened the door to the fortress. Treating their bodies like ragdolls, the fairies flung the álves every which way. Some hit the walls within the darkened room, and others flew out of the fortress and landed near Cymbelina's boot-clad feet.

Looking at the mass of allies that struggled to regain their composure, Cymbelina frantically turned to her partners, spitballing her newfound idea.

"This is where we split up!" the she-álf called out, her voice barely audible over the sounds of battle. "We should have three people stay here to aid our kin at the bottom of the stairs while the rest of us help the Magijarolk in the keep!"

"Go ahead!" Malaveen yelled, shooting another fairy in the head and watching it tumble back down the stairs, its limp frame joining the mass of bodies on the ground. "I'll stay here."

"As will I!" Dagver and Kayven offered simultaneously.

"Then that just leaves us," Cymbelina paused, her eyes filled with a mix of determination and worry as she glanced at her sister. Dried vilek blood coated her pale face, which bore an expression born of pure exhaustion.

"Are you ready?" the brunette asked in a way that was clear to the younger woman that 'no' was not an acceptable answer.

Inadvertently swiping a streak of dirt across her forehead as she wiped the sweat away, Una huffed, "I'm as ready as I'll ever be."

Without uttering another syllable, Cymbelina guided Una to the gigantic wooden doors, both álves glancing within the darkened estate.

The fray between the strengthed Dark Vilek and Magijarolk raged on, the silver-plated women dispatching álf after álf while somehow withstanding the countless attacks aimed in their direction. Their frames were cloaked in the familiar black aura, which rippled with each maneuver the vilek executed.

Of course, whoever is behind this would keep their strongest warriors back in the stronghold. It's a bloodbath in here, the brunette thought, a shot of pain running down her right arm as she reached for one of her daggers. *Might as well add to it.*

Flipping one of her daggers in her hand as she grabbed the hilt of the other, Cymbelina eyed a yellow-skinned fairy who stood proudly above a fallen Magijarolk. Attempting to draw the being away from her allies, she called out, "Hey! *Du mongra!*"

The yellow being jerked her head to the right and tilted it. She looked Cymbelina over, her eyes consumed by a type of darkness even the dead of night couldn't replicate. Short, white locks framed her dirty face, each strand covered in chunks of gore. She bared her sharpened teeth, a ferocious grin slowly spreading across her yellowish-gray face.

Una tensed as she harshly inquired, "Why are you luring it this way?! Why—"

"To lead her away from Emerik and the rest of the Magijarolk, why else?!"

The fairy's hand darted to the blade at her hip, her body pivoting to squarely face the sisters. Her wicked grin remained on her face as she nonchalantly brandished her sword. Crimson sprayed the ground as the vilek swung the weapon back and forth, creating a macabre path leading to the estate's entryway.

"Do I frighten you, little *álves*?!" The vilek shouted, her tone laced with malice clearly meant to antagonize the Sylvanrolk. "Are you afraid you'll end up like your dead brethren fertilizing Elderfell soil?"

I've had enough of these games, the eldest sibling thought to herself, a sneer spreading across her dirt and blood-stained face. *It's time to take this vermin down a notch.*

Bracing her sore legs, the brunette broke out into a dash toward their provoker. The yellow fairy followed suit.

"Cymbelina," Knight Commander Emerik called out, "stay back!"

The Dark Vilek's forward sprint was abruptly halted by a thick slab of rock, which came crashing down from the ceiling with a deafening thud, crushing the sanguine-soaked fairy.

"*Dihaal!*" the Half-Sylvanrolk shouted, digging her heels into the path to cease her movement.

Dust and dirt particles formed a dark cloud around Cymbelina's panting frame as she came to a halt, her green eyes fixed on the ground where the vilek once stood. Sparkly blue blood pooled out from underneath the rock and spread to the tips of her close-toed shoes. A yellowish-gray right arm was the only remnant of the fairy's corpse that could be seen from underneath the piece of ceiling, the brunette watching as a few of the being's digits continued to twitch. Slowly turning her eyes away from the scene of her enemy's brutal end, the Half-Sylvanrolk looked to the right.

The Magijarolk leader was sitting on the stone floor with his legs spread wide, his back propped against one of the interior corridor's walls. The grime coating his face hid his bright, pastel-green skin. A few of his white, disheveled locks formed a curtain over one of his soft, red eyes, which were framed by purplish-blue circles. One of Emerik's delicate hands cupped a deep gash carved into his stomach while the other slowly fell from its pointing position and landed by his leg.

"Knight Commander Emerik!"

The Half-Sylvanrolk rushed to the Elemental Àlf's side, ignoring the clash that raged on in the room ahead. Una joined her older sister's side by kneeling beside the injured man.

"Are you alright?"

"I'll... I'll survive," the man paused, breaking out into a coughing fit. "Forget about me, Cymbelina; I'll be ok. You...you need to charge forward. Help our kin defeat the remaining fairies and stop whatever monster is behind this."

"But Emerik, you saved me. I can't just—"

"He's right, Sis. Look!"

Cymbelina glanced at where her sister was pointing.

The Magijarolk had been able to take down one of the armored vilek terrorizing the throneroom, but one still remained at large. The bit of greenish-gray skin that peeked out between her armor plates was coated in blood, along with the spear that she clutched in her dirtied palms. Slicing the

Elemental Àlves that continuously tried to form a circle around her, the Dark Vilek continued to fight, her momentum seemingly endless.

"If you want to find a way to repay me for my assistance," Emerik paused, spitting blood, "help take down that fairy. Help...Help save my fellow Magijarolk."

With a curt nod, the brunette thanked the knight commander once more as she and her sister approached the throne room. However, before Cymbelina could formulate any sort of plans with her younger sister, she caught a glimpse of a strange figure she hadn't noticed before. Donning a gray coat, the mysterious individual dashed down a hallway at the opposite end of the room.

That could be the leader of the Dark Vilek army!

"Then what are you waiting for?" The familiar voice within her mind screamed. *"Chase after them!"*

As if in a trance, Cymbelina listened to the deep voice nestled within her mind without a sliver of hesitation, throwing her previous obligation to Emerik to the wind as she raced after the hooded person.

"Cymbelina, wait!"

Una's words fell on deaf, pointed ears as she chased after the retreating figure, desperate to know their identity. Refusing to leave the Magijarolk to their fate, Una helped the remaining álves fight the armored fairy, leaving Cymbelina to traverse the corridor alone.

The she-álf's boot-clad feet hit the ground in repetitive thumps, the plum-hued carpeting scrunching beneath her feet as she followed the cloaked figure through a series of winding hallways. The stranger's swift movement caused the torches on the wall to flicker and wave, their shifting shadows dancing over the dozens of ornate portraits hanging in solemn rows. Cymbelina's pulse pounded in her ears as she glanced from the pictures to the person ahead, her breath coming in rapid, shallow bursts.

I can't let them get away, I can't let them get away, I can't let them get away.

"Then don't! Keep following them!"

The pursuit abruptly ended as both people reached a dead end, the only thing on the wall being a window overlooking the tumultuous sea. Wind pouring through the window pummeled both figures, Cymbelina's hair swishing in the blustery breeze as a content smirk spread across her face.

"There's nowhere left for you to run!" The brunette called out, her breath coming out in short pants. Her hands hovered by the daggers on her hips. "It's time to reap what you have sown."

The stranger's cloak bathed their face in a pool of shadows, concealing all of their features besides their grayish-blue lips. The fairy's mouth parted in a sinister grin, revealing two rows of white teeth gleaming in the glow of the nearby torches.

"Not today, I think," the being announced, her feminine voice laced with arrogance. Slowly turning her back to the álf, the fairy faced the window.

She's going to jump!

"No!" Cymbelina cried out, her voice cutting through the air as she lunged toward the aperture in the wall, her arm outstretched in a desperate bid to snatch her foe. With a grunt of satisfaction, the being dove headfirst through the opening, her arms stretching above her as she vanished into the abyss.

With a resounding thud, Cymbelina collided with the windowsill, the impact jarring her as she leaned over the edge. Her heart raced as she peered down into the churning sea far below. The dark, tumultuous waves crashed violently against the jagged cliffside, sending up frothy sprays of foam. Cymbelina's eyes scanned the turbulent waters, darting anxiously across the surface, but she saw no signs of life.

"No, no, no, no, she can't escape!" The brunette screamed, pounding against the windowsill. The wind continuously whipped against her face as she looked down, her eyes filling to the brim with agitated tears. "Mother Terralynia, take me; we almost had her!"

"There's nothing we can do now," the voice within Cymbelina's head stated. *"Let us return to our allies. We can cripple the rest of their*

army and hope we won't have to battle the fairies again."

"I suppose you're right," Cymbelina uttered reluctantly, her gaze never wavering from the sea. "The Goddess will give that cloaked coward the death she deserves."

The Final Battle
17th of New Star, 1301 AC

After returning to the entry hall, Cymbelina raised hell, assisting her Magijarolk allies as they attempted to defeat the last of the vilek. The wind-controlling álves fell one by one until none of them remained, regardless of how hard the brunette tried to save them all. The only two álves left alive after the ceaseless slaughter besides the Half-Sylvanrolk were Una and Emerik, one of whom was still incapacitated from their injury.

Although the battle had dwindled to two against a formidable one, the armored fairy was slowly losing her strength. Her attacks became sloppy, as did her footwork. It reached the point where all the vilek could do was avoid the incoming blows from her adversaries instead of making her own.

We've got her now, Cymbelina thought, circling the still being. *One more swing, and she'll be done for.*

Sensing her impending doom, the green-skinned fairy rolled to the right as she dodged the brunette's forward thrust. Summoning the remainder of her dwindling stamina, the being dashed down one of the hallways that led into the depths of the castle.

Not again, the brunette internally groaned, snarling before she took off down the corridor in pursuit of the fairy. Una followed Cymbelina, the duo taking care to avoid the corpses littering the blood-spattered floor. Luckily for the álven warriors, the chase didn't last long, with the vilek turning into one of the rooms towards the end of the first passageway.

"What's the point in hiding? We know where you are!" The Half-Sylvanrolk called out to the tired woman.

Arriving at a pair of twin doors, Cymbelina and Una slammed against them, causing them to fly open. A thunderous crack rang out in the secluded chamber that the sisters intently gazed into.

Fading daylight filtered through stormy clouds and penetrated through a sheer set of curtains shrouding a pair of balcony doors, causing minimal sunlight to disperse throughout the room in a muted orange glow. Amidst a scattered array of tables and artifacts stood two shadowy figures, one kneeling in front of the other. The one on the floor had a large staff protruding from its chest, while the other stood above it, its head bent downwards. The injured figure slouched to the ground, presumably lifeless. The other turned their head to the side.

A roaring gale ruffled the curtains and seeped into the room, scattering loose papers and scrolls about. The balcony doors slammed shut with a flick of the mysterious form's wrist, their masculine voice bouncing off the dark room's walls.

"Truly useless, these servants of mine," the figure sneered, its voice dripping with disdain. "Unable to perform the simplest tasks I provide them with. Honestly, how pathetic. I guess I'll have to deal with this nuisance myself."

The two she-álves stood at the mouth of the room, their hands grasping their weapons.

"I take it you're the coward in charge here?" Cymbelina grimaced, her eyes squinting as she assessed the hidden being.

The concealed man chuckled, the sound followed by the shattering of a glass object he released from one of his hands.

"Coward? My, my, you might want to change how you speak to me, filth."

The individual turned to face the álves, his right hand coming up to his face. A bright flame danced in his palm after a snap of his fingers, lighting up the man's gray face. Coal-black eyes sat in deep-set sockets, a thin set of lips upturned into a sadistic grin. His snow-white hair was shaved on one side of his scalp, the rest flowing down over his shoulder in wintry waves. Two gauges adorned his pointed ears, which slightly twitched in the brilliant flame in his hand. Gigantic, moth-like wings were situated on his back, a point he accentuated with a quick flutter. After looking the fairy over, Cymbelina realized she had never seen a male vilek before.

"After all, I am the one who will decide how you'll die. If you want me to spare you from a painful death, I suggest you watch your tongue lest I pry it out of your insolent mouth."

"The man that stands before you must be the leader of the Dark Vilek," the anger-fueled voice rumbled inside the she-álf's head. *"End him, and your kin will never have to face another Dark Fairy again."*

"I don't think you'll be killing anyone else today," Una spoke, her knuckles turning white as she gripped the shaft of the sword she had plucked from one of the fairy's bodies.

"Oh?" The male chuckled, his eyes resting on the Wood Álf, a smirk slowly growing across his menacing features. "And who is going to stop me? You? You're a petite outsider who doesn't know how to properly handle a sword of that caliber," the fairy paused, pointing to the weapon in the younger sister's hand. "The notion of you being able to bring me down is simultaneously laughable and insulting."

Infuriated by the vilek's cockiness, Una charged at the gray-skinned man, shocking her older sibling.

"Una, stop! He wants you to engage; don't fall for it!"

Ignoring Cymbelina's plea to halt, the Sylvanrolk sprinted toward the Dark Fairy, who simply snickered.

When the inky-haired woman was within feet of her target, the fairy outstretched his hands. The air was sucked out of the room as violent gusts of wind poured forth from his spindly fingers, channeled directly at the young woman. Una flew backward into the hallway.

"Una!"

The eighteen-year-old's thin frame slammed against one of the stone walls, a resounding thump following the impact as her body limply fell to the cold floor.

"NO!" The brunette wailed, sprinting toward her sister's unconscious body.

Blood oozed from a gash on the back of her head, coating Cymbelina's hands in dark red lifeforce. As the older sibling attempted to prop her sleeping sister against the wall, fury and panic formed a sickening feeling in the pit of her stomach.

Hold on, Cymbelina thought, tears flooding her eyes as she cradled her younger sister's head in her hands. *Please stay strong for me while I kill this bastard.*

"Weeping won't heal her," the fairy taunted, taking a step toward the crouching woman. "But I will say, seeing a pitiful being on their knees brings me great pleasure."

Releasing her sister's battered body, the Half-Sylvanrolk stood up, her knees wobbly and her calves crying out in pain. A dull throbbing blossomed at the base of her skull as she wearily looked at her opponent.

"What are you waiting for?" the deep voice inquired, its tone shrill. *"Kill him! Avenge your friends and family, and ensure his treachery never touches the lands of Sacarnia again!"*

The male vilek's smile never faltered as he closely examined the brunette's face, counting every tear that dripped from her bloodshot, green eyes. He chuckled at her twitching limbs and rising chest, a depraved smile revealing his sharpened teeth. The being seemed to sense her frustration and fatigue, and he reveled in it.

After a swift, pained glance at the pool of blood spreading around her sister, Cymbelina's eyes locked onto the vilek standing across from her. She reflected on the hatred she felt towards the mysterious man as she stared into his soulless eyes. She dwelled on motivations for all the atrocities he committed as she looked at his blade. And after all of these ruminations, the brunette realized one thing: she would make him pay.

"What is your name?" Cymbelina asked hoarsely, her darkened eyes glued to the man's black ones.

"Vukasino. Monarch Vukasino. Not that you deserve to know, wretch. Why do you ask?"

The brunette grunted as she wobbled into the room the man was standing in. With quivering arms, she turned around, slamming the doors shut before turning back to face Vukasino. "Because I'd like to know the name of the murderous clod I'm about to kill."

"A clod?" Vukasino questioned, his expression muddying from delight to one of contempt. "I don't think you know the full extent of who you're speaking to, girl."

"I think I do," the brunette muttered as a shiver raced down her spine. She felt her eyes twitch, the once-green irises transforming into a shade akin to the blazing fires of Infernus. Her circular pupils now resembled those of a serpent. As she stared at the man, an orange glow, akin to a raging inferno, shrouded her frame, as it had during the battle at the Snøthorn Mountains. Anger bubbled inside her, her hatred lapping at the depths of her mind and soul.

"Kill him," the familiar voice whispered to her, its voice sending shockwaves down her spine. *"Kill him using the power I have bestowed upon you, animus hospi."*

"I will make you suffer just as you and your army of fairies have made my people suffer, Vukasino. When this is all over," the female paused, taking a step toward the ruler and looking him over. "You'll be slain, and your remains will be used as food for the seagulls."

The aura surrounding the Half-Sylvanrolk female flickered at her words, each syllable laced with malice. The leader of the Dark Vilek showed no signs of being horrified by Cymbelina's transformation or her choice of words. In fact, he looked delighted by the turn of events unfolding before him, as if she had proposed they play a game of chess.

"I highly doubt that, as I have my own tricks, you álven dog."

As soon as the threat left his darkened leer, Vukasino's face began to warp, his chiseled facial features sharpening. A rippling shroud of darkness enveloped the fairy, his sinewy muscles pulsating and twitching as the elixir coursed through his veins.

"So this is what it feels like to taste Annihilmon's greatest creation," the visi-vilek said to himself, forgetting where and when he was as he looked himself over in a moment of vanity. "I'll have to praise Tihana for finding the recipe for this potion later. If she still lives, that is."

As the man foolishly appreciated himself, Cymbelina reached down, grasping the bow and an arrow Una had dropped before she was flung backward.

"Thank her?" Cymbelina sneered, her weapon trained on the man. "I would dismiss her if I were you. You're now twice as ugly."

Releasing an arrow, the man deftly evaded it, emitting a piercing scream as he flew toward the brunette. The fairy's frighteningly sharp nails grazed her back as the she-álf swiftly rolled out of harm's way, relinquishing her bow in the process. Springing to her feet, she reached for her father's daggers and adopted a defensive stance.

"You might be quick," Vukasino observed, lifting his sharpened nails to his face and observing them, "but you're not fast enough to escape what I have in store for you."

A fiery sphere blossomed in the male's gray palm as he aimed and threw it at Cymbelina. Swiftly pirouetting out of the way of the fireball, the spell grazed her skin, the flames licking against her dirtied armor. Growling, the male unleashed a dozen more. Luckily for the brunette, she was able to dodge some of the incoming attacks while the rest of them did minimal damage due to the fiery aura encasing her.

Seeing that his attacks were ineffective, the male spat, black specks tinging his spittle as it hit the floor.

"*Ka welo kurvasti.* Stop this little game and meet your fate!"

"I plan to," the woman countered, playing with one of her daggers, "but I have to kill you first."

The fairy snarled, unsheathing his curved, steel blade and running toward Cymbelina again.

The two danced in a deadly waltz, neither warrior giving the other much time to respond. Their moves were accentuated by a metallic orchestra, the singing blades creating a jarring song of silver and steel. Cymbelina's heart thudded in her chest, her breaths heavy as she met every one of the vilek's attacks with her daggers, cutting it close a number of times. Her muscles cried out for mercy, a mixture of dirt and sweat clogging the pores on her face.

Mantras of self-assurance repeated in the patron-possessed she-álf's mind, her hands becoming a blur as she returned the blows the vilek aimed at her.

You have everything under control, Cymbelina. Vukasino will die just like the rest. He has to.

In a miscalculated attempt to parry one of the Dark Fairy's attacks, Cymbelina raised her right hand just in time for Vukasino to slice it clean off. Letting out a shaking howl of pain, the discarded appendage flew to the other side of the room, leaving the Half-Sylvanrolk to stare at her stump of an arm in horror.

No!

The sharp pang of agony in her core surged into a relentless tsunami of despair as Cymbelina stared at her injury. The contents of her stomach churned violently as tears of anguish streamed down her dirt-streaked cheeks. The brunette's knees felt incredibly weak, her knees buckling before she collapsed to the cold stone floor.

This can't be happening. I've come so far; this can't be the end.

Blood poured from the wound, the brunette's eyes squeezing shut as she tried to block the pain flooding her veins. Holding back the vomit threatening to spill from her cracked lips, she felt the bite of cold steel against her neck.

Cymbelina slowly opened her bleary eyes, her chest heaving. An overwhelming sense of vertigo clouded her thoughts as she averted her gaze from the curved sword at her neck to the man before her.

The slate-gray male looked down at the Half-Sylvanrolk in evil delight. A low chuckle poured forth from his mouth before crescendoing into a cackle as a wicked grin spread across his face.

"That is where you belong, vermin: on your knees. If I

didn't know better, I'd say Mother Terralynia made your kind specifically for this purpose."

"Why…Why are you…Doing this?"

The tip of his blade slid from the base of Cymbelina's neck to her narrow chin, the steel caressing her pounding pulse.

"Because I am sick of seeing my people sequestered on this damn island. I am sick of seeing álves prance about and flourish on the soil that belongs to my ancestors by birthright. We were the first race to grace Sacarnia, and by all the gods in the heavens, I promised myself I would reclaim my kin's rightful home on Florella."

"You were never banished! You could have…come home," the female paused, wincing as she became lightheaded. "Your ancestors decided to leave of their own accord. Besides, my ancestors were native to Florella, too. That island is as much ours as it is the vilek's rightful home."

"I don't care about any of that," the male spat. "As with all other races inhabiting Sacarnia, your race is nothing more than a stain on this world. I mean, why should I stop correcting the Godess' mistakes on Florella? Maybe once I've finished off all the álves on Florella, I can deal with the pests inhabiting the continent of Arcana!" The male laughed, a depraved thought crossing his mind. "And after Arcana, I'll head to the Ebon Strath! Or maybe even…."

The male trailed off during his triumphant tirade, his coal-black eyes drifting to Cymbelina's right arm.

Instead of staring at a handless arm, he and the she-álf stared in amazement as the appendage slowly reformed, starting with the palm and ending with the fingertips. Fully restored, the Wood Álf gazed up at the monarch, a victorious grin spreading across her face. Before giving her a chance to formulate a witty response, the male flung his sword to the side, rushing toward the female and snatching her by the throat.

"I shall end this squabble NOW!"

Channeling a rush of wind toward the balcony doors, the strengthened male glided out of the room with Cymbelina in tow. The cold winds battered Cymbelina's body as Vukasino soared over the castle, taking her to a spot hundreds of feet above the courtyard. Even while remaining still, the wind blew furiously around them, whipping around the duo's hair. The brunette stared from Vukasino to the dozens of soldiers fighting below. Fire engulfed the grass covering the island, making the frames of the soldiers appear as nothing more than souls fighting their damnation in the pits of Infernus.

"How does it feel to have your life completely in the hands of a superior being?" The male laughed, his fingers squeezing the Half-Sylvanrolk's neck. "I wouldn't know the feeling myself, so I'm curious."

The woman was motionless, weighing her options in her head. She could either fight back and quite possibly fall to her death, or she could be strangled to death in the hands of this deranged monster.

As the clock was ticking down, all the brunette could do was gasp and wriggle in her captor's hands. His grip around her neck was akin to a vise, leaving the thought of escaping his hold far from her mind.

"Oh, silly me. What am I thinking?" Vukasino laughed, squeezing harder as his eyes lit up in unholy glee. "You can't answer my question when you're on the verge of death."

The monarch's grasp on Cymbelina's throat remained firm as the brunette's serpentine eyes slowly rolled back in her skull. Her lungs spasmed for air, her heart palpitating in ways she had never felt before as waves of terror flowed through her. There was nowhere to go, no way for her to fight back. Her arms refused to move, no matter how hard the half-álf wanted to fight back.

This is the end, the woman thought to herself, staring into the eyes of her tormentor as her vision began to blur. *What happened? I was so close.*

"It's not over yet," the deep voice within her mind said as her heart began to slow down. *"The blood price has been paid. If you permit it, I can take over your body."*

Her head craned backward, her eyes gazing into the sky. She

could feel her body becoming weaker and weaker. *"How is that possible?"*

"There's no time to explain. Just say yes, and I'll be able to turn the tide quickly. I'll end this swine once and for all."

Sensing no other options, the she-álf wordlessly agreed, handing her corporeal faculties over to the voice within her head.

As soon as the thought left her mind, Cymbelina's body shook, startling the man whose grasp she was in. The Half-Sylvanrolk's eyes stirred behind her eyelids before she opened them wide. Her slit-like pupils looked into the vilek's abyssal ones. A look of horror crossed Vukasino's visage as he observed a dragon's face in the depths of the female's eyes, flames pouring from the creature's open maw. The creature's eyes seemed to stare into the fairy's soul, causing his grip on the female to loosen. It was clear he couldn't bear to look away, no matter how much he might've wanted to.

"What are you?" The male murmured, fear creeping into his voice for the first time in his life.

"I am your end, visi-vilek," Cymbelina answered, her once feminine voice distorted to match the menacing voice within her head.

Holding her left arm out, one of Ignatius' daggers manifested into the palm of Cymbelina's dirty hand, forming from the blood magically drawn from her skin. Clutching it tight, the possessed woman plunged the weapon deep into the fairy's heart. Cobalt lifeforce poured forth from the demented creature, coating the blade and making the runes on its sleek surface glow. A rumbling vocalization of content flowed from the she-álf's mouth, a wolfish smirk spreading across her face.

"Ast a bonara est sum retrana," Cymbelina deeply hummed, ripping the weapon out of the male's chest.

The Dark Vilek's wings stopped fluttering seconds later, causing Cymbelina and Vukasino to plummet to the ground.

Arching through the stormy sky like a meteor, Cymbelina's balled-up, flame-encased body left a large indent in the earth as she hit the island's surface, the sound echoing across the land.

The fiery silhouette surrounding her injured frame slowly died as the voice let the brunette reclaim her body.

Cymbelina's body ached as if she had been flogged a million times. Using the minimal strength she had left, she turned to face the crowd gathering around her. Faces of horror and confusion stared into the crater where the Half-Sylvanrolk lay. Cymbelina's now green eyes fluttered open and closed as she forced herself to look upon the broken body of the fairy beside her. The man's insides had become his outsides, his blue gore splattering the area around them.

It's done, the brunette thought, staring into the dark sky. *The war is over.*

Rain slowly began to fall, battering at the Half-Sylvanrolk's distressed frame. In her last few moments of consciousness, she heard the familiar, heart-rending screams of her mother, which pierced her heart before she fell into a deep slumber.

Peace At Last
17th of New Star, 1301 AC

Behind slumbering eyes, Cymbelina saw the monarch's death repeatedly. She felt the hellish satisfaction of his blood coating her blade as she plummeted to the ground. She could hear the echoing cries of her mother as she lay nearly paralyzed on the ground, her body weak with exhaustion. However, no matter how palpable these experiences seemed to be, she felt like a spectator during the entire debacle. Yet, it repeatedly played in a continuous loop within the confines of her mind, the sights and sounds engraving themselves into the she-álf's memory as she found herself in her dream again.

The dark room that had been the setting of her last vision had transformed into a well-lit chamber, with dozens of torches casting a blazing glow upon the center of the room. Within the light of the flickering firebrands sat the hellish creature that had remained dormant for the majority of Cymbelina's life.

The towering monster's dark, cyan scales glittered in the fierce glow of the nearby flames, its infernal serpentine eyes flickering with delight as it stared down at Cymbelina. Its long tail swept to the right, its razor-sharp claws scratching against the stone flooring as it adjusted its stance, a deep rumble emitting from its menacing maw.

"I'm not what you expected, am I?"

"I wasn't quite sure what to expect if I'm being honest," Cymbelina replied, her green eyes analyzing the creature. "But I didn't know Sylvanrolk could have a dragon patron."

358

The dragon chuckled, its smooth voice bouncing off the stone walls that enclosed the duo in the confined space. A circle of runes, similar in appearance to those on Ignatius' daggers, surrounded the sitting being, who did nothing but swish his tail from side to side.

"It dawned on me that I never asked what I should call you," Cymbelina continued, unperturbed by the creature's silence. "According to lore, most patrons have a name given to them by Mother Terralynia and share it with their hosts during their host's awakening. I've noticed that you have yet to say yours."

"Names are frivolous. Calling someone by their role is much more sensible. But, if it helps your mortal mind wrap itself around my presence, so be it. You shall call me Gehenomon."

"Well, Gehenomon," The she-álf said, finding the dragon's name displeasing on her tongue, "I think you owe me some answers now."

The being cackled, its forked tongue peeking out of its fanged mouth. "What answers do you think you deserve?"

"I gave you what you desired," the brunette answered. "I lent you my body so we could defeat Monarch Vukasino, which you clearly wanted to do. You were egging me on the entire time for me to kill him."

"So, because I came to your aid and offered advice in your time of need, I somehow owe you more assistance by giving you the answers you seek? That doesn't seem too reasonable, does it?"

"You said that by providing you with the things you seek, 'bloodshed, hatred, relentlessness,' you would supply me with the answer to what I crave to know the most?"

"Wasn't knowing your patron form what you wanted to know about the most?"

"You've been dwelling inside my mind for my entire life; you mean to tell me you can't decipher that for yourself?"

The dragon chuckled, its eyes closing in mirth. "You caught me. Well, at least I didn't say I would tell you right away, right?

After all, you'll find out eventually. You just need to be patient."

"What?!" Cymbelina screamed, the sound shaking the room and startling the dragon, its expression of merriment morphing into one of disgust at the female's outburst.

"You heard me, *animus hospi*," the creature spoke. All sense of humor evaporated from its countenance as the dragon approached the álf, its footsteps causing the ground underneath Cymbelina's feet to shake. "I did not say I would tell you right away. You let me take over your form once, and you think I should bow to your every whim?" The creature snorted, steam erupting from its nostrils. "Ah, mortals: you do one thing for them, and suddenly you owe them the rest of the world."

The she-álf grimaced. What the brunette desired the most, more than anything else in Sacarnia, was to know more about her father, Ignatius. And everywhere she turned, she met another being determined to tell her as little as possible about him or nothing at all.

Sensing the dragon was sensitive to being accused of not knowing something, Cymbelina smirked before questioning the colossal being.

"I don't think you owe me anything more than what you promised. I deserve to know the truth about Ignatius, facts that I long for more than anything in this godforsaken world. Information you implied you would supply me with. The more we talk, however, the more I'm convinced that you don't know as much about the situation as your mysterious retorts would lead me to believe."

The dragon's serpentine eyes narrowed, his fangs shining in the dim torchlight as he glanced at the Half-Sylvanrolk. His expression emanated a look of utter danger as he hissed, "Is that so?"

"It is," the brunette continued, crossing her arms over her chest. "Why else would you deny me answers at every turn? Why else would you be so mysterious about your origins? Why else would your communication with me be so inconsistent? It must be because you're clearly not as knowledgeable as you portray yourself to be."

The dragon's claws dug into the stony ground as he emitted a ferocious growl akin to a curse. The runic circle underneath Gehenomon glowed as he shifted his sharp talons between the grooves in the floor, cleaving the ground in two. The stony terrain shook as the crevice slowly grew into a great chasm, rapidly expanding and approaching Cymbelina. Immobile, the female watched in horror as the crack split the floor between her legs in two, a fearful gasp escaping her throat. Before the Half-Sylvanrolk could tumble into the hole, Gehenomon's wings flapped furiously, the wind whipping the she-álf's hair as he reached out a talon-clawed hand and plucked Cymbelina off her feet.

The duo hovered above a gigantic pit, smothering heat radiating from within. A whirlpool of lava gurgled and spat scalding liquid to and fro as Cymbelina gazed into the depths of the funnel, her heart pounding as sweat beaded on her brow. She heard screams and cries from within the molten rock as if the souls of those sent to Malignos were crying out for help.

"You presume much yet know little," the dragon spoke angrily, drawing the woman's attention away from the lava below. "I know everything there is to know about who you are as a person, as I've been with you since the beginning. From the moment your father impregnated your mother, I was there. I continued to grow from the moment you first looked into the blistering sun. And even now, after twenty-two years, I remain firmly rooted in your soul. And I will continue to be here, Cymbelina, until you draw your final breath." The dragon paused, letting its ominous words sink in. "If we are to work together, you will address me in a respectable manner. Is that understood?"

The woman's voice caught in her throat, her mind reeling from the dragon's words. She could only manage a trembly nod in response, her dry lips refusing to form with a retort.

"Good. Now leave me."

Cymbelina's eyes flew open as she returned to the land of the living. Along with her consciousness came stabbing pangs of discomfort, which rocked her shivering frame as she lay curled on the cold, wet deck of one of the ships built by her álven kin. The waves rocked violently against the vessel's sides as the moon hung in the sky, its twinkling glow illuminating her singing brethren as they rowed atop the savage sea.

Mother Terralynia, I'm alive?

Groaning, the woman sat up and rubbed her forehead, looking from side to side to get a sense of her surroundings.

The sky was painted the deepest shade of blue, with sparkling stars dotting its heavenly tapestry. The sails of the ship Cymbelina sat on fluttered and bent in the smooth winter winds, the occasional wave arching over the side of the boat and lapping at the feet of the rowers, none of which she recognized. The inability to name any of the álves beside her left a sinking feeling in the brunette's gut, her thoughts racing in her weary mind.

Which ship am I on? Where are the others?

Although Cymbelina didn't know the names of any of the álves surrounding her, they certainly knew who she was and what she had done during the battle. Recognizing that the brunette had woken from her slumber, one of the rowers shouted to a Sylvanrolk Cymbelina knew all too well.

"Deirdre, Cymbelina's awake!"

Mom?!

Although Cymbelina frantically searched for the woman the man called out for, she still missed her mother until a strong pair of arms wrapped around her sore torso, bringing the dazed álf in for a rough hug.

Tears dripped onto the brunette's armor-clad shoulders as Deirdre huffed, "I...I thought I had lost you."

Cymbelina wordlessly nodded, too dazed by her dream and too tired from the battle to speak. She turned around in her mother's embrace, wrapping her arms around her mother for a proper hug, squeezing her tightly.

The women sat in the center of the rocking ship, waves occasionally splashing onto the wooden floorboards as the sailors continued to row. Melodies of triumph echoed on the frosty sea air, neither female joining in with the chanting of their allies.

Although her kin sang songs of glorious battle, and even though Cymbelina was nestled in her mother's warm embrace, the brunette was not at peace. Her mind raced as she recalled the events that had occurred hours ago, and her heart pounded as Gehenomon's menacing words echoed within the depths of her mind.

"I know everything there is to know about who you are...I will be here, Cymbelina, until you draw your final breath."

The brunette shivered. Never once in Cymbelina's years of training had she heard about a patron being so antagonistic...so uncaring of their host's desires. But there were exceptions to every rule, and it was just Cymbelina's luck that she would end up with a patron who proved an exception to the standards.

Deirdre patted Cymbelina's back as she released her from the embrace, her pale hands landing on her daughter's bruised shoulders. Deirdre's eyes were bloodshot, her hands shaky and clammy as she addressed her oldest daughter.

"I was so worried about you. In my forty-seven years on this planet, I have never seen a being, let alone an álf, fall from such a height and survive. I still can't wrap my head around the fact that you're breathing right now." The older woman paused, sniffling. "It doesn't even appear like you've been heavily scathed. Besides a few bruises here and there, you appear to be alright."

The brunette began to laugh but quickly stopped when a pang of pain stabbed her chest. "Besides aching all over, yeah...I don't feel too bad."

"Your patron must be a strong one."

That's right, Cymbelina thought, her eyes briefly flickering from her mother to the álves around her. *No one here has seen the details of my patron form up close. They have no clue what it is or what it's capable of.*

"Yeah," Cymbelina mumbled, drying some of the tears that had streamed down her dirty face, "it is."

"Well, it would still be a good idea to have a healer look at you when we return to camp, just in case you have any underlying medical issues that need to be dealt with. I'm sure your grandfather would like to speak to you, too."

"Oh, I bet he will!" One of the sailors called, looking at Cymbelina and Deirdre as he continued to row. "Cymbelina helped save the day after all. I bet Kinlord Emyr will be a proud man."

"Maybe her brave actions will even help convince him to let her remain a member of the Glenrolk clan," another álf offered.

Cymbelina's heart sunk into her stomach once more. The brunette had forgotten all about her expulsion from her clan through the excitement of the battle. Although her purpose for defending her people was not to reclaim her status as a member of the Glenrolk, it would certainly be an outcome she would welcome with open arms.

"Hush, you two," Deirdre said, moving to cover her daughter's ears, "she doesn't need to hear—"

"It's not a problem, Mom," Cymbelina interrupted, removing Deirdre's hands from over her dirtied ears. "But, you do have a point. I don't feel like discussing that right now. In fact, I'd like to know where everyone else is. Where is Una, Kayven, and Malaveen? And is Una alright? She had a nasty cut on her head earlier."

"Everyone is fine, and Una will live, so don't worry about her, ok?"

The Half-Sylvanrolk didn't answer, opting to turn her weary gaze toward the western horizon. Even from miles away, she could see the ravenous flames dance across the island of Elderfell. Smoke billowed in the night wind as the brilliant conflagration roared like an angered beast, consuming the land the Dark Vilek called home. Cymbelina winced at the sight, turning away. She couldn't fathom the lives that had been lost earlier in the day.

Sensing her daughter's unease, Deirdre gently cupped the right side of Cymbelina's face, guiding the young she-álf to look into her cerulean eyes. "Don't think about what happened back on Elderfell, sweetheart. Now is the time to rest."

The green-eyed álf weakly nodded before turning her head to the east. She couldn't see her homeland from where the boat currently was, but she knew it was out there somewhere.

Mom's right, the brunette thought, allowing her mother to turn her around. Deirdre directed Cymbelina to lean against her, which she did with ease. The half-alf then clenched her eyes shut, allowing the god of slumber to lull her to sleep. *Now that the war is over, it's time for me to rest.*

* * *

The date was the twenty-first of New Star. Four Days had passed since the united álfrolk army had besieged the Dark Vilek's capital, setting most of the island up in smoke. Hundreds of álves who fought in the battle died, their departure from Sacarnia weighing heavily on the shoulders of those who survived. However, many fairies died that day, too, with the only survivors comprising a handful who had surrendered to the álven champions.

Although the heavy loss of álven life marred the momentous victory the army had achieved, the álven leaders organized a victory party to try and lift the spirits of the survivors. The gathering served as a way to recognize and thank the dead for their brave sacrifice while also celebrating the triumph the troops achieved.

Hundreds of álves relished the thought of escaping the grim reality of the battle they had just experienced, swarming the united army's camp and indulging in various festivities.

Instead of participating in said activities, Cymbelina stayed cooped up in her room, where she had been hidden for the past few days. Her motivation for hiding was to avoid the barrage of questions her allies liked to throw her way whenever she emerged from her home. Her avoidance of said inquiries was so severe that the only time she left was for the daily meals the camp's cooks prepared. However, she would break her schedule today just so she could follow through on a summons she had received from her grandfather's assistant, Phalena. Cymbelina hadn't seen or heard from her grandfather since before the battle, so she was guessing that was what the summons was about.

Hopefully, today won't be the day I'm evicted from the camp, the brunette thought, clutching the letter tightly in her fist. *Well, here goes nothing.*

Parting the entryway out of her family's home, Cymbelina became immersed in the celebration of her kin. A mixed aura of sadness and elation welled in her heart, the feelings of the álves around her palpable. A wintry gust of air swept through the field, causing the fabric of the tents and stalls nearby to ripple. The grass underneath the woman's feet swished in the blustery gale as she maneuvered through the dense crowd, beginning her walk to Kinlord Emyr's tent. Although the brunette tried to block out the words of those around her, she occasionally heard the conversations of her neighbors. Some didn't talk about her at all, while others whispered various contemplations, such as what Cymbelina's patron animal could be and why she didn't seem to have many signs of physical damage from her fight with Vukasino. Blocking out the words she didn't want to hear, the brunette pressed onwards, eventually arriving at her grandfather's tent.

Ringing the bell hanging from a pole outside of Emyr's abode, Cymbelina could only wait and glance around her anxiously.

Please come out soon, Phalena, so nobody has time to come up and start asking me questions.

As if Phalena was reading the brunette's thoughts, Cymbelina saw the folds of the clan leader's tent part, the redhead popping out to address Emyr's granddaughter.

"I thought I saw a shadow approaching," Phalena murmured, eyeing Cymbelina. "Kinlord Emyr will see you now."

Nodding her head, Cymbelina followed Phalena as she led her into Kinlord Emyr's quarters. Once inside, the assistant left the granddaughter alone with her grandfather, leaving a tense silence in her wake.

Giving a customary bow before the clan's leader, the Half-Sylvanrolk waited to move until she heard Emyr gruffly whisper, "You may be seated."

Sitting cross-legged on the large bear rug, the brunette looked up at the kinlord, noting his downcast gaze as he scanned over a pile of documents in his lap. The joyous cheering from the revelry outside bled through the thick fabric walls of the tent, marking the only sound audible to Cymbelina besides the occasional flipping of one of Emyr's pages.

What is he looking at? What does it have to do with me? Are those a copy of the Sylvan Tenets? Am I officially being banished?

After a few moments of silence, the elder gazed away from the composition, his mint-green eyes landing on the anxious she-álf seated before him.

"Some...monumental...rumors about you are floating around the campsite, Cymbelina," the man began, placing the pile of paper on a table beside his throne. "Not only did you and your friends directly disobey the orders the álven leaders and I crafted, but the antics of your little group of rebels could've caused the entire operation to fail. Out of all the silly things you've done before, this is by far the most egregious."

Taking a deep breath, the brunette held back the urge to interrupt her grandfather, figuring that practicing hearing room etiquette would be the best way to save the hides of herself and her friends.

"May I speak, Kinlord Emyr?"

"You may, in fact, I encourage it. I must know your thought process when you concocted and executed your reckless plan."

"Well, I have a question before I go on. Have you talked to anyone else who fought alongside me that day?"

"No. How this conversation goes determines if I need to speak to them."

"I see," the brunette paused, giving herself enough time to gather her thoughts and take a deep breath. "Well, to be honest, Kinlord Emyr, my brethren and I were not satisfied with our assigned stations. Not because we sought glory on the battlefield, but because we knew our talents would be most useful elsewhere."

"It would be nigh impossible to share how many of your álven brothers and sisters felt the same way, Cymbelina. I, along with the other leaders, received many pleas from your fellow warriors to be issued different assignments in the days leading up to the battle. With that being said, did the other people displeased with their positions abandon their posts? No. So, regardless of the logic behind why you and the others disobeyed the orders handed down to you, you still did. On top of that, two of your companions are dead because of your actions. Usenia and Kivi are in the Goddess' embrace tonight, as they shall be for the rest of eternity. All because your group decided to disobey commands."

"I can't say with confidence that I agree with your judgment, Kinlord Emyr. Look at all of the álves who died following the plans you and the other leaders drafted for them. Are you and the others to blame for their deaths? Of course not. Try as hard as we might, sir, but lives will always be lost during a battle. It's up to us to protect as many of our allies as possible and, if need be, remember their sacrifice after the fact."

The male pursed his lips, his eyes remaining on the she-álf. "That's a grim way to look at it."

"But it's the realistic way, sir. These past few battles have taught me that being optimistic is good, but being pragmatic is even better."

The man hummed, not uttering a single word as his gaze remained on his granddaughter. His bony fingers tapped against the right armrest of his throne as he mulled over something in his mind. Cymbelina returned his steady stare in kind, refusing to look away from Emyr's intense eyes.

He wants me to look away. He wants me to prove that my convictions are not as strong as I portray them to be, but I refuse to bend them. What my friends and I did was the right thing to do. I refuse to allow him to convince me otherwise.

There were no words spoken between the two álves for minutes on end, both individuals thinking through what should be said next. The first person to talk again was Kinlord Emyr, who leaned back on his throne before addressing Cymbelina.

"The other Sylvanrolk leaders and I discussed your banishment yesterday."

The brunette's heart skipped a beat. "May I know the details of your conversation?"

"Of course," the male replied, folding his hands in his lap. "Although I find it very displeasing that you directly disobeyed the Sylvan Tenets and went against the orders I laid out for you on the day of the battle, after much persuading from Kinlord Quindlen and Kinlady Nairna, I am allowing you to remain among the Glenrolk. Your unselfishness in repeatedly risking your life to defend your people is an admirable trait that I believe many could learn from."

Cymbelina's heart beat rapidly, her pulse thumping like the drums of a glorious war song. Although she didn't risk her life just to be accepted amongst her people once again, she certainly wouldn't turn this prize away, especially since it meant she could remain amongst her family and friends.

I can't believe it, the woman thought. *This doesn't seem real.*

A smile graced the brunette's tired face, prompting her grandfather to add, "Before you get too excited, your place amongst the Glenrolk has certain conditions attached to it."

"What sort of conditions?"

"Well, for starters, you will never be able to participate in *Cathanu* and take over the helm of clan leader once I pass away. You also forfeit the right to a trial should you disobey the Sylvan Tenets again. This means that if I say it's time for you to go, it's time for you to go. Do you understand?"

"Yes, Kinlord Emyr," the brunette enthusiastically agreed. "I understand and agree to your gracious terms. I thank you for allowing me to stay."

"Oh, and since you're no longer an álfing in the eyes of the law, you must take on patrol duties two times a week."

The woman smiled, wordlessly nodding.

For the first time in a while, Kinlord Emyr expressed a playful grin, replying, "Excellent. I'm glad we were able to reach an understanding. I'll send you your patrol assignment next week. For now, you may be dismissed."

With pep in her step, Cymbelina jumped to her feet before rushing toward the room's threshold, eager to share the good news with her friends and family. However, before she could exit Emyr's chambers, his voice stopped her in her tracks.

"I'm surprised you didn't share with me what it is?"

"What is what?" Cymbelina asked, turning around.

"Your patron guardian, of course. I have to know what spirit was able to avoid detection when you were an infant. I've also heard rumors that you were encased in a fiery aura while fighting the leader of the Dark Vilek army. An orange aura would indicate that your animal is fueled by anger. So, what is it?"

"Don't tell him," Gehenomon whispered, his tone imperative. *"If you share with him what I am, he will do nothing but worry. Do you wish to keep your newfound freedom intact, or do you want to remain on a leash for the rest of your life?"*

While thinking of how best to respond to her grandfather, Phalena popped her head into the hearing chambers, an apologetic look on her countenance.

"I'm sorry to interrupt your conversation, Kinlord Emyr, but Kinlady Nairna would like to speak to you. She said it's important."

The male dully nodded, turning his gaze from his assistant to Cymbelina.

"I guess we'll resume this conversation later. Goodbye, Cymbelina. Enjoy the festivities while you can."

"I will, and thank you again, Grand—I mean, Kinlord Emyr!"

Rushing out of the tent, Cymbelina felt a bit more whole than she did hours before. With exciting news to share with her allies, the brunette prepped to head to her family's tent. Turning abruptly to the right after exiting her grandfather's home, Cymbelina ran straight into the broad chest of a male.

"I'm sorry! I didn't see...oh." The female paused, her green eyes drifting upwards, meeting the marigold eyes of her companion, Kayven. The sun's xanthic rays beat down heavily upon the taller male as it sank toward the horizon, framing his obsidian locks in a halo-like glow. "It's you."

The male laughed, "Yes, it is me."

The woman smiled, shoving the male playfully. "How did you know where I was?"

"It's hard to be ignorant of your whereabouts when the entire town is whispering about you leaving your tent to get some fresh air."

Cymbelina snorted. "Fair point. Well, let me ask you this; why did you come searching for me?"

"I wanted to talk to you about something you asked me a while ago. Now that the war has settled, I feel that now is the right time to talk to you about it. Do you have time to talk?"

"I do."

"Awesome. But first," the male said, a mischievous grin creeping along his face, "what say you to a little race?"

The brunette smiled, her expression matching her companion's. "I'm game. Where to?"

"The hill we spent a lot of time on as kids, the one near Master Arvel's training grounds. The last person to get there takes over the other one's patrol duties next week. Also, we can't use our patron animals to help us during the race."

"I agree to those conditions."

"Then it's settled," the male said, lowering himself into a starting position. "On the count of three: one, two, thr—"

"I'm going to win this!" Cymbelina shouted, dashing through a crowd of people blocking the path ahead.

"Not if I have anything to say about it!"

The pair weaved in and out of stalls, a mix of cheers and startled yells following their trail. The smell of Tadhgmaris' cooking drifted on the cold winds, tempting the brunette to stray from the playful challenge she had been issued. Staying strong, she pushed onward, her feet slowly guiding her far ahead of Kayven.

Stopping at the top of the hill, Cymbelina shakily exhaled, looking down the grassy mound at her friend. Having given up, Kayven swiftly walked up the steep incline, his head bent down as he gazed at the tall grass underfoot. His obsidian locks swayed as he shook his head in playful disappointment, looking up at the Half-Sylvanrolk.

"I see the Glenrolk have a cheater amidst our ranks!"

"Hey, don't hate me just because I'm faster than you, Kayven."

"That's not why you won. You won because you started running before I could even finish saying three!"

"Yeah, yeah, whatever you say," Cymbelina chuckled, sitting down amongst the tall grass.. "I'll tell Grandpa to adjust the patrol schedule later in your favor because you do have a point."

"That's more like it," the male chuckled, sitting beside the brunette.

The two sat in blissful silence, the only noises nearby coming from the distant melodies from the band and the jocose cheering of their allies.

Cymbelina's green eyes remained on the setting sun as it slowly sank further into its bed along the horizon. Shades of pink, purple, and blue painted the sky above Florella, the sight of distant stars peeking through the vibrant colors.

A cold breeze swept across Terralynia's Folly, causing the grass to ripple. Cymbelina hugged her knees close to her chest as a shiver shot down her spine. Turning to her ally, the brunette whispered, "What did you want to talk to me about?"

"Back when we first started our adventure into the Glimmering Wilds, you asked me about why I was rejoining the Glenrolk," the male said, his eyes unwaveringly still on the horizon. "I told you the reason was that I was ready to come back to my birth clan."

"Was that not true?"

"It was a facet of the truth but not the entire one." He glanced at the female, a certain darkness clouding his yellowish-orange eyes. "My mother died last year, Cymbelina. She died on the twelfth of Baltalmun's Joy. Right toward the beginning of the Harvest Festival, her favorite time of year."

The brunette's gaze dropped, her face sullen. "I'm so sorry, Kayven. I know how close you were to Adair, and I just..."

"It's ok, Cymbelina. It's a part of life, is it not?" The male momentarily paused as he took in a deep breath. "I'm not telling you this because I want pity. I just wanted to share the entire truth of my return with you because I felt bad for not telling you before and because, well, I want you to know I'm here for you. You've lost a lot of people close to you these past few months, and I know how hard it is to process the loss of those closest to you, especially if you're locking up the pain within the depths of your soul. Grieving is hard when you share your pain with others, but it's unbearable if you keep it all within yourself."

The woman smiled weakly at her companion. "You have a point, Kayven. Thank you."

"You're welcome, Cymbelina. May I say one other thing?"

"Of course. What is it?"

"Their physical forms might not be with us anymore, but Idal and Master Arvel's spirits always will be. They will always be here, even if we can't feel, hear, or see them. And I know if Mother Terralynia gave them a chance to walk on Sacarnian soil again, they would happily stand by your side and celebrate the momentous victory you accomplished on Elderfell. Not just for all alven kind, but the personal victory of being able to finally manifest your patron animal." The male paused, a proud smile crossing his face. "Never forget that, Cymbelina. Never."

Cymbelina's eyes brimmed with tears as she stared at the male beside her. Unable to contain herself, the brunette brought the tall man in for a hug, her head resting on his shoulder.

"I'm glad you're living amongst the Glenrolk again, Kayven. I missed you."

"And I, you."

Smiling, the male leaned into his friend's hug as Cymbelina gazed at the horizon, hopes for continued peace lodged deeply in her heart.

Epilogue
21st of New Star, 1301 AC

Thunder rolled in the overcast sky as fluffy gray clouds scraped against the snow-capped pinnacles of the forgotten mountains overlooking the sparsely inhabited fields of the forbidden land, Xarthaxis. Tempestuous winds battered ceaseless rain against Tihana's torn, rippling hood. The gray fabric of the cloak repeatedly hit the side of the alchemist's black stallion, whose hooves stamped against a pebble-laden path that took the Dark Vilek over a series of undulating hills. Rock after rock cascaded down the sides of the mounds, falling into the dark, winding river below with cacophonous splashes.

Despite all the noise that threatened to distract her, the fairy's narrow escape from the island replayed as a montage in her mind, the feeling of the cold sea she had dived into etched into her bones. Although her escape from the castle didn't go exactly as planned, one thing certainly did: Monarch Vukasino was dead. She had seen it for herself as she swam away. The man who had been a thorn in her side for over a hundred years, the demon who tortured her fellow fae for years on end, the abomination she had helped to create, had perished. At the hands of the brunette álf, just like Tihana's newfound allies in Xarthaxis had forseen. And with the help of said friends, the alchemist could take over the Dark Vilek throne and rebuild Elderfell to its former glory. Or, at least, that was a part of the deal she had struck with the people of Xarthaxis.

Whatever they want to do with that girl is none of my business, the fairy thought, her eyes glued on the path ahead. *Once I've become the matriarch of the Dark Vilek, nothing else will matter.*

Tihana's orange eyes flicked to and fro, ensuring nobody followed her as she traveled around the bend and down into the fields at the base of the mountains. After days of traveling across an unfamiliar countryside, the Dark Vilek was beginning to get antsy, even a tad paranoid.

I can't wait to return to Elderfell. This place is far too open for my taste.

The cries of distant wolves echoed off the rocky slopes of the craggy peaks as the alchemist approached her destination. Harshly tugging at her horse's reins, the animal neighed indignantly as it came to a halt in front of a ring of pillars.

Dismounting her stallion, the woman landed on the muddy terrain with a squelch, pulling out the map hooked onto her belt. Unfurling the parchment, she looked at it and then at the monument.

The picture is identical to the stones in front of me; this has to be the place. Now I just need to worry about opening the damn door.

Hiding the rain-spattered document, the fairy slowly approached the standing stones. Her thin, grayish-blue fingers rubbed the red jewel dangling from her neck. The wind caused the necklace to sway to the side, the golden thorns that hugged the blood-red gem glowing brighter as the fairy approached the circle. Mysterious symbols etched on the tall pillars sparkled a fiery shade of orange as the woman stood in the center of the ring, just as the letter she had received instructed.

"Est ascenda, unaliut mustila primina descenda."

The carvings on the stones burned brightly as Tihana uttered the phrase she had been ordered to speak. The grooves in the rocks began to flicker as the stony foundation surrounding the center of the circle parted, revealing an ancient, winding staircase.

Cocking an eyebrow at the ingenuity of the group's entrance into their hideout, the fairy descended the steep, seemingly neverending, twisting steps.

The passageway led into an abyssal cave, lit only by two glowing pools of lava surrounding a runic bridge in the center of the antechamber. Approaching the stone structure, Tihana slowly crossed it, the runes underneath her feet glowing as the molten liquid on either side of her dangerously gurgled.

Two gigantic, hooded guards awaited her on the other side of the bridge. Standing beside two massive doors, the tall figures were hidden behind robes the color of blood and armed with shiny halberds.

Distant chants of shamans bled through the heavy doors as the fairy stood before the sentries and pulled back the hood of her cloak, revealing her grayish-blue face.

One of the tall figures glanced down at the fairy, who was dwarfed in size compared to the man in front of her. With a set of pale, corpse-like lips, the figure inquired, *"Quin diteth te sano unaliuf?"*

The woman bore a look of confusion on her face, her gaze turning toward the other figure. He remained motionless. "What did he say? I don't know any Infernal besides the phrase needed to enter the sanctum."

"What sayeth the elder one?" The second guard repeated in Common, his frustrated voice muffled by the mask concealing his face.

"To live in temperance is to not live at all," Tihana answered confidently, remembering the answer her contacts had given her.

Looking at each other and nodding, the guards opened the doors for the fairy, who seemed like a speck of dust in front of the large entryway. With an echoing bang, the structure parted for the female, whose eyes rested upon the cloaked figures seated deep within the cavernous room.

The concealed individuals sat in ominous silence at a long table in front of two empty diorite thrones on the opposite end of the main chamber. Their silence was palpable, broken only by the nearby gurgling lava and the chanting of worshippers. The light from the nearby pool cast a bright glow upon the silent people, who beckoned Tihana with a single, slow wave of their hands, inviting her to join them in the depths of the scalding room.

377

Stopping feet away from the table, Tihana reluctantly knelt, just as the letter said to do.

"Honor to the Temple of Malignos."

"You may rise," the individual seated in the center of the table spoke in a feminine voice, motioning for the fairy to stand up.

Tihana rose, internally cringing after bowing before the figures in front of her.

"What brings you before the Crimson Tribunal today, Initiate?"

"I was told by the High Priest to bring news of the task we discussed last year to this sanctum once it was completed. The letter I received confirms my story."

"Bring it here," the woman at the center of the table demanded.

Doing as the hooded figure instructed, Tihana handed the parchment over, watching as the person she passed it to study the wax seal at the bottom of the paper, which bore the shape of an unknown shape that was similar to an eye.

"And what task might that be?" Another individual asked in a deep, baritone voice as their comrade examined the parchment. From the lack of curiosity in the person's voice, Tihana could tell they already knew the answer; they were just trying to test her to see if she was who she said she was.

"I was assigned to report to this committee when Monarch Vukasino, leader of the Dark Vilek army, was slain. Well, here I am to share the good news."

"By whose hand was your leader slaughtered?" another figure questioned.

"The Half-Sylvanrolk the High Priest told me to look out for."

The figures fell silent, several turning towards the one examining the letter. With a curt nod, the female placed the document on the table, motioning to the others that the letter was legitimate.

"How do you know for certain that Vukasino died?" Another court member asked.

"I witnessed it for myself," Tihana replied. "I saw it happen, and not only that, when the current leader of the Dark Vilek dies, every living Dark Fairy can feel it. He is definitely dead. And, according to your leader, she could only have done that if she had been awakened."

Or whatever word the High Priest used.

The figure in the center of the table stood up, her face still masked by the hood. "That's quite a claim. I'm sure you understand that an assertion of that magnitude needs to be verified."

"I do, and I would heartily welcome any of your emissaries to Elderfell if that's what it takes to prove my statement."

"We shall take that into consideration. But there will need to be extra measures taken if we are to move forward."

Tihana paused, trying her best to formulate her question correctly to avoid offending any members of the tribunal. "Do you…mind if I inquire what those extra measures will be."

"You may not," the central figure answered. "Suffice it to say, we will speak to the High Priest and Priestess about what you've told us today. And then we will contact you about any future plans that require your knowledge."

"What should I do in the meantime?"

"Return to your homeland and gather all the notes and supplies you can muster; that way, you can start making more batches of the Elixir of Annihilmon according to the recipe we gave you. We shall then proceed with phase two."

Cast Of Characters

A

- **Adair** (uh-dare): Kayven's mother.
- **Andrzej** (aund-jay): One of the wind-controlling Magijarolk that accompanies Cymbelina to the Snøthorn Mountains and to Elderfell.
- **Annihilmon** (uh-nai-huhl-mon): The name of a famed magister from the continent of Arcana. He disappeared after his defeat in 500 AC.
- **Arvel** (arr-vuhl): The primary patron guide for the Glenrolk clan and one of Cymbelina's closest allies.
- **Astraliam** (ast-rahl-ee-um): A god who rules over the heavens and oversees the change between night and day. He is also known as the god of slumber. He is one of the Supreme Three.
- **Aurnia** (our-nia): A member of the Glenrolk clan.

B

- **Bela** (bay-lah): One of the wind-controlling Magijarolk that accompanies Cymbelina to the Snøthorn Mountains.
- **Bojana** (boi-anah): One of Monarch Vukasino's three knights.
- **Brynnor** (brin-or): The innkeeper of the Golden Pillow Inn located in the city of Krigdor.

C

- **Calina** (kuh-lee-nah): One of Monarch Vukasino's servants.
- **Calmar** (caal-maar): A Dokkalrolk guard stationed in the tunnels of Jordstand.
- **Cymbelina** (sim-bull-ee-nah): The protagonist.

D

- **Dagver** (daag-ver): One of Scoutmaster Estrasta's scouts who accompanies Cymbelina to Elderfell.
- **Danica** (duh-nee-tsah): One of the four surviving Light Vilek who inhabit Nebesati. A member of the Court of Mothers.
- **Deirdre** (deer-druh): the mother of Cymbelina and Una, the wife of Séacael, and the daughter of Kinlord Emyr.

E

- **Emerik Vesnavin** (em-er-ik ves-nah-vin): The knight commander of Gradgate and Nebesati, son of Mother Vesna.
- **Emyr** (em-eer): The kinlord of the Glenrolk clan and Cymbelina's maternal grandfather.
- **Estrasta Gundblad** (est-raa-sta gund-blaad): The scoutmaster of the Dokkalrolk army and Jarl Orsala's wife.

F

- **Fenrolf the Brave** (fen-rolf): The second son of Hakon the Last and the leader of the group of álves whose descendants would come to be known as the Magijarolk.
- **Findella** (fin-dell-ah): One of the seamstresses of the Glenrolk clan.
- **Flora** (flor-uh): A swan spirit who happens to be Malaveen's patron.

G

- **Gaildwynn** (gail-dwin): One of Malaveen's childhood friends and one of Cymbelina's bullies.
- **Gallven** (gall-ven): A member of the Glenrolk clan.
- **Gehenomon** (gi-hen-oh-mon): Cymbelina's patron.
- **Grigor** (grih-gor): An officer of the law in Gradgate.

H

- **Hakon the Last** (ha-kun): The last king of the united álfrolk people.
- **Hana** (ha-nah): An officer of the law in Gradgate.
- **Helda Stineeyes** (hell-da stine-eyes): The wife of Jarl Yngraham Stineeyes.
- **Hjaldar** (hyal-dar): A Dokkalrolk guard stationed in the city of Jordstand.

I

- **Idal** (ee-daal): Cymbelina's best friend.
- **Ignatius** (ig-nai-shihuhs): Cymbelina's biological father.
- **Ilmava** (ill-maa-vah): One of Kazimiera's scouts in Monarch Vukasino's army.
- **Inar** (eye-naar): One of Scoutmaster Estrasta's scouts.

J

- **Jadah** (yaa-dah): One of Kazimiera's scouts in Monarch Vukasino's army.
- **Jara** (yaa-raa): One of Kazimiera's scouts in Monarch Vukasino's army.
- **Jasmina** (yuhs-mee-nah): One of the four surviving Light Vilek who inhabit Nebesati. A member of the Court of Mothers.
- **Jelkaza** (yell-kaa-zaa): Mistress Tihana's aide.

K

- **Kayven** (kay-ven): A member of the Glenrolk clan and Cymbelina's childhood friend.
- **Kazimiera** (kaaz-ih-meer-ah): One of Monarch Vukasino's three knights.
- **Kivi** (key-vee): One of Scoutmaster Estrasta's scouts who accompanies Cymbelina to Elderfell.

L

- **Latava** (la-taa-vah): One of Monarch Vukasino's attendants.
- **Laufeia the Kind** (lau-fee-ah): The only daughter of Hakon the Last and the leader of the group of álves whose descendants would become the Sylvanrolk.
- **Lufor** (luu-for): One of the Dokkalrolk who acts as a guard for the city of Krigdor.

M

- **Malaveen** (mal-ah-veen): A member of the Glenrolk clan and Cymbelina's former bully.
- **Malignos** (mal-ih-nos): A god who rules over the hellscape known as Infernus and all of the demonic beings that come from within. He is one of The Supreme Three.
- **Milena** (mil-ayy-nah): One of the record keepers for the Court of Mothers in Nebesati.
- **Morana** (mor-aa-nah): One of Monarch Vukasino's three knights.

N

- **Nadasha** (nuh-dah-shuh): One of the four surviving Light Vilek who inhabit Nebesati. A member of the Court of Mothers.
- **Nairna** (nair-nah): Kinlady of the Forrolk clan.
- **Norsla Thornshield** (nors-lah thorn-shield): The queen of the Dokkalrolk and the Kingdom of Snøthorn. Wife of King Ragnar Thornshield.

O

- **Olenell** (ole-nell): One of Malaveen's childhood friends and one of Cymbelina's bullies.
- **Orsala Orrheart** (or-saal-ah or-heart): The jarl of Krigdor in the Kingdom of Snøthorn and Scoutmaster Estrasa's wife.

P

- **Pajana** (pa-yaa-nah): One of Kazimiera's scouts in Monarch Vukasino's army.
- **Petiča** (peh-teech-ah): A scout in Monarch Vukasino's army who was captured by the Glenrolk clan. She is also Urskana's sister.
- **Phalena** (fa-layn-ah): Kinlord Emyr's advisor.

Q

- **Quendol** (qwhen-doll): A Dokkalrolk guard stationed in the city of Jordstand.
- **Quindlen** (qwhen-dlin): Kinlord of the Durolk clan.

R

- **Ragnar Thornsheid** (raag-naar thorn-shield): The king of the Dokkalrolk and the Kingdom of Snøthorn. Husband of Queen Norsla Thornshield.
- **Rayna** (rain-uh): One of Monarch Vukasino's servants.
- **Rhoslyn** (rhoz-lin): Idal's mother.

S

- **Sanja** (sahn-yah): One of Monarch Vukasino's servants.
- **Saskia** (zahs-kee-ah): One of the wind-controlling Magijarolk that accompanies Cymbelina back to the Snøthorn Mountains.
- **Satula** (sah-too-lah): One of the Dokkalrolk who acts as a guard for the city of Krigdor.
- **Séacael** (shay-kayl): The husband of Deirdre, the stepfather of Cymbelina, and the biological father of Una.
- **Snaerr the Wise** (snair): The first son of Hakon the Last and the leader of the group of álves whose descendants would become the Dokkalrolk.

T

- **Tadhgmaris** (taig-maa-ris): The father of Kayven and the cook for the Glenrolk clan.
- **Tajni** (teye-nee): Vukasino's pet rook.
- **Talfryn** (tal-frin): A member of the Glenrolk clan.
- **Terralynia** (tair-uh-lyn-ee-uh): A goddess who created all life before 0 AC on Sacarnia. She is sometimes called Mother Terralynia, the Supreme Mother, or Goddess. She is one of The Supreme Three.
- **Tihana** (tee-haa-nah): The lead alchemist of the Dark Vilek army and creator of the visi-vilek.
- **Toryn** (tor-in): A brown wolf spirit who happens to be Kayven's patron.
- **Travana** (tra-vah-nah): One of the two vilek who terrorized the Sylvanrolk during the Eldenfield Festival.
- **Tully** (tuh-lee): A red squirrel spirit who happens to be Una's patron.

U

- **Ulfric** (ull-frick): A Dokkalrolk guard stationed in the tunnels of Jordstand.
- **Una** (oo-nah): The younger half-sibling of Cymbelina and daughter of Deirdre and Séacael.
- **Urskana** (ur-skaa-nah): Petiča's sister and a citizen of Elderfell.
- **Usenia** (uh-sen-ee-ah): One of the wind-controlling Magijarolk that accompanies Cymbelina back to the Snøthorn Mountains and to Elderfell.

V

- **Vatrina** (vuh-tree-nah): One of the two vilek who terrorized the Sylvanrolk during the Eldenfield Festival.
- **Vesna** (veh-snah): One of the four surviving Light Vilek who inhabit Nebesati. A member of the Court of Mothers and Emerik's mother.

- **Vevina** (veh-vee-nah): The healer for the Glenrolk clan.
- **Vukasino** (vuu-kaa-seen-oh): The visi-vilek monarch of Dark Vilek.

W

- **Wavoda** (waa-voe-dah): One of Kazimiera's scouts in Monarch Vukasino's army.
- **Wray Volsen** (ray vole-son): The jarl of Sølvcast in the Kingdom of Snøthorn.
- **Wynne** (win): A member of the Glenrolk clan.

Y

- **Yestin** (yes-tin): A member of the Glenrolk clan.
- **Yngraham Stineeyes** (ihng-grum stine-eyes): The jarl of Jordstand in the Kingdom of Snøthorn. Husband of Lady Helda Stineeyes.
- **Yulla** (yoo-lah): King Ragnar's adviser.

Z

- **Zhikavza** (shi-kav-zah): One of Kazimiera's scouts in Monarch Vukasino's army.
- **Zlatana** (zlaa-taan-ah): Monarch Vukasino's deceased mother and former Matriarch of the Dark Vilek.
- **Zosiana** (zoe-see-aan-ah): One of Monarch Vukasino's servants.

Notable Terms

A

- **AC**: The time period Legends of Sacarnia takes place in. It stands for "After Configuration," which references the time after the goddess Terralynia finished interfering with life on Sacarnia.
- **Álfrolk**: The second race of sentient beings created by the goddess Terralynia.

B

- **BC**: Stands for "Before Configuration," which references the time before the goddess Terralynia finished creating life on Sacarnia.

C

- **Cathanu**: Also known as the Proving Trials, Cathanu is an event where members of the Sylvanrolk clans compete in a series of tests in order to become the next kinlord or kinlady of their clan. This only happens once their clan leader has died.
- **The Court of Mothers**: The name of the remaining four Light Vilek who rule over the Glimmering Wilds and keep the creatures within safe.

D

- **Dokkalrolk**: Also known as Dark Álves, this race of sentient beings inhabits the Snøthorn Mountains.
- **Durolk**: Also known as the Jungle Folk, this clan is one of the three Sylvanrolk clans. They inhabit the region of Florella known as the Jungle of Solitude. Their clan colors are blue, purple, and black.

E

- **Eldenfield Festival**: A Sylvanrolk celebration that typically occurs in autumn in the region of Florella known as Eldenfield. The focus of this event is to celebrate the survival of the Wood Álves and their culture.

- **Elixir of Annihilmon**: A potion named after a famed magister of the continent of Arcana who sought to take over the world and destroy all non-magical beings in the year 500 AC.

F

- **Forrolk**: Also known as the Forest Folk, this clan is one of the three Sylvanrolk clans. They inhabit the southeastern reaches of the region of Florella known as the Sunshade Forest. Their clan colors are yellow, orange, and brown.

G

- **"The Garden"**: Specifically when referenced in phrases like *"Day'll sas du dan fairn,"* which, when translated from Sylvan to Common, means "I'll see you in the garden." This phrase refers to Terralynia's heavenly paradise. It is a widespread belief in Wood Álf culture that all deceased creatures return to the Supreme Mother's garden in the sky when they die so they can reunite with their creator and their loved ones.
- **Glenrolk**: Also known as the Valley Folk, this clan is one of the three Sylvanrolk clans. They inhabit the region of Florella known as Terralynia's Folly. Their clan colors are green, brown, and white.
- **The Great Dissolution**: The name of the event where a dragon destroyed the ancient álfrolkian capital of Snøvern and caused the ancient race of álfrolk to split off into three different groups across Florella.

I

- **Infernus**: A fiery domain ruled by the primordial god named Malignos. Damned souls inhabit this realm, as do the many demonic entities the hell god has created.

K

- **Kinlady/Kinlord**: The official title for the leader of a Sylvanrolk clan.

M

- **Magijarolk**: Also known as Elemental Álves, this race of sentient beings inhabits the Glimmering Wilds. They are the descendants of the Light Vilek and ancient álves.

P

- **Patron animal/patron**: An animal spirit that bonds to a Sylvanrolk álf while they are in their mother's womb. Through rigorous training, a Wood Álf and their patron can become one, and the álf can assume their patron's form (unless they're Half Sylvanrolk, in which case they can only take on certain characteristics of their patrons, such as eyes, ears, teeth, wings, etc.).
- **Patron teacher/guide**: A Sylvranrolk álf trained in the art of teaching Wood Álves to bond with their patron guardians.

S

- **Sip of Tranquility**: An apple cider-colored potion some Sylvanrolk take before conducting a soul reading in order to relax their minds.
- **Soul Bonding**: The name of the mating process the vilek undergo in order to reproduce. This practice replicates the process the goddess Terralynia followed to make life on Sacarnia but on a much smaller scale. Two fairies (or a fairy and her non-fae mate, which can be of any race) swap pieces of their soul and combine them to create a new fairy or half-fairy.
- **Soul Reading**: Known as *"anas tusinca"* in the Wood Álf language, this is a practice among the Sylvanrolk álves. It involves communicating with their soul to discern visions from their patron animals.

- **The Supreme Three**: The official name for the grouping of the three primordial gods Astraliam, Malignos, and Terralynia.
- **Sylvan Tenets**: Also known as the Old Laws, this is the body of rules the Sylvanrolk follow in order to remain a member of their clan.
- **Sylvanrolk**: Also known as Wood Álves, this race of sentient beings inhabits the mid to southern reaches of Florella.
- **Sylvanrolk Outcast/Nomad**: A Wood Álf who originally belonged to one of the three Sylvanrolk clans but was excommunicated for breaking the Sylvan Tenets. Most leave their clans and find solace in the Jungle of Solitude.
- **Terralynia's Chosen**: Another name for mages. These are magic users born with innate magical abilities that are not typical for the race the magic user belongs to. For example, vilek are not considered Terralynia's chosen, as all fairies are born with innate magical abilities.

V

- **Vilek**: The first race of sentient beings created by the goddess Terralynia. After the álves were introduced to the vilek, these fairy women split into two separate courts; The Light Vilek, or "Welcoming" fairies and the Dark Vilek, or "Unwelcoming" fairies.
- **Visi-Vilek**: A fairy created by Mistress Tihana using the DNA of a vilek mother and the DNA of a random, non-fae father. Vukasino was the first one to survive the first fifty years of life, a time period in which a fairy is still considered a child.

W

- **Well of Observation**: A rainbow-hued pond that allows members of the Court of Mothers to see almost anywhere on the face of Sacarnia as long as the location isn't charmed to keep prying eyes out.

Languages of Florella

Dark Álven

This language is spoken by the Dokkalrolk inhabiting the Snøthorn Mountains. It is the closest modern language to the ancient álfrolkian dialect.

- **An** (aan): it.
- **Blad** (blaad): blade.
- **Fordaastar** (for-daas-tar): traitor, betrayer.
- **Gund** (gund): god.
- **Huss** (huss): house
- **Inferdon** (in-fur-don): damn
- **Inferdon-an** (in-fur-don-aan): damn it.
- **Lov** (love): law.
- **Lovhuss** (love-huss): lawhouse.
- **Orr** (oar): eagle.
- **Sen** (sen): son.
- **Stine** (stine): stone.
- **Ute** (uut): out
- **Utelander** (uut-land-er): outlander, outsider.
- **Vol** (vole): night.

Hominan

This language is spoken primarily by human mages. Not only do certain magical houses speak this language, but their descendants across the world do, too, such as the Sylvanrolk.

- **Domi** (dome-ee): magic house. It specifically refers to the magical abilities a mage possesses. For example, if a mage says they are from the water domi, that means their abilities are water-based.

Infernal

This language is obscure to most of Sacarnia's inhabitants.

- **A** (ah): is.
- **Animus** (an-ih-mus): soul.
- **Ascenda** (ah-scend-ah): ascend, rise.
- **Ast** (ast): it.
- **Bonara** (bon-arr-ah): good.
- **Containeo** (kuhn-tayn-ee-oh): contained.
- **Descenda** (dih-scend-ah): descend, fall.
- **Dit** (deet), **diteth** (deet-eth): say, sayeth.
- **Draco** (dray-koh): dragon.
- **Dun** (dun): when, while.
- **Est** (est): to.
- **Hospi** (hos-pee): host.
- **Mustila** (must-ill-ah): must.
- **Primina** (prim-ee-nah): first.
- **Quin** (quin): what.
- **Retrana** (reh-traa-naah): return, back.
- **Sano** (saa-no): elder.
- **Servanus** (ser-vaan-us): servant.
- **Somnulli** (som-null-ee), **somnullis** (som-null-is): sleep, sleeps.
- **Sum** (sum): be.
- **Te** (teh): the.
- **Unaliut** (une-all-ee-ut): one, when in reference to a person.

Sylvan/Wood Álven

This language is spoken by the Sylvanrolk. It was formed by mixing certain Homian words with those of the ancient álfrolkian language.

- **Anas** (aan-aas): soul.

- **Berrica** (bear-eh-ka), **berricus** (bear-eh-kiss): berry, berries.
- **Brethan** (breath-aan), **brethanna** (breath-aan-ah), **brethany** (breath-aan-ee): kin, brethren. Brethan is masculine, brethanna is feminine, and brethany refers to multiple genders that are present.
- **Caa** (kaa), **caas** (kaas): idiot, idiots.
- **Cacas** (ka-kass): excrement, shit.
- **Dan** (daan): in, in the.
- **Day** (day): I.
- **Day'll** (dayl): I'll, I will.
- **Day'm** (daym): I'm, I am.
- **Dihaal** (dee-haal): damn.
- **Du** (due): you.
- **Em** (em): am.
- **Fairn** (fairn): garden.
- **Fokashel** (fock-ah-shell): an expletive akin to "fuck."
- **Ma** (ma): my.
- **Miln** (miln), **milnier** (miln-ear): surround, surrounded.
- **Mong** (mong), **mongra** (mong-raah): male dog, female dog. Can be used in the literal sense or as an insult.
- **Nill** (nill): will.
- **Sas** (saas): see.
- **Tarbal** (tar-buul): bull.
- **Tarbalcacas** (tar-buul-ka-kass): bullshit.
- **Tusine** (too-seen), **tusinca** (too-seen-ka): to read, reading.
- **Vala** (vaal-aa): by.

Vilean

This language is spoken by the vilek and the Magijarolk. It was the first language to be created outside of Common.

- **Casni** (ka-snee), **casna** (ka-snah): a male officer, a female officer.

- **Dana** (daa-naa): day.
- **Dobay** (dough-bay): good.
- **Espon** (ess-pon): rise. Usually used as a magical command.
- **Famija** (fa-me-yaa): family, kin, close allies.
- **Jetav** (yeh-taav): fuck, screw.
- **Ka** (ka): you.
- **Kurvasti** (kuur-vaa-stea): whore, harlot, slag.
- **Mamlazan** (maam-la-zaan): idiot, fool.
- **Mo** (mo), **Moa** (mo-ah): my. Mo is masculine, moa is feminine.
- **Na** (nah): to, to the.
- **Nak** (naak): non, not.
- **Ove** (ohve), **ova** (ohva): lamb, lambs.
- **Ravoyja** (ra-voy-yaa): monster, fiend.
- **Slanava** (sla-naa-vah): slaughter.
- **Spatazi** (spa-taa-zee): sleep. Usually used as a magical command.
- **Spratsina** (sprat-seen-ah): calming dust. Sourced from pollen, this sedative is used in places of healing in Nebesati.
- **Vasa** (vaa-saa): more.
- **Vatez** (va-tez): knight commander.
- **Vin** (veen): son, son of.
- **Vina** (veen-ah): daughter, daughter of.
- **Welo** (vell-oh): little.

Hayley Hawk is a dreamer and storyteller who crafts enchanting worlds and epic adventures. With a lifelong love for fantasy, Hayley brings to life rich, imaginative realms where heroes rise, magic flows, and the impossible becomes reality. When not writing, Hayley enjoys listening to music, exploring nature, searching for new books to read, and finding inspiration in the beauty of the everyday and the extraordinary.

Discover more about Hayley's magical journeys by checking out her Instagram page (@author_hayley_hawk) and her Facebook page.

Made in the USA
Middletown, DE
11 September 2024